THE COMPLETE TALES OF HENRY JAMES
VOLUME TWELVE: 1903–1910

THE COMPLETE TALES OF
HENRY JAMES

THE COMPLETE TALES OF

HENRY JAMES

EDITED WITH AN
INTRODUCTION BY

LEON EDEL

12

1903–1910

RUPERT HART-DAVIS

SOHO SQUARE LONDON

1964

Introduction © *Leon Edel, 1964*

B64-22249

PRINTED IN GREAT BRITAIN BY
WESTERN PRINTING SERVICES LTD BRISTOL

CONTENTS

INTRODUCTION: 1903-1910

IN 1904, on completing *The Golden Bowl*, Henry James sailed for America. He had last been in New York in 1883 when it had seemed to him a semi-provincial "Tiffany-city," crowded into its small island; he returned to find the new skyscrapers looking, he remarked, like pins casually thrust into a pincushion. His American impressions of the next year contain a certain exuberance of observation and comment; but the four American tales which he wrote on his return to England reflect a sense of shock. Indeed all his last tales have in them a barely concealed "sacred rage." The Olympian—the acknowledged "Master" of the new generation—sets aside his urbanity and his good humour and howls, like Lear: he sees the suffering and waste of human life, the loss of friendship and of personal identity, the loneliness of modern cities; he has the oppressive sense that all is "too late." Many things implied in his final masterpieces, *The Ambassadors*, *The Wings of the Dove* and *The Golden Bowl*, are stated in these tales crudely and at moments savagely. There is a single sentence in the last tale written by James which suggests the sadness woven into his final stories. "There was nothing like a crowd . . . for making one feel lonely." These are tales of individuals lost in the crowd; and of individuals without identity or self-awareness. They are also angry tales.

We have only to glance at a single paragraph in "Crapy Cornelia" to glimpse James's acute disillusion. It is one of the rare instances when he assumes the stance and tone of a prophet:

This was clearly going to be the music of the future—that if people were but rich enough and furnished enough and fed enough, exercised and sanitated and manicured and generally advised and advertised and made "knowing" enough, *avertis* enough, as the term

7

appeared to be nowadays in Paris, all they had to do for civility was to take the amused ironic view of those who might be less initiated. In *his* time, when he was young or even when he was only but a little less middle-aged, the best manners had been the best kindness, and the best kindness had mostly been some art of not insisting on one's luxurious differences, of concealing rather, for common humanity, if not for common decency, a part at least of the intensity or the ferocity with which one might be "in the know."

In James's last tale, "A Round of Visits," the young man, returning to New York after ten years abroad, discovers he has been robbed by one of his oldest and most cherished friends. What he experiences, however, is not so much the loss of his money as the personal betrayal. He wanders through the city, searching for someone to whom he might confide his secret sorrow. Manhattan turns a deaf ear. The women in particular are devoid of sympathy; fatuous, ugly, rich, common, they speak to him only in dreary generalities. Their drawing-rooms are places to flee; he cannot linger.

One does not need the resolution of this story to recognise its inner statement. Henry James had been robbed and betrayed; his patrimony was gone; he had lived in a treacherous world. Earlier, in "The Jolly Corner," he had described the more private wanderings of a repatriate, in a particular house, in the old part of Manhattan near Washington Square. There is no feeling of betrayal in this tale, but there is, for James's hero, self-doubt and a questioning of his identity. Spencer Brydon asks himself what he would have been like had he remained at home. Gradually he convinces himself that his American counterpart is somewhere in these old rooms which had nourished so much of his family history. He paces them at night; he stalks the ghost as if he were a hunter. It is indeed a tale both of a hunting and a haunting—of a man in quest of his Self.

"Fordham Castle" and "Julia Bride" are of a piece with

"The Jolly Corner"—sketches of Americans in a world of obscure or lost identities. There is the whimsical-pathetic shunted husband of the society-seeking matron, going through a series of name-changes imposed by his ambitious wife and trying to create a new self for each name. There is the beautiful Julia Bride, doomed to live up to her name; she will always have been a bride—but she will achieve no marriage; each prospective husband discovers her six broken engagements and her mother's three divorces. And in "The Velvet Glove," first of the group of tales in *The Finer Grain*, there is deception of identity: the beautiful Princess, who seems to offer the great author a promise of Romance, takes him on a long night drive through Paris; he has learned that she is really Amy Evans, a scribbler of novels, and her purpose has been to get him to write a "lovely, friendly, irresistible log-rolling preface" to her new novel. How, the great author asks himself, could a creature "so formed for living and breathing her Romance" be addicted to "the dreadful amateurish dance of ungrammatically scribbling it?"

The tales in *The Finer Grain*, as James explained, dealt with "the sentient, perceptive, reflective" individual involved in a challenging personal adventure; and he added that it was usually his hero who "exhibits this finer grain of accessibility to suspense or curiosity, to mystification or attraction." This was true; and his women, in this ultimate group of tales, are of coarser grain. James indeed casts aside all euphemism in describing them. Mrs Worthingham is simply "as ignorant as a fish"; Mrs Drack in "Julia Bride" looms before us with "a large innocent elephantine archness: she fairly rioted in that dimension of size"; and the lady in "A Round of Visits" who has been defrauded (but has plenty of money left) pretends she is reduced to a bare bone which she "pawed and tossed with her little extraordinarily gemmed and manicured hands." James writes with the same directness and anger that animated *The Bostonians* twenty-five years before. One feels he is too bitter and disillusioned to care what words he finds for these detestable persons. They are common and coarse, and he has no need for delicacy. In two of his subjects, however, he shows his compassionate and pitying side. "Mora Montravers" and "The Bench of Desolation" deal with human waste, mistaken lives, wrong decisions, lost opportunities. "The Bench of Desolation" belongs to the series of fictions which had their origin in the idea of "too late." It is allied to "The Beast in the Jungle"; however, its little passive bookseller, Herbert Dodd, has neither the obsessive "drive" nor the overpowering egotism of John Marcher. Weak, betrayed, lost, he will ultimately accept the comfort of the woman who has made his life wretched.

Henry James could sail to no Yeatsian Byzantium. For him, in his old age, there seems to have been only the cold bench and the desolation of the metropolitan jungles. There is terror behind the melodrama and the coincidences of these tales. And the crack of the pistol at the end of the final story is the crack of doom. By the time *The Finer Grain* was published, James had had his serious nervous illness of 1910. After that, he wrote no more tales. He chose instead to relive his past in his autobiographies, *A Small Boy and Others*, *Notes of a Son and Brother* and the unfinished *Middle Years*.

In these twelve volumes have been published all of Henry James's 112 tales—more than three million words of fiction. Their quality, their thematic consistency and art, have been suggested in the various prefaces; and it might be well to ask ourselves now what are their limitations. They do describe a narrow world; they deal with all too "special" types and almost exclusively with "the better sort"; they are "artificial"; they seem unduly introspective; they are sometimes transparently autobiographical. This latter is a part of their charm, but it may also be a flaw, if we agree with some critics that the intimate personal diminishes the "impersonal" in art. And the tales suffer, in their last stages, from an excess of style and decoration. Doubtless many more unfavourable things could be said, not least that some of them, in their leisurely elaborateness, try the patience of the impatient modern reader.

Nevertheless most of these tales have survived such limitations as they have and they emerged from the ephemeral pages of the magazines in which they first appeared. If one were to ask why, when so many other tales of gifted authors fall by the wayside, the answer would seem to be that James had the genius of the twice-told, the oft-repeated tale. His writings can be re-read; his pages contain richnesses of observation and insight which make us want to return to them. He is the born story-teller who, given the right audience, knows how to command its attention. And he is human and fertile, searching and sentient. If his world is "narrow," he made up for it by his grasp of motives, his understanding of man's inner world. For forty-six years he wrote these tales, reflecting in them the decades of his life and of his age. Now, a century after he began them, we can see that what he produced was not only "a multitude of pictures of my time," as he had promised long ago, but a large and splendid literary monument. In it is enshrined his consciousness, his creative imagination, the power of his "unageing intellect."

LEON EDEL

Gay Head, 1964

THE PAPERS

I

THERE was a longish period—the dense duration of a London winter, cheered, if cheered it could be called, with lurid electric, with fierce "incandescent" flares and glares—when they repeatedly met, at feeding-time, in a small and not quite savoury pothouse a stone's-throw from the Strand. They talked always of pothouses, of feeding-time—by which they meant any hour between one and four of the afternoon; they talked of most things, even of some of the greatest, in a manner that gave, or that they desired to show as giving, in respect to the conditions of their life, the measure of their detachment, their contempt, their general irony. Their general irony, which they tried at the same time to keep gay and to make amusing at least to each other, was their refuge from the want of savour, the want of napkins, the want, too often, of shillings, and of many things besides that they would have liked to have. Almost all they had with any security was their youth, complete, admirable, very nearly invulnerable, or as yet inattackable; for they didn't count their talent, which they had originally taken for granted and had since then lacked freedom of mind, as well indeed as any offensive reason, to reappraise. They were taken up with other questions and other estimates—the remarkable limits, for instance, of their luck, the remarkable smallness of the talent of their friends. They were above all in that phase of youth and in that state of aspiration in which "luck" is the subject of most frequent reference, as definite as the colour red, and in which it is the elegant name for money when people are as refined as they are

13

poor. She was only a suburban young woman in a sailor hat, and he a young man destitute, in strictness, of occasion for a "topper"; but they felt that they had in a peculiar way the freedom of the town, and the town, if it did nothing else, gave a range to the spirit. They sometimes went, on excursions that they groaned at as professional, far afield from the Strand, but the curiosity with which they came back was mostly greater than any other, the Strand being for them, with its ampler alternative Fleet Street, overwhelmingly the Papers, and the Papers being, at a rough guess, all the furniture of their consciousness.

The Daily Press played for them the part played by the embowered nest on the swaying bough for the parent birds that scour the air. It was, as they mainly saw it, a receptacle, owing its form to the instinct more remarkable, as they held the journalistic, than that even of the most highly organised animal, into which, regularly, breathlessly, contributions had to be dropped—odds and ends, all grist to the mill, all somehow digestible and convertible, all conveyed with the promptest possible beak and the flutter, often, of dreadfully fatigued little wings. If there had been no Papers there would have been no young friends for us of the figure we hint at, no chance mates, innocent and weary, yet acute even to penetration, who were apt to push off their plates and rest their elbows on the table in the interval between the turn-over of the pint-pot and the call for the awful glibness of their score. Maud Blandy drank beer—and welcome, as one may say; and she smoked cigarettes when privacy permitted, though she drew the line at this in the right place, just as she flattered herself she knew how to draw it, journalistically, where other delicacies were concerned. She was fairly a product of the day —so fairly that she might have been born afresh each morning, to serve, after the fashion of certain agitated ephemeral insects, only till the morrow. It was as if a past had been wasted on her and a future were not to be fitted; she was really herself, so far at least as her great preoccupation went, an edition, an "extra special," coming out at the loud hours and living its life, amid the roar of vehicles, the hustle of pavements, the shriek of newsboys, according to the quantity of shock to be proclaimed and distributed, the quantity to be administered, thanks to the varying temper of Fleet Street, to the nerves of the nation. Maud was a shocker, in short, in petticoats, and alike for the thoroughfare, the club, the suburban train and the humble home; though it must honestly be added that petticoats were not of her essence. This was one of the reasons, in an age of "emancipations," of her intense actuality, as well as, positively, of a good fortune to which, however impersonal she might have appeared, she was not herself in a position to do full justice; the felicity of her having about her naturally so much of the young bachelor that she was saved the disfigurement of any marked straddling or elbowing. It was literally true of her that she would have pleased less, or at least have offended more, had she been obliged, or been prompted, to assert—all too vainly, as it would have been sure to be—her superiority to sex. Nature, constitution, accident, whatever we happen to call it, had relieved her of this care; the struggle for life, the competition with men, the taste of the day, the fashion of the hour had *made* her superior, or had at any rate made her indifferent, and she had no difficulty in remaining so. The thing was therefore, with the aid of an extreme general flatness of person, directness of step and simplicity of motive, quietly enough done, without a grace, a weak inconsequence, a stray re-minder to interfere with the success; and it is not too much to say that the success—by which I mean the plainness of the type—would probably never have struck you as so great as at the moments of our young lady's chance comradeship with Howard Bight. For the young man, though his personal signs had not, like his friend's, especially the effect of one of the stages of an evolution, might have been noted as not so fiercely or so freshly a male as to distance Maud in the show.

She presented him in truth, while they sat together, as comparatively girlish. She fell naturally into gestures, tones, expressions, resemblances, that he either suppressed, from sensibility to her personal predominance, or that were merely latent in him through much taking for granted. Mild, sensitive, none too solidly nourished, and condemned, perhaps by a deep delusion as to the final issue of it, to perpetual coming and going, he was so resigned to many things, and so disgusted even with many others, that the least of his cares was the cultivation of a bold front. What mainly concerned him was its being bold enough to get him his dinner, and it was never more void of aggression than when he solicited in person those scraps of information, snatched at those floating particles of news, on which his dinner depended. Had he had time a little more to try his case, he would have made out that if he liked Maud Blandy it was partly by the impression of what she could do for him: what she could do for herself had never entered into his head. The positive quantity, moreover, was vague to his mind; it existed, that is, for the present, but as the proof of how, in spite of the want of encouragement, a fellow could keep going. She struck him in fact as the only encouragement he had, and this altogether by example, since precept, frankly, was deterrent on her lips, as speech was free, judgment prompt, and accent not absolutely pure. The point was that, as the easiest thing to be with her, he was so passive that it almost made him graceful and so attentive that it almost made him distinguished. She was herself neither of these things, and they were not of course what a man had most to be; whereby she contributed to their common view the impatiences required by a proper reaction, forming thus for him a kind of protective hedge behind which he could wait. Much waiting, for either, was, I hasten to add, always in order, inasmuch as their novitiate seemed to them interminable

and the steps of their ladder fearfully far apart. It rested
—the ladder—against the great stony wall of the public
attention—a sustaining mass which apparently wore somewhere, in the upper air, a big, thankless, expressionless face,
a countenance equipped with eyes, ears, an uplifted nose and
a gaping mouth—all convenient if they could only be reached.
The ladder groaned meanwhile, swayed and shook with the
weight of the close-pressed climbers, tier upon tier, occupying
the upper, the middle, the nethermost rounds and quite pre-
venting, for young persons placed as our young friends were
placed, any view of the summit. It was meanwhile moreover
only Howard Bight's perverse view—he was confessedly
perverse—that Miss Blandy had arrived at a perch superior
to his own.

She had hitherto recognised in herself indeed but a tighter
clutch and a grimmer purpose; she had recognised, she believed, in keen moments, a vocation; she had recognised that
there had been eleven of them at home, with herself as
youngest, and distinctions by that time so blurred in her that
she might as easily have been christened John. She had
recognised truly, most of all, that if they came to talk they
both were nowhere; yet this was compatible with her insisting
that Howard had as yet comparatively had the luck. When he
wrote to people they consented, or at least they answered;
almost always, for that matter, they answered with greed, so
that he was not without something of some sort to hawk
about to buyers. Specimens indeed of human greed—*the*
greed, the great one, the eagerness to figure, the snap at the
bait of publicity, he had collected in such store as to stock, as
to launch, a museum. In this museum the prize object, the
high rare specimen, had been for some time established; a
celebrity of the day enjoying, uncontested, a glass case all to
himself, more conspicuous than any other, before which the
arrested visitor might rebound from surprised recognition.
Sir A. B. C. Beadel-Muffet K.C.B., M.P., stood forth there as

large as life, owing indeed his particular place to the shade of
direct acquaintance with him that Howard Bight could boast,
yet with his eminent presence in such a collection but too
generally and notoriously justified. He was universal and
ubiquitous, commemorated, under some rank rubric, on every
page of every public print every day in every year, and as
inveterate a feature of each issue of any self-respecting sheet
as the name, the date, the tariffed advertisements. He had
always done something, or was about to do something,
round which the honours of announcement clustered, and
indeed, as he had inevitably thus become a subject of fallacious
report, one half of his chronicle appeared to consist of official
contradiction of the other half. His activity—if it had not
better been called his passivity—was beyond any other that
figured in the public eye, for no other assuredly knew so few
or such brief intermittences. Yet, as there was the inside as
well as the outside view of his current history, the quantity of
it was easy to analyse for the possessor of the proper crucible.
Howard Bight, with his arms on the table, took it apart and
put it together again most days in the year, so that an amused
comparison of notes on the subject often added a mild spice to
his colloquies with Maud Blandy. They knew, the young pair,
as they considered, many secrets, but they liked to think that
they knew none quite so scandalous as the way that, to put it
roughly, this distinguished person maintained his distinction.

It was known certainly to all who had to do with the
Papers, a brotherhood, a sisterhood of course interested—
for what was it, in the last resort, but the interest of their
bread and butter?—in shrouding the approaches to the oracle,
in not telling tales out of school. They all lived alike on the
solemnity, the sanctity of the oracle, and the comings and
goings, the doings and undoings, the intentions and retrac-
tations of Sir A. B. C. Beadel-Muffet K.C.B., M.P., were in their
degree a part of that solemnity. The Papers, taken together
the glory of the age, were, though superficially multifold,

fundamentally one, so that any revelation of their being pro-
cured or procurable to float an object not intrinsically buoyant
would very logically convey discredit from the circumference
—where the revelation would be likely to be made—to the
centre. Of so much as this our grim neophytes, in common
with a thousand others, were perfectly aware; but something
in the nature of their wit, such as it was, or in the condition
of their nerves, such as it easily might become, sharpened
almost to acerbity their relish of so artful an imitation of the
voice of fame. The fame was *all* voice, as they could guarantee
who had an ear always glued to the speaking-tube; the items
that made the sum were individually of the last vulgarity, but
the accumulation was a triumph—one of the greatest the age
could show—of industry and vigilance. It was after all not
true that a man had done nothing who for ten years had so
fed, so dyked and directed and distributed the fitful sources of
publicity. He had laboured, in his way, like a navvy with a
spade; he might be said to have earned by each night's work
the reward, each morning, of his small spurt of glory. Even
for such a matter as its not being true that Sir A. B. C.
Beadel-Muffet K.C.B., M.P., was to start on his visit to the
Sultan of Samarcand on the 23rd, *but* being true that he was
to start on the 29th, the personal attention required was no
small affair, taking the legend with the fact, the myth with the
meaning, the original artless error with the subsequent earnest
truth—allowing in fine for the statement still to come that the
visit would have to be relinquished in consequence of the
visitor's other pressing engagements, and bearing in mind
the countless channels to be successively watered. Our young
man, one December afternoon, pushed an evening paper
across to his companion, keeping his thumb on a paragraph at
which she glanced without eagerness. She might, from her manner, have known by instinct what it would be, and her exclama-
tion had the note of satiety. "Oh, he's working *them* now?"

"If he has begun he'll work them hard. By the time that

has gone round the world there'll be something else to say. 'We are authorised to state that the marriage of Miss Miranda Beadel-Muffet to Captain Guy Devereux, of the Fiftieth Rifles, will not take place.' Authorised to state—rather! when every wire in the machine has been pulled over and over. They're authorised to state something every day in the year, and the authorisation is not difficult to get. Only his daughters, now that they're coming on, poor things—and I believe there are many—will have to be chucked into the pot and produced on occasions when other matter fails. How pleasant for them to find themselves hurtling through the air, clubbed by the paternal hand, like golf-balls in a suburb! Not that I suppose they don't like it—why should one suppose anything of the sort?" Howard Bight's impression of the general appetite appeared to-day to be especially vivid, and he and his companion were alike prompted to one of those slightly violent returns on themselves and the work they were doing which none but the vulgar-minded altogether avoid. "People —as I see them—would almost rather be jabbered about unpleasantly than not be jabbered about at all: whenever you try them—whenever, at least, I do—I'm confirmed in that conviction. It isn't only that if one holds out the mere tip of the perch they jump at it like starving fish; it is that they leap straight out of the water themselves, leap in their thousands and come flopping, open-mouthed and goggle-eyed, to one's very door. What is the sense of the French expression about a person's making *des yeux de carpe?* It suggests the eyes that a young newspaper-man seems to see all round him, and I declare I sometimes feel that, if one has the courage not to blink at the show, the gilt is a good deal rubbed off the gingerbread of one's early illusions. They all do it, as the song is at the music-halls, and it's some of one's surprises that tell one most. You've thought there were some high souls that didn't do it—that wouldn't, I mean, to work the oracle, lift a little finger of their own. But, Lord bless you, give them a

chance—you'll find some of the greatest the greediest. I give
you my word for it, I haven't a scrap of faith left in a single
human creature. Except, of course," the young man added,
"the grand creature that *you* are, and the cold, calm, compre-
hensive one whom you thus admit to your familiarity. *We* face
the music. We see, we understand; we know we've got to
live, and how we do it. But at least, like this, alone together,
we take our intellectual revenge, we escape the indignity of
being fools dealing with fools. I don't say we shouldn't enjoy
it more if we *were*. But it can't be helped; we haven't the gift—
the gift, I mean, of not seeing. We do the worst we can for
the money."

"*You* certainly do the worst you can," Maud Blandy soon
replied, "when you sit there, with your wanton wiles, and
take the spirit out of me. I require a working faith, you know.
If one isn't a fool, in our world, where *is* one?"

"Oh, I say!" her companion groaned without alarm.
"Don't you fail *me*, mind you."

They looked at each other across their clean platters, and,
little as the light of romance seemed superficially to shine in
them or about them, the sense was visibly enough in each of
being involved in the other. He would have been sharply
alone, the softly sardonic young man, if the somewhat dry
young woman hadn't affected him, in a way he was even too
nervous to put to the test, as saving herself up for him; and
the consciousness of absent resources that was on her own
side quite compatible with this economy grew a shade or two
less dismal with the imagination of his somehow being at
costs for her. It wasn't an expense of shillings—there was not
much question of that; what it came to was perhaps nothing
more than that, being, as he declared himself, "in the know,"
he kept pulling her in too, as if there had been room for them
both. He told her everything, all his secrets. He talked and
talked, often making her think of herself as a lean, stiff person,
destitute of skill or art, but with ear enough to be performed

to, sometimes strangely touched, at moments completely ravished, by a fine violinist. He was her fiddler and genius; she was sure neither of her taste nor of his tunes, but if she could do nothing else for him she could hold the case while he handled the instrument. It had never passed between them that they could draw nearer, for they seemed near, near verily for pleasure, when each, in a decent young life, was so much nearer to the other than to anything else. There was no pleasure known to either that wasn't further off. What held them together was in short that they were in the same boat, a cockle-shell in a great rough sea, and that the movements required for keeping it afloat not only were what the situation safely permitted, but also made for reciprocity and intimacy. These talks over greasy white slabs, repeatedly mopped with moist grey cloths by young women in black uniforms, with inexorable braided "buns" in the nape of weak necks, these sessions, sometimes prolonged, in halls of oilcloth, among penal-looking tariffs and pyramids of scones, enabled them to rest on their oars; the more that they were on terms with the whole families, chartered companies, of food-stations, each a race of innumerable and indistinguishable members, and had mastered those hours of comparative elegance, the earlier and the later, when the little weary ministrants were limply sitting down and the occupants of the red benches bleakly interspaced. So it was, that, at times, they renewed their understanding, and by signs, mannerless and meagre, that would have escaped the notice of witnesses. Maud Blandy had no need to kiss her hand across to him to show she felt what he meant; she had moreover never in her life kissed her hand to anyone, and her companion couldn't have imagined it of her. His romance was so grey that it wasn't romance at all; it was a reality arrived at without stages, shades, forms. If he had been ill or stricken she would have taken him—other resources failing—into her lap; but would that, which would scarce even have been motherly, have been romantic? She nevertheless at this moment put in her plea for the general element. "I can't help it, about Beadel-Muffet; it's too magnificent—it appeals to me. And then I've a particular feeling about him—I'm waiting to see what will happen. It *is* genius, you know, to get yourself so celebrated for nothing—to carry out your idea in the face of everything. I mean your idea of *being* celebrated. It isn't as if he had done even one little thing. What *has* he done when you come to look?"

"Why, my dear chap, he has done everything. He has missed nothing. He has been in everything, *of* everything, *at* everything, *over* everything, *under* everything, that has taken place for the last twenty years. He's *always* present, and, though he never makes a speech, he never fails to get alluded to in the speeches of others. That's doing it cheaper than anyone else does it, but it's thoroughly doing it—which is what we're talking about. And so far," the young man contended, "from its being 'in the face' of anything, it's positively with the help of everything, since the Papers are everything and more. They're made for such people, though no doubt he's the person who has known best how to use them. I've gone through one of the biggest sometimes, from beginning to end—it's quite a thrilling little game—to catch him once out. It has happened to me to think I was near it when, on the last column of the last page—I count 'advertisements,' heaven help us, out!—I've found him as large as life and as true as the needle to the pole. But at last, in a way, it goes, it can't help going, of itself. He comes in, he breaks out, of himself; the letters, under the compositor's hand, form themselves, from the force of habit, into his name—any connection for it, any context, being as good as any other, and the wind, which he has originally 'raised,' but which continues to blow, setting perpetually in his favour. The thing would really be now, don't you see, for him to keep himself out. That would be, on my honour, it strikes me—his *getting* himself out—the biggest fact in his record."

The girl's attention, as her friend developed the picture, had become more present. "He *can't* get himself out. There he is." She had a pause; she had been thinking. "That's just my idea."

"Your idea? Well, an idea's always a blessing. What do you want for it?"

She continued to turn it over as if weighing its value. "Something perhaps *could* be done with it—only it would take imagination."

He wondered, and she seemed to wonder that he didn't see. "Is it a situation for a 'ply'?"

"No, it's too good for a ply—yet it isn't quite good enough for a short story."

"It would do then for a novel?"

"Well, I seem to see it," Maud said—"and with a lot *in* it to be got out. But I seem to see it as a question not of what you or I might be able to do with it, but of what the poor man himself may. That's what I meant just now," she explained, "by my having a creepy sense of what may happen for him. It has already more than once occurred to me. *Then*," she wound up, "we shall have real life, the case itself."

"Do you know *you've* got imagination?" Her friend, rather interested, appeared by this time to have seized her thought.

"I see him having for some reason, very imperative, to seek retirement, lie low, to hide, in fact, like a man 'wanted,' but pursued all the while by the lurid glare that he has himself so started and kept up, and at last literally devoured ('like Frankenstein,' of course!) by the monster he has created."

"I say, you *have* got it!"—and the young man flushed, visibly, artistically, with the recognition of elements which his eyes had for a minute earnestly fixed. "But it will take a lot of doing."

"Oh," said Maud, "*we* shan't have to do it. He'll do it himself."

"I wonder." Howard Bight really wondered. "The fun would be for him to do it *for* us. I mean for him to want us to help him somehow to get out."

"Oh, 'us'!" the girl mournfully sighed.

"Why not, when he comes to us to get in?"

Maud Blandy stared. "Do you mean to you personally? You surely know by this time that no one ever 'comes' to me."

"Why, I went to him in the first instance; I made up to him straight, I did him 'at home,' somewhere, as I've surely mentioned to you before, three years ago. He liked, I believe—for he's really a delightful old ass—the way I did it; he knows my name and has my address, and has written me three or four times since, with his own hand, a request to be so good as to make use of my (he hopes) still close connection with the daily Press to rectify the rumour that he has reconsidered his opinion on the subject of the blankets supplied to the Upper Tooting Workhouse Infirmary. He has reconsidered his opinion on no subject whatever—which he mentions, in the interest of historic truth, without further intrusion on my valuable time. And he regards that sort of thing as a commodity that I can dispose of—thanks to my 'close connection' —for several shillings."

"And can you?"

"Not for several pence. They're all tariffed, but he's tariffed low—having a value, apparently, that money doesn't represent. He's always welcome, but he isn't always paid for. The beauty, however, is in his marvellous memory, his keeping us all so apart and not muddling the fellow to whom he has written that he hasn't done this, that or the other with the fellow to whom he has written that he has. He'll write to me again some day about something else—about his alleged position on the date of the next school-treat of the Chelsea Cabmen's Orphanage. I shall seek a market for the precious item, and that will keep us in touch; so that if the complication

you have the sense of in your bones does come into play—
the thought's too beautiful!—he may once more remember
me. Fancy his coming to one with a 'What can you do for
me *now?*' " Bight lost himself in the happy vision; it gratified
so his cherished consciousness of the "irony of fate"—a consciousness so cherished that he never could write ten lines
without use of the words.

Maud showed however at this point a reserve which appeared to have grown as the possibility opened out. "I believe
in it—it must come. It can't not. It's the only end. He doesn't
know; nobody knows—the simple-minded all: only you and
I know. But it won't be nice, remember."

"It won't be funny?"

"It will be pitiful. There'll have to be a reason."

"For his turning round?" the young man nursed the
vision. "More or less—I see what you mean. But except for
a 'ply' will that so much matter? His reason will concern
himself. What will concern us will be his funk and his helplessness, his having to stand there in the blaze, with nothing
and nobody to put it out. We shall see him, shrieking for a
bucket of water, wither up in the central flame."

Her look had turned sombre. "It makes one cruel. That is
it makes *you.* I mean our trade does."

"I dare say—I see too much. But I'm willing to chuck it."

"Well," she presently replied, "I'm not willing to, but it
seems pretty well on the cards that I shall have to. *I* don't
see too much. I don't see enough. So, for all the good it does
me——!"

She had pushed back her chair and was looking round for
her umbrella. "Why, what's the matter?" Howard Bight too
blankly inquired.

She met his eyes while she pulled on her rusty old gloves.
"Well, I'll tell you another time."

He kept his place, still lounging, contented where she had
again become restless. "Don't you call it seeing enough to

see—to have had so luridly revealed to you—the doom of
Beadel-Muffet?"

"Oh, he's not my business, he's yours. You're his man, or
one of his men—he'll come back to you. Besides, he's a
special case, and, as I say, I'm too sorry for him."

"That's a proof then of what you do see."

Her silence for a moment admitted it, though evidently she
was making, for herself, a distinction, which she didn't express. "I don't then see what I want, what I require. And *he,*"
she added, "if he does have some reason, will have to have an
awfully strong one. To be strong enough it will have to be
awful."

"You mean he'll have done something?"

"Yes, that may remain undiscovered if he can only drop
out of the papers, sit for a while in darkness. You'll know what
it is; you'll not be able to help yourself. But I shan't want to,
for anything."

She had got up as she said it, and he sat looking at her,
thanks to her odd emphasis, with an interest that, as he also
rose, passed itself off as a joke. "Ah, then, you sweet sensitive
thing, I promise to keep it from you."

II

THEY met again a few days later, and it seemed the law of
their meetings that these should take place mainly within
moderate eastward range of Charing Cross. An afternoon
performance of a play translated from the Finnish, already
several times given, on a series of Saturdays, had held Maud
for an hour in a small, hot, dusty theatre where the air hung
as heavy about the great "trimmed" and plumed hats of the
ladies as over the flora and fauna of a tropical forest; at the
end of which she edged out of her stall in the last row, to join

a small band of unattached critics and correspondents, spectators with ulterior views and pencilled shirtcuffs, who, coming
together in the lobby for an exchange of ideas, were ranging
from "Awful rot" to "Rather jolly." Ideas, of this calibre,
rumbled and flashed, so that, lost in the discussion, our young
woman failed at first to make out that a gentleman on the
other side of the group, but standing a little off, had his eyes
on her for some extravagant, though apparently quite respectable, purpose. He had been waiting for her to recognise him,
and as soon as he had caught her attention he came round to
her with an eager bow. She had by this time entirely placed
him—placed him as the smoothest and most shining subject
with which, in the exercise of her profession, she had yet
experimented; but her recognition was accompanied with a
pang that his amiable address made but the sharper. She had
her reason for awkwardness in the presence of a rosy, glossy,
kindly, but discernibly troubled personage whom she had
waited on "at home" at her own suggestion—promptly
welcomed—and the sympathetic element in whose "personality," the Chippendale, the photographic, the autographic
elements in whose flat in the Earl's Court Road, she had commemorated in the liveliest prose of which she was capable.
She had described with humour his favourite pug, she had
revealed with permission his favourite make of Kodak, she
had touched upon his favourite manner of spending his
Sundays and had extorted from him the shy confession that
he preferred after all the novel of adventure to the novel of
subtlety. Her embarrassment was therefore now the greater as,
touching to behold, he so clearly had approached her with
no intention of asperity, not even at first referring at all to
the matter that couldn't have been gracefully explained.

She had seen him originally—had had the instinct of it in
making up to him—as one of the happy of the earth, and the
impression of him "at home," on his proving so good-
natured about the interview, had begotten in her a sharper

envy, a hungrier sense of the invidious distinctions of fate,
than any her literary conscience, which she deemed rigid, had
yet had to reckon with. He must have been rich, rich by such
estimates as hers; he at any rate had everything, while she
had nothing—nothing but the vulgar need of offering him to
brag, on his behalf, for money, if she could get it, about his
luck. She hadn't in fact got money, hadn't so much as managed
to work in her stuff anywhere; a practical comment sharp
enough on her having represented to him—with wasted
pathos, she was indeed soon to perceive—how "important"
it was to her that people should let her get at them. This dim
celebrity had not needed that argument; he had not only, with
his alacrity, allowed her, as she had said, to try her hand, but
had tried *with* her, quite feverishly, and all to the upshot of
showing her that there were even greater outsiders than herself. He could have put down money, could have published,
as the phrase was—a bare two columns—at his own expense;
but it was just a part of his rather irritating luxury that he had
a scruple about that, wanted intensely to taste the sweet, but
didn't want to owe it to any wire-pulling. He wanted the
golden apple straight from the tree, where it yet seemed so
unable to grow for him by any exuberance of its own. He had
breathed to her his real secret—that to be inspired, to work
with effect, he had to feel he was appreciated, to have it all
somehow come back to him. The artist, necessarily sensitive,
lived on encouragement, on knowing and being reminded that
people cared for him a little, cared even just enough to flatter
him a wee bit. They had talked that over, and he had really,
as he called it, quite put himself in her power. He had whis-
pered in her ear that it might be very weak and silly, but that
positively to be himself, to do anything, certainly to do his
best, he required the breath of sympathy. He did love notice,
let alone praise—there it was. To be systematically ignored—
well, blighted him at the root. He was afraid she would think
he had said too much, but she left him with his leave, none the

less, to repeat a part of it. They had agreed that she was to
bring in prettily, somehow, that he did love praise; for just
the right way he was sure he could trust to her taste.

She had promised to send him the interview in proof, but
she had been able, after all, to send it but in type-copy. If *she*,
after all, had had a flat adorned—as to the drawing-room
alone—with eighty-three photographs, and all in plush
frames; if she had lived in the Earl's Court Road, had been
rosy and glossy and well filled out; and if she had looked
withal, as she always made a point of calling it when she
wished to refer without vulgarity to the right place in the
social scale, "unmistakeably gentle"—if she had achieved
these things she would have snapped her fingers at all other
sweets, have sat as tight as possible and let the world wag,
have spent her Sundays in silently thanking her stars, and
not have cared to know one Kodak, or even one novelist's
"methods," from another. Except for his unholy itch he was
in short so just the person she would have liked to be that the
last consecration was given for her to his character by his
speaking quite as if he had accosted her only to secure her
view of the strange Finnish "soul." He had come each time—
there had been four Saturdays; whereas Maud herself had had
to wait till to-day, though her bread depended on it, for the
roundabout charity of her publicly bad seat. It didn't matter
why he had come—so that he might see it somewhere printed
of him that he was "a conspicuously faithful attendant" at
the interesting series; it only mattered that he was letting her
off so easily, and yet that there was a restless hunger, odd on
the part of one of the filled-out, in his appealing eye, which
she now saw not to be a bit intelligent, though that didn't
matter either. Howard Bight came into view while she dealt
with these impressions, whereupon she found herself edging
a little away from her patron. Her other friend, who had but
just arrived and was apparently waiting to speak to her,
would be a pretext for a break before the poor gentleman

should begin to accuse her of having failed him. She had failed herself so much more that she would have been ready to reply to him that *he* was scarce the one to complain; fortunately, however, the bell sounded the end of the interval and her tension was relaxed. They all flocked back to their places, and her *camarade*—she knew enough often so to designate him— was enabled, thanks to some shifting of other spectators, to occupy a seat beside her. He had brought with him the breath of business; hurrying from one appointment to another he might have time but for a single act. He had seen each of the others by itself, and the way he now crammed in the third, after having previously snatched the fourth, brought home again to the girl that he was leading the real life. Her own was a dull imitation of it. Yet it happened at the same time that before the curtain rose again he had, with a "Who's your fat friend?" professed to have caught her in the act of making her own brighter.

" 'Mortimer Marshal'?" he echoed after she had, a trifle dryly, satisfied him. "Never heard of him."

"Well, I shan't tell him that. But you *have*," she said; "you've only forgotten. I told you after I had been to him."

Her friend thought—it came back to him. "Oh yes, and showed me what you had made of it. I remember your stuff was charming."

"I see you remember nothing," Maud a little more dryly said. "I didn't show you what I had made of it. I've never made anything. You've not seen my stuff, and nobody has. They won't have it."

She spoke with a smothered vibration, but, as they were still waiting, it had made him look at her; by which she was slightly the more disconcerted. "Who won't?"

"Everyone, everything won't. Nobody, nothing will. He's hopeless, or rather *I* am. I'm no good. And he knows it."

"O—oh!" the young man kindly but vaguely protested. "Has he been making that remark to you?"

"No—that's the worst of it. He's too dreadfully civil. He thinks I can do something."

"Then why do you say he knows you can't?"

She was impatient; she gave it up. "Well, I don't know what he knows—except that he does want to be loved."

"Do you mean he has proposed to you to love him?"

"Loved by the great heart of the public—speaking through its natural organ. He wants to be—well, where Beadel-Muffet is."

"Oh, I hope not!" said Bight with grim amusement.

His friend was struck with his tone. "Do you mean it's coming on for Beadel-Muffet—what we talked about?" And then as he looked at her so queerly that her curiosity took a jump: "It really and truly *is?* Has anything happened?"

"The rummest thing in the world—since I last saw you. We're wonderful, you know, you and I together—we *see*. And what we see always takes place, usually within the week. It wouldn't be believed. But it will do for *us*. At any rate it's high sport."

"Do you mean," she asked, "that his scare has literally begun?"

He meant, clearly, quite as much as he said. "He has written to me again he wants to see me, and we've an appointment for Monday."

"Then why isn't it the old game?"

"Because it isn't. He wants to gather from me, as I *have* served him before, if something can't be done. *On a souvent besoin d'un plus petit que soi.* Keep quiet, and we shall see something."

This was very well; only his manner visibly had for her the effect of a chill in the air. "I hope," she said, "you're going at least to be decent to him."

"Well, you'll judge. Nothing at all can be done—it's too ridiculously late. And it serves him right. I shan't deceive him, certainly, but I might as well enjoy him."

The fiddles were still going, and Maud had a pause. "Well, you know you've more or less lived on him. I mean it's the kind of thing you *are* living on."

"Precisely—that's just why I loathe it."

Again she hesitated. "You mustn't quarrel, you know, with your bread and butter."

He looked straight before him, as if she had been consciously, and the least bit disagreeably, sententious. "What in the world's that but what I shall just be *not* doing? If our bread and butter is the universal push I consult our interest by not letting it trifle with us. They're not to blow hot and cold—it won't do. There he is—let him get out himself. What I call sport is to see if he can."

"And not—poor wretch—to help him?"

But Bight was ominously lucid. "The devil is that he can't *be* helped. His one idea of help, from the day he opened his eyes, has been to be prominently—damn the word!—mentioned: it's the only kind of help that exists in connection with him. What therefore is a fellow to do when he happens to want it to stop—wants a special sort of prominence that will work like a trap in a pantomime and enable him to vanish when the situation requires it? Is one to mention that he wants *not* to be mentioned—never, never, please, any more? Do you see the success of that, all over the place, do you see the headlines in the American papers? No, he must die as he has lived—the Principal Public Person of his time."

"Well," she sighed, "it's all horrible." And then without a transition: "What do you suppose has happened to him?"

"The dreadfulness I wasn't to tell you?"

"I only mean if you suppose him in a really bad hole."

The young man considered. "It can't certainly be that he has had a change of heart—never. It may be nothing worse than that the woman he wants to marry has turned against it."

"But I supposed him—with his children all so boomed—to *be* married."

"Naturally; else he couldn't have got such a boom from the poor lady's illness, death and burial. Don't you remember two years ago?—'We are given to understand that Sir A. B. C. Beadel-Muffet K.C.B., M.P., particularly desires that no flowers be sent for the late Hon. Lady Beadel-Muffet's funeral.' And then, the next day: 'We are authorised to state that the impression, so generally prevailing, that Sir A. B. C. Beadel-Muffet has expressed an objection to flowers in connection with the late Hon. Lady Beadel-Muffet's obsequies, rests on a misapprehension of Sir A. B. C. Beadel-Muffet's markedly individual views. The floral tributes already delivered in Queen's Gate Gardens, and remarkable for number and variety, have been the source of such gratification to the bereaved gentleman as his situation permits.' With a wind-up of course for the following week—the inevitable few heads of remark, on the part of the bereaved gentleman, on the general subject of Flowers at Funerals as a Fashion, vouchsafed, under pressure possibly indiscreet, to a rising young journalist always thirsting for the authentic word."

"I guess now," said Maud, after an instant, "the rising young journalist. You egged him on."

"Dear, no. I panted in his rear."

"It makes you," she added, "more than cynical."

"And what do you call 'more than' cynical?"

"It makes you sardonic. Wicked," she continued; "devilish."

"That's it—that *is* cynical. Enough's as good as a feast." But he came back to the ground they had quitted. "What were you going to say *he's* prominent for, Mortimer Marshal?"

She wouldn't, however, follow him there yet, her curiosity on the other issue not being spent. "Do you know then as a fact, that he's marrying again, the bereaved gentleman?"

Her friend, at this, showed impatience. "My dear fellow, do you *see* nothing? We had it all, didn't we, three months ago, and then we didn't have it, and then we had it again; and goodness knows where we are. But I throw out the possibility. I forget her bloated name, but she may be rich, and she may be decent. She may make it a condition that he keeps out—out, I mean, of the only things he has really ever been 'in.' "

"The Papers?"

"The dreadful, nasty, vulgar Papers. She may put it to him —I see it dimly and queerly, but I see it—that he must get out first, and then they'll talk; then she'll say yes, then he'll have the money. I see it—and much more sharply—that he *wants* the money, needs it, I mean, badly, desperately, so that this necessity may very well make the hole in which he finds himself. Therefore he must do something—what he's trying to do. It supplies the motive that our picture, the other day, rather missed."

Maud Blandy took this in, but it seemed to fail to satisfy her. "It must be something worse. You make it out *that*, so that your practical want of mercy, which you'll not be able to conceal from me, shall affect me as less inhuman."

"I don't make it out anything, and I don't care what it is; the queerness, the grand 'irony' of the case is itself enough for me. You, on your side, however, I think, make it out what you call 'something worse,' because of the romantic bias of your mind. You 'see red.' Yet isn't it, after all, sufficiently lurid that he shall lose his blooming bride?"

"You're sure," Maud appealed, "that he'll lose her?"

"Poetic justice screams for it; and my whole interest in the matter is staked on it."

But the girl continued to brood. "I thought you contend that nobody's half 'decent.' Where do you find a woman to make such a condition?"

"Not easily, I admit." The young man thought. "It will be *his* luck to have found her. That's his tragedy, say, that she can financially save him, but that she happens to be just the one freak, the creature whose stomach has turned. The spark—I mean of decency—has got, after all, somehow to be kept alive; and it may be lodged in this particular female form."

"I see. But why should a female form that's so particular confess to an affinity with a male form that's so fearfully general? As he's *all* self-advertisement, why isn't it much more natural to her simply to loathe him?"

"Well, because, oddly enough, it seems that people don't."

"*You* do," Maud declared. "You'll kill him."

He just turned a flushed cheek to her, and she saw that she had touched something that lived in him. "We *can*," he consciously smiled, "deal death. And the beauty is that it's in a perfectly straight way. We can lead them on. But have you ever seen Beadel-Muffet for yourself?" he continued.

"No. How often, please, need I tell you that I've seen nobody and nothing?"

"Well, if you had you'd understand."

"You mean he's so fetching?"

"Oh, he's great. He's not 'all' self-advertisement—or at least he doesn't seem to be: that's his pull. But I see, you female humbug," Bight pursued, "how much you'd like him yourself."

"I want, while I'm about it, to pity him in sufficient quantity."

"Precisely. Which means, for a woman, with extravagance and to the point of immorality."

"I ain't a woman," Maud Blandy sighed. "I wish I were!"

"Well, about the pity," he went on; "you shall be immoral, I promise you, before you've done. Doesn't Mortimer Marshal," he asked, "take you for a woman?"

"You'll have to ask *him*. How," she demanded, "does one know those things?" And she stuck to her Beadel-Muffet. "If you're to see him on Monday shan't you then get to the bottom of it?"

"Oh, I don't conceal from you that I promise myself larks,

but I won't tell you, positively I won't," Bight said, "what I
see. You're morbid. If it's only bad enough—I mean his
motive—you'll want to save him."

"Well, isn't that what you're to profess to him that *you*
want?"

"Ah," the young man returned, "I believe you'd really
invent a way."

"I would if I could." And with that she dropped it.
"There's my fat friend," she presently added, as the entr'acte
still hung heavy and Mortimer Marshal, from a row much in
advance of them, screwed himself round in his tight place
apparently to keep her in his eye.

"He does then," said her companion, "take you for a
woman. I seem to guess he's 'littery.' "

"That's it; so badly that he wrote that 'littery' ply *Corisanda*,
you must remember, with Beatrice Beaumont in the principal
part, which was given at three matinées in this very place and
which hadn't even the luck of being slated. Every creature
connected with the production, from the man himself and
Beatrice *her*self down to the mothers and grandmothers of
the sixpenny young women, the young women of the pro-
grammes, was interviewed both before and after, and he
promptly published the piece, pleading guilty to the 'littery'
charge—which is the great stand he takes and the subject of
the discussion."

Bight had wonderingly followed. "Of what discussion?"

"Why, the one he thinks there ought to have been. There
hasn't been any, of course, but he wants it, dreadfully misses
it. People won't keep it up—whatever they *did* do, though I
don't myself make out that they did anything. His state of
mind requires something to start with, which has got somehow to be provided. There must have been a noise made,
don't you see? to make him prominent; and in order to
remain prominent he has got to go for his enemies. The
hostility to his ply, and all *because* its 'littery,' we can do

nothing without that; but it's uphill work to come across it. We sit up nights trying, but we seem to get no for'arder. The public attention would seem to abhor the whole matter even as nature abhors a vacuum. We've nothing to go upon, otherwise we might go far. But there we are."

"I see," Bight commented. "You're nowhere at all."

"No; it isn't even that, for we're just where *Corisanda*, on the stage and in the closet, put us at a stroke. Only there we stick fast—nothing seems to happen, nothing seems to come or to be capable of being made to come. We wait."

"Oh, if he waits with *you!*" Bight amicably jibed.

"He may wait for ever?"

"No, but resignedly. You'll make him forget his wrongs."

"Ah, I'm not of that sort, and I could only do it by making him come into his rights. And I recognise now that that's impossible. There are different cases, you see, whole different classes of them, and his is the opposite to Beadel-Muffet's."

Howard Bight gave a grunt. "Why the opposite if you also pity him? I'll be hanged," he added, "if you won't save *him* too."

But she shook her head. She knew. "No; but it's nearly, in its way, as lurid. Do you know," she asked, "what he has done?"

"Why, the difficulty appears to be that he can't have done anything. He should strike once more—hard, and in the same place. He should bring out another ply."

"Why so? You can't be more than prominent, and he *is* prominent. You can't do more than subscribe, in your prominence, to thirty-seven 'press-cutting' agencies in England and America, and, having done so, you can't do more than sit at home with your ear on the postman's knock, looking out for results. *There* comes in the tragedy—there are no results. Mortimer Marshal's postman doesn't knock; the press-cutting agencies can't find anything to cut. With thirty-seven, in the whole English-speaking world, scouring millions of papers for him in vain, and with a big slice of his private income all the while going to it, the 'irony' is too cruel, and the way he looks at one, as in one's degree responsible, does make one wince. He expected, naturally, most from the Americans, but it's they who have failed him worst. Their silence is that of the tomb, and it seems to grow, if the silence of the tomb *can* grow. He won't admit that the thirty-seven look far enough or long enough, and he writes them, I infer, angry letters, wanting to know what the deuce they suppose he has paid them for. But what are they either, poor things, to do?"

"Do? They can print his angry letters. That, at least, will break the silence, and he'll like it better than nothing."

This appeared to strike our young woman. "Upon my word, I really believe he would." Then she thought better of it. "But they'd be afraid, for they do guarantee, you know, that there's something for everyone. They claim it's their strength—that there's enough to go round. They won't want to show that they break down."

"Oh, well," said the young man, "if he can't manage to smash a pane of glass somewhere——!"

"That's what he thought *I* would do. And it's what *I* thought I might," Maud added; "otherwise I wouldn't have approached him. I did it on spec, but I'm no use. I'm a fatal influence. I'm a non-conductor."

She said it with such plain sincerity that it quickly took her companion's attention. "I *say!*" he covertly murmured. "Have you a secret sorrow?"

"Of course I've a secret sorrow." And she stared at it, stiff and a little sombre, not wanting it to be too freely handled, while the curtain at last rose to the lighted stage.

III

SHE was later on more open about it, sundry other things, not
wholly alien, having meanwhile happened. One of these had
been that her friend had waited with her to the end of the
Finnish performance and that it had then, in the lobby, as
they went out, not been possible for her not to make him
acquainted with Mr Mortimer Marshal. This gentleman had
clearly waylaid her and had also clearly divined that her companion was of the Papers—papery all through; which doubtless
had something to do with his having handsomely proposed
to them to accompany him somewhere to tea. They hadn't
seen why they shouldn't, it being an adventure, all in their
line, like another; and he had carried them, in a four-wheeler,
to a small and refined club in a region which was as the fringe
of the Piccadilly region, where even their own presence scarce
availed to contradict the implication of the exclusive. The
whole occasion, they were further to feel, was essentially a
tribute to their professional connection, especially that side
of it which flushed and quavered, which panted and pined in
their host's personal nervousness. Maud Blandy now saw it
vain to contend with his delusion that *she*, underfed and un-
printed, who had never been so conscious as during these
bribed moments of her non-conducting quality, was papery
to any purpose—a delusion that exceeded, by her measure,
every other form of pathos. The decoration of the tea-room
was a pale, æsthetic green, the liquid in the delicate cups a
copious potent amber; the bread and butter was thin and
golden, the muffins a revelation to her that she was bar-
barously hungry. There were ladies at other tables with other
gentlemen—ladies with long feather boas and hats not of the
sailor pattern, and gentlemen whose straight collars were

doubled up much higher than Howard Bight's and their hair parted far more at the side. The talk was so low, with pauses somehow so not of embarrassment that it could only have been earnest, and the air, an air of privilege and privacy to our young woman's sense, seemed charged with fine things taken for granted. If it hadn't been for Bight's company she would have grown almost frightened, so much seemed to be offered her for something she couldn't do. That word of Bight's about smashing a window-pane had lingered with her; it had made her afterwards wonder, while they sat in their stalls, if there weren't some brittle surface in range of her own elbow. She had to fall back on the consciousness of how her elbow, in spite of her type, lacked practical point, and that was just why the terms in which she saw her services now, as she believed, bid for, had the effect of scaring her. They came out most, for that matter, in Mr Mortimer Marshal's dumbly-insistent eyes, which seemed to be perpetually saying: "You know what I mean when I'm too refined—like everything here, don't you see?—to say it out. You know there ought to be something about me somewhere, and that really, with the opportunities, the facilities you enjoy, it wouldn't be so much out of your way just to—well, reward this little attention."

The fact that he was probably every day, in just the same anxious flurry and with just the same superlative delicacy, paying little attentions with an eye to little rewards, this fact by itself but scantily eased her, convinced as she was that no luck but her own was as hopeless as his. He squared the clever young wherever he could get at them, but it was the clever young, taking them generally, who fed from his hand and then forgot him. She didn't forget him; she pitied him too much, pitied herself, and was more and more, as she found, now pitying everyone; only she didn't know how to say to him that she could do, after all, nothing for him. She oughtn't to have come, in the first place, and wouldn't if it hadn't been

for her companion. Her companion was increasingly sardonic
—which was the way in which, at best, she now increasingly
saw him; he was shameless in acceptance, since, as she knew,
as she felt at his side, he had come only, at bottom, to mislead
and to mystify. *He* was, as she wasn't, on the Papers and of
them, and their baffled entertainer knew it without either a
hint on the subject from herself or a need, on the young
man's own lips, of the least vulgar allusion. Nothing was so
much as named, the whole connection was sunk; they talked
about clubs, muffins, afternoon performances, the effect of the
Finnish soul upon the appetite, quite as if they had met in
society. Nothing could have been less like society—she inno-
cently supposed at least—than the real spirit of their meeting;
yet Bight did nothing that he might do to keep the affair
within bounds. When looked at by their friend so hard and so
hintingly, he only looked back, just as dumbly, but just as
intensely and, as might be said, portentously; ever so im-
penetrably, in fine, and ever so wickedly. He didn't smile—
as if to cheer—the least little bit; which he might be abstaining
from on purpose to make his promises solemn: so, as he tried
to smile—she couldn't, it was all too dreadful—she wouldn't
meet her friend's eyes, but kept looking, heartlessly, at the
"notes" of the place, the hats of the ladies, the tints of the
rugs, the intenser Chippendale, here and there, of the chairs
and tables, of the very guests, of the very waitresses. It had
come to her early: "I've done him, poor man, at home, and
the obvious thing now will be to do him at his club." But this
inspiration plumped against her fate even as an imprisoned
insect against the window-glass. She couldn't do him at his
club without decently asking leave; whereby he would know
of her feeble feeler, feeble because she was so sure of refusals.
She would rather tell him, desperately, what she thought of
him than expose him to see again that she was herself nowhere, herself nothing. Her one comfort was that, for the half-
hour—it had made the situation quite possible—he seemed

fairly hypnotised by her colleague; so that when they took
leave he as good as thanked her for what she had this time
done for him. It was one of the signs of his infatuated state
that he clearly viewed Bight as a mass of helpful cleverness,
though the cruel creature, uttering scarce a sound, had only
fixed him in a manner that might have been taken for the
fascination of deference. He might perfectly have been an
idiot for all the poor gentleman knew. But the poor gentleman saw a possible "leg up" in every bush; and nothing but
impertinence would have convinced him that she hadn't
brought him, compunctiously as to the past, a master of the
proper art. Now, more than ever, how he would listen for the
postman!

The whole occasion had broken so, for busy Bight, into
matters to be attended to before Fleet Street warmed to its
work, that the pair were obliged, outside, to part company on
the spot, and it was only on the morrow, a Saturday, that
they could taste again of that comparison of notes which
made for each the main savour, albeit slightly acrid, of their
current consciousness. The air was full, as from afar, of the
grand indifference of spring, of which the breath could be felt
so much before the face could be seen, and they had bicycled
side by side out to Richmond Park as with the impulse to
meet it on its way. They kept a Saturday, when possible,
sacred to the Suburbs as distinguished from the Papers—
when possible being largely when Maud could achieve the
use of the somewhat fatigued family machine. Many sisters
contended for it, under whose flushed pressure it might have
been seen spinning in many different directions. Superficially,
at Richmond, our young couple rested—found a quiet corner
to lounge deep in the Park, with their machines propped by
one side of a great tree and their associated backs sustained
by another. But agitation, finer than the finest scorching, was
in the air for them; it was made sharp, rather abruptly, by a
vivid outbreak from Maud. It was very well, she observed,

for her friend to be clever at the expense of the general "greed"; he saw it in the light of his own jolly luck, and what she saw, as it happened, was nothing but the general art of letting you starve, yourself, in your hole. At the end of five minutes her companion had turned quite pale with having to face the large extent of her confession. It was a confession for the reason that in the first place it evidently cost her an effort that pride had again and again successfully prevented, and because in the second she had thus the air of having lived overmuch on swagger. She could scarce have said at this moment what, for a good while, she had really lived on, and she didn't let him know now to complain either of her privation or of her disappointments. She did it to show why she couldn't go with him when he was so awfully sweeping. There were at any rate apparently, all over, two wholly different sets of people. If everyone rose to his bait no creature had ever risen to hers; and that was the grim truth of her position, which proved at the least that there were two quite different kinds of luck. They told two different stories of human vanity; they couldn't be reconciled. And the poor girl put it in a nutshell. "There's but one person I've *ever* written to who has so much as noticed my letter."

He wondered, painfully affected—it rather overwhelmed him; he took hold of it at the easiest point. "One person——?"

"The misguided man we had tea with. He alone—*he* rose."

"Well then, you see that when they do rise they *are* misguided. In other words they're donkeys."

"What I see is that I don't strike the right ones and that I haven't therefore your ferocity; that is my ferocity, if I have any, rests on a different ground. You'll say that I go for the wrong people; but I don't, God knows—witness Mortimer Marshal—fly too high. I picked him out, after prayer and fasting, as just the likeliest of the likely—not anybody a bit grand and yet not quite a nobody; and by an extraordinary chance I was justified. Then I pick out others who seem just as good, I pray and fast, and no sound comes back. But I work through my ferocity too," she stiffly continued, "though at first it was great, feeling as I did that when my bread and butter was in it people had no right not to oblige me. It was their duty—what they were prominent *for*—to be interviewed, so as to keep me going; and I did as much for them any day as they would be doing for me."

Bight heard her, but for a moment said nothing. "Did you tell them that? I mean say to them it was your little all?"

"Not vulgarly—I know how. There are ways of saying it's 'important'; and I hint it just enough to see that the importance fetches them no more than anything else. It isn't important to *them*. And I, in their place," Maud went on, "wouldn't answer either; I'll be hanged if ever I would. That's what it comes to, that there *are* two distinct lots, and that my luck, being born so, is always to try the snubbers. You were born to know by instinct the others. But it makes me more tolerant."

"More tolerant of what?" her friend asked.

"Well, of what you described to me. Of what you rail at."

"Thank you for *me!*" Bight laughed.

"Why not? Don't you live on it?"

"Not in such luxury—you surely must see for yourself— as the distinction you make seems to imply. It isn't luxury to be nine-tenths of the time sick of everything. People more-over are worth to me but tuppence apiece; there are too many, confound them—so many that I don't see really how any can be left over for *your* superior lot. It *is* a chance," he pursued—"I've had refusals too—though I confess they've sometimes been of the funniest. Besides, I'm getting out of it," the young man wound up. "God knows I want to. My advice to you," he added in the same breath, "is to sit tight. There are as good fish in the sea——!"

She waited a moment. "You're sick of everything and you're getting out of it; it's not good enough for you, in other words, but it's still good enough for me. Why am I to sit tight when you sit so loose?"

"Because what you want will come—can't help coming. Then, in time, you'll also get out of it. But then you'll have had it, as I have, and the good of it."

"But what, really, if it breeds nothing but disgust," she asked, "do you *call* the good of it?"

"Well, two things. First the bread and butter, and then the fun. I repeat it—sit tight."

"Where's the fun," she asked again, "of learning to despise people?"

"You'll see when it comes. It will all be upon you, it will change for you any day. Sit tight, sit tight."

He expressed such confidence that she might for a minute have been weighing it. "If you get out of it, what will you do?"

"Well, imaginative work. This job has made me at least *see*. It has given me the loveliest tips."

She had still another pause. "It has given me—*my* experience has—a lovely tip too."

"And what's that?"

"I've told you before—the tip of pity. I'm so much sorrier for them all—panting and gasping for it like fish out of water —than I am anything else."

He wondered. "But I thought that was what just isn't your experience."

"Oh, I mean then," she said impatiently, "that my tip is from yours. It's only a different tip. I want to save them."

"Well," the young man replied, and as if the idea had had a meaning for him, "saving them may perhaps work out as a branch. The question is can you be paid for it?"

"Beadel-Muffet would pay me," Maud suddenly suggested.

"Why, that's just what I'm expecting," her companion laughed, "that he will, after to-morrow—directly or indirectly —do *me*."

"Will you take it from him then only to get him in deeper, as that's what you perfectly know you'll do? You won't save him; you'll lose him."

"What then would you, in the case," Bight asked, "do for your money?"

Well, the girl thought. "I'd get him to see me—I should have first, I recognise, to catch my hare—and then I'd work up my stuff. Which would be boldly, quite by a master-stroke, a statement of his fix—of the fix, I mean, of his want-ing, his supplicating to be dropped. I'd give out that it would really oblige. Then I'd send my copy about, and the rest of the matter would take care of itself. I don't say *you* could do it that way—you'd have a different effect. But I should be able to trust the thing, being mine, not to be looked at, or, if looked at, chucked straight into the basket. I should so have, to that extent, handled the matter, and I should so, by merely touching it, have broken the spell. That's my one line—I stop things off by touching them. There'd never be a word about him more."

Her friend, with his legs out and his hands locked at the back of his neck, had listened with indulgence. "Then hadn't I better arrange it for you that Beadel-Muffet shall see you?"

"Oh, not after you've damned him!"

"You want to see him first?"

"It will be the only way—to be of any use to him. You ought to wire him in fact not to open his mouth till he has seen me."

"Well, I will," said Bight at last. "But, you know, we shall lose something very handsome—his struggle, all in vain, with his fate. Noble sport, the sight of it all." He turned a little, to rest on his elbow, and, cycling suburban young man as he was, he might have been, outstretched under his tree, melancholy Jacques looking off into a forest glade, even as sailor-hatted Maud, in—for elegance—a new cotton blouse and a long-limbed angular attitude, might have prosefully suggested the mannish Rosalind. He raised his face in appeal to her. "Do you really ask me to sacrifice it?"

"Rather than sacrifice *him?* Of course I do."

He said for a while nothing more; only, propped on his elbow, lost himself again in the Park. After which he turned back to her. "Will you have me?" he suddenly asked.

"'Have you'——?"

"Be my bonny bride. For better, for worse. I hadn't, upon my honour," he explained with obvious sincerity, "understood you were so down."

"Well, it isn't so bad as that," said Maud Blandy.

"So bad as taking up with *me?*"

"It isn't as bad as having let you know—when I didn't want you to."

He sank back again with his head dropped, putting himself more at his ease. "You're too proud—that's what's the matter with you. And I'm too stupid."

"No, you're not," said Maud grimly. "Not stupid."

"Only cruel, cunning, treacherous, cold-blooded, vile?" He drawled the words out softly, as if they sounded fair.

"And I'm not stupid either," Maud Blandy went on. "We just, poor creatures—well, we just *know.*"

"Of course we do. So why do you want us to drug ourselves with rot? to go on as if we didn't know?"

She made no answer for a moment; then she said: "There's good to be known too."

"Of course, again. There are all sorts of things, and some much better than others. That's why," the young man added, "I just put that question to you."

"Oh no, it isn't. You put it to me because you think I feel I'm no good."

"How so, since I keep assuring you that you've only to wait? How so, since I keep assuring you that if you do wait it will all come with a rush? But say I *am* sorry for you," Bight lucidly pursued; "how does that prove either that my motive is base or that I do you a wrong?"

The girl waived this question, but she presently tried another. "Is it your idea that we should live on all the people——?"

"The people we catch? Yes, old man, till we can do better."

"My conviction is," she soon returned, "that if I were to marry you I should dish you. I should spoil the business. It would fall off; and, as I can do nothing myself, then where should we be?"

"Well," said Bight, "we mightn't be quite so high up in the scale of the morbid."

"It's you that are morbid," she answered. "You've, in your way—like everyone else, for that matter, all over the place—'sport' on the brain."

"Well," he demanded, "what is sport but success? What is success but sport?"

"Bring that out somewhere. If it be true," she said, "I'm glad I'm a failure."

After which, for a longish space, they sat together in silence, a silence finally broken by a word from the young man. "But about Mortimer Marshal—how do you propose to save *him?*"

It was a change of subject that might, by its so easy introduction of matter irrelevant, have seemed intended to dissipate whatever was left of his proposal of marriage. That proposal, however, had been somehow both too much in the tone of familiarity to linger and too little in that of vulgarity to drop. It had had no form, but the mild air kept perhaps thereby the better the taste of it. This was sensibly moreover in what the girl found to reply. "I think, you know, that he'd be no such bad friend. I mean that, with his appetite, there would be something to be done. He doesn't half hate me."

"Ah, my dear," her friend ejaculated, "don't, for God's sake, be low."

12:D

But she kept it up. "He clings to me. You saw. It's hideous, the way he's able to 'do' himself."

Bight lay quiet, then spoke as with a recall of the Chippendale Club. "Yes, I couldn't 'do' you as he could. But if you don't bring it off——?"

"Why then does he cling? Oh, because, all the same, I'm potentially the Papers still. I'm at any rate the nearest he has got to them. And then I'm other things."

"I see."

"I'm so awfully attractive," said Maud Blandy. She got up with this and, shaking out her frock, looked at her resting bicycle, looked at the distances possibly still to be gained. Her companion paused, but at last also rose, and by that time she was awaiting him, a little gaunt and still not quite cool, as an illustration of her last remark. He stood there watching her, and she followed this remark up. "I do, you know, really pity him."

It had almost a feminine fineness, and their eyes continued to meet. "Oh, you'll work it!" And the young man went to his machine.

IV

It was not till five days later that they again came together, and during these days many things had happened. Maud Blandy had, with high elation, for her own portion, a sharp sense of this; if it had at the time done nothing more intimate for her the Sunday of bitterness just spent with Howard Bight had started, all abruptly, a turn of the tide of her luck. This turn had not in the least been in the young man's having spoken to her of marriage—since she hadn't even, up to the late hour of their parting, so much as answered him straight: she dated the sense of difference much rather from the throb of a happy thought that had come to her while she cycled home to Kilburnia in the darkness. The throb had made her for the few minutes, tired as she was, put on speed, and it had been the cause of still further proceedings for her the first thing the next morning. The active step that was the essence of these proceedings had almost got itself taken before she went to bed; which indeed was what had happened to the extent of her writing, on the spot, a meditated letter. She sat down to it by the light of the guttering candle that awaited her on the dining-room table and in the stale air of family food that only *had* been—a residuum so at the mercy of mere ventilation that she didn't so much as peep into a cupboard; after which she had been on the point of nipping over, as she would have said, to drop it into that opposite pillar-box whose vivid maw, opening out through thick London nights, had received so many of her fruitless little ventures. But she had checked herself and waited, waited to be sure, with the morning, that her fancy wouldn't fade; posting her note in the end, however, with a confident jerk, as soon as she was up. She had, later on, had business, or at least had sought it, among the haunts that she had taught herself to regard as professional; but neither on the Monday nor on either of the days that directly followed had she encountered there the friend whom it would take a difference in more matters than could as yet be dealt with to enable her to regard, with proper assurance or with proper modesty, as a lover. Whatever he was, none the less, it couldn't otherwise have come to her that it was possible to feel lonely in the Strand. That showed, after all, how thick they must constantly have been—which *was* perhaps a thing to begin to think of in a new, in a steadier light. But it showed doubtless still more that her companion was probably up to something rather awful; it made her wonder, holding her breath a little, about Beadel-Muffet, made her certain that he and his affairs would partly account for Bight's whirl of absence.

Ever conscious of empty pockets, she had yet always a penny, or at least a ha'penny, for a paper, and those she now scanned, she quickly assured herself, were edited quite as usual. Sir A. B. C. Beadel-Muffet K.C.B., M.P. had returned on Monday from Undertone, where Lord and Lady Wispers had, from the previous Friday, entertained a very select party; Sir A. B. C. Beadel-Muffet K.C.B., M.P. was to attend on Tuesday the weekly meeting of the society of the Friends of Rest; Sir A. B. C. Beadel-Muffet K.C.B., M.P. had kindly consented to preside on Wednesday, at Samaritan House, at the opening of the Sale of Work of the Middlesex Incurables. These familiar announcements, however, far from appeasing her curiosity, had an effect upon her nerves; she read into them mystic meanings that she had never read before. Her freedom of mind in this direction was indeed at the same time limited, for her own horizon was already, by the Monday night, bristling with new possibilities, and the Tuesday itself —well, what had the Tuesday itself become, with this eruption, from within, of interest amounting really to a revelation, what had the Tuesday itself become but the greatest day yet of her life? Such a description of it would have appeared to apply predominantly to the morning had she not, under the influence, precisely, of the morning's thrill, gone, towards evening, with her design, into the Charing Cross Station. There, at the bookstall, she bought them all, every rag that was hawked; and there, as she unfolded one at a venture, in the crowd and under the lamps, she felt her consciousness further, felt it for the moment quite impressively, enriched. "Personal Peeps—Number Ninety-Three: a Chat with the New Dramatist" needed neither the "H. B." as a terminal signature nor a text spangled, to the exclusion of almost everything else, with Mortimer Marshals that looked as tall as if lettered on posters, to help to account for her young man's use of his time. And yet, as she soon made out, it had been used with an economy that caused her both to wonder and to wince; the "peep" commemorated being none other than their tea with the artless creature the previous Saturday, and the meagre incidents and pale impressions of that occasion furnishing forth the picture.

Bight had solicited no new interview; he hadn't been such a fool—for she saw, soon enough, with all her intelligence, that this was what he would have been, and that a repetition of contact would have dished him. What he *had* done, she found herself perceiving—and perceiving with an emotion that caused her face to glow—was journalism of the intensest essence; a column concocted of nothing, an omelette made, as it were, without even the breakage of the egg or two that might have been expected to be the price. The poor gentleman's whereabouts at five o'clock was the only egg broken, and this light and delicate crash was the sound in the world that would be sweetest to him. What stuff it had to be, since the writer really knew nothing about him, yet how its being just such stuff made it perfectly serve its purpose! She might have marvelled afresh, with more leisure, at such purposes, but she was lost in the wonder of seeing how, without matter, without thought, without an excuse, without a fact and yet at the same time sufficiently without a fiction, he had managed to be as resonant as if he had beaten a drum on the platform of a booth. And he had not been too personal, not made anything awkward for *her*, had given nothing and nobody away, had tossed the Chippendale Club into the air with such a turn that it had fluttered down again, like a blown feather, miles from its site. The thirty-seven agencies would already be posting to their subscriber thirty-seven copies, and their subscriber, on his side, would be posting, to his acquaintance, many times thirty-seven, and thus at least getting something for his money; but this didn't tell her why her friend had taken the trouble—if it had *been* a trouble; why at all events he had taken the time, pressed as he apparently was for that commodity. These things she was indeed presently to learn, but they were meanwhile part of a suspense composed of more elements than any she had yet tasted. And the suspense was prolonged, though other affairs too, that were not part of it, almost equally crowded upon her; the week having almost waned when relief arrived in the form of a cryptic post-card. The post-card bore the H. B., like the precious "Peep," which had already had a wondrous sequel, and it appointed, for the tea-hour, a place of meeting familiar to Maud, with the simple addition of the significant word "Larks!"

When the time he had indicated came she waited for him, at their small table, swabbed like the deck of a steam-packet, nose to nose with a mustard-pot and a price-list, in the consciousness of perhaps after all having as much to tell him as to hear from him. It appeared indeed at first that this might well be the case, for the questions that came up between them when he had taken his place were overwhelmingly those he himself insisted on putting. "What has he done, what *has* he, and what will he?"—that inquiry, not loud but deep, had met him as he sat down; without however producing the least recognition. Then she as soon felt that his silence and his manner were enough for her, or that, if they hadn't been, his wonderful look, the straightest she had ever had from him, would instantly have made them so. He looked at her hard, hard, as if he had meant "I say, mind your eyes!" and it amounted really to a glimpse, rather fearful, of the subject. It was no joke, the subject, clearly, and her friend had fairly gained age, as he had certainly lost weight, in his recent dealings with it. It struck her even, with everything else, that this was positively the way she would have liked him to show if their union had taken the form they hadn't reached the point of discussing; wearily coming back to her from the thick of things, wanting to put on his slippers and have his tea, all prepared by her and in their place, and beautifully to be trusted to regale her in his turn. He was excited, disavowedly, and it took more disavowal still after she had opened her budget—which she did, in truth, by saying to him as her first alternative: "What did you do him *for*, poor Mortimer Marshal? It isn't that he's not in the seventh heaven——!"

"He *is* in the seventh heaven!" Bight quickly broke in. "He doesn't want my blood?"

"Did you do him," she asked, "that he should want it? It's splendid how you could—simply on that show."

"That show? Why," said Howard Bight, "that show was an immensity. That show was volumes, stacks, abysses."

He said it in such a tone that she was a little at a loss. "Oh, you don't want abysses."

"Not much, to knock off such twaddle. There isn't a breath in it of what I saw. What I saw is my own affair. I've got the abysses for myself. They're in my head—it's always something. But the monster," he demanded, "has written you?"

"How couldn't he—that night? I got it the next morning, telling me how much he wanted to thank me and asking me where he might see me. So I went," said Maud, "to see him."

"At his own place again?"

"At his own place again. What do I yearn for but to be received at people's own places?"

"Yes, for the stuff. But when you've had—as you had had from him—the stuff?"

"Well, sometimes, you see, I get more. He gives me all I can take." It was in her head to ask if by chance Bight were jealous, but she gave it another turn. "We had a big palaver, partly about you. He appreciates."

"Me?"

"Me—first of all, I think. All the more that I've had—fancy!—a proof of my stuff, the despised and rejected, as originally concocted, and that he has now seen it. I tried it on again with *Brains*, the night of your thing—sent it off with your thing enclosed as a rouser. They took it, by return, like a shot—you'll see on Wednesday. And if the dear man lives till then, for impatience, I'm to lunch with him that day."

"I see," said Bight. "Well, that was what I did it for. It shows how right I was."

They faced each other, across their thick crockery, with eyes that said more than their words, and that, above all, said, and asked, other things. So she went on in a moment: "I don't know what he doesn't expect. And he thinks I can keep it up."

"Lunch with him *every* Wednesday?"

"Oh, he'd give me my lunch, and more. It was last Sunday that you were right—about my sitting close," she pursued. "I'd have been a pretty fool to jump. Suddenly, I see, the music begins. I'm awfully obliged to you."

"You feel," he presently asked, "quite differently—so differently that I've missed my chance? I don't care for *that* serpent, but there's something else that you don't tell me." The young man, detached and a little spent, with his shoulder against the wall and a hand vaguely playing over the knives, forks and spoons, dropped his succession of sentences without an apparent direction. "Something else has come up, and you're as pleased as Punch. Or, rather, you're not quite entirely so, because you can't goad me to fury. You can't worry me as much as you'd like. Marry me first, old man, and *then* see if I mind. Why shouldn't you keep it up?—I mean lunching with him?" His questions came as in play that was a little pointless, without his waiting more than a moment for answers; though it was not indeed that she might not have answered even in the moment, had not the pointless play been more what she wanted. "Was it at the place," he went on, "that he took us to?"

"Dear no—at his flat, where I've been before. You'll see, in *Brains*, on Wednesday. I don't think I've muffed it—it's really rather there. But he showed me everything this time—the bathroom, the refrigerator, and the machines for stretching his trousers. He has nine, and in constant use."

"Nine?" said Bight gravely.

"Nine."

"Nine trousers?"

"Nine machines. I don't know how many trousers."

"Ah, my dear," he said, "that's a grave omission; the want of the information will be felt and resented. But does it all, at any rate," he asked, "sufficiently fetch you?" After which, as she didn't speak, he lapsed into helpless sincerity. "Is it really, you think, his dream to secure you?"

She replied, on this, as if his tone made it too amusing. "Quite. There's no mistaking it. He sees me as, most days in the year, pulling the wires and beating the drum somewhere; that is he sees me of course not exactly as writing about 'our home'—once I've got one—myself, but as procuring others to do it through my being (as *you've* made him believe) in with the Organs of Public Opinion. He doesn't see, if I'm half decent, why there shouldn't be something about him every day in the week. He's all right, and he's all ready. And who, after all, *can* do him so well as the partner of his flat? It's like making, in one of those big domestic siphons, the luxury of the poor, your own soda-water. It comes cheaper, and it's always on the sideboard. '*Vichy chez soi.*' The interviewer at home."

Her companion took it in. "Your place is on *my* sideboard —you're really a first-class fizz! He steps then, at any rate, into Beadel-Muffet's place."

"That," Maud assented, "is what he would like to do." And she knew more than ever there was something to wait for.

"It's a lovely opening," Bight returned. But he still said, for the moment, nothing else; as if, charged to the brim though he had originally been, she had rather led his thought away.

"What have you done with poor Beadel?" she consequently asked. "What is it, in the name of goodness, you're doing *to* him? It's worse than ever."

"Of course it's worse than ever."

"He capers," said Maud, "on every housetop—he jumps

out of every bush." With which her anxiety really broke out. "*Is* it you that are doing it?"

"If you mean am I seeing him, I certainly am. I'm seeing nobody else. I assure you he's spread thick."

"But you're acting for him?"

Bight waited. "Five hundred people are acting for him; but the difficulty is that what he calls the 'terrific forces of publicity'—by which he means ten thousand *other* persons—are acting against him. We've all in fact been turned on—to turn everything off, and that's exactly the job that makes the biggest noise. It appears everywhere, in every kind of connection and every kind of type, that Sir A. B. C. Beadel-Muffet K.C.B., M.P. desires to cease to appear *anywhere;* and then it appears that his desiring to cease to appear is observed to conduce directly to his more tremendously appearing, or certainly, and in the most striking manner, to his not in the least *dis*appearing. The workshop of silence roars like the Zoo at dinner-time. He *can't* disappear; he hasn't weight enough to sink; the splash the diver makes, you know, tells where he is. If you ask me what I'm doing," Bight wound up, "I'm holding him under water. But we're in the middle of the pond, the banks are thronged with spectators, and I'm expecting from day to day to see stands erected and gate-money taken. There," he wearily smiled, "you have it. Besides," he then added with an odd change of tone, "I rather think you'll see to-morrow."

He had made her at last horribly nervous. "What shall I see?"

"It will all be out."

"Then why shouldn't you tell me?"

"Well," the young man said, "he *has* disappeared. There you are. I mean personally. He's not to be found. But nothing could make more, you see, for ubiquity. The country will ring with it. He vanished on Tuesday night—was then last seen at his club. Since then he has given no sign. How can a man disappear who does *that* sort of thing? It is, as you say, to caper on the housetops. But it will only be known to-night."

"Since when, then," Maud asked, "have you known it?"

"Since three o'clock to-day. But I've kept it. I *am*—a while longer—keeping it."

She wondered; she was full of fears. "What do you expect to get for it?"

"Nothing—if you spoil my market. I seem to make out that you want to."

She gave this no heed; she had her thought. "Why then did you three days ago wire me a mystic word?"

"Mystic——?"

"What do you call 'Larks'?"

"Oh, I remember. Well, it was because I saw larks coming; because I saw, I mean, what has happened. I was sure it would have to happen."

"And what the mischief *is* it?"

Bight smiled. "Why, what I tell you. That he has gone."

"Gone where?"

"Simply bolted to parts unknown. 'Where' is what nobody who belongs to him is able in the least to say, or seems likely to be able."

"Any more than why?"

"Any more than why."

"Only *you* are able to say that?"

"Well," said Bight, "I can say what has so lately stared me in the face, what he has been thrusting at me in all its grotesqueness: his desire for a greater privacy worked through the Papers themselves. He came to me with it," the young man presently added. "I didn't go to *him*."

"And he trusted you," Maud replied.

"Well, you see what I have given him—the very flower of my genius. What more do you want? I'm spent, seedy, sore. I'm sick," Bight declared, "of his beastly funk."

Maud's eyes, in spite of it, were still a little hard. "Is he thoroughly sincere?"

"Good God, no! How *can* he be? Only trying it—as a cat, for a jump, tries too smooth a wall. He drops straight back."

"Then isn't his funk real?"

"As real as he himself is."

Maud wondered. "Isn't his flight——?"

"That's what we shall see!"

"Isn't," she continued, "his reason?"

"Ah," he laughed out, "there you are again!"

But she had another thought and was not discouraged. "Mayn't he be, honestly, mad?"

"Mad—oh yes. But not, I think, honestly. He's not honestly anything in the world but the Beadel-Muffet of our delight."

"Your delight," Maud observed after a moment, "revolts me." And then she said: "When did you last see him?"

"On Tuesday at six, love. I was one of the last."

"Decidedly, too, then, I judge, one of the worst." She gave him her idea. "You hounded him on."

"I reported," said Bight, "success. Told him how it was going."

"Oh, I can see you! So that if he's dead——"

"Well?" asked Bight blandly.

"His blood is on your hands."

He eyed his hands a moment. "They *are* dirty for him! But now, darling," he went on, "be so good as to show me yours."

"Tell me first," she objected, "what you believe. *Is* it suicide?"

"I think that's the thing for us to make it. Till somebody," he smiled, "makes it something else." And he showed how he warmed to the view. "There are weeks of it, dearest, yet."

He leaned more toward her, with his elbows on the table, and in this position, moved by her extreme gravity, he lightly flicked her chin with his finger. She threw herself, still grave, back from his touch, but they remained thus a while closely confronted. "Well," she at last remarked, "I shan't pity you."

"You make it, then, everyone except me?"

"I mean," she continued, "if you do have to loathe yourself."

"Oh, I shan't miss it." And then as if to show how little, "I did mean it, you know, at Richmond," he declared.

"I won't have you if you've killed him," she presently returned.

"You'll decide in that case for the *nine?*" And as the allusion, with its funny emphasis, left her blank: "You want to wear *all* the trousers?"

"You deserve," she said, when light came, "that I should take him." And she kept it up. "It's a lovely flat."

Well, he could do as much. "Nine, I suppose, appeals to you as the number of the muses?"

This short passage, remarkably, for all its irony, brought them together again, to the extent at least of leaving Maud's elbows on the table and of keeping her friend, now a little back in his chair, firm while he listened to her. So the girl came out. "I've seen Mrs Chorner three times. I wrote that night, after our talk at Richmond, asking her to oblige. And I put on cheek as I had never, never put it. I said the public would be so glad to hear from her 'on the occasion of her engagement.'"

"Do you call that cheek?" Bight looked amused. "She at any rate rose straight."

"No, she rose crooked; but she rose. What you had told me there in the Park—well, immediately happened. She did consent to see me, and so far you had been right in keeping me up to it. But what do you think it was for?"

"To show you *her* flat, *her* tub, *her* petticoats?"

"She doesn't live in a flat; she lives in a house of her own, and a jolly good one, in Green Street, Park Lane; though I did, as happened, see her tub, which is a dream—all marble and silver, like a kind of a swagger sarcophagus, a thing for the Wallace Collection; and though her petticoats, as she first shows, seem all that, if you wear petticoats yourself, you can look at. There's no doubt of her money—given her place and her things, and given her appearance too, poor dear, which would take some doing."

"She squints?" Bight sympathetically asked.

"She's so ugly that she *has* to be rich—she couldn't afford it on less than five thousand a year. As it is, I could well see, she can afford anything—even such a nose. But she's funny and decent; sharp, but a really good sort. And they're *not* engaged."

"She told you so? Then there you are!"

"It all depends," Maud went on; "and you don't know where I am at all. *I* know what it depends on."

"Then there you are again! It's a mine of gold."

"Possibly, but not in your sense. She wouldn't give me the first word of an interview—it wasn't for that she received me. It was for something much better."

Well, Bight easily guessed. "For *my* job?"

"To see what can be done. She loathes his publicity."

The young man's face lighted. "She told you so?"

"She received me on purpose to tell me."

"Then why do you question my 'larks'? What do you want more?"

"I want nothing—with what I have: nothing, I mean, but to help her. We made friends—I like her. And she likes *me*," said Maud Blandy.

"Like Mortimer Marshal, precisely."

"No, precisely not like Mortimer Marshal. I caught, on the spot, her idea—*that* was what took her. Her idea is that I can help her—help her to keep them quiet about Beadel: for which purpose I seem to have struck her as falling from the skies, just at the right moment, into her lap."

Howard Bight followed, yet lingered by the way. "To keep *whom* quiet——?"

"Why, the beastly Papers—what we've been talking about. She wants him straight out of them—*straight*."

"She too?" Bight wondered. "Then *she's* in terror?"

"No, not in terror—or it wasn't that when I last saw her. But in mortal disgust. She feels it has gone too far—which is what she wanted me, as an honest, decent, likely young woman, up to my neck in it, as she supposed, to understand from her. My relation with her is now that I do understand and that if an improvement takes place I shan't have been the worse for it. Therefore you see," Maud went on, "you simply cut my throat when you prevent improvement."

"Well, my dear," her friend returned, "I won't let you bleed to death." And he showed, with this, as confessedly struck. "She doesn't then, you think, *know*——?"

"Know what?"

"Why, what, about him, there may *be* to be known. Doesn't know of his flight."

"She didn't—certainly."

"Nor of anything to make it likely?"

"What you call his queer reason? No—she named it to me no more than you have; though she does mention, distinctly, that he himself hates, or pretends to hate, the exhibition daily made of him."

"She speaks of it," Bight asked, "as pretending——?"

Maud straightened it out. "She feels him—*that* she practically told me—as rather ridiculous. She honestly has her feeling; and, upon my word, it's what I like her for. Her stomach has turned and she has made it her condition. 'Muzzle your Press,' she says; '*then* we'll talk.' She gives him three months—she'll give him even six. And this, meanwhile —when he comes to *you*—is how you forward the muzzling."

"The Press, my child," Bight said, "is the watchdog of civilisation, and the watchdog happens to be—it can't be helped—in a chronic state of *rabies*. Muzzling is easy talk; one can but keep the animal on the run. Mrs Chorner, however," he added, "seems a figure of fable."

"It's what I told you she would have to be when, some time back, you threw out, as a pure hypothesis, to supply the man with a motive, your exact vision of her. Your motive has come true," Maud went on—"with the difference only, if I understand you, that this doesn't appear the whole of it. That doesn't matter"—she frankly paid him a tribute. "Your forecast was inspiration."

"A stroke of genius"—he had been the first to feel it. But there were matters less clear. "When did you see her last?"

"Four days ago. It was the third time."

"And even then she didn't imagine the truth about him?"

"I don't know, you see," said Maud, "what you *call* the truth."

"Well, that he—quite by that time—didn't know where the deuce to turn. That's truth enough."

Maud made sure. "I don't see how she can have known it and not have been upset. She wasn't," said the girl, "upset. She *isn't* upset. But she's original."

"Well, poor thing," Bight remarked, "she'll have to be."

"Original?"

"Upset. Yes, and original too, if she doesn't give up the job." It had held him an instant—but there were many things. "She sees the wild ass he is, and yet she's willing——?"

" 'Willing' is just what I asked *you* three months ago," Maud returned, "how she *could* be."

He had lost it—he tried to remember. "What then did I say?"

"Well, practically, that women are idiots. Also, I believe, that he's a dazzling beauty."

"Ah yes, he *is*, poor wretch, though beauty to-day in distress."

"Then there you are," said Maud. They had got up, as at the end of their story, but they stood a moment while he waited for change. "If it comes out," the girl dropped, "*that* will save him. If he's dishonoured—as I see her—she'll have him, because then he won't be ridiculous. And I can understand it."

Bight looked at her in such appreciation that he forgot, as he pocketed it, to glance at his change. "Oh, you creatures——!"

"Idiots, aren't we?"

Bight let the question pass, but still with his eyes on her, "You ought to want him to *be* dishonoured."

"I can't want him, then—if he's to get the good of it—to be dead."

Still for a little he looked at her. "And if *you're* to get the good?" But she had turned away, and he went with her to the door, before which, when they had passed out, they had in the side-street, a backwater to the flood of the Strand, a further sharp colloquy. They were alone, the small street for a moment empty, and they felt at first that they had adjourned to a greater privacy, of which, for that matter, he took prompt advantage. "You're to lunch again with the man of the flat?"

"Wednesday, as I say; 1.45."

"Then oblige me by stopping away."

"You don't like it?" Maud asked.

"Oblige me, oblige me," he repeated.

"And disoblige *him?*"

"Chuck him. We've started him. It's enough."

Well, the girl but wanted to be fair. "It's *you* who started him; so I admit you're quits."

"That then started *you*—made *Brains* repent; so you see what you both owe me. I let the creature off, but I hold you to your debt. There's only one way for you to meet it." And then as she but looked into the roaring Strand: "With worship." It made her, after a minute, meet his eyes, but something just then occurred that stayed any word on the lips of either. A sound reached their ears, as yet unheeded, the sound of newsboys in the great thoroughfare shouting "extra-specials" and mingling with the shout a catch that startled them. The expression in their eyes quickened as they heard, borne on the air, "Mysterious Disappearance——!" and then lost it in the hubbub. It was easy to complete the cry, and Bight himself gasped. "Beadel-Muffet? Confound them!"

"Already?" Maud had turned positively pale.

"They've got it first—be hanged to them!"

Bight gave a laugh—a tribute to their push—but her hand was on his arm for a sign to listen again. It was there, in the raucous throats; it was there, for a penny, under the lamps and in the thick of the stream that stared and passed and left it. They caught the whole thing—"Prominent Public Man!" And there was something brutal and sinister in the way it was given to the flaring night, to the other competing sounds, to the general hardness of hearing and sight which was yet, on London pavements, compatible with an interest sufficient for cynicism. He had been, poor Beadel, public and prominent, but he had never affected Maud Blandy at least as so marked with this character as while thus loudly committed to extinction. It was horrid—it was tragic; yet her lament for him was dry. "If he's gone I'm dished."

"Oh, he's gone—now," said Bight.

"I mean if he's dead."

"Well, perhaps he isn't. I see," Bight added, "what you do mean. If he's dead you can't kill him."

"Oh, she wants him alive," said Maud.

"Otherwise she can't chuck him?"

To which the girl, however, anxious and wondering, made no direct reply. "Good-bye to Mrs Chorner. And I owe it to *you.*"

"Ah, my love!" he vaguely appealed.

"Yes, it's you who have destroyed him, and it makes up for what you've done *for* me."

"I've done it, you mean, against you? I didn't know," he said, "you'd take it so hard."

Again, as he spoke, the cries sounded out: "Mysterious Disappearance of Prominent Public Man!" It seemed to swell as they listened; Maud started with impatience. "I hate it too much," she said, and quitted him to join the crowd.

He was quickly at her side, however, and before she reached the Strand he had brought her again to a pause. "Do you mean you hate it so much you won't have me?"

It had pulled her up short, and her answer was proportionately straight. "I won't have you if he's dead."

"Then will you if he's not?"

At this she looked at him hard. "Do you *know*, first?"

"No—blessed if I do."

"On your honour?"

"On my honour."

"Well," she said after a hesitation, "if *she* doesn't drop me——"

"It's an understood thing?" he pressed.

But again she hung fire. "Well, produce him first."

They stood there striking their bargain, and it was made, by the long look they exchanged, a question of good faith. "I'll produce him," said Howard Bight.

V

IF it had not been a disaster, Beadel-Muffet's plunge into the obscure, it would have been a huge success; so large a space did the prominent public man occupy, for the next few days, in the Papers, so near did he come, nearer certainly than ever before, to supplanting other topics. The question of his whereabouts, of his antecedents, of his habits, of his possible

motives, of his probable, or improbable, embarrassments,
fairly raged, from day to day and from hour to hour, making
the Strand, for our two young friends, quite fiercely, quite
cruelly vociferous. They met again promptly, in the thick of
the uproar, and no other eyes could have scanned the current
rumours and remarks so eagerly as Maud's unless it had been
those of Maud's companion. The rumours and remarks were
mostly very wonderful, and all of a nature to sharpen the
excitement produced in the comrades by their being already,
as they felt, "in the know." Even for the girl this sense
existed, so that she could smile at wild surmises; she struck
herself as knowing much more than she did, especially as, with
the alarm once given, she abstained, delicately enough, from
worrying, from catechising Bight. She only looked at him as
to say "See, while the suspense lasts, how generously I spare
you," and her attitude was not affected by the interested
promise he had made her. She believed he knew more than he
said, though he had sworn as to what he didn't; she saw him
in short as holding some threads but having lost others, and
his state of mind, so far as she could read it, represented in
equal measure assurances unsupported and anxieties uncon-
fessed. He would have liked to pass for having, on cynical
grounds, and for the mere ironic beauty of it, believed that
the hero of the hour was only, as he had always been, "up
to" something from which he would emerge more than ever
glorious, or at least conspicuous; but, knowing the gentleman
was more than anything, more than all else, asinine, he was
not deprived of ground in which fear could abundantly grow.
If Beadel, in other words, was ass enough, as was conceivable,
to be working the occasion, he was by the same token ass
enough to have lost control of it, to have committed some folly
from which even fools don't rebound. That was the spark of
suspicion lurking in the young man's ease, and that, Maud
knew, explained something else.

The family and friends had but too promptly been

approached, been besieged; yet Bight, in all the promptness, had markedly withdrawn from the game—had had, one could easily judge, already too much to do with it. Who but he, otherwise, would have been so naturally let loose upon the forsaken home, the bewildered circle, the agitated club, the friend who had last conversed with the eminent absentee, the waiter, in exclusive halls, who had served him with five-o'clock tea, the porter, in august Pall Mall, who had called his last cab, the cabman, supremely privileged, who had driven him—where? "The Last Cab" would, as our young woman reflected, have been a heading so after her friend's own heart, and so consonant with his genius, that it took all her discretion not to ask him how he had resisted it. She didn't ask, she but herself noted the title for future use—she would have at least got that, "The Last Cab," out of the business; and, as the days went by and the extra-specials swarmed, the situation between them swelled with all the unspoken. Matters that were grave depended on it for each—and nothing so much, for instance, as her seeing Mrs Chorner again. To see that lady as things *had* been had meant that the poor woman might have been helped to believe in her. Believing in her she would have paid her, and Maud, disposed as she was, really had felt capable of earning the pay. Whatever, as the case stood, was caused to hang in the air, nothing dangled more free than the profit derivable from muzzling the Press. With the watchdog to whom Bight had compared it barking for dear life, the moment was scarcely adapted for calling afresh upon a person who had offered a reward for silence. The only silence, as we say, was in the girl's not mentioning to her friend how these embarrassments affected her. Mrs Chorner was a person she liked—a connection more to her taste than any she had professionally made, and the thought of her now on the rack, tormented with suspense, might well have brought to her lips a "See *there* what you've done!"

There was, for that matter, in Bight's face—he couldn't keep it out—precisely the look of seeing it; which was one of her reasons too for not insisting on her wrong. If he couldn't conceal it this was a part of the rest of the unspoken; he didn't allude to the lady lest it might be too sharply said to him that it was on *her* account he should most blush. Last of all he was hushed by the sense of what he had himself said when the news first fell on their ears. His promise to "produce" the fugitive was still in the air, but with every day that passed the prospect turned less to redemption. Therefore if her own promise, on a different head, depended on it, he was naturally not in a hurry to bring the question to a test. So it was accordingly that they but read the Papers and looked at each other. Maud felt in truth that these organs had never been so worth it, nor either she or her friend—whatever the size of old obligations—so much beholden to them. They helped them to wait, and the better, really, the longer the mystery lasted. It grew of course daily richer, adding to its mass as it went and multiplying its features, looming especially larger through the cloud of correspondence, communication, suggestion, supposition, speculation, with which it was presently suffused. Theories and explanations sprouted at night and bloomed in the morning, to be overtopped at noon by a still thicker crop and to achieve by evening the density of a tropical forest. These, again, were the green glades in which our young friends wandered.

Under the impression of the first night's shock Maud had written to Mortimer Marshal to excuse herself from her engagement to luncheon—a step of which she had promptly advised Bight as a sign of her playing fair. He took it, she could see, for what it was worth, but she could see also how little he now cared. He was thinking of the man with whose strange agitation he had so cleverly and recklessly played, and, in the face of the catastrophe of which they were still so likely to have news, the vanities of smaller fools, the conveniences of first-class flats, the memory of Chippendale teas, ceased to be actual or ceased at any rate to be importunate. Her old interview, furbished into freshness, had appeared, on its Wednesday, in *Brains*, but she had not received in person the renewed homage of its author—she had only, once more, had the vision of his inordinate purchase and diffusion of the precious number. It was a vision, however, at which neither Bight nor she smiled; it was funny on so poor a scale compared with their other show. But it befell that when this latter had, for ten days, kept being funny to the tune that so lengthened their faces, the poor gentleman glorified in *Brains* succeeded in making it clear that he was not easily to be dropped. He wanted now, evidently, as the girl said to herself, to live at concert pitch, and she gathered, from three or four notes, to which, at short intervals, he treated her, that he was watching in anxiety for reverberations not as yet perceptible. His expectation of results from what our young couple had done for him would, as always, have been a thing for pity with a young couple less imbued with the comic sense; though indeed it would also have been a comic thing for a young couple less attentive to a different drama. Disappointed of the girl's company at home the author of *Corisanda* had proposed fresh appointments, which she had desired at the moment, and indeed more each time, not to take up; to the extent even that, catching sight of him, unperceived, on one of these occasions, in her inveterate Strand, she checked on the spot a first impulse to make herself apparent. He was before her, in the crowd, and going the same way. He had stopped a little to look at a shop, and it was then that she swerved in time not to pass close to him. She turned and reversed, conscious and convinced that he was, as she mentally put it, on the prowl for her.

She herself, poor creature—as she also mentally put it—she herself was shamelessly on the prowl, but it wasn't, for her self-respect, to get herself puffed, it wasn't to pick up a personal advantage. It was to pick up news of Beadel-Muffet, to be near the extra-specials, and it was, also—as to this she was never blind—to cultivate that nearness by chances of Howard Bight. The blessing of blindness, in truth, at this time, she scantily enjoyed—being perfectly aware of the place occupied, in her present attitude to that young man, by the simple impossibility of not seeing him. She had done with him, certainly, if he *had* killed Beadel, and nothing was now growing so fast as the presumption in favour of some catastrophe, yet shockingly to be revealed, enacted somewhere in desperate darkness—though probably "on lines," as the Papers said, anticipated by none of the theorists in their own columns, any more than by clever people at the clubs, where the betting was so heavy. She had done with him, indubitably, but she had not—it was equally unmistakeable—done with letting him see how thoroughly she *would* have done; or, to feel about it otherwise, she was laying up treasure in time—as against the privations of the future. She was affected moreover —perhaps but half-consciously—by another consideration; her attitude to Mortimer Marshal had turned a little to fright; she wondered, uneasily, at impressions she might have given him; and she had it, finally, on her mind that, whether or no the vain man believed in them, there must be a limit to the belief she had communicated to her friend. He *was* her friend, after all—whatever should happen; and there were things that, even in that hampered character, she couldn't allow him to suppose. It was a queer business now, in fact, for her to ask herself if she, Maud Blandy, had produced on any sane human sense an effect of flirtation.

She saw herself in this possibility as in some grotesque reflector, a full-length looking-glass of the inferior quality that deforms and discolours. It made her, as a flirt, a figure for frank derision, and she entertained, honest girl, none of the self-pity that would have spared her a shade of this sharpened consciousness, have taken an inch from facial proportion where it would have been missed with advantage, or added one in such other quarters as would have welcomed the gift. She might have counted the hairs of her head, for any wish she could have achieved to remain vague about them, just as she might have rehearsed, disheartened, postures of grace, for any dream she could compass of having ever accidentally struck one. Void, in short, of a personal illusion, exempt with an exemption which left her not less helplessly aware of where her hats and skirts and shoes failed, than of where her nose and mouth and complexion, and, above all, where her poor figure, without a scrap of drawing, did, she blushed to bethink herself that she might have affected her young man as really bragging of a conquest. Her *other* young man's pursuit of her, what was it but rank greed—not in the least for her person, but for the connection of which he had formed so preposterous a view? She was ready now to say to herself that she had swaggered to Bight for the joke—odd indeed though the wish to undeceive him at the moment when he would have been more welcome than ever to think what he liked. The only thing she wished him not to think, as she believed, was that she thought Mortimer Marshal thought her —or anyone on earth thought her—intrinsically charming. She didn't want to put to him "Do you suppose I suppose that if it came to the point——?" her reasons for such avoidance being easily conceivable. He was not to suppose that, in any such quarter, she struck herself as either casting a spell or submitting to one; only, while their crisis lasted, rectifications were scarce in order. She couldn't remind him even, without a mistake, that she had but wished to worry him; because in the first place that suggested again a pretension in her (so at variance with the image in the mirror) to put forth arts—suggested possibly even that she used similar ones when she lunched, in bristling flats, with the pushing; and because in the second it would have seemed a sort of challenge to him to renew his appeal.

Then, further and most of all, she had a doubt which by

itself would have made her wary, as it distinctly, in her present suspended state, made her uncomfortable; she was haunted by the after-sense of having perhaps been fatuous. A spice of conviction, in respect to what was open to her, an element of elation, in her talk to Bight about Marshal, had there not, after all, been? Hadn't she a little liked to think the wretched man *could* cling to her? and hadn't she also a little, for herself, filled out the future, in fancy, with the picture of the droll relation? She had seen it as droll, evidently; but had she seen it as impossible, unthinkable? It had become unthinkable now, and she was not wholly unconscious of how the change had worked. Such workings were queer—but there they were; the foolish man had become odious to her precisely *because* she was hardening her face for Bight. The latter was no foolish man, but this it was that made it the more a pity he should have placed the impassable between them. That was what, as the days went on, she felt herself take in. It was there, the impassable—she couldn't lucidly have said why, couldn't have explained the thing on the real scale of the wrong her comrade had done. It was a wrong, it was a wrong—she couldn't somehow get out of that; which was a proof, no doubt, that she confusedly tried. The author of *Corisanda* was sacrificed in the effort—for ourselves it may come to that. Great to poor Maud Blandy as well, for that matter, great, yet also attaching, were the obscurity and ambiguity in which some impulses lived and moved—the rich gloom of their combinations, contradictions, inconsistencies, surprises. It rested her verily a little from her straightness—the line of a character, she felt, markedly like the line of the Edgware Road and of Maida Vale—that she *could* be queerly inconsistent, and inconsistent in the hustling Strand, where, if anywhere, you had, under pain of hoofs and wheels, to decide whether or no you would cross. She had moments, before shop-windows, into which she looked without seeing, when all the unuttered came over her. She had once told her friend that she pitied everyone, and at these moments, in sharp unrest, she pitied Bight for their tension, in which nothing was relaxed.

It was all too mixed and too strange—each of them in a different corner with a different impossibility. There was her own, in far Kilburnia; and there was her friend's, everywhere —for where didn't he go? and there was Mrs Chorner's, on the very edge of Park "Line," in spite of all petticoats and marble baths; and there was Beadel-Muffet's, the wretched man, God only knew where—which was what made the whole show supremely incoherent: he ready to give his head, if, as seemed so unlikely, he still *had* a head, to steal into cover and keep under, out of the glare; he having scoured Europe, it might so well be guessed, for some hole in which the Papers wouldn't find him out, and then having—what else was there by this time to presume?—died, in the hole, as the only way not to see, to hear, to know, let alone *be* known, heard, seen. Finally, while he lay there relieved by the only relief, here was poor Mortimer Marshal, undeterred, undismayed, unperceiving, so hungry to be paragraphed in something like the same fashion and published on something like the same scale, that, for the very blindness of it, he couldn't read the lesson that was in the air, and scrambled, to his utmost, toward the boat itself that ferried the warning ghost. Just *that*, beyond everything, was the incoherence that made for rather dismal farce, and on which Bight had put his finger in naming the author of *Corisanda* as a candidate, in turn, for the comic, the tragic vacancy. It was a wonderful moment for such an ideal, and the sight was not really to pass from her till she had seen the whole of the wonder. A fortnight had elapsed since the night of Beadel's disappearance, and the conditions attending the afternoon performances of the Finnish drama had in some degree reproduced themselves—to the extent, that is, of the place, the time and several of the actors involved; the audience, for reasons traceable, being differently composed. A lady of "high social position," desirous still further to elevate that

character by the obvious aid of the theatre, had engaged a
playhouse for a series of occasions on which she was to affront
in person whatever volume of attention she might succeed in
collecting. Her success had not immediately been great, and
by the third or the fourth day the public consciousness was so
markedly astray that the means taken to recover it penetrated,
in the shape of a complimentary ticket, even to our young
woman. Maud had communicated with Bight, who could be
sure of a ticket, proposing to him that they should go together and offering to await him in the porch of the theatre.
He joined her there, but with so queer a face—for her
subtlety—that she paused before him, previous to their going
in, with a straight "You *know* something!"

"About that rank idiot?" He shook his head, looking kind
enough; but it didn't make him, she felt, more natural. "My
dear, it's all beyond me."

"I mean," she said with a shade of uncertainty, "about poor
dear Beadel."

"So do I. So does everyone. No one now, at any moment,
means anything about anyone else. But I've lost intellectual
control—of the extraordinary case. I flattered myself I still
had a certain amount. But the situation at last escapes me. I
break down. Non comprenny? I give it up."

She continued to look at him hard. "Then what's the matter
with you?"

"Why, just *that*, probably—that I feel like a clever man
'done,' and that your tone with me adds to the feeling. Or,
putting it otherwise, it's perhaps only just one of the ways in
which I'm so interesting; that, with the life we lead and the age
we live in, there's *always* something the matter with me—there
can't help being: some rage, some disgust, some fresh amazement against which one hasn't, for all one's experience, been
proof. That sense—of having been sold again—produces
emotions that may well, on occasion, be reflected in the
countenance. There you are."

Well, he might say that, "There you are," as often as he liked without, at the pass they had come to, making her in the least see where she was. She was only just where she stood, a little apart in the lobby, listening to his words, which she found eminently characteristic of him, struck with an odd impression of his talking against time, and, most of all, tormented to recognise that she could fairly do nothing better, at such a moment, than feel he was awfully nice. The moment —that of his most blandly (she would have said in the case of another most impudently) failing, all round, to satisfy her— was appropriate only to some emotion consonant with her dignity. It was all crowded and covered, hustled and interrupted now; but what really happened in this brief passage, and with her finding no words to reply to him, was that dignity quite appeared to collapse and drop from her, to sink to the floor, under the feet of people visibly bristling with "paper," where the young man's extravagant offer of an arm, to put an end and help her in, had the effect of an invitation to leave it lying to be trampled on.

Within, once seated, they kept their places through two intervals, but at the end of the third act—there were to be no less than five—they fell in with a movement that carried half the audience to the outer air. Howard Bight desired to smoke, and Maud offered to accompany him, for the purpose, to the portico, where, somehow, for both of them, the sense was immediately strong that *this*, the squalid Strand, damp yet incandescent, ugly yet eloquent, familiar yet fresh, was life, palpable, ponderable, possible, much more than the stuff, neither scenic nor cosmic, they had quitted. The difference came to them, from the street, in a moist mild blast, which they simply took in, at first, in a long draught, as more amusing than their play, and which, for the moment, kept them conscious of the voices of the air as of something mixed and vague. The next thing, of course, however, was that they heard the hoarse newsmen, though with the special sense of the sound not standing out—which, so far as it did come, made them exchange a look. There was no hawker just then within call.

"What are they crying?"

"Blessed if I care!" Bight said while he got his light—which he had but just done when they saw themselves closely approached. The Papers had come into sight in the form of a small boy bawling the "Winner" of something, and at the same moment they recognised their reprieve they recognised also the presence of Mortimer Marshal.

He had no shame about it. "I fully believed I should find you."

"But you haven't been," Bight asked, "inside?"

"Not at to-day's performance—I only just thought I'd pass. But at each of the others," Mortimer Marshal confessed.

"Oh, you're a devotee," said Bight, whose reception of the poor man contended, for Maud's attention, with this extravagance of the poor man's own importunity. Their friend had sat through the piece three times on the chance of her being there for one or other of the acts, and if he had given that up in discouragement he still hovered and waited. Who now, moreover, was to say he wasn't rewarded? To find her companion as well as at last to find herself gave the reward a character that it took, somehow, for her eye, the whole of this misguided person's curiously large and flat, but distinctly bland, sweet, solicitous countenance to express. It came over the girl with horror that here was a material object—the incandescence, on the edge of the street, didn't spare it—which she had had perverse moments of seeing fixed before her for life. She asked herself, in this agitation, what she would have likened it to; more than anything perhaps to a large clean china plate, with a neat "pattern," suspended, to the exposure of hapless heads, from the centre of the domestic ceiling. Truly she was, as by the education of the strain undergone, learning something every hour—it seemed so to be the case that a strain enlarged the mind, formed the taste, enriched, even, the imagination. Yet in spite of this last fact, it must be added, she continued rather mystified by the actual pitch of her comrade's manner, Bight really behaving as if he enjoyed their visitor's "note." He treated him so decently, as they said, that he might suddenly have taken to liking his company; which was an odd appearance till Maud understood it—whereupon it became for her a slightly sinister one. For the effect of the honest gentleman, she by that time saw, was to make her friend nervous and vicious, and the form taken by his irritation was just this dangerous candour, which encouraged the candour of the victim. She had for the latter a residuum of pity, whereas Bight, she felt, had none, and she didn't want him, the poor man, absolutely to pay with his life.

It was clear, however, within a few minutes, that this was what he was bent on doing, and she found herself helpless before his smug insistence. She had taken his measure; he was *made* incorrigibly to try, irredeemably to fail—to be, in short, eternally defeated and eternally unaware. He wouldn't rage —he *couldn't*, for the citadel might, in that case, have been carried by his assault; he would only spend his life in walking round and round it, asking everyone he met how in the name of goodness one did get in. And everyone would make a fool of him—though no one so much as her companion now—and everything would fall from him but the perfection of his temper, of his tailor, of his manners, of his mediocrity. He evidently rejoiced at the happy chance which had presented him again to Bight, and he lost as little time as possible in proposing, the play ended, an adjournment again to tea. The spirit of malice in her comrade, now inordinately excited, met this suggestion with an amendment that fairly made her anxious; Bight threw out, in a word, the idea that he himself surely, this time, should entertain Mr Marshal.

"Only I'm afraid I can take you but to a small pothouse that we poor journalists haunt."

"They're just the places I delight in—it would be of an extraordinary interest. I sometimes venture into them—feeling awfully strange and wondering, I do assure you, who people are. But to go there with *you*——!" And he looked from Bight to Maud and from Maud back again with such abysses of appreciation that she knew him as lost indeed.

VI

It was demonic of Bight, who immediately answered that he would tell him with pleasure who everyone was, and she felt this the more when her friend, making light of the rest of the entertainment they had quitted, advised their sacrificing it and proceeding to the other scene. He was really too eager for his victim—she wondered what he wanted to do with him. He could only play him at the most a practical joke—invent appetising identities, once they were at table, for the dull consumers around. No one, at the place they most frequented, had an identity in the least appetising, no one was anyone or anything. It was apparently of the essence of existence on such terms—the terms, at any rate, to which *she* was reduced—that people comprised in it couldn't even minister to each other's curiosity, let alone to envy or awe. She would have wished therefore, for their pursuer, to intervene a little, to warn him against beguilement; but they had moved together along the Strand and then out of it, up a near cross street, without her opening her mouth. Bight, as she felt, was acting to prevent this; his easy talk redoubled, and he led his lamb to the shambles. The talk had jumped to poor Beadel—her friend had startled her by causing it, almost with violence, at a given moment, to take that direction, and he thus quite sufficiently stayed her speech. The people she lived with mightn't make you curious, but there was of course always a sharp exception

for *him*. She kept still, in fine, with the wonder of what he
wanted; though indeed she might, in the presence of their
guest's response, have felt he was already getting it. He was
getting, that is—and *she* was, into the bargain—the fullest
illustration of the ravage of a passion; so sublimely Marshal
rose to the proposition, infernally thrown off, that, in whatever queer box or tight place Beadel might have found
himself, it was something, after all, to have so powerfully interested the public. The insidious artless way in which Bight
made his point!—"I don't know that I've ever known the
public (and I watch it, as in my trade we have to, day and
night) *so* consummately interested." They had that phenomenon—the present consummate interest—well before them
while they sat at their homely meal, served with accessories
so different from those of the sweet Chippendale (another
chord on which the young man played with just the right
effect!), and it would have been hard to say if the guest were,
for the first moments, more under the spell of the marvellous
"hold" on the town achieved by the great absentee, or of that
of the delicious coarse tablecloth, the extraordinary form of
the saltcellars, and the fact that he had within range of sight,
at the other end of the room, in the person of the little quiet
man with blue spectacles and an obvious wig, the greatest
authority in London about the inner life of the criminal
classes. Beadel, none the less, came up again and stayed up—
would clearly so have been *kept* up, had there been need, by
their host, that the girl couldn't at last fail to see how much
it was for herself that his intention worked. What *was* it, all
the same—since it couldn't be anything so simple as to
expose their hapless visitor? What had she to learn about
him?—especially at the hour of seeing what there was still
to learn about Bight. She ended by deciding—for his appearance bore her out—that his explosion was but the form taken
by an inward fever. The fever, on this theory, was the result
of the final pang of responsibility. The mystery of Beadel had

grown too dark to be borne—which they would presently feel; and he was meanwhile in the phase of bluffing it off, precisely because it was to overwhelm him.

"And do you mean you too would pay with your *life?*" He put the question, agreeably, across the table to his guest; agreeably of course in spite of his eye's dry glitter.

His guest's expression, at this, fairly became beautiful. "Well, it's an awfully nice point. Certainly one would like to *feel* the great murmur surrounding one's name, to *be* there, more or less, so as not to lose the sense of it, and as I really think, you know, the pleasure; the great city, the great empire, the world itself for the moment, hanging literally on one's personality and giving a start, in its suspense, whenever one is mentioned. Big sensation, you know, that," Mr Marshal pleadingly smiled, "and of course if one were dead one wouldn't enjoy it. One would have to come to life for that."

"Naturally," Bight rejoined—"only that's what the dead don't do. You can't eat your cake and have it. The question is," he good-naturedly explained, "whether you'd be willing, for the certitude of the great murmur you speak of, to part with your life under circumstances of extraordinary mystery."

His guest earnestly fixed it. "Whether *I* would be willing?"

"Mr Marshal wonders," Maud said to Bight, "if you are, as a person interested in his reputation, definitely proposing to him some such possibility."

He looked at her, on this, with mild, round eyes, and she felt, wonderfully, that he didn't quite see her as joking. He smiled—he always smiled, but his anxiety showed, and he turned it again to their companion. "You mean—a—the knowing how it might be *going* to be felt?"

"Well, yes—call it that. The consciousness of what one's unexplained extinction—given, to start with, one's high position—would mean, wouldn't be able to *help* meaning, for millions and millions of people. The point is—and I admit it's, as you call it, a 'nice' one—if you can think of the impression so made as worth the purchase. *Naturally*, naturally, there's but the impression you make. You don't receive any. You can't. You've only your confidence—so far as that's an impression. Oh, it *is* indeed a nice point; and I only put it to you," Bight wound up, "because, you know, you do like to be recognised."

Mr Marshal was bewildered, but he was not so bewildered as not to be able, a trifly coyly, but still quite bravely, to confess to that. Maud, with her eyes on her friend, found herself thinking of him as of some plump, innocent animal, more or less of the pink-eyed rabbit or sleek guinea-pig order, involved in the slow spell of a serpent of shining scales. Bight's scales, truly, had never so shone as this evening, and he used to admiration—which was just a part of the lustre— the right shade of gravity. He was neither so light as to fail of the air of an attractive offer, nor yet so earnest as to betray a gibe. He might conceivably have been, as an undertaker of improvements in defective notorieties, placing before his guest a practical scheme. It was really quite as if he were ready to guarantee the "murmur" if Mr Marshal was ready to pay the price. And the price wouldn't of course be only Mr Marshal's existence. All this, at least, if Mr Marshal felt moved to take it so. The prodigious thing, next, was that Mr Marshal *was* so moved—though, clearly, as was to be expected, with important qualifications. "Do you really mean," he asked, "that one would excite *this* delightful interest?"

"You allude to the charged state of the air on the subject of Beadel?" Bight considered, looking volumes. "It would depend a good deal upon who one *is*."

He turned, Mr Marshal, again to Maud Blandy, and his eyes seemed to suggest to her that she should put his question for him. They forgave her, she judged, for having so oddly forsaken him, but they appealed to her now not to leave him to struggle alone. Her own difficulty was, however, meanwhile, that she feared to serve him as he suggested without too much, by way of return, turning his case to the comic; whereby she only looked at him hard and let him revert to their friend. "Oh," he said, with a rich wistfulness from which the comic was not absent, "of course everyone can't pretend to be Beadel."

"Perfectly. But we're speaking, after all, of those who do count."

There was quite a hush, for the minute, while the poor man faltered. "Should you say that *I*—in any appreciable way— count?"

Howard Bight distilled honey. "Isn't it a little a question of how much we should find you *did*, or, for that matter, might, as it were, be made to, in the event of a real catastrophe?"

Mr Marshal turned pale, yet he met it too with sweetness. "I like the way"—and he had a glance for Maud—"you talk of catastrophes!"

His host did the comment justice. "Oh, it's only because, you see, we're so peculiarly in the presence of one. Beadel shows so tremendously what a catastrophe does for the right person. His absence, you may say, doubles, quintuples, his presence."

"I see, I see!" Mr Marshal was all there. "It's awfully interesting to be so present. And yet it's rather dreadful to be so absent." It had set him fairly musing; for couldn't the opposites be reconciled? "If he *is*," he threw out, "absent——!"

"Why, he's absent, of course," said Bight, "if he's dead."

"And really dead is what you believe him to be?"

He breathed it with a strange break, as from a mind too full. It was on the one hand a grim vision for his own case, but was on the other a kind of clearance of the field. With Beadel out of the way his own case could live, and he was obviously thinking what it might be to be as dead as that and yet as much alive. What his demand first did, at any rate, was to make Howard Bight look straight at Maud. Her own look met him, but she asked nothing now. She felt him somehow fathomless, and his practice with their infatuated guest created a new suspense. He might indeed have been looking at her to learn how to reply, but even were this the case she had still nothing to answer. So in a moment he had spoken without her. "I've quite given him up."

It sank into Marshal, after which it produced something. "He ought then to come back. I mean," he explained, "to see for himself—to *have* the impression."

"Of the noise he has made? Yes"—Bight weighed it— "that would be the ideal."

"And it would, if one must call it 'noise,'" Marshal limpidly pursued, "make—a—more."

"Oh, but if you *can't!*"

"Can't, you mean, through having already made so much, add to the quantity?"

"Can't"—Bight was a wee bit sharp—"come back, confound it, at all. Can't return from the dead!"

Poor Marshal had to take it. "No—not if you *are* dead."

"Well, that's what we're talking about."

Maud, at this, for pity, held out a perch. "Mr Marshal, I think, is talking a little on the basis of the possibility of your not being!" He threw her an instant glance of gratitude, and it gave her a push. "So long as you're not quite too utterly, you *can* come back."

"Oh," said Bight, "in time for the fuss?"

"Before"—Marshal met it—"the interest has subsided. It naturally then *wouldn't*—would it?—subside!"

"No," Bight granted; "not if it hadn't, through wearing out—I mean your being lost too long—already died out."

"Oh, of course," his guest agreed, "you mustn't be lost *too* long." A vista had plainly opened to him, and the subject led him on. He had, before its extent, another pause. "About how long, do you think——?"

Well, Bight *had* to think. "I should say Beadel had rather overdone it."

The poor gentleman stared. "But if he can't help him-self——?"

Bight gave a laugh. "Yes; but in case he could."

Maud again intervened, and, as her question was for their host, Marshal was all attention. "Do you consider Beadel has overdone it?"

Well, once more, it took consideration. The issue of Bight's, however, was not of the clearest. "I don't think we can tell unless he *were* to. I don't think that, without seeing it, and judging by the special case, one can quite know how it would be taken. He might, on the one side, have spoiled, so to speak, his market; and he might, on the other, have scored as never before."

"It might be," Maud threw in, "just the making of him."

"Surely"—Marshal glowed—"there's just that chance."

"What a pity then," Bight laughed, "that there isn't some-one to take it! For the light it would throw, I mean, on the laws—so mysterious, so curious, so interesting—that govern the great currents of public attention. They're not wholly whimsical—wayward and wild; they have their strange logic, their obscure reason—if one could only get *at* it! The man who does, you see—and who can keep his discovery to him-self!—will make his everlasting fortune, as well, no doubt, as that of a few others. It's *our* branch, *our* preoccupation, in fact, Miss Blandy's and mine—this pursuit of the incalculable, this study, to that end, of the great forces of publicity. Only, of course, it must be remembered," Bight went on, "that in the case we're speaking of—the man disappearing as Beadel has now disappeared, and supplanting for the time every other topic—must have someone on the spot for him, to keep the pot boiling, someone acting, with real intelligence, in his interest. I mean if he's to get the good of it when he does turn up. It would never do, you see, that *that* should be flat!"

"Oh no, not *flat*, never!" Marshal quailed at the thought. Held as in a vise by his host's high lucidity, he exhaled his interest at every pore. "It wouldn't be flat for Beadel, would it?—I mean if he *were* to come."

"Not much! It wouldn't be flat for Beadel—I think I can undertake." And Bight undertook so well that he threw himself back in his chair with his thumbs in the armholes of his waistcoat and his head very much up. "The only thing is that for poor Beadel it's a luxury, so to speak, wasted—and so dreadfully, upon my word, that one quite regrets there's no one to step in."

"To step in?" His visitor hung upon his lips.

"To do the thing better, so to speak—to do it right; to—having raised the whirlwind—really *ride* the storm. To seize the psychological hour."

Marshal met it, yet he wondered. "You speak of the reappearance? I see. But the man of the reappearance would have, wouldn't he?—or perhaps I don't follow?—to be the same as the man of the *dis*appearance. It wouldn't do as well —would it?—for *somebody else* to turn up?"

Bight considered him with attention—as if there were fine possibilities. "No; unless such a person should turn up, say —well, with news of him."

"But what news?"

"With lights—the more lurid the better—*on* the darkness. With the facts, don't you see, *of* the disappearance."

Marshal, on his side, threw himself back. "But he'd have to know them!"

"Oh," said Bight, with prompt portentousness, "that could be managed."

It was too much, by this time, for his victim, who simply turned on Maud a dilated eye and a flushed cheek. "Mr Marshal," it made her say—"Mr Marshal would like to turn up."

Her hand was on the table, and the effect of her words,

combined with this, was to cause him, before responsive speech could come, to cover it respectfully but expressively with his own. "Do you mean," he panted to Bight, "that you have, amid the general collapse of speculation, facts to give?"

"I've always facts to give."

It begot in the poor man a large hot smile. "But—how shall I say?—authentic, or as I believe you clever people say, 'inspired' ones?"

"If I should undertake such a case as we're supposing, I would of course by that circumstance undertake that my facts should be—well, worthy of it. I would take," Bight on his own part modestly smiled, "pains with them."

It finished the business. "Would you take pains for *me?*"

Bight looked at him now hard. "Would you like to appear?"

"Oh, 'appear'!" Marshal weakly murmured.

"Is it, Mr Marshal, a real proposal? I mean are you prepared——?"

Wonderment sat in his eyes—an anguish of doubt and desire. "But wouldn't you prepare me——?"

"Would you prepare *me*—that's the point," Bight laughed —"*to* prepare you?"

There was a minute's mutual gaze, but Marshal took it in. "I don't know what you're making me say; I don't know what you're making me *feel*. When one is with people so up in these things——" and he turned to his companions, alternately, a look as of conscious doom lighted with suspicion, a look that was like a cry for mercy—"one feels a little as if one ought to be saved from one's self. For I dare say one's foolish enough with one's poor little wish——"

"The little wish, my dear sir"—Bight took him up—"to stand out in the world! Your wish is the wish of all high spirits."

"It's dear of you to say it." Mr Marshal was all response.

"I shouldn't want, even if it *were* weak or vain, to have lived wholly unknown. And if what you ask is whether I understand you to speak, as it were, professionally——"

"You *do* understand me?" Bight pushed back his chair.

"Oh, but so well!—when I've already seen what you can do. I need scarcely say, that having seen it, I shan't bargain."

"Ah, then, *I* shall," Bight smiled. "I mean with the Papers. It must be half profits."

" 'Profits'?" His guest was vague.

"Our friend," Maud explained to Bight, "simply wants the position."

Bight threw her a look. "Ah, he must take what I give him."

"But what you give me," their friend handsomely contended, "*is* the position."

"Yes; but the terms that I shall get! I don't produce you, of course," Bight went on, "till I've prepared you. But when I do produce you it will be as a value."

"You'll get so much for me?" the poor gentleman quavered.

"I shall be able to get, I think, anything I ask. So we divide." And Bight jumped up.

Marshal did the same, and, while, with his hands on the back of his chair, he steadied himself from the vertiginous view, they faced each other across the table. "Oh, it's too wonderful!"

"You're not afraid?"

He looked at a card on the wall, framed, suspended and marked with the word "Soups." He looked at Maud, who had not moved. "I don't know; I may be; I must feel. What I *should* fear," he added, "would be his coming back."

"Beadel's? Yes, that would dish you. But since he can't——!"

"I place myself," said Mortimer Marshal, "in your hands."

Maud Blandy still hadn't moved; she stared before her at

the cloth. A small sharp sound, unheard, she saw, by the
others, had reached her from the street, and with her mind
instinctively catching at it, she waited, dissimulating a little,
for its repetition or its effect. It was the howl of the Strand,
it was news of the absent, and it would have a bearing. She
had a hesitation, for she winced even now with the sense of
Marshal's intensest look at her. He couldn't be saved from
himself, but he might be, still, from Bight; though it hung of
course, her chance to warn him, on what the news would be.
She thought with concentration, while her friends unhooked
their overcoats, and by the time these garments were donned
she was on her feet. Then she spoke. "I don't want you to be
'dished.'"

He allowed for her alarm. "But how *can* I be?"

"Something has come."

"Something——?" The men had both spoken.

They had stopped where they stood; she again caught the
sound. "Listen! They're crying."

They waited then, and it came—came, of a sudden, with
a burst and as if passing the place. A hawker, outside, with
his "extra," called by someone and hurrying, bawled it as he
moved. "Death of Beadel-Muffet—Extraordinary News!"

They all gasped, and Maud, with her eyes on Bight, saw
him, to her satisfaction at first, turn pale. But his guest drank
it in. "If it's true then?"—Marshal triumphed at her—"I'm
not dished."

But she only looked hard at Bight, who struck her as
having, at the sound, fallen to pieces, and as having above all,
on the instant, turned cold for his worried game. "Is it true?"
she austerely asked.

His white face answered. "It's true."

VII

THE first thing, on the part of our friends—after each inter-
locutor, producing a penny, had plunged into the unfolded
"Latest"—was this very evidence of their dispensing with
their companion's further attendance on their agitated state,
and all the more that Bight was to have still, in spite of agitation, his function with him to accomplish: a result much
assisted by the insufflation of wind into Mr Marshal's sails
constituted by the fact before them. With Beadel publicly
dead this gentleman's opportunity, on the terms just arranged,
opened out; it was quite as if they had seen him, then and
there, step, with a kind of spiritual splash, into the empty
seat of the boat so launched, scarcely even taking time to
master the essentials before he gave himself to the breeze.
The essentials indeed he was, by their understanding, to
receive in full from Bight at their earliest leisure; but nothing
could so vividly have marked his confidence in the young
man as the promptness with which he appeared now ready to
leave him to his inspiration. The news moreover, as yet, was
the rich, grim fact—a sharp flare from an Agency, lighting
into blood-colour the locked room, finally, with the police
present, forced open, of the first hotel at Frankfort-on-the-
Oder; but there was enough of it, clearly, to bear scrutiny,
the scrutiny represented in our young couple by the act of
perusal prolonged, intensified, repeated, so repeated that it
was exactly perhaps with this suggestion of doubt that poor
Mr Marshal had even also a little lost patience. He vanished,
at any rate, while his supporters, still planted in the side-street
into which they had lately issued, stood extinguished, as to
any facial communion, behind the array of printed columns.
It was only after he had gone that, whether aware or not,

the other lowered, on either side, the absorbing page and knew that their eyes had met. A remarkable thing, for Maud Blandy, then happened, a thing quite as remarkable at least as poor Beadel's suicide, which we recall her having so considerably discounted.

Present as they thus were at the tragedy, present in far Frankfort just where they stood, by the door of their stale pothouse and in the thick of London air, the logic of her situation, she was sharply conscious, would have been an immediate rupture with Bight. He was scared at what he had done—he looked his scare so straight out at her that she might almost have seen in it the dismay of his question of how far his responsibility, given the facts, might, if pried into, be held—and not only at the judgment-seat of mere morals—to reach. The dismay was to that degree illuminating that she had had from him no such avowal of responsibility as this amounted to, and the limit to any laxity on her own side had therefore not been set for her with any such sharpness. It put her at last in the right, his scare—quite richly in the right; and as that was naturally but where she had waited to find herself, everything that now silently passed between them had the merit, if it had none other, of simplifying. Their hour had struck, the hour after which she was definitely not to have forgiven him. Yet what occurred, as I say, was that, if, at the end of five minutes, she had moved much further, it proved to be, in spite of logic, not in the sense away from him, but in the sense nearer. He showed to her, at these strange moments, as blood-stained and literally hunted; the yell of the hawkers, repeated and echoing round them, was like a cry for his life; and there was in particular a minute during which, gazing down into the roused Strand, all equipped both with mob and with constables, she asked herself whether she had best get off with him through the crowd, where they would be least noticed, or get him away through quiet Covent Garden, empty at that hour, but with policemen to watch a furtive couple, and with the news, more bawled at their heels in the stillness, acquiring the sound of the very voice of justice. It was this last sudden terror that presently determined her, and determined with it an impulse of protection that had somehow to do with pity without having to do with tenderness. It settled, at all events, the question of leaving him; she couldn't leave him there and so; she must see at least what would have come of his own sense of the shock.

The way he took it, the shock, gave her afresh the measure of how perversely he had played with Marshal—of how he had tried so, on the very edge of his predicament, to cheat his fears and beguile his want of ease. He had insisted to his victim on the truth he had now to reckon with, but had insisted only because he didn't believe it. Beadel, by that attitude, was but lying low; so that he would have no promise really to redeem. At present he had one, indeed, and Maud could ask herself if the redemption of it, with the leading of their wretched friend a further fantastic dance, would be what he depended on to drug the pain of remorse. By the time she had covered as much ground as this, however, she had also, standing before him, taken his special out of his hand and, folding it up carefully with her own and smoothing it down, packed the two together into such a small tight ball as she might toss to a distance without the air, which she dreaded, of having, by any looser proceeding, disowned or evaded the news. Howard Bight, helpless and passive, putting on the matter no governed face, let her do with him as she liked, let her, for the first time in their acquaintance, draw his hand into her arm as if he were an invalid or as if she were a snare. She took with him, thus guided and sustained, their second plunge; led him, with decision, straight to where their shock was shared and amplified, pushed her way, guarding him, across the dense thoroughfare and through the great westward current which fairly seemed to meet and challenge them, and then, by reaching Waterloo Bridge with him and descending

the granite steps, set him down at last on the Embankment.
It was a fact, none the less, that she had in her eyes, all the
while, and too strangely for speech, the vision of the scene
in the little German city: the smashed door, the exposed
horror, the wondering, insensible group, the English gentleman, in the disordered room, driven to bay among the
scattered personal objects that only too floridly announced
and emblazoned him, and several of which the Papers were
already naming—the poor English gentleman, hunted and
hiding, done to death by the thing he yet, for so long, always
would have, and stretched on the floor with his beautiful little
revolver still in his hand and the effusion of his blood, from
a wound taken, with rare resolution, full in the face, extraordinary and dreadful.

She went on with her friend, eastward and beside the river,
and it was as if they both, for that matter, had, in their silence,
the dire material vision. Maud Blandy, however, presently
stopped short—one of the connections of the picture so
brought her to a stand. It had come over her, with a force she
couldn't check, that the catastrophe itself would have been,
with all the unfathomed that yet clung to it, just the thing
for her companion's professional hand; so that, queerly but
absolutely, while she looked at him again in reprobation and
pity, it was as much as she could do not to feel it for him as
something missed, not to wish he might have been there to
snatch his chance, and not, above all, to betray to him this
reflection. It had really risen to her lips—"Why aren't *you*,
old man, on the spot?" and indeed the question, had it broken
forth, might well have sounded as a provocation to him to
start without delay. Such was the effect, in poor Maud, for the
moment, of the habit, so confirmed in her, of seeing time
marked only by the dial of the Papers. She had admired in
Bight the true journalist that she herself was so clearly not—
though it was also not what she had *most* admired in him; and
she might have felt, at this instant, the charm of putting true

journalism to the proof. She might have been on the point of saying: "Real business, you know, would be for you to start *now*, just as you are, before anyone else, sure as you can so easily be of having the pull"; and she might, after a moment, while they paused, have been looking back, through the river-mist, for a sign of the hour, at the blurred face of Big Ben. That she grazed this danger yet avoided it was partly the result in truth of her seeing for herself quickly enough that the last thing Bight could just then have thought of, even under provocation of the most positive order, was the chance thus failing him, or the train, the boat, the advantage, that the true journalist wouldn't have missed. He quite, under her eyes, while they stood together, ceased to be the true journalist; she saw him, as she felt, put off the character as definitely as she might have seen him remove his coat, his hat, or the contents of his pockets, in order to lay them on the parapet before jumping into the river. Wonderful was the difference that this transformation, marked by no word and supported by no sign, made in the man she had hitherto known. Nothing, again, could have so expressed for her his continued inward dismay. It was as if, for that matter, she couldn't have asked him a question without adding to it; and she didn't wish to add to it, since she was by this time more fully aware that she wished to be generous. When she at last uttered other words it was precisely so that she mightn't press him.

"I think of *her*—poor thing: that's what it makes me do. I think of her there at this moment—just out of the 'Line'—with this stuff shrieked at her windows." With which, having so at once contained and relieved herself, she caused him to walk on.

"Are you talking of Mrs Chorner?" he after a moment asked. And then, when he had had her quick "Of course—of who else?" he said what she didn't expect. "Naturally one thinks of her. But she has herself to blame. I mean she drove him——" What he meant, however, Bight suddenly dropped, taken as he was with another idea, which had brought them the next minute to a halt. "Mightn't you, by the way, see her?"

"See her *now*——?"

" 'Now' or never—for the good of it. Now's just your time."

"But how can it be hers, in the very midst——?"

"*Because* it's in the very midst. She'll tell you things to-night that she'll never tell again. To-night she'll be great."

Maud gàped almost wildly. "You want me, at such an hour, to *call*——?"

"And send up your card with the word—oh, of course the right one!—on it."

"What do you suggest," Maud asked, "as the right one?"

"Well, 'The world *wants* you'—that usually does. I've seldom known it, even in deeper distress than is, after all, here supposable, to fail. Try it, at any rate."

The girl, strangely touched, intensely wondered. "Demand of her, you mean, to let me explain for her?"

"There you are. You catch on. Write *that*—if you like—'Let me explain.' She'll want to explain."

Maud wondered at him more—he had somehow so turned the tables on her. "But she doesn't. It's exactly *what* she doesn't; she never *has*. And that he, poor wretch, was always wanting to——"

"Was precisely what made her hold off? I grant it." He had waked up. "But that was before she had killed him. Trust me, she'll chatter now."

This, for his companion, simply forced it out. "It wasn't *she* who killed him. That, my dear, you know."

"You mean it was I who did? Well then, my child, interview *me*." And, with his hands in his pockets and his idea apparently genuine, he smiled at her, by the grey river and under the high lamps, with an effect strange and suggestive. "*That* would be a go!"

"You mean"—she jumped at it—"you'll tell me what you know?"

"Yes, and even what I've done! But—if you'll take it so—for the Papers. Oh, for the Papers only!"

She stared. "You mean you want me to get it in——?"

"I don't 'want' you to do anything, but I'm ready to help you, ready to get it in for you, like a shot, myself, if it's a thing you yourself want."

"A thing I want—to give you away?"

"Oh," he laughed, "I'm just now worth giving! You'd really do it, you know. And, to help you, here I am. It *would* be for you—only judge!—a leg up."

It would indeed, she really saw; somehow, on the spot, she believed it. But his surrender made her tremble. It wasn't a joke—she *could* give him away; or rather she could sell him for money. Money, thus, was what he offered her, or the value of money, which was the same; it was what he wanted her to have. She was conscious already, however, that she could have it only as he offered it, and she said therefore, but half-heartedly, "I'll keep your secret."

He looked at her more gravely. "Ah, as a secret I can't give it." Then he hesitated. "I'll get you a hundred pounds for it."

"Why don't you," she asked, "get them for yourself?"

"Because I don't care for myself. I care only for you."

She waited again. "You mean for my taking you?" And then as he but looked at her: "How should I take you if I had dealt with you that way?"

"What do I lose by it," he said, "if, by our understanding of the other day, since things have so turned out, you're not to take me at all? So, at least, on my proposal, you get something else."

"And what," Maud returned, "do you get?"

"I *don't* 'get'; I lose. I *have* lost. So I don't matter." The eyes with which she covered him at this might have signified either that he didn't satisfy her or that his last word—*as* his word—rather imposed itself. Whether or no, at all events, she decided that he still did matter. She presently moved again, and they walked some minutes more. He had made her tremble, and she continued to tremble. So unlike anything that had ever come to her was, if seriously viewed, his proposal. The quality of it, while she walked, grew intenser with each step. It struck her as, when one came to look at it, unlike any offer any man could ever have made or any woman ever have received; and it began accordingly, on the instant, to affect her as almost inconceivably romantic, absolutely, in a manner, and quite out of the blue, *dramatic;* immeasurably more so, for example, than the sort of thing she had come out to hear in the afternoon—the sort of thing that was already so far away. If he was joking it was poor, but if he was serious it was, properly, sublime. And he wasn't joking. He was, however, after an interval, talking again, though, trembling still, she had not been attentive; so that she was unconscious of what he had said until she heard him once more sound Mrs Chorner's name. "If you don't, you know, someone else will, and someone much worse. You told me she likes you." She had at first no answer for him, but it presently made her stop again. It was beautiful, if she would, but it was odd—this pressure for *her* to push at the very hour he himself had renounced pushing. A part of the whole sublimity of his attitude, so far as she was concerned, it clearly was; since, obviously, he was not now to profit by anything she might do. She seemed to see that, as the last service he could render, he wished to launch her and leave her. And that came out the more as he kept it up. "If she likes you, you know, she really wants you. Go to her as a friend."

"And bruit her abroad as one?" Maud Blandy asked.

"Oh, as a friend *from* the Papers—from them and *for* them, and with just your half-hour to give her before you rush back to them. Take it even—oh, you can safely"—the young man developed—"a little high with her. That's the way—the real way." And he spoke the next moment as if almost losing his patience. "You ought by this time, you know, to understand."

There was something in her mind that it still charmed—his mastery of the horrid art. He could see, always, the superior way, and it was as if, in spite of herself, she were getting the truth from him. Only she didn't want the truth—at least not that one. "And if she simply, for my impudence, chucks me out of window? A short way is easy for them, you know, when one doesn't scream or kick, or hang on to the furniture or the banisters. And I usually, you see"—she said it pensively—"don't. I've always, from the first, had my retreat prepared for any occasion, and flattered myself that, whatever hand I might, or mightn't, become at getting in, no one would ever be able so beautifully to get out. Like a flash, simply. And if she does, as I say, chuck me, it's *you* who fall to the ground."

He listened to her without expression, only saying "If you feel for her, as you insist, it's your duty." And then later, as if he had made an impression, "Your duty, I mean, to try. I admit, if you will, that there's a risk, though I don't, with my experience, feel it. Nothing venture, at any rate, nothing have; and it's all, isn't it? at the worst, in the day's work. There's but one thing you can go on, but it's enough. The greatest probability."

She resisted, but she was taking it in. "The probability that she will throw herself on my neck?"

"It will be either one thing or the other," he went on as if he had not heard her. "She'll not receive you, or she will. But if she does your fortune's made, and you'll be able to look higher than the mere *common* form of donkey." She recognised the reference to Marshal, but that was a thing she needn't mind now, and he had already continued. "She'll keep *nothing* back. And you mustn't either."

"Oh, won't I?" Maud murmured.

"Then you'll break faith with her."

And, as if to emphasise it, he went on, though without leaving her an infinite time to decide, for he looked at his watch as they proceeded, and when they came, in their spacious walk, abreast of another issue, where the breadth of the avenue, the expanses of stone, the stretch of the river, the dimness of the distance, seemed to isolate them, he appeared, by renewing their halt and looking up afresh toward the town, to desire to speed her on her way. Many things meanwhile had worked within her, but it was not till she had kept him on past the Temple Station of the Underground that she fairly faced her opportunity. Even then too there were still other things, under the assault of which she dropped, for the moment, Mrs Chorner. "Did you really," she asked, "believe he'd turn up alive?"

With his hands in his pockets he continued to gloom at her. "Up there, just now, with Marshal—what did you take me as believing?"

"I gave you up. And I do give you. You're beyond me. Only," she added, "I seem to have made you out since then as really staggered. Though I don't say it," she ended, "to bear hard upon you."

"Don't bear hard," said Howard Bight very simply.

It moved her, for all she could have said; so that she had for a moment to wonder if it were bearing hard to mention some features of the rest of her thought. If she was to have him, certainly, it couldn't be without knowing, as she said to herself, something—something she might perhaps mitigate a little the solitude of his penance by possessing. "There were moments when I even imagined that, up to a certain point, you were still in communication with him. Then I seemed to see that you lost touch—though you braved it out for me; that you had begun to be really uneasy and were giving him up. I seemed to see," she pursued after a hesitation, "that it was coming home to you that you had worked him up too high—that you were feeling, if I may say it, that you had better have stopped short. I mean short of *this*."

"You may say it," Bight answered. "I *had* better."

She looked at him a moment. "There was more of him than you believed."

"There was more of him. And now," Bight added, looking across the river, "here's *all* of him."

"Which you feel you have on your heart?"

"I don't know where I have it." He turned his eyes to her. "I must wait."

"For more facts?"

"Well," he returned after a pause, "hardly perhaps for 'more' if—with what we have—this *is* all. But I've things to think out. I must wait to see how I feel. I did nothing but what he wanted. But we were behind a bolting horse—whom neither of us could have stopped."

"And *he*," said Maud, "is the one dashed to pieces."

He had his grave eyes on her. "Would you like it to have been me?"

"Of course not. But you enjoyed it—the bolt; everything up to the smash. Then, with that ahead, you were nervous."

"I'm nervous still," said Howard Bight.

Even in his unexpected softness there was something that escaped her, and it made in her, just a little, for irritation. "What I mean is that you enjoyed his terror. That was what led you on."

"No doubt—it was so grand a case. But do you call charging me with it," the young man asked, "*not* bearing hard——?"

"No"—she pulled herself up—"it *is*. I don't charge you. Only I feel how little—about what has been, all the while, *behind*—you tell me. Nothing explains."

"Explains what?"

"Why, his act."

He gave a sign of impatience. "Isn't the explanation what I offered a moment ago to give you?"

It came, in effect, back to her. "For use?"

"For use."

"Only?"

"Only." It was sharp.

They stood a little, on this, face to face; at the end of which she turned away. "I'll go to Mrs Chorner." And she was off while he called after her to take a cab. It was quite as if she were to come upon him, in his strange insistence, for the fare.

VIII

IF she kept to herself, from the morrow on, for three days, her adoption of that course was helped, as she thankfully felt, by the great other circumstance and the great public commotion under cover of which it so little mattered what became of private persons. It was not simply that she had her reasons, but she couldn't during this time have descended again to Fleet Street even had she wished, though she said to herself often enough that her behaviour was rank cowardice. She left her friend alone with what he had to face, since, as she found, she could in absence from him a little recover herself. In his presence, the night of the news, she knew she had gone to pieces, had yielded, all too vulgarly, to a weakness proscribed by her original view. Her original view had been that if poor Beadel, worked up, as she inveterately kept seeing him, *should* embrace the tragic remedy, Howard Bight wouldn't be able not to show as practically compromised. He wouldn't be able not to smell of the wretched man's blood, morally speaking, too strongly for condonations or complacencies. There were other things, truly, that, during their minutes on the Embankment, he *had* been able to do, but they constituted just the sinister subtlety to which it was well that she should not again, yet awhile, be exposed. They were of the order— from the safe summit of Maida Hill she could make it out— that had proved corrosive to the muddled mind of the Frankfort fugitive, deprived, in the midst of them, of any honest issue. Bight, of course, rare youth, had *meant* no harm; but what was precisely queerer, what, when you came to judge, less human, than to be formed for offence, for injury, by the mere inherent play of the spirit of observation, of criticism, by the inextinguishable flame, in fine, of the ironic passion? The ironic passion, in such a world as surrounded one, might assert itself as half the dignity, the decency, of life; yet, none the less, in cases where one had seen it prove gruesomely fatal (and not to one's self, which was nothing, but to others, even the stupid and the vulgar) one was plainly admonished to— well, stand off a little and think.

This was what Maud Blandy, while the Papers roared and resounded more than ever with the new meat flung to them, tried to consider that she was doing; so that the attitude held her fast during the freshness of the event. The event grew, as she had felt it would, with every further fact from Frankfort and with every extra-special, and reached its maximum, inevitably, in the light of comment and correspondence. These features, before the catastrophe, had indubitably, at the last, flagged a little, but they revived so prodigiously, under the well-timed shock, that, for the period we speak of, the poor gentleman seemed, with a continuance, with indeed an enhancement, of his fine old knack, to have the successive editions *all* to himself. They had been always of course, the Papers, very largely about him, but it was not too much to say that at this crisis they were about nothing else worth speaking of; so that our young woman could but groan in spirit at the direful example set to the emulous. She spared an occasional moment to the vision of Mortimer Marshal, saw him drunk, as she might have said, with the mere fragrance of the wine of glory, and asked herself what art Bight would now use to furnish him forth as he had promised. The mystery of Beadel's course loomed, each hour, so much larger and darker that the plan would have to be consummate, or the private knowledge alike beyond cavil and beyond calculation, which should attempt either to sound or to mask the appearances. Strangely enough, none the less, she even now found herself thinking of her rash colleague as attached, for the benefit of his surviving victim, to this idea; she went in fact so far as to imagine him half-upheld, while the public wonder spent itself, by the prospect of the fun he might still have with Marshal. This implied, she was not unconscious, that his notion of fun was infernal, and would of course be especially so were his knowledge as real as she supposed it. He would inflate their foolish friend with knowledge that was false and so start him as a balloon for the further gape of the world. This was the image, in turn, that would yield the last sport—the droll career of the wretched man as wandering forever through space under the apprehension, in time duly gained, that the least touch of earth would involve the smash of his car. Afraid, thus, to drop, but at the same time equally out of conceit of the chill air of the upper and increasing solitudes to which he had soared, he would become such a diminishing speck, though traceably a prey to wild human gyrations, as she might conceive Bight to keep in view for future recreation.

It wasn't however the future that was actually so much in question for them all as the immediately near present, offered to her as the latter was in the haunting light of the inevitably unlimited character of any real inquiry. The inquiry of the Papers, immense and ingenious, had yet for her the saving quality that she didn't take it as real. It abounded, truly, in hypotheses, most of them lurid enough, but a certain ease of mind as to what these might lead to was perhaps one of the advantages she owed to her constant breathing of Fleet Street air. She couldn't quite have said why, but she felt it wouldn't be the Papers that, proceeding from link to link, would arrive vindictively at Bight's connection with his late client. The enjoyment of that consummation would rest in another quarter, and if the young man were as uneasy now as she thought he ought to be even while she hoped he wasn't, it would be from the fear in his eyes of such justice as was shared with the vulgar. The Papers held an inquiry, but the Authorities, as they vaguely figured to her, would hold an inquest; which was a matter—even when international, complicated and arrangeable, between Frankfort and London, only on some system unknown to her—more in tune with possibilities of exposure. It was not, as need scarce be said, from the exposure of Beadel that she averted herself; it was from the exposure of the person who had made of Beadel's danger, Beadel's dread—whatever these really represented—the use that the occurrence at Frankfort might be shown to certify. It was well before her, at all events, that if Howard Bight's reflections, so stimulated, kept pace at all with her own, he would at the worst, or even at the best, have been glad to meet her again. It was her knowing that and yet lying low that she privately qualified as cowardice; it was the instinct of watching and waiting till she should see how great the danger might become. And she had moreover another reason, which we shall presently learn. The extra-specials meanwhile were to be had in Kilburnia almost as soon as in the Strand; the little ponied and painted carts, tipped at an extraordinary angle, by which they were disseminated, had for that matter, she observed, never rattled up the Edgware Road at so furious a rate. Each evening, it was true, when the flare of Fleet Street would have begun really to smoke, she had, in resistance to old habit, a little to hold herself; but for three successive days she tided over that crisis. It was not till the fourth night that her reaction suddenly declared itself, determined as it partly was by the latest poster that dangled free at the door of a small shop just out of her own street. The establishment dealt in buttons, pins, tape, and silver bracelets, but the branch of its industry she patronised was that of telegrams, stamps, stationery, and the "Edinburgh rock" offered to the appetite of the several small children of her next-door neighbour but one. "The Beadel-Muffet Mystery, Startling Disclosures, Action of the Treasury"—at these words she anxiously gazed; after which she decided. It was as if from her hilltop, from her very housetop, to which the window of her little room was contiguous, she had seen the red light in the east. It *had*, this time, its colour. She went on, she went far, till she met a cab, which she hailed, "regardless," she felt, as she had hailed one after leaving Bight by the river. "To Fleet Street" she simply said, and it took her—that she felt too—back into life.

Yes, it was life again, bitter, doubtless, but with a taste, when, having stopped her cab, short of her indication, in Covent Garden, she walked across southward and to the top of the street in which she and her friend had last parted with Mortimer Marshal. She came down to their favoured pothouse, the scene of Bight's high compact with that worthy, and here, hesitating, she paused, uncertain as to where she had best look out. Her conviction, on her way, had but grown; Howard Bight would be looking out—*that* to a certainty; something more, something portentous, had happened (by her evening paper, scanned in the light of her little shop window, she had taken instant possession of it), and this would have made him know that she couldn't keep up what he would naturally call her "game." There were places where they often met, and the diversity of these—not too far apart, however—would be his only difficulty. He was on the prowl, in fine, with his hat over his eyes; and she hadn't known, till this vision of him came, what seeds of romance were in her soul. Romance, the other night, by the river, had brushed them with a wing that was like the blind bump of a bat, but that had been something on *his* part, whereas this thought of

bringing him succour as to a Russian anarchist, to some victim
of society or subject of extradition, was all her own, and was
of this special moment. She *saw* him with his hat over his eyes;
she saw him with his overcoat collar turned up; she saw him
as a hunted hero cleverly drawn in one of the serialising
weeklies or, as they said, in some popular "ply," and the
effect of it was to open to her on the spot a sort of happy sense
of all her possible immorality. That was the romantic sense,
and everything vanished but the richness of her thrill. She
knew little enough what she might have to do for him, but her
hope, as sharp as a pang, was that, if anything, it would put
her in danger too. The hope, as it happened then, was crowned
on the very spot; she had never so felt in danger as when, just
now, turning to the glazed door of their cookshop, she saw a
man, within, close behind the glass, still, stiff and ominous,
looking at her hard. The light of the place was behind him, so
that his face, in the dusk of the side-street, was dark, but it
was visible that she showed for him as an object of interest.
The next thing, of course, she had seen more—seen she
could be such an object, in such a degree, only to her friend
himself, and that Bight had been thus sure of her; and the
next thing after that had passed straight in and been met by
him, as he stepped aside to admit her, in silence. He *had* his
hat pulled down and, quite forgetfully, in spite of the warmth
within, the collar of his mackintosh up.

It was his silence that completed the perfection of these
things—the perfection that came out most of all, oddly, after
he had corrected them by removal and was seated with her,
in their common corner, at tea, with the room almost to
themselves and no one to consider but Marshal's little man
in the obvious wig and the blue spectacles, the great authority
on the inner life of the criminal classes. Strangest of all, nearly,
was it, that, though now essentially belonging, as Maud felt,
to this order, they were not conscious of the danger of his
presence. What she had wanted most immediately to learn

was how Bight had known; but he made, and scarce to her surprise, short work of that. "I've known every evening— known, that is, that you've wanted to come; and I've been here every evening, waiting just there till I should see you. It was but a question of time. To-night, however, I was sure —for there's, after all, *something* of me left. Besides, be- sides——!" He had, in short, another certitude. "You've been ashamed—I knew, when I saw nothing come, that you would be. But also that that would pass."

Maud found him, as she would have said, all there. "I've been ashamed, you mean, of being afraid?"

"You've been ashamed about Mrs Chorner; that is, about *me*. For that you did go to her I know."

"Have you been then yourself?"

"For what do you take me?" He seemed to wonder. "What had I to do with her—except *for* you?" And then before she could say: "Didn't she receive you?"

"Yes, as you said, she 'wanted' me."

"She jumped at you?"

"Jumped at me. She gave me an hour."

He flushed with an interest that, the next moment, had flared in spite of everything into amusement. "So that I was right, in my perfect wisdom, up to the hilt?"

"Up to the hilt. She took it from me."

"That the public wants her?"

"That it won't take a refusal. So she opened up."

"Overflowed?"

"Prattled."

"Gushed?"

"Well, recognised and embraced her opportunity. Kept me there till midnight. Told me, as she called it, everything about everything."

They looked at each other long on it, and it determined in Bight at last a brave clatter of his crockery. "They're stupen- dous!"

"It's *you* that are," Maud replied, "to have found it out so. You know them down to the ground."

"Oh, what I've found out——!" But it was more than he could talk of then. "If I hadn't really felt sure, I wouldn't so have urged you. Only now, if you please, I don't understand your having apparently but kept her in your pocket."

"Of course you don't," said Maud Blandy. To which she added, "And I don't quite myself. I only know that now that I have her there nothing will induce me to take her out."

"Then you potted her, permit me to say," he answered, "on absolutely false pretences."

"Absolutely; which is precisely why I've been ashamed. I made for home with the whole thing," she explained, "and there, that night, in the hours till morning, when, turning it over, I saw all it really was, I knew that I *couldn't*—that I would rather choose *that* shame, that of not doing for her what I had offered, than the hideous honesty of bringing it out. Because, you see," Maud declared, "it was—well, it was too much."

Bight followed her with a sharpness! "It was so good?"

"Quite beautiful! Awful!"

He wondered. "Really charming?"

"Charming, interesting, horrible. It was *true*—and it was the whole thing. It was herself—and it was *him*, all of him too. Not a bit made up, but just the poor woman melted and overflowing, yet at the same time raging—like the hot-water tap when it boils. I never saw anything like it; everything, as you guaranteed, came out; it has made me know things. So, to have come down here with it, to have begun to hawk it, either through you, as you kindly proposed, or in my own brazen person, to the highest bidder—well, I felt that I didn't *have* to, after all, if I didn't want to, and that if it's the only way I can get money I would much rather starve."

"I see." Howard Bight saw all. "And that's why you're ashamed?"

She hesitated—she was both so remiss and so firm. "I knew that by my not coming back to you, you would have guessed, have found me wanting; just, for that matter, as *she* has found me. And I couldn't explain. I can't—I can't to *her*. So that," the girl went on, "I shall have done, so far as her attitude to me was to be concerned, something more indelicate, something more indecent, than if I had passed her on. I shall have wormed it all out of her, and then, by not having carried it to market, disappointed and cheated her. She was to have heard it cried like fresh herring."

Bight was immensely taken. "Oh, beyond all doubt. You're in a fix. You've played, you see, a most unusual game. The code allows everything *but* that."

"Precisely. So I must take the consequences. I'm dishonoured, but I shall have to bear it. And I shall bear it by getting *out*. Out, I mean, of the whole thing. I shall chuck them."

"Chuck the *Papers?*" he asked in his simplicity.

But his wonder, she saw, was overdone—their eyes too frankly met. "Damn the Papers!" said Maud Blandy.

It produced in his sadness and weariness the sweetest smile that had yet broken through. "We *shall*, between us, if we keep it up, ruin them! And you make nothing," he went on, "of one's having at last so beautifully started you? Your complaint," he developed, "was that you couldn't get in. Then suddenly, with a splendid jump, you *are* in. Only, however, to look round you and say with disgust 'Oh, here?' Where the devil do you *want* to be?"

"Ah, that's another question. At least," she said, "I can scrub floors. I can take it out perhaps—my swindle of Mrs Chorner," she pursued—"in scrubbing *hers*."

He only, after this, looked at her a little. "She has written to you?"

"Oh, in high dudgeon. I was to have attended to the 'press-cutting' people as well, and she was to have seen herself, at the furthest, by the second morning (that was day-before-yesterday) all over the place. She wants to know what I mean."

"And what do you answer?"

"That it's hard, of course, to make her understand, but that I've felt her, since parting with her, simply to be too good."

"Signifying by it, naturally," Bight amended, "that you've felt yourself to be so."

"Well, that too if you like. But she was exquisite."

He considered. "Would she do for a ply?"

"Oh God, no!"

"Then for a tile?"

"Perhaps," said Maud Blandy at last.

He understood, visibly, the shade, as well as the pause; which, together, held him a moment. But it was of something else he spoke. "And you who had found they would never bite!"

"Oh, I was wrong," she simply answered. "Once they've *tasted* blood——!"

"They want to devour," her friend laughed, "not only the bait and the hook, but the line and the rod and the poor fisherman himself? Except," he continued, "that poor Mrs Chorner hasn't yet even 'tasted.' However," he added, "she obviously will."

Maud's assent was full. "She'll find others. She'll appear."

He waited a moment—his eye had turned to the door of the street. "Then she must be quick. These are things of the hour."

"You hear something?" she asked, his expression having struck her.

He listened again, but it was nothing. "No—but it's some-how in the air."

"What is?"

"Well, that she must hurry. She must get in. She must get

out." He had his arms on the table, and, locking his hands and inclining a little, he brought his face nearer to her. "My sense to-night's of an openness——! I don't know what's the matter. Except, that is, that you're great."

She looked at him, not drawing back. "You know everything—so immeasurably more than you admit or than you tell me. You mortally perplex and worry me."

It made him smile. "You're great, you're great," he only repeated. "You know it's quite awfully swagger, what you've done."

"What I haven't, you mean; what I never shall. Yes," she added, but now sinking back—"of course you see that too. What *don't* you see, and what, with such ways, is to be the end of you?"

"You're great, you're great"—he kept it up. "And I like you. That's to be the end of me."

So, for a minute, they left it, while she came to the thing that, for the last half-hour, had most been with her. "What *is* the 'action,' announced to-night, of the Treasury?"

"Oh, they've sent somebody out, partly, it would seem, at the request of the German authorities, to take possession."

"Possession, you mean, of his effects?"

"Yes, and legally, administratively, of the whole matter."

"Seeing, you mean, that there's still more in it——?"

"Than meets the eye," said Bight, "precisely. But it won't be till the case is transferred, as it presently will be, to this country, that they *will* see. Then it will be funny."

"Funny?" Maud Blandy asked.

"Oh, lovely."

"Lovely for *you?*"

"Why not? The bigger the whole thing grows, the lovelier."

"You've odd notions," she said, "of loveliness. Do you expect his situation won't be traced to you? Don't you suppose you'll be forced to speak?"

"To 'speak'——?"

"Why, if it *is* traced. What do you make, otherwise, of the facts to-night?"

"Do you call them facts?" the young man asked.

"I mean the Astounding Disclosures."

"Well, do you only read your headlines? 'The most astounding disclosures are expected'—*that's* the valuable text. Is *it*," he went on, "what fetched you?"

His answer was so little of one that she made her own scant. "What fetched me is that I can't rest."

"No more can I," he returned. "But in what danger do you think me?"

"In any in which you think yourself. Why not, if I don't mean in danger of hanging?"

He looked at her so that she presently took him for serious at last—which was different from his having been either worried or perverse. "Of public discredit, you mean—for having so unmercifully baited him? Yes," he conceded with a straightness that now surprised her, "I've thought of that. But how can the baiting be proved?"

"If they take possession of his effects won't his effects be partly his papers, and won't they, among them, find letters from you, and won't your letters show it?"

"Well, show what?"

"Why, the frenzy to which you worked him—and thereby your connection."

"They won't show it to dunderheads."

"And are they all dunderheads?"

"Every mother's son of them—where anything so beautiful is concerned."

"Beautiful?" Maud murmured.

"Beautiful, my letters are—gems of the purest ray. I'm covered."

She let herself go—she looked at him long. "You're a wonder. But all the same," she added, "you don't like it."

"Well, I'm not sure." Which clearly meant, however, that he almost *was*, from the way in which, the next moment, he had exchanged the question for another. "You haven't anything to tell me of Mrs Chorner's explanation?"

Oh, as to this, she had already considered and chosen. "What do you want of it when you know so much more? So much more, I mean, than even she has known."

"Then she *hasn't* known——?"

"There you are! What," asked Maud, "are you talking about?"

She had made him smile, even though his smile was perceptibly pale; and he continued. "Of what was behind. Behind any game of mine. Behind everything."

"So am I then talking of that. No," said Maud, "she hasn't known, and she doesn't know I judge, to this hour. Her explanation therefore doesn't bear upon that. It bears upon something else."

"Well, my dear, on what?"

He was not, however, to find out by simply calling her his dear; for she had not sacrificed the reward of her interview in order to present the fine flower of it, unbribed, even to *him*. "You know how little you've ever told me, and you see how, at this instant, even while you press me to gratify you, you give me nothing. I give," she smiled—yet not a little flushed —"nothing *for* nothing."

He showed her he felt baffled, but also that she was perverse. "What you want of me is what, originally, you wouldn't hear of: anything so dreadful, that is, as his predicament must be. You saw that to make him want to keep quiet he must have something to be ashamed of, and that was just what, in pity, you positively objected to learning. You've grown," Bight smiled, "more interested since."

"If I have," said Maud, "it's because *you* have. Now, at any rate, I'm not afraid."

He waited a moment. "Are you very sure?"

"Yes, for my mystification is greater at last than my deli-cacy. I don't know till I do know"—and she expressed this even with difficulty—"what it has been, all the while, that it was a question of, and what, consequently, all the while, we've been talking about."

"Ah, but why should you know?" the young man in-quired. "I can understand your needing to, or somebody's needing to, if we were in a ply, or even, though in a less degree, if we were in a tile. But since, my poor child, we're only in the delicious muddle of life itself——!"

"You may have all the plums of the pudding, and I nothing but a mouthful of cold suet?" Maud pushed back her chair; she had taken up her old gloves; but while she put them on she kept in view both her friend and her grievance. "I don't believe," she at last brought out, "that there *is*, or that there ever was, anything."

"Oh, oh, oh!" Bight laughed.

"There's nothing," she continued, " 'behind.' There's no horror."

"You hold, by that," said Bight, "that the poor man's deed is *all* me? That does make it, you see, bad for me."

She got up and, there before him, finished smoothing her creased gloves. "Then we *are*—if there's such richness—in a ply."

"Well, we are not, at all events—so far as we ourselves are concerned—the spectators." And he also got up. "The spectators must look out for themselves."

"Evidently, poor things!" Maud sighed. And as he still stood as if there might be something for him to come from her, she made her attitude clear—which was quite the attitude now of tormenting him a little. "If you know something about him which she doesn't, and also which *I* don't, she knows something about him—as I do too—which *you* don't."

"Surely: when it's exactly what I'm trying to get out of you. Are you afraid *I'll* sell it?"

But even this taunt, which she took moreover at its worth, didn't move her. "You definitely then won't tell me?"

"You mean that if I will you'll tell *me?*"

She thought again. "Well—yes. But on that condition alone."

"Then you're safe," said Howard Bight. "I *can't*, really, my dear, tell you. Besides, if it's to come out——!"

"I'll wait in that case till it does. But I must warn you," she added, "that *my* facts *won't* come out."

He considered. "Why not, since the rush at her is probably even now being made? Why not, if she receives others?"

Well, Maud could think too. "She'll receive them, but they won't receive *her*. Others are like *your* people—dunderheads. Others won't understand, won't count, won't exist." And she moved to the door. "There *are* no others." Opening the door, she had reached the street with it, even while he replied, overtaking her, that there were certainly none such as herself; but they had scarce passed out before her last remark was, to their somewhat disconcerted sense, sharply enough refuted. There was still the other they had forgotten, and that neglected quantity, plainly in search of them and happy in his instinct of the chase, now stayed their steps in the form of Mortimer Marshal.

IX

H E was coming in as they came out; and his "I *hoped* I might find you," an exhalation of cool candour that they took full in the face, had the effect, the next moment, of a great soft carpet, all flowers and figures, suddenly unrolled for them to walk upon and before which they felt a scruple. Their ejaculation, Maud was conscious, couldn't have passed for a welcome, and it wasn't till she saw the poor gentleman checked a little, in turn, by their blankness, that she fully perceived how interesting they had just become to themselves. His face, however, while, in their arrest, they neither proposed to re-enter the shop with him nor invited him to proceed with them anywhere else—his face, gaping there, for Bight's promised instructions, like a fair receptacle, shallow but with all the capacity of its flatness, brought back so to our young woman the fond fancy her companion had last excited in him that he profited just a little—and for sympathy in spite of his folly— by her sense that with her too the latter had somehow amused himself. This placed her, for the brief instant, in a strange fellowship with their visitor's plea, under the impulse of which, without more thought, she had turned to Bight. "Your eager claimant," she, however, simply said, "for the opportunity now so beautifully created."

"I've ventured," Mr Marshal glowed back, "to come and remind you that the hours are fleeting."

Bight had surveyed him with eyes perhaps equivocal. "You're afraid someone else will step in?"

"Well, with the place so tempting and so empty——!"

Maud made herself again his voice. "Mr Marshal sees it empty itself perhaps too fast."

He acknowledged, in his large, bright way, the help afforded him by her easy lightness. "I do want to get in, you know, before anything happens."

"And what," Bight inquired, "are you afraid *may* happen?"

"Well, to make sure," he smiled, "I want myself, don't you see, to happen first."

Our young woman, at this, fairly fell, for her friend, into his sweetness. "*Do* let him happen!"

"*Do* let me happen!" Mr Marshal followed it up.

They stood there together, where they had paused, in their strange council of three, and their extraordinary tone, in connection with their number, might have marked them, for some passer catching it, as persons not only discussing questions supposedly reserved for the Fates, but absolutely enacting some encounter of these portentous forces. "Let you —let you?" Bight gravely echoed, while on the sound, for the moment, immensities might have hung. It was as far, however, as he was to have time to speak, for even while his voice was in the air another, at first remote and vague, joined it there on an ominous note and hushed all else to stillness. It came, through the roar of thoroughfares, from the direction of Fleet Street, and it made our interlocutors exchange an altered look. They recognised it, the next thing, as the howl, again, of the Strand, and then but an instant elapsed before it flared into the night. "Return of Beadel-Muffet! Tremenjous Sensation!"

Tremenjous indeed, so tremenjous that, each really turning as pale with it as they had turned, on the same spot, the other time and with the other news, they stood long enough stricken and still for the cry, multiplied in a flash, again to reach them. They couldn't have said afterwards who first took it up. "Return——?"

"From the *Dead*—I *say!*" poor Marshal piercingly quavered.

"Then he *hasn't* been——?" Maud gasped it with him at Bight.

But that genius, clearly, was not less deeply affected. "He's alive?" he breathed in a long, soft wail in which admiration appeared at first to contend with amazement and then the sense of the comic to triumph over both. Howard Bight uncontrollably—it might have struck them as almost hysterically —laughed.

The others could indeed but stare. "Then who's dead?" piped Mortimer Marshal.

"I'm afraid, Mr Marshal, that *you* are," the young man returned, more gravely, after a minute. He spoke as if he saw *how* dead.

Poor Marshal was lost. "But someone was killed——!"

"Someone undoubtedly was, but Beadel somehow has survived it."

"Has he, then, been playing the game——?" It baffled comprehension.

Yet it wasn't even that what Maud most wondered. "Have you all the while really known?" she asked of Howard Bight.

He met it with a look that puzzled her for the instant, but that she then saw to mean, half with amusement, half with sadness, that his genius was, after all, simpler. "I wish I had. I really believed."

"All along?"

"No; but after Frankfort."

She remembered things. "You haven't had a notion this evening?"

"Only from the state of my nerves."

"Yes, your nerves must be in a state!" And somehow now she had no pity for him. It was almost as if she were, frankly, disappointed. "*I*," she then boldly said, "didn't believe."

"If you had mentioned that then," Marshal observed to her, "you would have saved me an awkwardness."

But Bight took him up. "She did believe—so that she might punish me."

"Punish you——?"

Maud raised her hand at her friend. "He doesn't understand."

He was indeed, Mr Marshal, fully pathetic now. "No, I don't understand. Not a wee bit."

"Well," said Bight kindly, "we none of us do. We must give it up."

"You think *I* really must——?"

"You, sir," Bight smiled, "most of all. The places seem so taken."

His client, however, clung. "He won't die again——?"

"If he does he'll again come to life. He'll never die. Only *we* shall die. He's immortal."

He looked up and down, this inquirer; he listened to the howl of the Strand, not yet, as happened, brought nearer to them by one of the hawkers. And yet it was as if, overwhelmed by his lost chance, he knew himself too weak even for *their* fond aid. He still therefore appealed. "Will *this* be a boom for him?"

"His return? Colossal. For—fancy!—it was exactly what we talked of, you remember, the other day, as the ideal. I mean," Bight smiled, "for a man to be lost, and yet at the same time——"

"To be found?" poor Marshal too hungrily mused.

"To be boomed," Bight continued, "by his smash and yet never to have been too smashed to know how he was booming."

It was wonderful for Maud too. "To have given it all up, and yet to have it all."

"Oh, better than that," said her friend: "to have *more* than all, and more than you gave up. Beadel," he was careful to explain to their companion, "will have more."

Mr Marshal struggled with it. "More than if he were dead?"

"More," Bight laughed, "than if he weren't! It's what *you* would have liked, as I understand you, isn't it? and what you would have got. It's what *I* would have helped you to."

"But who then," wailed Marshal, "helps *him?*"

"Nobody. His star. His genius."

Mortimer Marshal glared about him as for some sign of such aids in his own sphere. It embraced, his own sphere too, the roaring Strand, yet—mystification and madness!—it was with Beadel the Strand was roaring. A hawker, from afar, at sight of the group, was already scaling the slope. "Ah, but *how* the devil——?"

Bight pointed to this resource. "Go and see."

"But don't *you* want them?" poor Marshal asked as the others retreated.

"The Papers?" They stopped to answer. "No, never again. We've done with them. We give it up."

"I mayn't again see you?"

Dismay and a last clutch were in Marshal's face, but Maud, who had taken her friend's meaning in a flash, found the word to meet them. "We retire from business."

With which they turned again to move in the other sense, presenting their backs to Fleet Street. They moved together up the rest of the hill, going on in silence, not arrested by another little shrieking boy, not diverted by another extra-special, not pausing again till, at the end of a few minutes, they found themselves in the comparative solitude of Covent Garden, encumbered with the traces of its traffic, but now given over to peace. The howl of the Strand had ceased, their client had vanished forever, and from the centre of the empty space they could look up and see stars. One of these was of course Beadel-Muffet's, and the consciousness of that, for the moment, kept down any arrogance of triumph. He still hung above them, he ruled, immortal, the night; they were far beneath, and he now transcended their world; but a sense of relief, of escape, of the light, still unquenched, of their old irony, made them stand there face to face. There was more between them now than there had ever been, but it had ceased to separate them, it sustained them in fact like a deep water on which they floated closer. Still, however, there was something Maud needed. "It had been all the while worked?"

"Ah, not, before God—since I lost sight of him—by *me*."

"Then by himself?"

"I dare say. But there are plenty for him. He's beyond me."

"But you thought," she said, "it *would* be so. You thought," she declared, "something."

Bight hesitated. "I thought it would be great if he *could*. And *as* he could—why, it *is* great. But all the same I too was sold. I *am* sold. That's why I give up."

"Then it's why *I* do. We must do something," she smiled at him, "that requires less cleverness."

"We must love each other," said Howard Bight.

"But can we live by that?"

He thought again; then he decided. "Yes."

"Ah," Maud amended, "we must be 'littery.' We've now got stuff."

"For the dear old ply, for the rattling good tile? Ah, they take better stuff than this—though this too is good."

"Yes," she granted on reflection, "this is good, but it has bad holes. *Who was the dead man in the locked hotel room?*"

"Oh, I don't mean that. *That*," said Bight, "he'll splendidly explain."

"But how?"

"Why, in the Papers. To-morrow."

Maud wondered. "So soon?"

"If he returned to-night, and it's not yet ten o'clock, there's plenty of time. It will be in *all* of them—while the universe waits. He'll hold us in the hollow of his hand. His chance is just there. And there," said the young man, "will be his greatness."

"Greater than ever then?"

"Quadrupled."

She followed; then it made her seize his arm. "*Go* to him!"

Bight frowned. "'Go'——?"

"This instant. *You* explain!"

He understood, but only to shake his head. "Never again. I bow to him."

Well, she after a little understood; but she thought again. "You mean that the great hole is that he really had no reason, no funk——?"

"I've wondered," said Howard Bight.

"Whether he *had* done anything to make publicity embarrassing?"

"I've wondered," the young man repeated.

"But I thought you knew!"

"So did I. But I thought also I knew he was dead. However," Bight added, "he'll explain that too."

"To-morrow?"

"No—as a different branch. Say day after."

"Ah, then," said Maud, "if he explains——!"

"There's no hole? I don't know!"—and it forced from him at last a sigh. He was impatient of it, for he had done with it; it would soon bore him. So fast they lived. "It will take," he only dropped, "much explaining."

His detachment was logical, but she looked a moment at his sudden weariness. "There's always, remember, Mrs Chorner."

"Oh yes, Mrs Chorner; we luckily invented *her*."

"Well, if she drove him to his death——?"

Bight, with a laugh, caught at it. "Is that it? *Did* she drive him?"

It pulled her up, and, though she smiled, they stood again, a little, as on their guard. "Now, at any rate," Maud simply said at last, "she'll marry him. So you see how right I was."

With a preoccupation that had grown in him, however, he had already lost the thread. "How right——?"

"Not to sell my Talk."

"Oh yes,"—he remembered. "Quite right." But it all came to something else. "Whom will *you* marry?"

She only, at first, for answer, kept her eyes on him. Then she turned them about the place and saw no hindrance, and then, further, bending with a tenderness in which she felt so transformed, so won to something she had never been before, that she might even, to other eyes, well have looked so, she gravely kissed him. After which, as he took her arm, they walked on together. "That, at least," she said, "we'll put in the Papers."

FORDHAM CASTLE

SHARP little Madame Massin, who carried on the pleasant pension and who had her small hard eyes everywhere at once, came out to him on the terrace and held up a letter addressed in a manner that he recognised even from afar, held it up with a question in her smile, or a smile, rather a pointed one, in her question—he could scarce have said which. She was looking, while so occupied, at the German group engaged in the garden, near by, with aperitive beer and disputation—the noonday luncheon being now imminent; and the way in which she could show prompt lips while her observation searchingly ranged might have reminded him of the object placed by a spectator at the theatre in the seat he desires to keep during the entr'acte. Conscious of the cross-currents of international passion, she tried, so far as possible, not to mix her sheep and her goats. The view of the bluest end of the Lake of Geneva—she insisted in persuasive circulars that it *was* the bluest—had never, on her high-perched terrace, wanted for admirers, though thus early in the season, during the first days of May, they were not so numerous as she was apt to see them at midsummer. This precisely, Abel Taker could infer, was the reason of a remark she had made him before the claims of the letter had been settled. "I shall put you next the American lady—the one who arrived yesterday. I know you'll be kind to her; she had to go to bed, as soon as she got here, with a sick-headache brought on by her journey. But she's better. Who isn't better as soon as they get here? She's coming down, and I'm sure she'd like to know you."

Taker had now the letter in his hand—the letter intended for "Mr C. P. Addard"; which was not the name inscribed in the two or three books he had left out in his room, any more than it matched the initials, "A. F. T." attached to the few pieces of his modest total of luggage. Moreover, since Madame Massin's establishment counted, to his still somewhat bewildered mind, so little for an hotel, as hotels were mainly known to him, he had avoided the act of "registering," and the missive with which his hostess was practically testing him represented the very first piece of postal matter taken in since his arrival that hadn't been destined to some one else. He had privately blushed for the meagreness of his mail, which made him look unimportant. That however was a detail, an appearance he was used to; indeed the reasons making for such an appearance might never have been so pleasant to him as on this vision of his identity formally and legibly denied. It was denied there in his wife's large straight hand; his eyes, attached to the envelope, took in the failure of any symptom of weakness in her stroke; she at least had the courage of his passing for somebody he wasn't, of his passing rather for nobody at all, and he felt the force of her character more irresistibly than ever as he thus submitted to what she was doing with him. He wasn't used to lying; whatever his faults—and he was used, perfectly, to the idea of his faults—he hadn't made them worse by any perverse theory, any tortuous plea, of innocence; so that probably, with every inch of him giving him away, Madame Massin didn't believe him a bit when he appropriated the letter. He was quite aware he could have made no fight if she had challenged his right to it. That would have come of his making no fight, nowadays, on any ground, with any woman; he had so lost the proper spirit, the necessary confidence. It was true that he had had to do for a long time with no woman in the world but Sue, and of the practice of opposition so far as Sue was concerned the end had been determined early in his career. His hostess fortunately accepted his word, but the way in which her momentary attention bored into his secret like the turn of a gimlet gave him a sense of the quantity of life that passed before her as a dealer with all comers—gave him almost an awe of her power of not wincing. She knew he wasn't, he couldn't be, C. P. Addard, even though she mightn't know, or still less care, who he was; and there was therefore something queer about him if he pretended to be. That was what she didn't mind, there being something queer about him; and what was further present to him was that she would have known when to mind, when really to be on her guard. She attached no importance to his trick; she had doubtless somewhere at the rear, amid the responsive underlings with whom she was sometimes heard volubly, yet so obscurely, to chatter, her clever French amusement about it. He couldn't at all events have said if the whole passage with her most brought home to him the falsity of his position or most glossed it over. On the whole perhaps it rather helped him, since from this moment his masquerade had actively begun.

Taking his place for luncheon, in any case, he found himself next the American lady, as he conceived, spoken of by Madame Massin—in whose appearance he was at first as disappointed as if, a little, though all unconsciously, he had been building on it. Had she loomed into view, on their hostess's hint, as one of the vague alternatives, the possible beguilements, of his leisure—presenting herself solidly where so much else had refused to crystallise? It was certain at least that she presented herself solidly, being a large mild smooth person with a distinct double chin, with grey hair arranged in small flat regular circles, figures of a geometrical perfection; with diamond earrings, with a long-handled eye-glass, with an accumulation of years and of weight and presence, in fine, beyond what his own rather melancholy consciousness acknowledged. He was forty-five, and it took every year of his life, took all he hadn't done with them, to account for his present situation—since you couldn't be, conclusively, of so little use, of so scant an application, to any mortal career, above all to your own, unless you had been given up and cast aside after a long succession of experiments tried with you. But the American lady with the mathematical hair which reminded him in a manner of the old-fashioned "work," the weeping willows and mortuary urns represented by the little glazed-over flaxen or auburn or sable or silvered convolutions and tendrils, the capillary flowers, that he had admired in the days of his innocence—the American lady had probably seen her half-century; all the more that before luncheon was done she had begun to strike him as having, like himself, slipped slowly down over its stretched and shiny surface, an expanse as insecure to fumbling feet as a great cold curved ice-field, into the comparatively warm hollow of resignation and obscurity. She gave him from the first—and he was afterwards to see why—an attaching impression of being, like himself, in exile, and of having like himself learned to butter her bread with a certain acceptance of fate. The only thing that puzzled him on this head was that to parallel his own case she would have had openly to consent to be shelved; which made the difficulty, here, that that was exactly what, as between wife and husband, remained unthinkable on the part of the wife. The necessity for the shelving of one or the other was a case that appeared often to arise, but this wasn't the way he had in general seen it settled. She made him in short, through some influence he couldn't immediately reduce to its elements, vaguely think of her as sacrificed—without blood, as it were; as obligingly and persuadedly passive. Yet this effect, a reflexion of his own state, would doubtless have been better produced for him by a mere melancholy man. She testified unmistakeably to the greater energy of women; for he could think of no manifestation of spirit on his own part that might pass for an equivalent, in the way of resistance, of protest, to the rhythmic though rather wiggy water-waves

that broke upon her bald-looking brow as upon a beach bared
by a low tide. He had cocked up often enough—and as with
the intention of doing it still more under Sue's nose than under
his own—the two ends of his half-"sandy" half-grizzled
moustache, and he had in fact given these ornaments an extra
twist just before coming in to luncheon. That however was
but a momentary flourish; the most marked ferocity of which
hadn't availed not to land him—well, where he was landed
now.

His new friend mentioned that she had come up from
Rome and that Madame Massin's establishment had been
highly spoken of to her there, and this, slight as it was,
straightway contributed in its degree for Abel Taker to the
idea that they had something in common. He was in a condition in which he could feel the drift of vague currents, and
he knew how highly the place had been spoken of to *him*.
There was but a shade of difference in his having had his
lesson in Florence. He let his companion know, without
reserve, that he too had come up from Italy, after spending three or four months there: though he remembered in
time that, being now C. P. Addard, it was only as C. P.
Addard he could speak. He tried to think, in order to give
himself something to say, what C. P. Addard would have
done; but he was doomed to feel always, in the whole connexion, his lack of imagination. He had had many days to
come to it and nothing else to do; but he hadn't even yet made
up his mind who C. P. Addard was or invested him with any
distinguishing marks. He felt like a man who, moving in this,
that or the other direction, saw each successively lead him to
some danger; so that he began to ask himself why he shouldn't
just lie outright, boldly and inventively, and see what that
could do for him. There was an excitement, the excitement of
personal risk, about it—much the same as would belong for
an ordinary man to the first trial of a flying-machine; yet it
was exactly such a course as Sue had prescribed on his asking

12:1

her what he should do. "Anything in the world you like but talk about *me:* think of some other woman, as bad and bold as you please, and say you're married to *her.*" Those had been literally her words, together with others, again and again repeated, on the subject of his being free to "kill and bury" her as often as he chose. This was the way she had met his objection to his own death and interment; she had asked him, in her bright hard triumphant way, why he couldn't defend himself by shooting back. The real reason was of course that he was nothing without her, whereas she was everything, could be anything in the wide world she liked, without him. That question precisely had been a part of what was before him while he strolled in the projected green gloom of Madame Massin's plane-trees; he wondered what she *was* choosing to be and how good a time it was helping her to have. He could be sure she was rising to it, on some line or other, and that was what secretly made him say: "Why shouldn't I get something out of it too, just for the harmless fun——?"

It kept coming back to him, naturally, that he hadn't the breadth of fancy, that he knew himself as he knew the taste of ill-made coffee, that he was the same old Abel Taker he had ever been, in whose aggregation of items it was as vain to feel about for latent heroisms as it was useless to rummage one's trunk for presentable clothes that one didn't possess. But did that absolve him (having so definitely Sue's permission) from seeing to what extent he might temporarily make believe? If he were to flap his wings very hard and crow very loud and take as long a jump as possible at the same time—if he were to do all that perhaps he should achieve for half a minute the sensation of soaring. He knew only one thing Sue couldn't do, from the moment she didn't divorce him: she couldn't get rid of his name, unaccountably, after all, as she hated it; she couldn't get rid of it because she would have always sooner or later to come back to it. She might consider that her being a thing so dreadful as Mrs Abel Taker was a stumbling-block in her social path that nothing but his real, his official, his advertised circulated demise (with "American papers please copy") would avail to dislodge: she would have none the less to reckon with his continued existence as the drop of bitterness in her cup that seasoned undisguiseably each draught. He might make use of his present opportunity to row out into the lake with his pockets full of stones and there quietly slip overboard; but he could think of no shorter cut for her ceasing to be what her marriage and the law of the land had made her. She was not an inch less Mrs Abel Taker for these days of his sequestration, and the only thing she indeed claimed was that the concealment of the source of her shame, the suppression of the person who had divided with her his inherited absurdity, made the difference of a shade or two for getting honourably, as she called it, "about." How she had originally come to incur this awful inconvenience—*that* part of the matter, left to herself, she would undertake to keep vague; and she wasn't really left to herself so long as he too flaunted the dreadful flag.

This was why she had provided him with another and placed him out at board, to constitute, as it were, a permanent *alibi;* telling him she should quarrel with no colours under which he might elect to sail, and promising to take him back when she had got where she wanted. She wouldn't mind so much then—she only wanted a fair start. It wasn't a fair start —*was* it? she asked him frankly—so long as he was always there, so terribly cruelly there, to speak of what she *had* been. She had been nothing worse, to his sense, than a very pretty girl of eighteen out in Peoria, who had seen at that time no one else she wanted more to marry, nor even any one who had been so supremely struck by her. That, absolutely, was the worst that could be said of her. It was so bad at any rate in her own view—it had grown so bad in the widening light of life—that it had fairly become more than she could bear and that something, as she said, had to be done about it. She hadn't known herself originally any more than she had known him—hadn't foreseen how much better she was going to come out, nor how, for her individually, as distinguished from him, there might be the possibility of a big future. He couldn't be explained away—he cried out with all his dreadful presence that she *had* been pleased to marry him; and what they therefore had to do must transcend explaining. It was perhaps now helping her, off there in London, and especially at Fordham Castle—she was staying last at Fordham Castle, Wilts—it was perhaps inspiring her even more than she had expected, that they were able to try together this particular substitute: news of her progress in fact—her progress on from Fordham Castle, if anything could be higher—would not improbably be contained in the unopened letter he had lately pocketed.

There was a given moment at luncheon meanwhile, in his talk with his countrywoman, when he did try that flap of the wing—did throw off, for a flight into the blue, the first falsehood he could think of. "I stopped in Italy, you see, on my way back from the East, where I had gone—to Constantinople"—he rose actually to Constantinople—"to visit Mrs Addard's grave." And after they had all come out to coffee in the rustling shade, with the vociferous German tribe at one end of the terrace, the English family keeping silence with an English accent, as it struck him, in the middle, and his direction taken, by his new friend's side, to the other unoccupied corner, he found himself oppressed with what he had on his hands, the burden of keeping up this expensive fiction. He had never been to Constantinople—it could easily be proved against him; he ought to have thought of something better, have got his effect on easier terms. Yet a funnier thing still than this quick repentance was the quite equally fictive ground on which his companion had affected him—when he came to think of it—as meeting him.

"Why you know that's very much the same errand that

took me to Rome. I visited the grave of my daughter—whom I lost there some time ago."

She had turned her face to him after making this statement, looked at him with an odd blink of her round kind plain eyes, as if to see how he took it. He had taken it on the spot, for this was the only thing to do; but he had felt how much deeper down he was himself sinking as he replied: "Ah it's a sad pleasure, isn't it? But those are places one doesn't want to neglect."

"Yes—that's what I feel. I go," his neighbour had solemnly pursued, "about every two years."

With which she had looked away again, leaving him really not able to emulate her. "Well, I hadn't been before. You see it's a long way."

"Yes—that's the trying part. It makes you feel you'd have done better—"

"To bring them right home and have it done over there?" he had asked as she let the sad subject go a little. He quite agreed. "Yes—that's what many do."

"But it gives of course a peculiar interest." So they had kept it up. "I mean in places that mightn't have so *very* much."

"Places like Rome and Constantinople?" he had rejoined while he noticed the cautious anxious sound of her "very." The tone was to come back to him, and it had already made him feel sorry for her, with its suggestion of her being at sea like himself. Unmistakeably, poor lady, she too was trying to float—was striking out in timid convulsive movements. Well, he wouldn't make it difficult for her, and immediately, so as not to appear to cast any ridicule, he observed that, wherever great bereavements might have occurred, there was no place so remarkable as not to gain an association. Such memories made at the least another object for coming. It was after this recognition, on either side, that they adjourned to the garden —Taker having in his ears again the good lady's rather troubled or muddled echo: "Oh yes, when you come to all the *objects*—!" The grave of one's wife or one's daughter was an object quite as much as all those that one looked up in Baedeker—those of the family of the Castle of Chillon and the Dent du Midi, features of the view to be enjoyed from different parts of Madame Massin's premises. It was very soon, none the less, rather as if these latter presences, diffusing their reality and majesty, had taken the colour out of all other evoked romance; and to that degree that when Abel's fellow guest happened to lay down on the parapet of the terrace three or four articles she had brought out with her, her fan, a couple of American newspapers and a letter that had obviously come to her by the same post as his own, he availed himself of the accident to jump at a further conclusion. Their coffee, which was "extra," as he knew and as, in the way of benevolence, he boldly warned her, was brought forth to them, and while she was giving her attention to her demi-tasse he let his eyes rest for three seconds on the superscription of her letter. His mind was by this time made up, and the beauty of it was that he couldn't have said why: the letter was from her daughter, whom she had been burying for him in Rome, and it would be addressed in a name that was really no more hers than the name his wife had thrust upon him was his. Her daughter had put *her* out at cheap board, pending higher issues, just as Sue had put him—so that there was a logic not other than fine in his notifying her of what coffee every day might let her in for. She was addressed on her envelope as "Mrs Vanderplank," but he had privately arrived, before she so much as put down her cup, at the conviction that this was a borrowed and lawless title, for all the world as if, poor dear innocent woman, she were a bold bad adventuress. He had acquired furthermore the moral certitude that he was on the track, as he would have said, of her true identity, such as it might be. He couldn't think of it as in itself either very mysterious or very impressive; but, whatever it was, her duplicity had as yet mastered no finer art than his own, inasmuch as she had positively not escaped, at table, inadvertently dropping a name which, while it lingered on Abel's ear, gave her quite away. She had spoken, in her solemn sociability and as by the force of old habit, of "Mr Magaw," and nothing was more to be presumed than that this gentleman was her defunct husband, not so very long defunct, who had permitted her while in life the privilege of association with him, but whose extinction had left her to be worked upon by different ideas.

These ideas would have germed, infallibly, in the brain of the young woman, her only child, under whose rigid rule she now—it was to be detected—drew her breath in pain. Madame Massin would abysmally know, Abel reflected, for he was at the end of a few minutes more intimately satisfied that Mrs Magaw's American newspapers, coming to her straight from the other side and not yet detached from their wrappers, would not be directed to Mrs Vanderplank, and that, this being the case, the poor lady would have had to invent some pretext for a claim to goods likely still perhaps to be lawfully called for. And she wasn't formed for duplicity, the large simple scared foolish fond woman, the vague anxiety in whose otherwise so uninhabited and unreclaimed countenance, as void of all history as an expanse of Western prairie seen from a car-window, testified to her scant aptitude for her part. He was far from the desire to question their hostess, however—for the study of his companion's face on its mere inferred merits had begun to dawn upon him as the possible resource of his ridiculous leisure. He might verily have some fun with her—or he would so have conceived it had he not become aware before they separated, half an hour later, of a kind of fellow-feeling for her that seemed to plead for her being spared. She *wasn't* being, in some quarter still indistinct to him—and so no more was he, and these things were precisely a reason. Her sacrifice, he divined, was an act of devotion, a state not yet disciplined to the state of confidence. She had presently, as from a return of vigilance, gathered in her postal property, shuffling it together at her further side and covering it with her pocket-handkerchief—though this very betrayal indeed but quickened his temporary impulse to break out to her, sympathetically, with a "Had you the misfortune to *lose* Magaw?" or with the effective production of his own card and a smiling, an inviting, a consoling "That's who *I* am if you want to know!" He really made out, with the idle human instinct, the crude sense for other people's pains and pleasures that had, on his showing, to his so great humiliation, been found an inadequate outfit for the successful conduct of the coal, the commission, the insurance and, as a last resort, desperate and disgraceful, the book-agency business—he really made out that she didn't want to know, or wouldn't for some little time; that she was decidedly afraid in short, and covertly agitated, and all just because she too, with him, suspected herself dimly in presence of that mysterious "more" than, in the classic phrase, met the eye. They parted accordingly, as if to relieve, till they could recover themselves, the conscious tension of their being able neither to hang back with grace nor to advance with glory; but flagrantly full, at the same time, both of the recognition that they couldn't in such a place avoid each other even if they had desired it, and of the suggestion that they wouldn't desire it, after such subtlety of communion, even were it to be thought of.

Abel Taker, till dinner-time, turned over his little adventure and extracted, while he hovered and smoked and mused, some refreshment from the impression the subtlety of communion had left with him. Mrs Vanderplank was his senior by several years, and was neither fair nor slim nor "bright" nor truly, nor even falsely, elegant, nor anything that Sue had taught him, in her wonderful way, to associate with the American woman at the American woman's best—that best than which there was nothing better, as he had so often heard

her say, on God's great earth. Sue would have banished her
to the wildest waste of the unknowable, would have looked
over her head in the manner he had often seen her use—as if
she were in an exhibition of pictures, were in front of something bad and negligible that had got itself placed on the line,
but that had the real thing, the thing of interest for those who
knew (and when didn't Sue know?) hung above it. In Mrs
Magaw's presence everything would have been of more interest to Sue than Mrs Magaw; but that consciousness failed
to prevent his feeling the appeal of this inmate much rather
confirmed than weakened when she reappeared for dinner. It
was impressed upon him, after they had again seated themselves side by side, that she was reaching out to him indirectly, guardedly, even as he was to her; so that later on, in
the garden, where they once more had their coffee together—
it *might* have been so free and easy, so wildly foreign, so
almost Bohemian—he lost all doubt of the wisdom of his
taking his plunge. This act of resolution was not, like the
other he had risked in the morning, an upward flutter into
fiction, but a straight and possibly dangerous dive into the
very depths of truth. Their instinct was unmistakeably to
cling to each other, but it was as if they wouldn't know where
to take hold till the air had really been cleared. Actually, in
fact, they required a light—the aid prepared by him in the
shape of a fresh match for his cigarette after he had extracted,
under cover of the scented dusk, one of his cards from his
pocket-book.

"There I honestly am, you see—Abel F. Taker; which I
think you ought to know." It was relevant to nothing,
relevant only to the grope of their talk, broken with sudden
silences where they stopped short for fear of mistakes; but
as he put the card before her he held out to it the little momentary flame. And this was the way that, after a while and from
one thing to another, he himself, in exchange for what he had
to give and what he gave freely, heard all about "Mattie"—

Mattie Magaw, Mrs Vanderplank's beautiful and high-spirited daughter, who, as he learned, found her two names, so dreadful even singly, a combination not to be borne, and carried on a quarrel with them no less desperate than Sue's quarrel with—well, with everything. She had, quite as Sue had done, declared her need of a free hand to fight them, and she was, for all the world like Sue again, now fighting them to the death. This similarity of situation was wondrously completed by the fact that the scene of Miss Magaw's struggle was, as her mother explained, none other than that uppermost walk of "high" English life which formed the present field of Mrs Taker's operations; a circumstance on which Abel presently produced his comment. "Why if they're after the same thing in the same place, I wonder if we shan't hear of their meeting."

Mrs Magaw appeared for a moment to wonder too. "Well, if they do meet I guess we'll hear. I will say for Mattie that she writes me pretty fully. And I presume," she went on, "Mrs Taker keeps *you* posted?"

"No," he had to confess—"I don't hear from her in much detail. She knows I back her," Abel smiled, "and that's enough for her. 'You be quiet and I'll let you know when you're wanted'—that's her motto; I'm to wait, wherever I am, till I'm called for. But I guess she won't be in a hurry to call for me"—this reflexion he showed he was familiar with. "I've stood in her light so long—her 'social' light, outside of which everything is for Sue black darkness—that I don't really see the reason she should ever want me back. That at any rate is what I'm doing—I'm just waiting. And I didn't expect the luck of being able to wait in your company. I couldn't suppose—that's the truth," he added—"that there was another, anywhere about, with the same ideas or the same strong character. It had never seemed to be possible," he ruminated, "that there could be any one like Mrs Taker."

He was to remember afterwards how his companion had

appeared to consider this approximation. "Another, you mean, like my Mattie?"

"Yes—like my Sue. Any one that really comes up to her. It will be," he declared, "the first one I've struck."

"Well," said Mrs Vanderplank, "my Mattie's remarkably handsome."

"I'm sure—! But Mrs Taker's remarkably handsome too. Oh," he added, both with humour and with earnestness, "if it wasn't for that I wouldn't trust her so! Because, for what she wants," he developed, "it's a great help to be fine-looking."

"Ah it's always a help for a lady!"—and Mrs Magaw's sigh fluttered vaguely between the expert and the rueful. "But what is it," she asked, "that Mrs Taker wants?"

"Well, she could tell you herself. I don't think she'd trust me to give an account of it. Still," he went on, "she *has* stated it more than once for my benefit, and perhaps that's what it all finally comes to. She wants to get where she truly belongs."

Mrs Magaw had listened with interest. "That's just where Mattie wants to get! And she seems to know just where it is."

"Oh Mrs Taker knows—you can bet your life," he laughed, "on that. It seems to be somewhere in London or in the country round, and I dare say it's the same place as your daughter's. Once she's there, as I understand it, she'll be all right; but she has got to get there—that is to be seen there thoroughly fixed and photographed, and have it in all the papers—first. After she's fixed, she says, we'll talk. We *have* talked a good deal: when Mrs Taker says 'We'll talk' I know what she means. But this time we'll have it out."

There were communities in their fate that made his friend turn pale. "Do you mean she won't want you to come?"

"Well, for me to 'come,' don't you see? will be for me to come to life. How can I come to life when I've been as dead as I am now?"

Mrs Vanderplank looked at him with a dim delicacy. "But surely, sir, I'm not conversing with the remains—!"

"You're conversing with C. P. Addard. *He* may be alive —but even this I don't know yet; I'm just trying him," he said: "I'm trying him, Mrs Magaw, on you. Abel Taker's in his grave, but does it strike you that Mr Addard is at all above ground?"

He had smiled for the slightly gruesome joke of it, but she looked away as if it made her uneasy. Then, however, as she came back to him, "Are you going to wait here?" she asked.

He held her, with some gallantry, in suspense. "Are you?"

She postponed her answer, visibly not quite comfortable now; but they were inevitably the next day up to their necks again in the question; and then it was that she expressed more of her sense of her situation. "Certainly I feel as if I must wait —as long as I *have* to wait. Mattie likes this place—I mean she likes it for *me*. It seems the right *sort* of place," she opined with her perpetual earnest emphasis.

But it made him sound again the note. "The right sort to pass for dead in?"

"Oh she doesn't want me to pass for *dead*."

"Then what does she want you to pass for?"

The poor lady cast about. "Well, only for Mrs Vanderplank."

"And who or what is Mrs Vanderplank?"

Mrs Magaw considered this personage, but didn't get far. "She isn't any one in particular, I guess."

"That means," Abel returned, "that she isn't alive."

"She isn't more than *half* alive," Mrs Magaw conceded. "But it isn't what I *am*—it's what I'm passing for. Or rather" —she worked it out—"what I'm just not. I'm not passing— I don't, can't here, where it doesn't matter, you see—for her mother."

Abel quite fell in. "Certainly—she doesn't want to have any mother."

"She doesn't want to have *me*. She wants me to lay low. If I lay low, she says——"

"Oh I know what she says"—Abel took it straight up. "It's the very same as what Mrs Taker says. If you lie low she can fly high."

It kept disconcerting her in a manner, as well as steadying, his free possession of their case. "I don't feel as if I *was* lying —I mean as low as she wants—when I talk to you so." She broke it off thus, and again and again, anxiously, responsibly; her sense of responsibility making Taker feel, with his braver projection of humour, quite ironic and sardonic; but as for a week, for a fortnight, for many days more, they kept frequently and intimately meeting, it was natural that the so extraordinary fact of their being, as he put it, in the same sort of box, and of their boxes having so even more remarkably bumped together under Madame Massin's *tilleuls*, shouldn't only make them reach out to each other across their queer coil of communications, cut so sharp off in other quarters, but should prevent their pretending to any real consciousness but that of their ordeal. It was Abel's idea, promptly enough expressed to Mrs Magaw, that they ought to get something out of it; but when he had said that a few times over (the first time she had met it in silence), she finally replied, and in a manner that he thought quite sublime: "Well, we *shall*—if they do all they want. We shall feel we've helped. And it isn't so *very* much to do."

"You think it isn't so very much to do—to lie down and die for them?"

"Well, if I don't hate it any worse when I'm really dead—!" She took herself up, however, as if she had skirted the profane. "I don't say that if I didn't *believe* in Mat—! But I do believe, you see. That's where she *has* me."

"Oh I see more or less. That's where Sue has *me*."

Mrs Magaw fixed him with a milder solemnity. "But what has Mrs Taker against you?"

"It's sweet of you to ask," he smiled; while it really came to him that he was living with her under ever so much less strain than what he had been feeling for ever so long before from Sue. Wouldn't he have liked it to go on and on—wouldn't that have suited C. P. Addard? He seemed to be finding out who C. P. Addard was—so that it came back again to the way Sue fixed things. She had fixed them so that C. P. Addard could become quite interested in Mrs Vanderplank and quite soothed by her—and so that Mrs Vanderplank as well, wonderful to say, had lost her impatience for Mattie's summons a good deal more, he was sure, than she confessed. It was from this moment none the less that he began, with a strange but distinct little pang, to see that he couldn't be sure of her. Her question had produced in him a vibration of the sensibility that even the long series of mortifications, of publicly proved inaptitudes, springing originally from his lack of business talent, but owing an aggravation of aspect to an absence of nameable "type" of which he hadn't been left unaware, wasn't to have wholly toughened. Yet it struck him positively as the prettiest word ever spoken to him, so straight a surprise at his wife's dissatisfaction; and he was verily so unused to tributes to his adequacy that this one lingered in the air a moment and seemed almost to create a possibility. He wondered, honestly, what she could see in him, in whom Sue now at last saw really less than nothing; and his fingers instinctively moved to his moustache, a corner of which he twiddled up again, also wondering if it were perhaps only *that*—though Sue had as good as told him that the undue flourish of this feature but brought out to her view the insignificance of all the rest of him. Just to hang in the iridescent ether with Mrs Vanderplank, to whom he wasn't insignificant, just for them to sit on there together, protected, indeed positively ennobled, by their loss of identity, struck him as the foretaste of a kind of felicity that he hadn't in the past known enough about really to miss it. He appeared to have become aware that he should miss it quite sharply, that he would find how he had already learned to, if she should go; and the very sadness of his apprehension quickened his vision of what would work with her. She would want, with all the roundness of her kind, plain eyes, to see Mattie fixed—whereas he'd be hanged if he wasn't willing, on his side, to take Sue's elevation quite on trust. For the instant, however, he said nothing of that; he only followed up a little his acknowledgement of her having touched him. "What you ask me, you know, is just what I myself was going to ask. What has Miss Magaw got against *you?*"

"Well, if you were to see her I guess you'd know."

"Why I should think she'd like to show you," said Abel Taker.

"She doesn't so much mind their *seeing* me—when once she has had a look at me first. But she doesn't like them to hear me—though I don't talk so very much. Mattie speaks in the real English style," Mrs Magaw explained.

"But ain't the real English style not to speak at all?"

"Well, she's having the best kind of time, she writes me—so I presume there must be some talk in which she can shine."

"Oh I've no doubt at all Miss Magaw *talks!*"—and Abel, in his contemplative way, seemed to have it before him.

"Well, don't you go and believe she talks too much," his companion rejoined with spirit; and this it was that brought to a head his prevision of his own fate.

"I see what's going to happen. You only want to go to her. You want to get your share, after all. You'll leave me without a pang."

Mrs Magaw stared. "But won't you be going too? When Mrs Taker sends for you?"

He shook, as by a rare chance, a competent head. "Mrs Taker won't send for me. I don't make out the use Mrs Taker can ever have for me again."

Mrs Magaw looked grave. "But not to enjoy your seeing—?"

"My seeing where she has come out? Oh that won't be necessary to *her* enjoyment of it. It would be well enough perhaps if I could see without being seen; but the trouble with me—for I'm worse than you," Abel said—"is that it doesn't do for me either to be heard *or* seen. I haven't got *any* side—!" But it dropped; it was too old a story.

"Not any possible side at all?" his friend, in her candour, doubtingly echoed. "Why what do they want over there?"

It made him give a comic pathetic wail. "Ah to know a person who says such things as that to me, and to have to give her up—!"

She appeared to consider with a certain alarm what this might portend, and she really fell back before it. "Would you think I'd be able to give up Mattie?"

"Why not—if she's successful? The thing you wouldn't like—*you* wouldn't, I'm sure—would be to give her up if she should find, or if you should find, she wasn't."

"Well, I guess Mattie will be successful," said Mrs Magaw.

"Ah you're a worshipper of success!" he groaned. "I'd give Mrs Taker up, definitely, just to remain C. P. Addard with you."

She allowed it her thought; but, as he felt, superficially. "She's your wife, sir, you know, whatever you do."

" 'Mine'? Ah but whose? She isn't C. P. Addard's."

She rose at this as if they were going too far; yet she showed him, he seemed to see, the first little concession— which was indeed to be the only one—of her inner timidity; something that suggested how she must have preserved as a token, laid away among spotless properties, the visiting-card he had originally handed her. "Well, I guess the one I feel for is Abel F. Taker!"

This, in the end, however, made no difference; since one of the things that inevitably came up between them was that

if Mattie had a quarrel with her name her most workable idea
would be to get somebody to give her a better. That, he easily
made out, was fundamentally what she was after, and, though,
delicately and discreetly, as he felt, he didn't reduce Mrs
Vanderplank to so stating the case, he finally found himself
believing in Miss Magaw with just as few reserves as those
with which he believed in Sue. If it was a question of her
"shining" she would indubitably shine; she was evidently,
like the wife by whom he had been, in the early time, too
provincially, too primitively accepted, of the great radiating
substance, and there were times, here at Madame Massin's,
while he strolled to and fro and smoked, when Mrs Taker's
distant lustre fairly peeped at him over the opposite mountain-
tops, fringing their silhouettes as with the little hard bright
rim of a coming day. It was clear that Mattie's mother
couldn't be expected not to want to see her married; the
shade of doubt bore only on the stage of the business at which
Mrs Magaw might safely be let out of the box. Was she to
emerge abruptly *as* Mrs Magaw?—or was the lid simply to be
tipped back so that, for a good look, she might sit up a little
straighter? She had got news at any rate, he inferred, which
suggested to her that the term of her suppression was in sight;
and she even let it out to him that, yes, certainly, for Mattie
to be ready for her—and she did look as if she were going to
be ready—she must be right down sure. They had had further
lights by this time moreover, lights much more vivid always
in Mattie's bulletins than in Sue's; which latter, as Abel
insistently imaged it, were really each time, on Mrs Taker's
part, as limited as a peep into a death-chamber. The death-
chamber was Madame Massin's terrace; and—he completed
the image—how could Sue *not* want to know how things were
looking for the funeral, which was in any case to be thoroughly
"quiet"? *The* vivid thing seemed to pass before Abel's eyes
the day he heard of the bright compatriot, just the person to
go round with, a charming handsome witty widow, whom

Miss Magaw had met at Fordham Castle, whose ideas were, on all important points, just the same as her own, whose means also (so that they could join forces on an equality) matched beautifully, and whose name in fine was Mrs Sherrington Reeve. "Mattie has felt the want," Mrs Magaw explained, "of some lady, some real lady like that, to go round with: she says she sometimes doesn't find it very pleasant going round alone."

Abel Taker had listened with interest—this information left him staring. "By Gosh then, she has struck Sue!"

"'Struck' Mrs Taker—?"

"She isn't Mrs Taker now—she's Mrs Sherrington Reeve." It had come to him with all its force—as if the glare of her genius were, at a bound, high over the summits. "Mrs Taker's dead: I thought, you know, all the while, she must be, and this makes me sure. She died at Fordham Castle. So we're both dead."

His friend, however, with her large blank face, lagged behind. "At Fordham Castle too—died there?"

"Why she has been as good as *living* there!" Abel Taker emphasised. "'Address Fordham Castle'—that's about all she has written me. But perhaps she died before she went"— he had it before him, he made it out. "Yes, she must have gone as Mrs Sherrington Reeve. She had to die to go—as it would be for her like going to heaven. Marriages, sometimes, they say, are made up there; and so, sometimes then, apparently, are friendships—that, you see, for instance, of our two shining ones."

Mrs Magaw's understanding was still in the shade. "But are you sure—?"

"Why Fordham Castle settles it. If she wanted to get where she truly belongs she has got *there*. She belongs at Fordham Castle."

The noble mass of this structure seemed to rise at his words, and his companion's grave eyes, he could see, to rest on its towers. "But how has she become Mrs Sherrington Reeve?"

"By my death. And also after that by her own. I had to die first, you see, for *her* to be able to—that is for her to be sure. It's what she has been looking for, as I told you—to *be* sure. But oh—she was sure from the first. She knew I'd die off, when she had made it all right for me—so she felt no risk. She simply became, the day I became C. P. Addard, something as different as possible from the thing she had always so hated to be. She's what she always would have liked to be —so why shouldn't we rejoice for her? Her baser part, her vulgar part, has ceased to be, and she lives only as an angel."

It affected his friend, this elucidation, almost with awe; she took it at least, as she took everything, stolidly. "Do you call Mrs Taker an angel?"

Abel had turned about, as he rose to the high vision, moving, with his hands in his pockets, to and fro. But at Mrs Magaw's question he stopped short—he considered with his head in the air. "Yes—now!"

"But do you mean it's her idea to marry?"

He thought again. "Why for all I know she is married."

"With you, Abel Taker, living?"

"But I ain't living. That's just the point."

"Oh you're too dreadful"—and she gathered herself up. "And I won't," she said as she broke off, "help to bury you!"

This office, none the less, as she practically had herself to acknowledge, was in a manner, and before many days, forced upon her by further important information from her daughter, in the light of the true inevitability of which they had, for that matter, been living. She was there before him with her telegram, which she simply held out to him as from a heart too full for words. "Am engaged to Lord Dunderton, and Sue thinks you can come."

Deep emotion sometimes confounds the mind—and Mrs Magaw quite flamed with excitement. But on the other hand it sometimes illumines, and she could see, it appeared, what Sue meant. "It's because he's so much in love."

"So far gone that she's safe?" Abel frankly asked.

"So far gone that she's safe."

"Well," he said, "if Sue feels it—!" He had so much, he showed, to go by. "Sue *knows*."

Mrs Magaw visibly yearned, but she could look at all sides. "I'm bound to say, since you speak of it, that I've an idea Sue has helped. She'll like to have her there."

"Mattie will like to have Sue?"

"No, Sue will like to have Mattie." Elation raised to such a point was in fact already so clarifying that Mrs Magaw could come all the way. "As Lady Dunderton."

"Well," Abel smiled, "one good turn deserves another!" If he meant it, however, in any such sense as that Mattie might be able in due course to render an equivalent of aid, this notion clearly had to reckon with his companion's sense of its strangeness, exhibited in her now at last upheaved countenance. "Yes," he accordingly insisted, "it will work round to that—you see if it doesn't. If that's where they were to come out, and they *have* come—by which I mean if Sue has realised it for Mattie and acted as she acts when she does realise, then she can't neglect it in her own case: she'll just *have* to realise it for herself. And, for that matter, you'll help her too. You'll be able to tell her, you know, that you've seen the last of me." And on the morrow, when, starting for London, she had taken her place in the train, to which he had accompanied her, he stood by the door of her compartment and repeated this idea. "Remember, for Mrs Taker, that you've seen the last—!"

"Oh but I hope I haven't, sir."

"Then you'll come back to me? If you only will, you know, Sue will be delighted to fix it."

"To fix it—how?"

"Well, she'll tell you how. You've seen how she can

fix things, and that will be the way, as I say, you'll help her."

She stared at him from her corner, and he could see she was sorry for him; but it was as if she had taken refuge behind her large high-shouldered reticule, which she held in her lap, presenting it almost as a bulwark. "Mr Taker," she launched at him over it, "I'm afraid of you."

"Because I'm dead?"

"Oh sir!" she pleaded, hugging her morocco defence. But even through this alarm her finer thought came out. "Do you suppose I shall go to Fordham Castle?"

"Well, I guess that's what they're discussing now. You'll know soon enough."

"If I write you from there," she asked, "won't you come?"

"I'll come as the ghost. Don't old castles always have one?"

She looked at him darkly; the train had begun to move. "I *shall* fear you!" she said.

"Then there you are." And he moved an instant beside the door. "You'll be glad, when you get there, to be able to say—" But she got out of hearing, and, turning away, he felt as abandoned as he had known he should—felt left, in his solitude, to the sense of his extinction. He faced it completely now, and to himself at least could express it without fear of protest. "Why certainly I'm dead."

JULIA BRIDE

I

SHE had walked with her friend to the top of the wide steps of the Museum, those that descend from the galleries of painting, and then, after the young man had left her, smiling, looking back, waving all gaily and expressively his hat and stick, had watched him, smiling too, but with a different intensity—had kept him in sight till he passed out of the great door. She might have been waiting to see if he would turn there for a last demonstration; which was exactly what he did, renewing his cordial gesture and with his look of glad devotion, the radiance of his young face, reaching her across the great space, as she felt, in undiminished truth. Yes, so she could feel, and she remained a minute even after he was gone; she gazed at the empty air as if he had filled it still, asking herself what more she wanted and what, if it didn't signify glad devotion, his whole air could have represented.

She was at present so anxious that she could wonder if he stepped and smiled like that for mere relief at separation; yet if he wanted in such a degree to break the spell and escape the danger why did he keep coming back to her, and why, for that matter, had she felt safe a moment before in letting him go? She felt safe, felt almost reckless—that was the proof—so long as he was with her; but the chill came as soon as he had gone, when she instantly took the measure of all she yet missed. She might now have been taking it afresh, by the testimony of her charming clouded eyes and of the rigour that had already replaced her beautiful play of expression. Her radiance, for the minute, had "carried" as far as his, travelling on the light wings of her brilliant prettiness—he on his side not being facially handsome, but only sensitive clean and eager. Then with its extinction the sustaining wings dropped and hung.

She wheeled about, however, full of a purpose; she passed back through the pictured rooms, for it pleased her, this idea of a talk with Mr Pitman—as much, that is, as anything could please a young person so troubled. It had happened indeed that when she saw him rise at sight of her from the settee where he had told her five minutes before that she would find him, it was just with her nervousness that his presence seemed, as through an odd suggestion of help, to connect itself. Nothing truly would be quite so odd for her case as aid proceeding from Mr Pitman; unless perhaps the oddity would be even greater for himself—the oddity of her having taken into her head an appeal to him.

She had had to feel alone with a vengeance—inwardly alone and miserably alarmed—to be ready to "meet," that way, at the first sign from him, the successor to her dim father in her dim father's lifetime, the second of her mother's two divorced husbands. It made a queer relation for her; a relation that struck her at this moment as less edifying, less natural and graceful, than it would have been even for her remarkable mother—and still in spite of this parent's third marriage, her union with Mr Connery, from whom she was informally separated. It was at the back of Julia's head as she approached Mr Pitman, or it was at least somewhere deep within her soul, that if this last of Mrs Connery's withdrawals from the matrimonial yoke had received the sanction of the Court (Julia had always heard, from far back, so much about the "Court") she herself, as after a fashion, in that event, a party to it, wouldn't have had the cheek to make up—which was how she inwardly phrased what she was doing—to the long lean loose slightly cadaverous gentleman who was a memory, for her, of the period from her twelfth to her seventeenth year.

She had got on with him, perversely, much better than her mother had, and the bulging misfit of his duck waistcoat, with his trick of swinging his eye-glass, at the end of an extraordinarily long string, far over the scene, came back to her as positive features of the image of her remoter youth. Her present age—for her later time had seen so many things happen—gave her a perspective.

Fifty things came up as she stood there before him, some of them floating in from the past, others hovering with freshness: how she used to dodge the rotary movement made by his pince-nez while he always awkwardly, and kindly, and often funnily, talked—it had once hit her rather badly in the eye; how she used to pull down and straighten his waistcoat, making it set a little better, a thing of a sort her mother never did; how friendly and familiar she must have been with him for that, or else a forward little minx; how she felt almost capable of doing it again now, just to sound the right note, and how sure she was of the way he would take it if she did; how much nicer he had clearly been, all the while, poor dear man, than his wife and the Court had made it possible for him publicly to appear; how much younger too he now looked, in spite of his rather melancholy, his mildly-jaundiced, humorously-determined sallowness and his careless assumption, everywhere, from his forehead to his exposed and relaxed blue socks, almost sky-blue, as in past days, of creases and folds and furrows that would have been perhaps tragic if they hadn't seemed rather to show, like his whimsical black eyebrows, the vague interrogative arch.

Of course he wasn't wretched if he wasn't more sure of his wretchedness than that! Julia Bride would have been sure—had she been through what she supposed *he* had! With his thick loose black hair, in any case, untouched by a thread of grey, and his kept gift of a certain big-boyish awkwardness—that of his taking their encounter, for instance, so amusedly, so crudely, though, as she was not unaware, so eagerly too—

he could by no means have been so little his wife's junior as it had been that lady's habit, after the divorce, to represent him. Julia had remembered him as old, since she had so constantly thought of her mother as old; which Mrs Connery was indeed now, for her daughter, with her dozen years of actual seniority to Mr Pitman and her exquisite hair, the densest, the finest tangle of arranged silver tendrils that had ever enhanced the effect of a preserved complexion.

Something in the girl's vision of her quondam stepfather as still comparatively young—with the confusion, the immense element of rectification, not to say of rank disproof, that it introduced into Mrs Connery's favourite picture of her own injured past—all this worked, even at the moment, to quicken once more the clearness and harshness of judgement, the retrospective disgust, as she might have called it, that had of late grown up in her, the sense of all the folly and vanity and vulgarity, the lies, the perversities, the falsification of all life in the interest of who could say what wretched frivolity, what preposterous policy, amid which she had been condemned so ignorantly, so pitifully to sit, to walk, to grope, to flounder, from the very dawn of her consciousness. Didn't poor Mr Pitman just touch the sensitive nerve of it when, taking her in with his facetious cautious eyes, he spoke to her, right out, of the old, old story, the everlasting little wonder of her beauty?

"Why, you know, you've grown up so lovely—you're the prettiest girl I've ever seen!" Of course she was the prettiest girl he had ever seen; she was the prettiest girl people much more privileged than he had ever seen; since when hadn't she been passing for the prettiest girl any one had ever seen? She had lived in that, from far back, from year to year, from day to day and from hour to hour—she had lived for it and literally *by* it, as who should say; but Mr Pitman was somehow more illuminating than he knew, with the present lurid light that he cast upon old dates, old pleas, old values and old mysteries, not to call them old abysses: it had rolled over her in a swift wave, with the very sight of him, that her mother couldn't possibly have been right about him—as about what in the world had she ever been right?—so that in fact he was simply offered her there as one more of Mrs Connery's lies. She might have thought she knew them all by this time; but he represented for her, coming in just as he did, a fresh discovery, and it was this contribution of freshness that made her somehow feel she liked him. It was she herself who, for so long, with her retained impression, had been right about him; and the rectification he represented had *all* shone out of him, ten minutes before, on his catching her eye while she moved through the room with Mr French. She had never doubted of his probable faults—which her mother had vividly depicted as the basest of vices; since some of them, and the most obvious (not the vices, but the faults) were written on him as he stood there: notably, for instance, the exasperating "business slackness" of which Mrs Connery had, before the tribunal, made so pathetically much. It might have been, for that matter, the very business slackness that affected Julia as presenting its friendly breast, in the form of a cool loose sociability, to her own actual tension; though it was also true for her, after they had exchanged fifty words, that he had as well his inward fever and that, if he was perhaps wondering what was so particularly the matter with her, she could make out not less than something was the matter with *him*. It had been vague, yet it had been intense, the mute reflexion, "Yes, I'm going to like him, and he's going somehow to help me!" that had directed her steps so straight to him. She was sure even then of this, that he wouldn't put to her a query about his former wife, that he took to-day no grain of interest in Mrs Connery; that his interest, such as it was—and he couldn't look *quite* like that, to Julia Bride's expert perception, without something in the nature of a new one—would be a thousand times different.

It was as a value of *disproof* that his worth meanwhile so
rapidly grew: the good sight of him, the good sound and
sense of him, such as they were, demolished at a stroke so
blessedly much of the horrid inconvenience of the past that
she thought of him, she clutched at him, for a *general* saving
use, an application as sanative, as redemptive, as some universal healing wash, precious even to the point of perjury if
perjury should be required. That was the terrible thing, that
had been the inward pang with which she watched Basil
French recede: perjury would have to come in somehow and
somewhere—oh so quite certainly!—before the so strange,
so rare young man, truly smitten though she believed him,
could be made to rise to the occasion, before her measureless
prize could be assured. It was present to her, it had been
present a hundred times, that if there had only been some one
to (as it were) "deny everything" the situation might yet be
saved. She so needed some one to lie for her—ah she so
needed some one to lie! Her mother's version of everything,
her mother's version of anything, had been at the best, as
they said, discounted; and she herself could but show of course
for an interested party, however much she might claim to be
none the less a decent girl—to whatever point, that is, after
all that had both remotely and recently happened, presump-
tions of anything to be called decency could come in.

After what had recently happened—the two or three indirect but so worrying questions Mr French had put to her—
it would only be some thoroughly detached friend or witness
who might effectively testify. An odd form of detachment
certainly would reside, for Mr Pitman's evidential character,
in her mother's having so publicly and so brilliantly—though,
thank the powers, all off in North Dakota!—severed their
connexion with him; and yet mightn't it do *her* some good,
even if the harm it might do her mother were so little am-
biguous? The more her mother had got divorced—with her
dreadful cheap-and-easy second performance in that line and

her present extremity of alienation from Mr Connery, which enfolded beyond doubt the germ of a third petition on one side or the other—the more her mother had distinguished herself in the field of folly the worse for her own prospect with the Frenches, whose minds she had guessed to be accessible, and with such an effect of dissimulated suddenness, to some insidious poison.

It was all unmistakeable, in other words, that the more dismissed and detached Mr Pitman should have come to appear, the more as divorced, or at least as divorcing, his before-time wife would by the same stroke figure—so that it was here poor Julia could but lose herself. The crazy divorces only, or the half-dozen successive and still crazier engagements only —gathered fruit, bitter fruit, of her own incredibly allowed, her own insanely fostered frivolity—either of these two groups of skeletons at the banquet might singly be dealt with; but the combination, the fact of each party's having been so mixed-up with whatever was least presentable for the other, the fact of their having so shockingly amused themselves together, made all present steering resemble the classic middle course between Scylla and Charybdis.

It was not, however, that she felt wholly a fool in having obeyed this impulse to pick up again her kind old friend. *She* at least had never divorced him, and her horrid little filial evidence in Court had been but the chatter of a parrakeet, of precocious plumage and croak, repeating words earnestly taught her and that she could scarce even pronounce. Therefore, as far as steering went, he *must* for the hour take a hand. She might actually have wished in fact that he shouldn't now have seemed so tremendously struck with her; since it was an extraordinary situation for a girl, this crisis of her fortune, this positive wrong that the flagrancy, what she would have been ready to call the very vulgarity, of her good looks might do her at a moment when it was vital she should hang as straight as a picture on the wall. Had it ever yet befallen any young woman in the world to wish with secret intensity that she might have been, for her convenience, a shade less inordinately pretty? She had come to that, to this view of the bane, the primal curse, of their lavishly physical outfit, which had included everything and as to which she lumped herself resentfully with her mother. The only thing was that her mother was, thank goodness, still so much prettier, still so assertively, so publicly, so trashily, so ruinously pretty. Wonderful the small grimness with which Julia Bride put off on this parent the middle-aged maximum of their case and the responsibility of their defect. It cost her so little to recognise in Mrs Connery at forty-seven, and in spite, or perhaps indeed just by reason, of the arranged silver tendrils which were so like some rare bird's-nest in a morning frost, a facile supremacy for the dazzling effect—it cost her so little that her view even rather exaggerated the lustre of the different maternal items. She would have put it *all* off if possible, all off on other shoulders and on other graces and other morals than her own, the burden of physical charm that had made so easy a ground, such a native favouring air, for the aberrations which, apparently inevitable and without far consequences at the time, had yet at this juncture so much better not have been.

She could have worked it out at her leisure, to the last link of the chain, the way their prettiness had set them trap after trap, all along—had foredoomed them to awful ineptitude. When you were as pretty as that you could, by the whole idiotic consensus, be nothing *but* pretty; and when you were nothing "but" pretty you could get into nothing but tight places, out of which you could then scramble by nothing but masses of fibs. And there was no one, all the while, who wasn't eager to egg you on, eager to make you pay to the last cent the price of your beauty. What creature would ever for a moment help you to behave as if something that dragged in its wake a bit less of a lumbering train would, on the whole, have been better for you? The consequences of being plain

were only negative—you failed of this and that; but the consequences of being as *they* were, what were these but endless?
though indeed, as far as failing went, your beauty too could
let you in for enough of it. Who, at all events, would ever for
a moment credit you, in the luxuriance of that beauty, with
the study, on your own side, of such truths as these? Julia
Bride could, at the point she had reached, positively ask herself this even while lucidly conscious of the inimitable, the
triumphant and attested projection, all round her, of her
exquisite image. It was only Basil French who had at last, in
his doubtless dry but all distinguished way—the way, surely
as it was borne in upon her, of all the blood of all the Frenches
—stepped out of the vulgar rank. It was only he who, by the
trouble she discerned in him, had made her see certain things.
It was only for him—and not a bit ridiculously, but just beautifully, almost sublimely—that their being "nice," her mother
and she between them, had *not* seemed to profit by their being
so furiously handsome.

This had, ever so grossly and ever so tiresomely, satisfied
every one else; since every one had thrust upon them, had
imposed upon them as by a great cruel conspiracy, their
silliest possibilities; fencing them in to these, and so not
only shutting them out from others, but mounting guard at
the fence, walking round and round outside it to see they
didn't escape, and admiring them, talking to them, through the
rails, in mere terms of chaff, terms of chucked cakes and
apples—as if they had been antelopes or zebras, or even some
superior sort of performing, of dancing, bear. It had been
reserved for Basil French to strike her as willing to let go, so
to speak, a pound or two of this fatal treasure if he might only
have got in exchange for it an ounce or so more of their so
much less obvious and less published personal history. Yes,
it described him to say that, in addition to all the rest of him,
and of *his* personal history, and of his family, and of theirs,
in addition to their social posture, as that of a serried phalanx,

and to their notoriously enormous wealth and crushing respectability, she might have been ever so much less lovely for him if she had been only—well, a little prepared to answer questions. And it wasn't as if, quiet, cultivated, earnest, public-spirited, brought up in Germany, infinitely travelled, awfully like a high-caste Englishman, and all the other pleasant things, it wasn't as if he didn't love to be with her, to look at her, just as she was; for he loved it exactly as much, so far as that footing simply went, as any free and foolish youth who had ever made the last demonstration of it. It was that marriage was for him—and for them all, the serried Frenches—a great matter, a goal to which a man of intelligence, a real shy beautiful man of the world, didn't hop on one foot, didn't skip and jump, as if he were playing an urchins' game, but toward which he proceeded with a deep and anxious, a noble and highly just deliberation.

For it was one thing to stare at a girl till she was bored at it, it was one thing to take her to the Horse Show and the Opera, and to send her flowers by the stack, and chocolates by the ton, and "great" novels, the very latest and greatest, by the dozen; but something quite other to hold open for her, with eyes attached to eyes, the gate, moving on such stiff silver hinges, of the grand square forecourt of the palace of wedlock. The state of being "engaged" represented to him the introduction to this precinct of some young woman with whom his outside parley would have had the duration, distinctly, of his own convenience. That might be cold-blooded if one choose to think so; but nothing of another sort would equal the high ceremony and dignity and decency, above all the grand gallantry and finality, of their then passing in. Poor Julia could have blushed red, before that view, with the memory of the way the forecourt, as she now imagined it, had been dishonoured by her younger romps. She had tumbled over the wall with this, that and the other raw playmate, and had played "tag" and leap-frog, as she might say,

from corner to corner. That would be the "history" with
which, in case of definite demand, she should be able to
supply Mr French: that she had already, again and again, any
occasion offering, chattered and scuffled over ground provided, according to his idea, for walking the gravest of
minuets. If that then had been all their *kind* of history, hers
and her mother's, at least there was plenty of it: it was the
superstructure raised on the other group of facts, those of the
order of their having been always so perfectly pink and white,
so perfectly possessed of clothes, so perfectly splendid, so
perfectly idiotic. These things had been the "points" of ante-
lope and zebra; putting Mrs Connery for the zebra, as the
more remarkably striped or spotted. Such were the data Basil
French's enquiry would elicit: her own six engagements and
her mother's three nullified marriages—nine nice distinct
little horrors in all. What on earth was to be done about
them?

II

It was notable, she was afterwards to recognise, that there
had been nothing of the famous business slackness in the
positive pounce with which Mr Pitman put it to her that, as
soon as he had made her out "for sure," identified her there
as old Julia grown-up and gallivanting with a new admirer, a
smarter young fellow than ever yet, he had had the inspiration
of her being exactly the good girl to help him. She certainly
found him strike the hour again with these vulgarities of tone
—forms of speech that her mother had anciently described as
by themselves, once he had opened the whole battery, sufficient ground for putting him away. Full, however, of the use
she should have for him, she wasn't going to mind trifles.
What she really gasped at was that, so oddly, he was ahead of
her at the start. "Yes, I want something of you, Julia, and I

want it right now: you can do me a turn, and I'm blest if my luck—which has once or twice been pretty good, you know —hasn't sent you to me." She knew the luck he meant—that of her mother's having so enabled him to get rid of her; but it was the nearest allusion of the merely invidious kind that he would make. It had thus come to our young woman on the spot and by divination: the service he desired of her matched with remarkable closeness what she had so promptly taken into her head to name to himself—to name in her own interest, though deterred as yet from having brought it right out. She had been prevented by his speaking, the first thing, in that way, as if he had known Mr French—which surprised her till he explained that every one in New York knew by appearance a young man of his so quoted wealth ("What did she take them all in New York then *for?*") and of whose marked attention to her he had moreover, for himself, round at clubs and places, lately heard. This had accompanied the inevitable free question "Was she engaged to *him* now?"— which she had in fact almost welcomed as holding out to her the perch of opportunity. She was waiting to deal with it properly, but meanwhile he had gone on, and to such effect that it took them but three minutes to turn out, on either side, like a pair of pickpockets comparing, under shelter, their day's booty, the treasures of design concealed about their persons.

"I want you to tell the truth for me—as you only can. I want you to say that I was really all right—as right as you know; and that I simply acted like an angel in a story-book, gave myself away to have it over."

"Why my dear man," Julia cried, "you take the wind straight out of my sails! What I'm here to ask of *you* is that you'll confess to having been even a worse fiend than you were shown up for; to having made it impossible mother should *not* take proceedings." There!—she had brought it out, and with the sense of their situation turning to high excitement for her in the teeth of his droll stare, his strange grin, his characteristic "Lordy, lordy! What good will that do you?" She was prepared with her clear statement of reasons for her appeal, and feared so he might have better ones for his own that all her story came in a flash. "Well, Mr Pitman, I want to get married this time, by way of a change; but you see we've been such fools that, when something really good at last comes up, it's too dreadfully awkward. The fools we were capable of being—well, you know better than any one; unless perhaps not quite so well as Mr Connery. It has got to be denied," said Julia ardently—"it has got to be denied flat. But I can't get hold of Mr Connery—Mr Connery has gone to China. Besides, if he were here," she had ruefully to confess, "he'd be no good on the contrary. He wouldn't deny anything—he'd only tell more. So thank heaven he's away—there's *that* amount of good! I'm not engaged yet," she went on—but he had already taken her up.

"You're not engaged to Mr French?" It was all, clearly, a wondrous show for him, but his immediate surprise, oddly, might have been greatest for that.

"No, not to any one—for the seventh time!" She spoke as with her head held well up both over the shame and the pride. "Yes, the next time I'm engaged I want something to happen. But he's afraid; he's afraid of what may be told him. He's dying to find out, and yet he'd die if he did! He wants to be talked to, but he has got to be talked to right. You could talk to him right, Mr Pitman—if you only *would!* He can't get over mother—that I feel: he loathes and scorns divorces, and we've had first and last too many. So if he could hear from you that you just made her life a hell—why," Julia concluded, "it would be too lovely. If she *had* to go in for another—after having already, when I was little, divorced father—it would 'sort of' make, don't you see? one less. You'd do the high-toned thing by her: you'd say what a wretch you then were, and that she had had to save her life. In that way he mayn't mind it. Don't you see, you sweet man?" poor Julia pleaded. "Oh," she wound up as if his fancy lagged or his scruple looked out, "of course I want you to *lie* for me!"

It did indeed sufficiently stagger him. "It's a lovely idea for the moment when I was just saying to myself—as soon as I saw you—that you'd speak the truth for *me!*"

"Ah what's the matter with 'you'?" Julia sighed with an impatience not sensibly less sharp for her having so quickly scented some lion in her path.

"Why, do you think there's no one in the world but you who has seen the cup of promised affection, of something really to be depended on, only, at the last moment, by the horrid jostle of your elbow, spilled all over you? I want to provide for my future too as it happens; and my good friend who's to help me to that—the most charming of women this time—disapproves of divorce quite as much as Mr French. Don't you see," Mr Pitman candidly asked, "what that by itself must have done toward attaching me to her? *She* has got to be talked to—to be told how little I could help it."

"Oh lordy, lordy!" the girl emulously groaned. It was such a relieving cry. "Well, *I* won't talk to her!" she declared.

"You *won't*, Julia?" he pitifully echoed. "And yet you ask of *me*—!"

His pang, she felt, was sincere, and even more than she had guessed, for the previous quarter of an hour, he had been building up his hope, building it with her aid for a foundation. Yet was he going to see how their testimony, on each side, would, if offered, *have* to conflict? If he was to prove himself for her sake—or, more queerly still, for that of Basil French's high conservatism—a person whom there had been but that one way of handling, how could she prove him, in this other and so different interest, a mere gentle sacrifice to his wife's perversity? She had, before him there, on the instant, all acutely, a sense of rising sickness—a wan glimmer of foresight as to the end of the fond dream. Everything else was

against her, everything in her dreadful past—just as if she
had been a person represented by some "emotional actress,"
some desperate erring lady "hunted down" in a play; but
was that going to be the case too with her own very decency,
the fierce little residuum deep within her, for which she was
counting, when she came to think, on so little glory or even
credit? Was this also going to turn against her and trip her up
—just to show she was really, under the touch and the test,
as decent as any one; and with no one but herself the wiser
for it meanwhile, and no proof to show but that, as a consequence, she should be unmarried to the end? She put it to
Mr Pitman quite with resentment: "Do you mean to say
you're going to be married—?"

"Oh my dear, I too must get engaged first!"—he spoke
with his inimitable grin. "But that, you see, is where you
come in. I've told her about you. She wants awfully to meet
you. The way it happens is too lovely—that I find you just
in this place. She's coming," said Mr Pitman—and as in all
the good faith of his eagerness now; "she's coming in about
three minutes."

"Coming here?"

"Yes, Julia—right here. It's where we usually meet;" and
he was wreathed again, this time as if for life, in his large slow
smile. "She loves this place—she's awfully keen on art. Like
you, Julia, if you haven't changed—I remember how you did
love art." He looked at her quite tenderly, as to keep her up
to it. "You must still of course—from the way you're here.
Just let her *feel* that," the poor man fantastically urged. And
then with his kind eyes on her and his good ugly mouth
stretched as for delicate emphasis from ear to ear: "Every
little helps!"

He made her wonder for him, ask herself, and with a certain
intensity, questions she yet hated the trouble of; as whether
he were still as moneyless as in the other time—which was
certain indeed, for any fortune he ever would have made. His

slackness on that ground stuck out of him almost as much as if he had been of rusty or "seedy" aspect—which, luckily for him, he wasn't at all: he looked, in his way, like some pleasant eccentric ridiculous but real gentleman, whose taste might be of the queerest, but his credit with his tailor none the less of the best. She wouldn't have been the least ashamed, had their connexion lasted, of going about with him: so that what a fool, again, her mother had been—since Mr Connery, sorry as one might be for him, was irrepressibly vulgar. Julia's quickness was, for the minute, charged with all this; but she had none the less her feeling of the right thing to say and the right way to say it. If he was after a future financially assured, even as she herself so frantically was, she wouldn't cast the stone. But if he had talked about her to strange women she couldn't be less than a little majestic. "Who then is the person in question for you—?"

"Why such a dear thing, Julia—Mrs David E. Drack. Have you heard of her?" he almost fluted.

New York was vast, and she hadn't had that advantage. "She's a widow—?"

"Oh yes: she's not—!" He caught himself up in time. "She's a real one." It was as near as he came. But it was as if he had been looking at her now so pathetically hard. "Julia, she has millions."

Hard, at any rate—whether pathetic or not—was the look she gave him back. "Well, so has—or so *will* have—Basil French. And more of them than Mrs Drack, I guess," Julia quavered.

"Oh I know what *they've* got!" He took it from her—with the effect of a vague stir, in his long person, of unwelcome embarrassment. But was she going to give up because he was embarrassed? He should know at least what he was costing her. It came home to her own spirit more than ever; but meanwhile he had found his footing. "I don't see how your mother matters. It isn't a question of his marrying *her*."

"No; but, constantly together as we've always been, it's a question of there being so disgustingly much to get over. If we had, for people like them, but the one ugly spot and the one weak side; if we had made, between us, but the one vulgar *kind* of mistake: well, I don't say!" She reflected with a wistfulness of note that was in itself a touching eloquence. "To have our reward in this world we've had too sweet a time. We've had it all right down here!" said Julia Bride. "I should have taken the precaution to have about a dozen fewer lovers."

"Ah my dear, 'lovers'—!" He ever so comically attenuated.

"Well they *were!*" She quite flared up. "When you've had a ring from each (three diamonds, two pearls and a rather bad sapphire: I've kept them all, and they tell my story!) what are you to call them?"

"Oh rings—!" Mr Pitman didn't call rings anything. "I've given Mrs Drack a ring."

Julia stared. "Then aren't you her lover?"

"That, dear child," he humorously wailed, "is what I want you to find out! But I'll handle your rings all right," he more lucidly added.

"You'll 'handle' them?"

"I'll fix your lovers. I'll lie about *them*, if that's all you want."

"Oh about 'them'—!" She turned away with a sombre drop, seeing so little in it. "That wouldn't count—from *you!*" She saw the great shining room, with its mockery of art and "style" and security, all the things she was vainly after, and its few scattered visitors who had left them, Mr Pitman and herself, in their ample corner, so conveniently at ease. There was only a lady in one of the far doorways, of whom she took vague note and who seemed to be looking at them. "They'd have to lie for themselves!"

"Do you mean he's capable of putting it to them?"

Mr Pitman's tone threw discredit on that possibility, but she knew perfectly well what she meant. "Not of getting at them directly, not, as mother says, of nosing round himself; but of listening—and small blame to him!—to the horrible things other people say of me."

"But what other people?"

"Why Mrs George Maule, to begin with—who intensely loathes us, and who talks to his sisters, so that they may talk to *him:* which they do, all the while, I'm morally sure (hating me as they also must). But it's she who's the real reason—I mean of his holding off. She poisons the air he breathes."

"Oh well," said Mr Pitman with easy optimism, "if Mrs George Maule's a cat—!"

"If she's a cat she has kittens—four little spotlessly white ones, among whom she'd give her head that Mr French should make his pick. He could do it with his eyes shut—you can't tell them apart. But she has every name, every date, as you may say, for my dark 'record'—as of course they all call it: she'll be able to give him, if he brings himself to ask her, every fact in its order. And all the while, don't you see? there's no one to speak *for* me."

It would have touched a harder heart than her loose friend's to note the final flush of clairvoyance witnessing this assertion and under which her eyes shone as with the rush of quick tears. He stared at her, and what this did for the deep charm of her prettiness, as in almost witless admiration. "But can't you— lovely as you are, you beautiful thing!—speak for yourself?"

"Do you mean can't I tell the lies? No then, I can't—and I wouldn't if I could. I don't lie myself you know—as it happens; and it could represent to him then about the only thing, the only bad one, I don't do. I *did*—'lovely as I am'!— have my regular time; I wasn't so hideous that I couldn't! Besides, do you imagine he'd come and ask me?"

"Gad, I wish he would, Julia!" said Mr Pitman with his kind eyes on her.

"Well then I'd tell him!" And she held her head again high. "But he won't."

It fairly distressed her companion. "Doesn't he want then to know——?"

"He wants *not* to know. He wants to be told without asking—told, I mean, that each of the stories, those that have come to him, is a fraud and a libel. *Qui s'excuse s'accuse*, don't they say?—so that do you see me breaking out to him, un-provoked, with four or five what-do-you-call-'ems, the things mother used to have to prove in Court, a set of neat little 'alibis' in a row? How can I get hold of so *many* precious gentlemen, to turn them on? How can *they* want everything fished up?"

She had paused for her climax, in the intensity of these considerations; which gave Mr Pitman a chance to express his honest faith. "Why, my sweet child, they'd be just glad——!"

It determined in her loveliness almost a sudden glare. "Glad to swear they never had anything to do with such a creature? Then I'd be glad to swear they had lots!"

His persuasive smile, though confessing to bewilderment, insisted. "Why, my love, they've got to swear either one thing or the other."

"They've got to keep out of the way—that's *their* view of it, I guess," said Julia. "Where *are* they, please—now that they *may* be wanted? If you'd like to hunt them up for me you're very welcome." With which, for the moment, over the difficult case, they faced each other helplessly enough. And she added to it now the sharpest ache of her despair. "He knows about Murray Brush. The others"—and her pretty white-gloved hands and charming pink shoulders gave them up—"may go hang!"

"Murray Brush——?" It had opened Mr Pitman's eyes.

"Yes—yes; I do mind *him*."

"Then what's the matter with his at least rallying——?"

"The matter is that, being ashamed of himself, as he well

might, he left the country as soon as he could and has stayed away. The matter is that he's in Paris or somewhere, and that if you expect him to come home for me—!" She had already dropped, however, as at Mr Pitman's look.

"Why, you foolish thing, Murray Brush is in New York!" It had quite brightened him up.

"He has come back—?"

"Why sure! I saw him—when was it? Tuesday!—on the Jersey boat." Mr Pitman rejoiced in his news. "*He's* your man!"

Julia too had been affected by it; it had brought in a rich wave her hot colour back. But she gave the strangest dim smile. "He *was!*"

"Then get hold of him, and—if he's a gentleman—he'll prove for you, to the hilt, that he wasn't."

It lighted in her face, the kindled train of this particular sudden suggestion, a glow, a sharpness of interest, that had deepened the next moment, while she gave a slow and sad headshake, to a greater strangeness yet. "He isn't a gentleman."

"Ah lordy, lordy!" Mr Pitman again sighed. He struggled out of it but only into the vague. "Oh then if he's a pig—!"

"You see there are only a few gentlemen—not enough to go round—and that makes them count so!" It had thrust the girl herself, for that matter, into depths; but whether most of memory or of roused purpose he had no time to judge—aware as he suddenly was of a shadow (since he mightn't perhaps too quickly call it a light) across the heaving surface of their question. It fell upon Julia's face, fell with the sound of the voice he so well knew, but which could only be odd to her for all it immediately assumed.

"There are indeed very few—and one mustn't try *them* too much!" Mrs Drack, who had supervened while they talked, stood, in monstrous magnitude—at least to Julia's reimpressed eyes—between them: she was the lady our young

woman had descried across the room, and she had drawn
near while the interest of their issue so held them. We have
seen the act of observation and that of reflexion alike swift in
Julia—once her subject was within range—and she had now,
with all her perceptions at the acutest, taken in, by a single
stare, the strange presence to a happy connexion with which
Mr Pitman aspired and which had thus sailed, with placid
majesty, into their troubled waters. She was clearly not shy,
Mrs David E. Drack, yet neither was she ominously bold;
she was bland and "good," Julia made sure at a glance, and of
a large complacency, as the good and the bland are apt to
be—a large complacency, a large sentimentality, a large innocent elephantine archness: she fairly rioted in that dimension
of size. Habited in an extraordinary quantity of stiff and lustrous
black brocade, with enhancements, of every description, that
twinkled and tinkled, that rustled and rumbled with her least
movement, she presented a huge hideous pleasant face, a
featureless desert in a remote quarter of which the dispro-
portionately small eyes might have figured a pair of rash
adventurers all but buried in the sand. They reduced themselves when she smiled to barely discernible points—a couple
of mere tiny emergent heads—though the foreground of the
scene, as if to make up for it, gaped with a vast benevolence.
In a word Julia saw—and as if she had needed nothing more;
saw Mr Pitman's opportunity, saw her own, saw the exact
nature both of Mrs Drack's circumspection and of Mrs
Drack's sensibility, saw even, glittering there in letters of
gold and as a part of the whole metallic coruscation, the
large figure of her income, largest of all her attributes, and
(though perhaps a little more as a luminous blur beside all
this) the mingled ecstasy and agony of Mr Pitman's hope and
Mr Pitman's fear.

He was introducing them, with his pathetic belief in the
virtue for every occasion, in the solvent for every trouble, of
an extravagant genial professional humour; he was naming

her to Mrs Drack as the charming young friend he had told
her so much about and who had been as an angel to him in a
weary time; he was saying that the loveliest chance in the
world, this accident of a meeting in those promiscuous halls,
had placed within his reach the pleasure of bringing them
together. It didn't indeed matter, Julia felt, what he was
saying: he conveyed everything, as far as she was concerned,
by a moral pressure as unmistakeable as if, for a symbol of it,
he had thrown himself on her neck. Above all, meanwhile,
this high consciousness prevailed—that the good lady herself,
however huge she loomed, had entered, by the end of a
minute, into a condition as of suspended weight and arrested
mass, stilled to artless awe by the effect of her vision. Julia
had practised almost to lassitude the art of tracing in the
people who looked at her the impression promptly sequent;
but it was a singular fact that if, in irritation, in depression,
she felt that the lighted eyes of men, stupid at their clearest,
had given her pretty well all she should ever care for, she
could still gather a freshness from the tribute of her own sex,
still care to see her reflexion in the faces of women. Never,
probably, never would that sweet be tasteless—with such a
straight grim spoon was it mostly administered, and so
flavoured and strengthened by the competence of their eyes.
Women knew so much best *how* a woman surpassed—how
and where and why, with no touch or torment of it lost on
them; so that as it produced mainly and primarily the instinct
of aversion, the sense of extracting the recognition, of gouging
out the homage, was on the whole the highest crown one's
felicity could wear. Once in a way, however, the grimness
beautifully dropped, the jealousy failed: the admiration was
all there and the poor plain sister handsomely paid it. It had
never been so paid, she was presently certain, as by this great
generous object of Mr Pitman's flame, who without optical
aid, it well might have seemed, nevertheless entirely grasped
her—might in fact, all benevolently, have been groping her

over as by some huge mild proboscis. She gave Mrs Drack
pleasure in short; and who could say of what other pleasures
the poor lady hadn't been cheated?

It was somehow a muddled world in which one of her
conceivable joys, at this time of day, would be to marry Mr
Pitman—to say nothing of a state of things in which this
gentleman's own fancy could invest such a union with
rapture. That, however, was their own mystery, and Julia,
with each instant, was more and more clear about hers: so
remarkably primed in fact, at the end of three minutes, that
though her friend, and though *his* friend, were both saying
things, many things and perhaps quite wonderful things, she
had no free attention for them and was only rising and soaring.
She was rising to her value, she was soaring *with* it—the value
Mr Pitman almost convulsively imputed to her, the value that
consisted for her of being so unmistakeably the most dazzling
image Mrs Drack had ever beheld. These were the uses, for
Julia, in fine, of adversity; the range of Mrs Drack's experience might have been as small as the measure of her presence
was large: Julia was at any rate herself in face of the occasion
of her life, and, after all her late repudiations and reactions,
had perhaps never yet known the quality of this moment's
success. She hadn't an idea of what, on either side, had been
uttered—beyond Mr Pitman's allusion to her having be-
friended him of old: she simply held his companion with her
radiance and knew she might be, for her effect, as irrelevant
as she chose. It was relevant to do what he wanted—it was
relevant to dish herself. She did it now with a kind of passion,
to say nothing of her knowing, with it, that every word of it
added to her beauty. She gave him away in short, up to the
hilt, for any use of her own, and should have nothing to
clutch at now but the possibility of Murray Brush.

"He says I was good to him, Mrs Drack; and I'm sure I
hope I was, since I should be ashamed to be anything else. If
I could be good to him now I should be glad—that's just

what, a while ago, I rushed up to him here, after so long, to
give myself the pleasure of saying. I saw him years ago very
particularly, very miserably tried—and I saw the way he took
it. I did see it, you dear man," she sublimely went on—"I saw
it for all you may protest, for all you may hate me to talk
about you! I saw you behave like a gentleman—since Mrs
Drack agrees with me so charmingly that there are not many
to be met. I don't know whether you care, Mrs Drack"—
she abounded, she revelled in the name—"but I've always
remembered it of him: that under the most extraordinary
provocation he was decent and patient and brave. No appearance of anything different matters, for I speak of what I
know. Of course I'm nothing and nobody; I'm only a poor
frivolous girl, but I was very close to him at the time. That's
all my little story—if it *should* interest you at all." She measured every beat of her wing, she knew how high she was
going and paused only when it was quite vertiginous. Here
she hung a moment as in the glare of the upper blue; which
was but the glare—what else could it be?—of the vast and
magnificent attention of both her auditors, hushed, on their
side, in the splendour she emitted. She had at last to steady
herself, and she scarce knew afterwards at what rate or in
what way she had still inimitably come down—her own eyes
fixed all the while on the very figure of her achievement. She
had sacrificed her mother on the altar—proclaimed her false
and cruel; and if that didn't "fix" Mr Pitman, as he would
have said—well, it was all she could do. But the cost of her
action already somehow came back to her with increase; the
dear gaunt man fairly wavered, to her sight, in the glory of it,
as if signalling at her, with wild gleeful arms, from some mount
of safety, while the massive lady just spread and spread like a
rich fluid a bit helplessly spilt. It was really the outflow of
the poor woman's honest response, into which she seemed to
melt, and Julia scarce distinguished the two apart even for her
taking gracious leave of each. "Good-bye, Mrs Drack; I'm

awfully happy to have met you"—like as not it was for this
she had grasped Mr Pitman's hand. And then to him or to her,
it didn't matter which, "Good-bye, dear good Mr Pitman—
hasn't it been nice after so long?"

III

JULIA floated even to her own sense swanlike away—she left
in her wake their fairly stupefied submission: it was as if she
had, by an exquisite authority, now *placed* them, each for
each, and they would have nothing to do but be happy together. Never had she so exulted as on this ridiculous occasion
in the noted items of her beauty. *Le compte y était,* as they
used to say in Paris—every one of them, for her immediate
employment, was there; and there was something in it after
all. It didn't necessarily, this sum of thumping little figures,
imply charm—especially for "refined" people: nobody knew
better than Julia that inexpressible charm and quoteable
"charms" (quoteable like prices, rates, shares, or whatever,
the things they dealt in downtown) are two distinct categories; the safest thing for the latter being, on the whole, that
it might include the former, and the great strength of the
former being that it might perfectly dispense with the latter.
Mrs Drack wasn't refined, not the least little bit; but what
would be the case with Murray Brush now—after his three
years of Europe? He had done so what he liked with her—
which had seemed so then just the meaning, hadn't it? of their
being "engaged"—that he had made her not see, while the
absurdity lasted (the absurdity of their pretending to believe
they could marry without a cent) how little he was of metal
without alloy: this had come up for her, remarkably, but
afterwards—come up for her as she looked back. Then she
had drawn her conclusion, which was one of the many that

Basil French had made her draw. It was a queer service Basil was going to have rendered her, this having made everything she had ever done impossible, if he wasn't going to give her a new chance. If he was it was doubtless right enough. On the other hand Murray might have improved, if such a quantity of alloy, as she called it, *were*, in any man, reducible, and if Paris were the place all happily to reduce it. She had her doubts —anxious and aching on the spot, and had expressed them to Mr Pitman: certainly, of old, he had been more open to the quoteable than to the inexpressible, to charms than to charm. If she could try the quoteable, however, and with such a grand result, on Mrs Drack, she couldn't now on Murray— in respect to whom everything had changed. So that if he hadn't a sense for the subtler appeal, the appeal appreciable by people *not* vulgar, on which alone she could depend, what on earth would become of her? She could but yearningly hope, at any rate, as she made up her mind to write to him immediately at his club. It was a question of the right sensibility in him. Perhaps he would have acquired it in Europe.

Two days later indeed—for he had promptly and charmingly replied, keeping with alacrity the appointment she had judged best to propose, a morning hour in a sequestered alley of the Park—two days later she was to be struck well-nigh to alarm by everything he had acquired: so much it seemed to make that it threatened somehow a complication, and her plan, so far as she had arrived at one, dwelt in the desire above all to simplify. She wanted no grain more of extravagance or excess in anything—risking as she had done, none the less, a recall of ancient licence in proposing to Murray such a place of meeting. She had her reasons—she wished intensely to discriminate: Basil French had several times waited on her at her mother's habitation, their horrible flat which was so much too far up and too near the East Side; he had dined there and lunched there and gone with her thence to other places, notably to see pictures, and had in particular adjourned with her twice to the Metropolitan Museum, in which he took a great interest, in which she professed a delight, and their second visit to which had wound up in her encounter with Mr Pitman, after her companion had yielded, at her urgent instance, to an exceptional need of keeping a business engagement. She mightn't in delicacy, in decency, entertain Murray Brush where she had entertained Mr French—she was given over now to these exquisite perceptions and proprieties and bent on devoutly observing them; and Mr French, by good luck, had never been with her in the Park: partly because he had never pressed it, and partly because she would have held off if he had, so haunted were those devious paths and favouring shades by the general echo of her untrammelled past. If he had never suggested their taking a turn there this was because, quite divineably, he held it would commit him further than he had yet gone; and if she on her side had practised a like reserve it was because the place reeked for her, as she inwardly said, with old associations. It reeked with nothing so much perhaps as with the memories evoked by the young man who now awaited her in the nook she had been so competent to indicate; but in what corner of the town, should she look for them, wouldn't those footsteps creak back into muffled life, and to what expedient would she be reduced should she attempt to avoid all such tracks? The Museum was full of tracks, tracks by the hundred—the way really she had knocked about!—but she had to see people somewhere, and she couldn't pretend to dodge every ghost.

All she could do was not to make confusion, make mixtures, of the living; though she asked herself enough what mixture she mightn't find herself to have prepared if Mr French should, not so very impossibly for a restless roaming man—*her* effect on him!—happen to pass while she sat there with the moustachioed personage round whose name Mrs Maule would probably have caused detrimental anecdote most thickly to cluster. There existed, she was sure, a mass

12:M

of luxuriant legend about the "lengths" her engagement with
Murray Brush had gone; she could herself fairly feel them in
the air, these streamers of evil, black flags flown as in warning,
the vast redundancy of so cheap and so dingy social bunting,
in fine, that flapped over the stations she had successively
moved away from and which were empty now, for such an
ado, even to grotesqueness. The vivacity of that conviction
was what had at present determined her, while it was the way
he listened after she had quickly broken ground, while it was
the special character of the interested look in his handsome
face, handsomer than ever yet, that represented for her the
civilisation he had somehow taken on. Just so it was the
quantity of that gain, in its turn, that had at the end of ten
minutes begun to affect her as holding up a light to the wide
reach of her step. "There was never anything the least serious
between us, not a sign or a scrap, do you mind? of anything
beyond the merest pleasant friendly acquaintance; and if
you're not ready to go to the stake on it for me you may as
well know in time what it is you'll probably cost me."

She had immediately plunged, measuring her effect and
having thought it well over; and what corresponded to her
question of his having become a better person to appeal to
was the appearance of interest she had so easily created in
him. She felt on the spot the difference that made—it was
indeed his form of being more civilised: it was the sense in
which Europe in general and Paris in particular had made him
develop. By every calculation—and her calculations, based
on the intimacy of her knowledge, had been many and deep—
he would help her the better the more intelligent he should
have become; yet she was to recognise later on that the first
chill of foreseen disaster had been caught by her as, at a given
moment, this greater refinement of his attention seemed to
exhale it. It was just what she had wanted—"if I can only
get him interested—!" so that, this proving quite vividly
possible, why did the light it lifted strike her as lurid? Was

it partly by reason of his inordinate romantic good looks, those of a gallant genial conqueror, but which, involving so glossy a brownness of eye, so manly a crispness of curl, so red-lipped a radiance of smile, so natural a bravery of port, prescribed to any response he might facially, might expressively make a sort of florid disproportionate amplitude? The explanation, in any case, didn't matter; he was going to mean well—that she could feel, and also that he had meant better in the past, presumably, than he had managed to convince her of his doing at the time: the oddity she hadn't now reckoned with was this fact that from the moment he did advertise an interest it should show almost as what she would have called weird. It made a change in him that didn't go with the rest— as if he had broken his nose or put on spectacles, lost his handsome hair or sacrificed his splendid moustache: her conception, her necessity, as she saw, had been that something should be added to him for her use, but nothing for his own alteration.

He had affirmed himself, and his character, and his temper, and his health, and his appetite, and his ignorance, and his obstinacy, and his whole charming coarse heartless personality, during their engagement, by twenty forms of natural emphasis, but never by emphasis of interest. How in fact could you feel interest unless you should know, within you, some dim stir of imagination? There was nothing in the world of which Murray Brush was less capable than of such a dim stir, because you only began to imagine when you felt some approach to a need to understand. *He* had never felt it; for hadn't he been born, to his personal vision, with that perfect intuition of everything which reduces all the suggested preliminaries of judgement to the impertinence—when it's a question of your entering your house—of a dumpage of bricks at your door? He had had, in short, neither to imagine nor to perceive, because he had, from the first pulse of his intelligence, simply and supremely known: so that, at this

hour, face to face with him, it came over her that she had in
their old relation dispensed with any such convenience of
comprehension on his part even to a degree she had not
measured at the time. What therefore must he not have
seemed to her as a form of life, a form of avidity and activity,
blatantly successful in its own conceit, that he could have
dazzled her so against the interest of her very faculties and
functions? Strangely and richly historic all that backward
mystery, and only leaving for her mind the wonder of such
a mixture of possession and detachment as they would clearly
to-day both know. For each to be so little at last to the other
when, during months together, the idea of all abundance, all
quantity, had been, for each, drawn from the other and
addressed to the other—what was it monstrously like but
some fantastic act of getting rid of a person by going to lock
yourself up in the *sanctum sanctorum* of that person's house,
amid every evidence of that person's habits and nature? What
was going to happen, at any rate, was that Murray would
show himself as beautifully and consciously understanding—
and it would be prodigious that Europe should have inocu-
lated him with that delicacy. Yes, he wouldn't claim to know
now till she had told him—an aid to performance he had surely
never before waited for or been indebted to from any one;
and then, so knowing, he would charmingly endeavour to
"meet," to oblige and to gratify. He would find it, her case,
ever so worthy of his benevolence, and would be literally
inspired to reflect that he must hear about it first.

She let him hear then everything, in spite of feeling herself
slip, while she did so, to some doom as yet incalculable; she
went on very much as she had done for Mr Pitman and Mrs
Drack, with the rage of desperation and, as she was afterwards
to call it to herself, the fascination of the abyss. She didn't
know, couldn't have said at the time, *why* his projected
benevolence should have had most so the virtue to scare her:
he would patronise her, as an effect of her vividness, if not of

her charm, and would do this with all high intention, finding
her case, or rather *their* case, their funny old case, taking on of
a sudden such refreshing and edifying life, to the last degree
curious and even important; but there were gaps of connexion
between this and the intensity of the perception here overtaking her that she shouldn't be able to move in *any* direction
without dishing herself. That she couldn't afford it where she
had got to—couldn't afford the deplorable vulgarity of having
been so many times informally affianced and contracted (putting it only at that, at its being by the new lights and fashions
so unpardonably vulgar): he took this from her without
turning, as she might have said, a hair; except just to indicate,
with his new superiority, that he felt the distinguished appeal
and notably the pathos of it. He still took it from her that she
hoped nothing, as it were, from any other *alibi*—the people to
drag into court being too many and too scattered; but that,
as it was with him, Murray Brush, she had been *most* vulgar,
most everything she had better not have been, so she depended on him for the innocence it was actually vital she
should establish. He blushed or frowned or winced no more
at that than he did when she once more fairly emptied her
satchel and, quite as if they had been Nancy and the Artful
Dodger, or some nefarious pair of that sort, talking things
over in the manner of "Oliver Twist," revealed to him the
fondness of her view that, could she but have produced a
cleaner slate, she might by this time have pulled it off with
Mr French. Yes, he let her in that way sacrifice her honourable
connexion with him—all the more honourable for being so
completely at an end—to the crudity of her plan for not
missing another connexion, so much more brilliant than
what he offered, and for bringing another man, with whom
she so invidiously and unflatteringly compared him, into her
greedy life.

There was only a moment during which, by a particular
lustrous look she had never had from him before, he just

made her wonder which turn he was going to take; she felt, however, as safe as was consistent with her sense of having probably but added to her danger, when he brought out, the next instant: "Don't you seem to take the ground that we were guilty—that *you* were ever guilty—of something we shouldn't have been? What did we ever do that was secret, or underhand, or any way not to be acknowledged? What did we do but exchange our young vows with the best faith in the world—publicly, rejoicingly, with the full assent of every one connected with us? I mean of course," he said with his grave kind smile, "till we broke off so completely because we found that—practically, financially, on the hard worldly basis—we couldn't work it. What harm, in the sight of God or man, Julia," he asked in his fine rich way, "did we ever do?"

She gave him back his look, turning pale. "Am I talking of *that?* Am I talking of what *we* know? I'm talking of what others feel—of what they *have* to feel; of what it's just enough for them to know not to be able to get over it, once they do really know it. How do they know what *didn't* pass between us, with all the opportunities we had? That's none of their business—if we were idiots enough, on the top of everything! What you may or mayn't have done doesn't count, for *you;* but there are people for whom it's loathsome that a girl should have gone on like that from one person to another and still pretend to be—well, all that a nice girl is supposed to be. It's as if we had but just waked up, mother and I, to such a remarkable prejudice; and now we have it—when we could do so well without it!—staring us in the face. That mother should have insanely *let* me, should so vulgarly have taken it for my natural, my social career—*that's* the disgusting humiliating thing: with the lovely account it gives of both of us! But mother's view of a delicacy in things!" she went on with scathing grimness; "mother's measure of anything, with her grand 'gained cases' (there'll be another yet, she finds them so easy!) of which she's so publicly proud! You see I've no margin," said Julia; letting him take it from her flushed face as much as he would that her mother hadn't left her an inch. It was that he should make use of the spade with her for the restoration of a bit of a margin just wide enough to perch on till the tide of peril should have ebbed a little, it was that he should give her *that* lift——!

Well, it was all there from him after these last words; it was before her that he really took hold. "Oh, my dear child, I can see! Of course there are people—ideas change in our society so fast!—who are not in sympathy with the old American freedom and who read, I dare say, all sorts of un- canny things into it. Naturally you must take them as they are—from the moment," said Murray Brush, who had lighted, by her leave, a cigarette, "your life-path does, for weal or for woe, cross with theirs." He had every now and then such an elegant phrase. "Awfully interesting, certainly, your case. It's enough for me that it *is* yours—I make it my own. I put myself absolutely in your place; you'll understand from me, without professions, won't you? that I do. Command me in every way! What I do like is the sympathy with which you've inspired *him*. I don't, I'm sorry to say, happen to know him personally"—he smoked away, looking off; "but of course one knows all about him generally, and I'm sure he's right for you, I'm sure it would be charming, if you yourself think so. Therefore trust me and even—what shall I say?— leave it to me a little, won't you?" He had been watching, as in his fumes, the fine growth of his possibilities; and with this he turned on her the large warmth of his charity. It was like a subscription of a half a million. "I'll take care of you."

She found herself for a moment looking up at him from as far below as the point from which the school-child, with round eyes raised to the wall, gazes at the particoloured map of the world. Yes, it was a warmth, it was a special benignity, that had never yet dropped on her from any one; and she wouldn't for the first few moments have known how to describe it or even quite what to do with it. Then as it still rested, his fine improved expression aiding, the sense of what had happened came over her with a rush. She was being, yes, patronised; and that was really as new to her—the freeborn American girl who might, if she had wished, have got engaged and disengaged not six times but sixty—as it would have been to be crowned or crucified. The Frenches themselves didn't do it—the Frenches themselves didn't dare it. It was as strange as one would: she recognised it when it came, but anything might have come rather—and it was coming by (of all people in the world) Murray Brush! It overwhelmed her; still she could speak, with however faint a quaver and however sick a smile. "You'll lie for me like a gentleman?"

"As far as that goes till I'm black in the face!" And then while he glowed at her and she wondered if he would pointedly look his lies that way, and if, in fine, his florid gallant knowing, almost winking intelligence, *common* as she had never seen the common vivified, would represent his notion of "blackness": "See here, Julia; I'll do more."

" 'More'—?"

"Everything. I'll take it right in hand. I'll fling over you—"

"Fling over me—?" she continued to echo as he fascinatingly fixed her.

"Well, the biggest *kind* of rose-coloured mantle!" And this time, oh, he did wink: it *would* be the way he was going to wink (and in the grandest good faith in the world) when indignantly denying, under inquisition, that there had been "a sign or a scrap" between them. But there was more to come; he decided she should have it all. "Julia, you've got to know now." He hung fire but an instant more. "Julia, I'm going to be married." His "Julias" were somehow death to her; she could feel that even *through* all the rest. "Julia, I announce my engagement."

"Oh lordy, lordy!" she wailed: it might have been addressed to Mr Pitman.

The force of it had brought her to her feet, but he sat there smiling up as at the natural tribute of her interest. "I tell you before any one else; it's not to be 'out' for a day or two yet. But we want you to know; *she* said that as soon as I mentioned to her that I had heard from you. I mention to her everything, you see!"—and he almost simpered while, still in his seat, he held the end of his cigarette, all delicately and as for a form of gentle emphasis, with the tips of his fine fingers. "You've not met her, Mary Lindeck, I think: she tells me she hasn't the pleasure of knowing you, but she desires it so much—particularly longs for it. She'll take an interest too," he went on; "you must let me immediately bring her to you. She has heard so much about you and she really wants to see you."

"Oh mercy *me!*" poor Julia gasped again—so strangely did history repeat itself and so did this appear the echo, on Murray Brush's lips, and quite to drollery, of that sympathetic curiosity of Mrs Drack's which Mr Pitman, as they said, voiced. Well, there had played before her the vision of a ledge of safety in face of a rising tide; but this deepened quickly to a sense more forlorn, the cold swish of waters already up to her waist and that would soon be up to her chin. It came really but from the air of her friend, from the perfect benevolence and high unconsciousness with which he kept his posture—as if to show he could patronise her from below upward quite as well as from above down. And as she took it all in, as it spread to a flood, with the great lumps and masses of truth it was floating, she knew inevitable submission, not to say submersion, as she had never known it in her life; going down and down before it, not even putting out her hands to resist or cling by the way, only reading into the young man's very face an immense fatality and, for all his bright nobleness, his absence of rancour or of protesting pride, the great grey blankness of her doom. It was as if the earnest Miss Lindeck, tall and mild, high and lean, with eye-glasses and a big nose, but "marked" in a noticeable way, elegant and distinguished and refined, as you could see from a mile off, and as graceful, for common despair of imitation, as the curves of the "copy" set of old by one's writing-master—it was as if this stately well-wisher, whom indeed she had never exchanged a word with, but whom she had recognised and placed and winced at as soon as he spoke of her, figured there beside him now as also in portentous charge of her case.

He had ushered her into it in that way, as if his mere right word sufficed; and Julia could see them throned together, beautifully at one in all the interests they now shared, and regard her as an object of almost tender solicitude. It was positively as if they had become engaged for her good—in such a happy light as it shed. That was the way people you had known, known a bit intimately, looked at you as soon as they took on the high matrimonial propriety that sponged over the more or less wild past to which you belonged and of which, all of a sudden, they were aware only through some suggestion it made them for reminding you definitely that you still had a place. On her having had a day or two before to meet Mrs Drack and to rise to her expectation she had seen and felt herself act, had above all admired herself, and had at any rate known what she said, even though losing, at her altitude, any distinctness in the others. She could have re-peated afterwards the detail of her performance—if she hadn't preferred to keep it with her as a mere locked-up, a mere unhandled treasure. At present, however, as everything was for her at first deadened and vague, true to the general effect of sounds and motions in water, she couldn't have said after-wards what words she spoke, what face she showed, what impression she made—at least till she had pulled herself round to precautions. She only knew she had turned away, and that this movement must have sooner or later determined

his rising to join her, his deciding to accept it, gracefully and
condoningly—condoningly in respect to her natural emotion,
her inevitable little pang—for an intimation that they would
be better on their feet.

They trod then afresh their ancient paths; and though it
pressed upon her hatefully that he must have taken her
abruptness for a smothered shock, the flare-up of her old
feeling at the breath of his news, she had still to see herself
condemned to allow him this, condemned really to encourage
him in the mistake of believing her suspicious of feminine
spite and doubtful of Miss Lindeck's zeal. She was so far from
doubtful that she was but too appalled at it and at the officious
mass in which it loomed, and this instinct of dread, before
their walk was over, before she had guided him round to one
of the smaller gates, there to slip off again by herself, was
positively to find on the bosom of her flood a plank under aid
of which she kept in a manner and for the time afloat. She
took ten minutes to pant, to blow gently, to paddle dis-
guisedly, to accommodate herself, in a word, to the elements
she had let loose; but as a reward of her effort at least she then
saw how her determined vision accounted for everything.
Beside her friend on the bench she had truly felt all his cables
cut, truly swallowed down the fact that if he still perceived she
was pretty—and *how* pretty!—it had ceased appreciably to
matter to him. It had lighted the folly of her preliminary fear,
the fear of his even yet, to some effect of confusion or other
inconvenience for her, proving more alive to the quoteable
in her, as she had called it, than to the inexpressible. She had
reckoned with the awkwardness of that possible lapse of his
measure of her charm, by which his renewed apprehension of
her grosser ornaments, those with which he had most affinity,
might too much profit; but she need have concerned herself
as little for his sensibility on one head as on the other. She
had ceased personally, ceased materially—in respect, as who
should say, to any optical or tactile advantage—to exist for

him, and the whole office of his manner had been the more
piously and gallantly to dress the dead presence with flowers.
This was all to his credit and his honour, but what it clearly
certified was that their case was at last not even one of spirit
reaching out to spirit. *He* had plenty of spirit—had all the
spirit required for his having engaged himself to Miss Lindeck; into which result, once she had got her head well up
again, she read, as they proceeded, one sharp meaning after
another. It was therefore toward the subtler essence of that
mature young woman alone that he was occupied in stretching; what was definite to him about Julia Bride being merely,
being entirely—which was indeed thereby quite enough—that
she *might* end by scaling her worldly height. They would
push, they would shove, they would "boost," they would
arch both their straight backs as pedestals for her tiptoe; and
at the same time, by some sweet prodigy of mechanics, she
would pull them up and up with her.

Wondrous things hovered before her in the course of this
walk; her consciousness had become, by an extraordinary
turn, a music-box in which, its lid well down, the most
remarkable tunes were sounding. It played for her ear alone,
and the lid, as she might have figured, was her firm plan of
holding out till she got home, of not betraying—to her companion at least—the extent to which she was demoralised. To
see him think her demoralised by mistrust of the sincerity of
the service to be meddlesomely rendered her by his future
wife—she would have hurled herself publicly into the lake
there at their side, would have splashed, in her beautiful
clothes, among the frightened swans, rather than invite him
to that ineptitude. Oh her sincerity, Mary Lindeck's—she
would be drenched with her sincerity, and she would be
drenched, yes, with *his;* so that, from inward convulsion to
convulsion, she had, before they reached their gate, pulled up
in the path. There was something her head had been full of
these three or four minutes, the intensest little tune of the

music-box, and it had made its way to her lips now; belonging
—for all the good it could do her!—to the two or three sorts
of solicitude she might properly express.

"I hope *she* has a fortune, if you don't mind my speaking
of it: I mean some of the money we didn't in *our* time have—
and that we missed, after all, in our poor way and for what we
then wanted of it, so quite dreadfully."

She had been able to wreathe it in a grace quite equal to any
he himself had employed; and it was to be said for him also
that he kept up, on this, the standard. "Oh she's not, thank
goodness, at all badly off, poor dear. We shall do very well.
How sweet of you to have thought of it! May I tell her that
too?" he splendidly glared. Yes, he glared—how couldn't he,
with what his mind was really full of? But, all the same, he
came just here, by her vision, nearer than at any other point
to being a gentleman. He came quite within an ace of it—
with his taking from her thus the prescription of humility of
service, his consenting to act in the interest of her avidity, his
letting her mount that way, on his bowed shoulders, to the
success in which he could suppose she still believed. He
couldn't know, he would never know, that she had then and
there ceased to believe in it—that she saw as clear as the sun
in the sky the exact manner in which, between them, before
they had done, the Murray Brushes, all zeal and sincerity, all
interest in her interesting case, would dish, would ruin, would
utterly destroy her. He wouldn't have needed to go on, for
the force and truth of this; but he did go on—he was as
crashingly consistent as a motor-car without a brake. He was
visibly in love with the idea of what they might do for her
and of the rare "social" opportunity that they would, by the
same stroke, embrace. How he had been offhand with it, how
he had made it parenthetic, that he didn't happen "personally"
to know Basil French—as if it would have been at all likely
he *should* know him, even *im*personally, and as if he could
conceal from her the fact that, since she had made him her

overture, this gentleman's name supremely baited her hook! Oh they would help Julia Bride if they could—they would do their remarkable best; but they would at any rate have made his acquaintance over it, and she might indeed leave the rest to their thoroughness. He would already have known, he would already have heard; her appeal, she was more and more sure, wouldn't have come to him as a revelation. He had already talked it over with *her*, with Miss Lindeck, to whom the Frenches, in their fortress, had never been accessible, and his whole attitude bristled, to Julia's eyes, with the betrayal of her hand, her voice, her pressure, her calculation. His tone in fact, as he talked, fairly thrust these things into her face. "But you must see her for yourself. You'll judge her. You'll love her. My dear child"—he brought it all out, and if he spoke of children he might, in his candour, have been himself infantine—"my dear child, she's the person to do it for you. Make it over to her; but," he laughed, "of course see her first! Couldn't you," he wound up—for they were now near their gate, where she was to leave him—"couldn't you just simply make us meet him, at tea, say, informally; just *us* alone, as pleasant old friends of whom you'd have so naturally and frankly spoken to him; and then see what we'd *make* of that?"

It was all in his expression; he couldn't keep it undetected, and his shining good looks couldn't: ah he was so fatally much too handsome for her! So the gap showed just there, in his admirable mask and his admirable eagerness; the yawning little chasm showed where the gentleman fell short. But she took this in, she took everything in, she felt herself do it, she heard herself say, while they paused before separation, that she quite saw the point of the meeting, as he suggested, at her tea. She would propose it to Mr French and would let them know; and he must assuredly bring Miss Lindeck, bring her "right away," bring her soon, bring *them*, his fiancée and her, together somehow, and as quickly as possible—so that they *should* be old friends before the tea. She would propose it to Mr French, propose it to Mr French: that hummed in her ears as she went—after she had really got away; hummed as if she were repeating it over, giving it out to the passers, to the pavement, to the sky, and all as in wild discord with the intense little concert of her music-box. The extraordinary thing too was that she quite believed she should do it, and fully meant to; desperately, fantastically passive—since she almost reeled with it as she proceeded—she was capable of proposing anything to any one: capable too of thinking it likely Mr French would come, for he had never on her previous proposals declined anything. Yes, she would keep it up to the end, this pretence of owing them salvation, and might even live to take comfort in having done for them what they wanted. What they wanted *couldn't* but be to get at the Frenches, and what Miss Lindeck above all wanted, baffled of it otherwise, with so many others of the baffled, was to get at Mr French—for all Mr French would want of either of them!—still more than Murray did. It wasn't till after she had got home, got straight into her own room and flung herself on her face, that she yielded to the full taste of the bitterness of missing a connexion, missing the man himself, with power to create such a social appetite, such a grab at what might be gained by them. He could make people, even people like these two and whom there were still other people to envy, he could make them push and snatch and scramble like that—and then remain as incapable of taking her from the hands of such patrons as of receiving her straight, say, from those of Mrs Drack. It was a high note, too, of Julia's wonderful composition that, even in the long lonely moan of her conviction of her now certain ruin, all this grim lucidity, the perfect clearance of passion, but made her supremely proud of him.

THE JOLLY CORNER

I

"Every one asks me what I 'think' of everything," said
Spencer Brydon; "and I make answer as I can—begging or
dodging the question, putting them off with any nonsense.
It wouldn't matter to any of them really," he went on, "for,
even were it possible to meet in that stand-and-deliver way
so silly a demand on so big a subject, my 'thoughts' would
still be almost altogether about something that concerns only
myself." He was talking to Miss Staverton, with whom for a
couple of months now he had availed himself of every possible
occasion to talk; this disposition and this resource, this comfort and support, as the situation in fact presented itself,
having promptly enough taken the first place in the considerable array of rather unattenuated surprises attending his so
strangely belated return to America. Everything was somehow a surprise; and that might be natural when one had so
long and so consistently neglected everything, taken pains
to give surprises so much margin for play. He had given
them more than thirty years—thirty-three, to be exact; and
they now seemed to him to have organised their performance
quite on the scale of that licence. He had been twenty-three
on leaving New York—he was fifty-six to-day: unless indeed
he were to reckon as he had sometimes, since his repatriation,
found himself feeling; in which case he would have lived
longer than is often allotted to man. It would have taken a
century, he repeatedly said to himself, and said also to Alice
Staverton, it would have taken a longer absence and a more

averted mind than those even of which he had been guilty, to pile up the differences, the newnesses, the queernesses, above all the bignesses, for the better or the worse, that at present assaulted his vision wherever he looked.

The great fact all the while however had been the incalculability; since he *had* supposed himself, from decade to decade, to be allowing, and in the most liberal and intelligent manner, for brilliancy of change. He actually saw that he had allowed for nothing; he missed what he would have been sure of finding, he found what he would never have imagined. Proportions and values were upside-down; the ugly things he had expected, the ugly things of his far-away youth, when he had too promptly waked up to a sense of the ugly—these uncanny phenomena placed him rather, as it happened, under the charm; whereas the "swagger" things, the modern, the monstrous, the famous things, those he had more particularly, like thousands of ingenuous enquirers every year, come over to see, were exactly his sources of dismay. They were as so many set traps for displeasure, above all for reaction, of which his restless tread was constantly pressing the spring. It was interesting, doubtless, the whole show, but it would have been too disconcerting hadn't a certain finer truth saved the situation. He had distinctly not, in this steadier light, come over *all* for the monstrosities; he had come, not only in the last analysis but quite on the face of the act, under an impulse with which they had nothing to do. He had come—putting the thing pompously—to look at his "property," which he had thus for a third of a century not been within four thousand miles of; or, expressing it less sordidly, he had yielded to the humour of seeing again his house on the jolly corner, as he usually, and quite fondly, described it—the one in which he had first seen the light, in which various members of his family had lived and had died, in which the holidays of his overschooled boyhood had been passed and the few social flowers of his chilled adolescence gathered, and which,

alienated then for so long a period, had, through the successive deaths of his two brothers and the termination of old
arrangements, come wholly into his hands. He was the owner
of another, not quite so "good"—the jolly corner having
been, from far back, superlatively extended and consecrated;
and the value of the pair represented his main capital, with
an income consisting, in these later years, of their respective
rents which (thanks precisely to their original excellent type)
had never been depressingly low. He could live in "Europe,"
as he had been in the habit of living, on the product of these
flourishing New York leases, and all the better since, that of
the second structure, the mere number in its long row, having
within a twelvemonth fallen in, renovation at a high advance
had proved beautifully possible.

These were items of property indeed, but he had found
himself since his arrival distinguishing more than ever between
them. The house within the street, two bristling blocks westward, was already in course of reconstruction as a tall mass of
flats; he had acceded, some time before, to overtures for this
conversion—in which, now that it was going forward, it had
been not the least of his astonishments to find himself able,
on the spot, and though without a previous ounce of such
experience, to participate with a certain intelligence, almost
with a certain authority. He had lived his life with his back so
turned to such concerns and his face addressed to those of so
different an order that he scarce knew what to make of this
lively stir, in a compartment of his mind never yet penetrated,
of a capacity for business and a sense for construction. These
virtues, so common all round him now, had been dormant in
his own organism—where it might be said of them perhaps
that they had slept the sleep of the just. At present, in the
splendid autumn weather—the autumn at least was a pure
boon in the terrible place—he loafed about his "work"
undeterred, secretly agitated; not in the least "minding" that
the whole proposition, as they said, was vulgar and sordid,

and ready to climb ladders, to walk the plank, to handle materials and look wise about them, to ask questions, in fine, and challenge explanations and really "go into" figures.

It amused, it verily quite charmed him; and, by the same stroke, it amused, and even more, Alice Staverton, though perhaps charming her perceptibly less. She wasn't however going to be better-off for it, as *he* was—and so astonishingly much: nothing was now likely, he knew, ever to make her better-off than she found herself, in the afternoon of life, as the delicately frugal possessor and tenant of the small house in Irving Place to which she had subtly managed to cling through her almost unbroken New York career. If he knew the way to it now better than to any other address among the dreadful multiplied numberings which seemed to him to reduce the whole place to some vast ledger-page, overgrown, fantastic, of ruled and criss-crossed lines and figures—if he had formed, for his consolation, that habit, it was really not a little because of the charm of his having encountered and recognised, in the vast wilderness of the wholesale, breaking through the mere gross generalisation of wealth and force and success, a small still scene where items and shades, all delicate things, kept the sharpness of the notes of a high voice perfectly trained, and where economy hung about like the scent of a garden. His old friend lived with one maid and herself dusted her relics and trimmed her lamps and polished her silver; she stood off, in the awful modern crush, when she could, but she sallied forth and did battle when the challenge was really to "spirit," the spirit she after all confessed to, proudly and a little shyly, as to that of the better time, that of *their* common, their quite far-away and antediluvian social period and order. She made use of the street-cars when need be, the terrible things that people scrambled for as the panic-stricken at sea scramble for the boats; she affronted, inscrutably, under stress, all the public concussions and ordeals; and yet, with that slim mystifying grace of her appearance, which defied you to say if she were a fair young woman who looked older through trouble, or a fine smooth older one who looked young through successful indifference; with her precious reference, above all, to memories and histories into which he could enter, she was as exquisite for him as some pale pressed flower (a rarity to begin with), and, failing other sweetnesses, she was a sufficient reward of his effort. They had communities of knowledge, "their" knowledge (this discriminating possessive was always on her lips) of presences of the other age, presences all overlaid, in his case, by the experience of a man and the freedom of a wanderer, overlaid by pleasure, by infidelity, by passages of life that were strange and dim to her, just by "Europe" in short, but still unobscured, still exposed and cherished, under that pious visitation of the spirit from which she had never been diverted.

She had come with him one day to see how his "apartment-house" was rising; he had helped her over gaps and explained to her plans, and while they were there had happened to have, before her, a brief but lively discussion with the man in charge, the representative of the building-firm that had undertaken his work. He had found himself quite "standing-up" to this personage over a failure on the latter's part to observe some detail of one of their noted conditions, and had so lucidly argued his case that, besides ever so prettily flushing, at the time, for sympathy in his triumph, she had afterwards said to him (though to a slightly greater effect of irony) that he had clearly for too many years neglected a real gift. If he had but stayed at home he would have anticipated the inventor of the sky-scraper. If he had but stayed at home he would have discovered his genius in time really to start some new variety of awful architectural hare and run it till it burrowed in a gold-mine. He was to remember these words, while the weeks elapsed, for the small silver ring they had sounded over the queerest and deepest of his own lately most disguised and most muffled vibrations.

It had begun to be present to him after the first fortnight, it had broken out with the oddest abruptness, this particular wanton wonderment: it met him there—and this was the image under which he himself judged the matter, or at least, not a little, thrilled and flushed with it—very much as he might have been met by some strange figure, some unexpected occupant, at a turn of one of the dim passages of an empty house. The quaint analogy quite hauntingly remained with him, when he didn't indeed rather improve it by a still intenser form: that of his opening a door behind which he would have made sure of finding nothing, a door into a room shuttered and void, and yet so coming, with a great suppressed start, on some quite erect confronting presence, something planted in the middle of the place and facing him through the dusk. After that visit to the house in construction he walked with his companion to see the other and always so much the better one, which in the eastward direction formed one of the corners, the "jolly" one precisely, of the street now so generally dishonoured and disfigured in its westward reaches, and of the comparatively conservative Avenue. The Avenue still had pretensions, as Miss Staverton said, to decency; the old people had mostly gone, the old names were unknown, and here and there an old association seemed to stray, all vaguely, like some very aged person, out too late, whom you might meet and feel the impulse to watch or follow, in kindness, for safe restoration to shelter.

They went in together, our friends; he admitted himself with his key, as he kept no one there, he explained, preferring, for his reasons, to leave the place empty, under a simple arrangement with a good woman living in the neighbourhood and who came for a daily hour to open windows and dust and sweep. Spencer Brydon had his reasons and was growingly aware of them; they seemed to him better each time he was there, though he didn't name them all to his companion, any more than he told her as yet how often, how quite absurdly often, he himself came. He only let her see for the present, while they walked through the great blank rooms, that absolute vacancy reigned and that, from top to bottom, there was nothing but Mrs Muldoon's broomstick, in a corner, to tempt the burglar. Mrs Muldoon was then on the premises, and she loquaciously attended the visitors, preceding them from room to room and pushing back shutters and throwing up sashes— all to show them, as she remarked, how little there was to see. There was little indeed to see in the great gaunt shell where the main dispositions and the general apportionment of space, the style of an age of ampler allowances, had nevertheless for its master their honest pleading message, affecting him as some good old servant's, some lifelong retainer's appeal for a character, or even for a retiring-pension; yet it was also a remark of Mrs Muldoon's that, glad as she was to oblige him by her noonday round, there was a request she greatly hoped he would never make of her. If he should wish her for any reason to come in after dark she would just tell him, if he "plased," that he must ask it of somebody else.

The fact that there was nothing to see didn't militate for the worthy woman against what one *might* see, and she put it frankly to Miss Staverton that no lady could be expected to like, could she? "craping up to thim top storeys in the ayvil hours." The gas and the electric light were off the house, and she fairly evoked a gruesome vision of her march through the great grey rooms—so many of them as there were too!—with her glimmering taper. Miss Staverton met her honest glare with a smile and the profession that she herself certainly would recoil from such an adventure. Spencer Brydon meanwhile held his peace—for the moment; the question of the "evil" hours in his old home had already become too grave for him. He had begun some time since to "crape," and he knew just why a packet of candles addressed to that pursuit had been stowed by his own hand, three weeks before, at the back of a drawer of the fine old sideboard that occupied, as a "fixture," the deep recess in the dining-room. Just now he laughed at his companions—quickly however changing the subject; for the reason that, in the first place, his laugh struck him even at that moment as starting the odd echo, the conscious human resonance (he scarce knew how to qualify it) that sounds made while he was there alone sent back to his ear or his fancy; and that, in the second, he imagined Alice Staverton for the instant on the point of asking him, with a divination, if he ever so prowled. There were divinations he was unprepared for, and he had at all events averted enquiry by the time Mrs Muldoon had left them, passing on to other parts.

There was happily enough to say, on so consecrated a spot, that could be said freely and fairly; so that a whole train of declarations was precipitated by his friend's having herself broken out, after a yearning look round: "But I hope you don't mean they want you to pull *this* to pieces!" His answer came, promptly, with his re-awakened wrath: it was of course exactly what they wanted, and what they were "at" him for, daily, with the iteration of people who couldn't for their life understand a man's liability to decent feelings. He had found the place, just as it stood and beyond what he could express, an interest and a joy. There were values other than the beastly rent-values, and in short, in short—! But it was thus Miss Staverton took him up. "In short you're to make so good a thing of your sky-scraper that, living in luxury on *those* ill-gotten gains, you can afford for a while to be sentimental here!" Her smile had for him, with the words, the particular mild irony with which he found half her talk suffused; an irony without bitterness and that came, exactly, from her having so much imagination—not, like the cheap sarcasms with which one heard most people, about the world of "society," bid for the reputation of cleverness, from nobody's really having any. It was agreeable to him at this very moment to be sure that when he had answered, after a brief demur,

"Well yes: so, precisely, you may put it!" her imagination would still do him justice. He explained that even if never a dollar were to come to him from the other house he would nevertheless cherish this one; and he dwelt, further, while they lingered and wandered, on the fact of the stupefaction he was already exciting, the positive mystification he felt himself create.

He spoke of the value of all he read into it, into the mere sight of the walls, mere shapes of the rooms, mere sound of the floors, mere feel, in his hand, of the old silver-plated knobs of the several mahogany doors, which suggested the pressure of the palms of the dead; the seventy years of the past in fine that these things represented, the annals of nearly three generations, counting his grandfather's, the one that had ended there, and the impalpable ashes of his long-extinct youth, afloat in the very air like microscopic motes. She listened to everything; she was a woman who answered intimately but who utterly didn't chatter. She scattered abroad therefore no cloud of words; she could assent, she could agree, above all she could encourage, without doing that. Only at the last she went a little further than he had done himself. "And then how do you know? You may still, after all, want to live here." It rather indeed pulled him up, for it wasn't what he had been thinking, at least in her sense of the words. "You mean I may decide to stay on for the sake of it?"

"Well, *with* such a home—!" But, quite beautifully, she had too much tact to dot so monstrous an *i*, and it was precisely an illustration of the way she didn't rattle. How could any one—of any wit—insist on any one else's "wanting" to live in New York?

"Oh," he said, "I *might* have lived here (since I had my opportunity early in life); I might have put in here all these years. Then everything would have been different enough— and, I dare say, 'funny' enough. But that's another matter.

And then the beauty of it—I mean of my perversity, of my refusal to agree to a 'deal'—is just in the total absence of a reason. Don't you see that if I had a reason about the matter at all it would *have* to be the other way, and would then be inevitably a reason of dollars? There are no reasons here *but* of dollars. Let us therefore have none whatever—not the ghost of one."

They were back in the hall then for departure, but from where they stood the vista was large, through an open door, into the great square main saloon, with its almost antique felicity of brave spaces between windows. Her eyes came back from that reach and met his own a moment. "Are you very sure the 'ghost' of one doesn't, much rather, serve—?"

He had a positive sense of turning pale. But it was as near as they were then to come. For he made answer, he believed, between a glare and a grin: "Oh ghosts—of course the place must swarm with them! I should be ashamed of it if it didn't. Poor Mrs Muldoon's right, and it's why I haven't asked her to do more than look in."

Miss Staverton's gaze again lost itself, and things she didn't utter, it was clear, came and went in her mind. She might even for the minute, off there in the fine room, have imagined some element dimly gathering. Simplified like the death-mask of a handsome face, it perhaps produced for her just then an effect akin to the stir of an expression in the "set" commemorative plaster. Yet whatever her impression may have been she produced instead a vague platitude. "Well, if it were only furnished and lived in—!"

She appeared to imply that in case of its being still furnished he might have been a little less opposed to the idea of a return. But she passed straight into the vestibule, as if to leave her words behind her, and the next moment he had opened the house-door and was standing with her on the steps. He closed the door and, while he re-pocketed his key, looking up and down, they took in the comparatively harsh actuality of the

Avenue, which reminded him of the assault of the outer light of the Desert on the traveller emerging from an Egyptian tomb. But he risked before they stepped into the street his gathered answer to her speech. "For me it *is* lived in. For me it *is* furnished." At which it was easy for her to sigh "Ah yes—!" all vaguely and discreetly; since his parents and his favourite sister, to say nothing of other kin, in numbers, had run their course and met their end there. That represented, within the walls, ineffaceable life.

It was a few days after this that, during an hour passed with her again, he had expressed his impatience of the too flattering curiosity—among the people he met—about his appreciation of New York. He had arrived at none at all that was socially producible, and as for that matter of his "thinking" (thinking the better or the worse of anything there) he was wholly taken up with one subject of thought. It was mere vain egoism, and it was moreover, if she liked, a morbid obsession. He found all things come back to the question of what he personally might have been, how he might have led his life and "turned out," if he had not so, at the outset, given it up. And confessing for the first time to the intensity within him of this absurd speculation—which but proved also, no doubt, the habit of too selfishly thinking—he affirmed the impotence there of any other source of interest, any other native appeal. "What would it have made of me, what would it have made of me? I keep for ever wondering, all idiotically; as if I could possibly know! I see what it has made of dozens of others, those I meet, and it positively aches within me, to the point of exasperation, that it would have made something of me as well. Only I can't make out *what*, and the worry of it, the small rage of curiosity never to be satisfied, brings back what I remember to have felt, once or twice, after judging best, for reasons, to burn some important letter unopened. I've been sorry, I've hated it—I've never known what was in the letter. You may of course say it's a trifle—!"

"I don't say it's a trifle," Miss Staverton gravely inter-rupted.

She was seated by her fire, and before her, on his feet and restless, he turned to and fro between this intensity of his idea and a fitful and unseeing inspection, through his single eye-glass, of the dear little old objects on her chimney-piece. Her interruption made him for an instant look at her harder. "I shouldn't care if you did!" he laughed, however; "and it's only a figure, at any rate, for the way I now feel. *Not* to have followed my perverse young course—and almost in the teeth of my father's curse, as I may say; not to have kept it up, so, 'over there,' from that day to this, without a doubt or a pang; not, above all, to have liked it, to have loved it, so much, loved it, no doubt, with such an abysmal conceit of my own preference: some variation from *that*, I say, must have pro-duced some different effect for my life and for my 'form.' I should have stuck here—if it had been possible; and I was too young, at twenty-three, to judge, *pour deux sous*, whether it *were* possible. If I had waited I might have seen it was, and then I might have been, by staying here, something nearer to one of these types who have been hammered so hard and made so keen by their conditions. It isn't that I admire them so much—the question of any charm in them, or of any charm, beyond that of the rank money-passion, exerted by their conditions *for* them, has nothing to do with the matter: it's only a question of what fantastic, yet perfectly possible, development of my own nature I mayn't have missed. It comes over me that I had then a strange *alter ego* deep down somewhere within me, as the full-blown flower is in the small tight bud, and that I just took the course, I just transferred him to the climate, that blighted him for once and for ever."

"And you wonder about the flower," Miss Staverton said. "So do I, if you want to know; and so I've been wondering these several weeks. I believe in the flower," she continued,

"I feel it would have been quite splendid, quite huge and monstrous."

"Monstrous above all!" her visitor echoed; "and I imagine, by the same stroke, quite hideous and offensive."

"You don't believe that," she returned; "if you did you wouldn't wonder. You'd know, and that would be enough for you. What you feel—and what I feel *for* you—is that you'd have had power."

"You'd have liked me that way?" he asked.

She barely hung fire. "How should I not have liked you?"

"I see. You'd have liked me, have preferred me, a billionaire!"

"How should I not have liked you?" she simply again asked.

He stood before her still—her question kept him motionless. He took it in, so much there was of it; and indeed his not otherwise meeting it testified to that. "I know at least what I am," he simply went on; "the other side of the medal's clear enough. I've not been edifying—I believe I'm thought in a hundred quarters to have been barely decent. I've followed strange paths and worshipped strange gods; it must have come to you again and again—in fact you've admitted to me as much—that I was leading, at any time these thirty years, a selfish frivolous scandalous life. And you see what it has made of me."

She just waited, smiling at him. "You see what it has made of *me*."

"Oh you're a person whom nothing can have altered. You were born to be what you are, anywhere, anyway: you've the perfection nothing else could have blighted. And don't you see how, without my exile, I shouldn't have been waiting till now—?" But he pulled up for the strange pang.

"The great thing to see," she presently said, "seems to me to be that it has spoiled nothing. It hasn't spoiled your being here at last. It hasn't spoiled this. It hasn't spoiled your speaking—" She also however faltered.

He wondered at everything her controlled emotion might mean. "Do you believe then—too dreadfully!—that I *am* as good as I might ever have been?"

"Oh no! Far from it!" With which she got up from her chair and was nearer to him. "But I don't care," she smiled.

"You mean I'm good enough?"

She considered a little. "Will you believe it if I say so? I mean will you let that settle your question for you?" And then as if making out in his face that he drew back from this, that he had some idea which, however absurd, he couldn't yet bargain away: "Oh you don't care either—but very differently: you don't care for anything but yourself."

Spencer Brydon recognised it—it was in fact what he had absolutely professed. Yet he importantly qualified. "*He* isn't myself. He's the just so totally other person. But I do want to see him," he added. "And I can. And I shall."

Their eyes met for a minute while he guessed from something in hers that she divined his strange sense. But neither of them otherwise expressed it, and her apparent understanding, with no protesting shock, no easy derision, touched him more deeply than anything yet, constituting for his stifled perversity, on the spot, an element that was like breatheable air. What she said however was unexpected. "Well, *I've* seen him."

"You—?"

"I've seen him in a dream."

"Oh a 'dream'—!" It let him down.

"But twice over," she continued. "I saw him as I see you now."

"You've dreamed the same dream—?"

"Twice over," she repeated. "The very same."

This did somehow a little speak to him, as it also gratified him. "You dream about me at that rate?"

"Ah about *him!*" she smiled.

His eyes again sounded her. "Then you know all about him." And as she said nothing more: "What's the wretch like?"

She hesitated, and it was as if he were pressing her so hard that, resisting for reasons of her own, she had to turn away. "I'll tell you some other time!"

II

IT was after this that there was most of a virtue for him, most of a cultivated charm, most of a preposterous secret thrill, in the particular form of surrender to his obsession and of address to what he more and more believed to be his privilege. It was what in these weeks he was living for—since he really felt life to begin but after Mrs Muldoon had retired from the scene and, visiting the ample house from attic to cellar, making sure he was alone, he knew himself in safe possession and, as he tacitly expressed it, let himself go. He sometimes came twice in the twenty-four hours; the moments he liked best were those of gathering dusk, of the short autumn twilight; this was the time of which, again and again, he found himself hoping most. Then he could, as seemed to him, most intimately wander and wait, linger and listen, feel his fine attention, never in his life before so fine, on the pulse of the great vague place: he preferred the lampless hour and only wished he might have prolonged each day the deep crepuscular spell. Later—rarely much before midnight, but then for a considerable vigil—he watched with his glimmering light; moving slowly, holding it high, playing it far, rejoicing above all, as much as he might, in open vistas, reaches of communication between rooms and by passages; the long straight chance or show, as he would have called it, for the revelation he pretended to invite. It was a practice he found he could perfectly "work" without exciting remark; no one was in the least the wiser for it; even Alice Staverton, who was moreover a well of discretion, didn't quite fully imagine.

He let himself in and let himself out with the assurance of calm proprietorship; and accident so far favoured him that, if a fat Avenue "officer" had happened on occasion to see him entering at eleven-thirty, he had never yet, to the best of his belief, been noticed as emerging at two. He walked there on the crisp November nights, arrived regularly at the evening's end; it was as easy to do this after dining out as to take his way to a club or to his hotel. When he left his club, if he hadn't been dining out, it was ostensibly to go to his hotel; and when he left his hotel, if he had spent a part of the evening there, it was ostensibly to go to his club. Everything was easy in fine; everything conspired and promoted: there was truly even in the strain of his experience something that glossed over, something that salved and simplified, all the rest of consciousness. He circulated, talked, renewed, loosely and pleasantly, old relations—met indeed, so far as he could, new expectations and seemed to make out on the whole that in spite of the career, of such different contacts, which he had spoken of to Miss Staverton as ministering so little, for those who might have watched it, to edification, he was positively rather liked than not. He was a dim secondary social success— and all with people who had truly not an idea of him. It was all mere surface sound, this murmur of their welcome, this popping of their corks—just as his gestures of response were the extravagant shadows, emphatic in proportion as they meant little, of some game of *ombres chinoises*. He projected himself all day, in thought, straight over the bristling line of hard unconscious heads and into the other, the real, the waiting life; the life that, as soon as he had heard behind him the click of his great house-door, began for him, on the jolly corner, as beguilingly as the slow opening bars of some rich music follows the tap of the conductor's wand.

He always caught the first effect of the steel point of his stick on the old marble of the hall pavement, large black-and-white squares that he remembered as the admiration of his childhood and that had then made in him, as he now saw, for the growth of an early conception of style. This effect was the dim reverberating tinkle as of some far-off bell hung who should say where?—in the depths of the house, of the past, of that mystical other world that might have flourished for him had he not, for weal or woe, abandoned it. On this impression he did ever the same thing; he put his stick noiselessly away in a corner—feeling the place once more in the likeness of some great glass bowl, all precious concave crystal, set delicately humming by the play of a moist finger round its edge. The concave crystal held, as it were, this mystical other world, and the indescribably fine murmur of its rim was the sigh there, the scarce audible pathetic wail to his strained ear, of all the old baffled forsworn possibilities. What he did therefore by this appeal of his hushed presence was to wake them into such measure of ghostly life as they might still enjoy. They were shy, all but unappeasably shy, but they weren't really sinister; at least they weren't as he had hitherto felt them—before they had taken the Form he so yearned to make them take, the Form he at moments saw himself in the light of fairly hunting on tiptoe, the points of his evening-shoes, from room to room and from storey to storey.

That was the essence of his vision—which was all rank folly, if one would, while he was out of the house and otherwise occupied, but which took on the last verisimilitude as soon as he was placed and posted. He knew what he meant and what he wanted; it was as clear as the figure on a cheque presented in demand for cash. His *alter ego* "walked"—that was the note of his image of him, while his image of his motive for his own odd pastime was the desire to waylay him and meet him. He roamed, slowly, warily, but all restlessly, he himself did—Mrs Muldoon had been right, absolutely, with her figure of their "craping"; and the presence he watched for would roam restlessly too. But it would be as cautious and as shifty; the conviction of its probable, in fact its already quite sensible, quite audible evasion of pursuit grew for him from night to night, laying on him finally a rigour to which nothing in his life had been comparable. It had been the theory of many superficially-judging persons, he knew, that he was wasting that life in a surrender to sensations, but he had tasted of no pleasure so fine as his actual tension, had been introduced to no sport that demanded at once the patience and the nerve of this stalking of a creature more subtle, yet at bay perhaps more formidable, than any beast of the forest. The terms, the comparisons, the very practices of the chase positively came again into play; there were even moments when passages of his occasional experience as a sportsman, stirred memories, from his younger time, of moor and mountain and desert, revived for him—and to the increase of his keenness—by the tremendous force of analogy. He found himself at moments—once he had placed his single light on some mantel-shelf or in some recess—stepping back into shelter or shade, effacing himself behind a door or in an embrasure, as he had sought of old the vantage of rock and tree; he found himself holding his breath and living in the joy of the instant, the supreme suspense created by big game alone.

He wasn't afraid (though putting himself the question as he believed gentlemen on Bengal tiger-shoots or in close quarters with the great bear of the Rockies had been known to confess to having put it); and this indeed—since here at least he might be frank!—because of the impression, so intimate and so strange, that he himself produced as yet a dread, produced certainly a strain, beyond the liveliest he was likely to feel. They fell for him into categories, they fairly became familiar, the signs, for his own perception, of the alarm his presence and his vigilance created; though leaving him always to remark, portentously, on his probably having formed a relation, his probably enjoying a consciousness, unique in the experience of man. People enough, first and last, had been in terror of apparitions, but who had ever before so turned the tables and become himself, in the apparitional world, an incalculable terror? He might have found this sublime had he quite dared to think of it; but he didn't too much insist, truly, on that side of his privilege. With habit and repetition he gained to an extraordinary degree the power to penetrate the dusk of distances and the darkness of corners, to resolve back into their innocence the treacheries of uncertain light, the evil-looking forms taken in the gloom by mere shadows, by accidents of the air, by shifting effects of perspective; putting down his dim luminary he could still wander on without it, pass into other rooms and, only knowing it was there behind him in case of need, see his way about, visually project for his purpose a comparative clearness. It made him feel, this acquired faculty, like some monstrous stealthy cat; he wondered if he would have glared at these moments with large shining yellow eyes, and what it mightn't verily be, for the poor hard-pressed *alter ego*, to be confronted with such a type.

He liked however the open shutters; he opened everywhere those Mrs Muldoon had closed, closing them as carefully afterwards, so that she shouldn't notice: he liked—oh this he did like, and above all in the upper rooms!—the sense of the hard silver of the autumn stars through the window-panes, and scarcely less the flare of the street-lamps below, the white electric lustre which it would have taken curtains to keep out. This was human actual social; this was of the world he had lived in, and he was more at his ease certainly for the countenance, coldly general and impersonal, that all the while and in spite of his detachment it seemed to give him. He had support of course mostly in the rooms at the wide front and the prolonged side; it failed him considerably in the central shades and the parts at the back. But if he sometimes, on his rounds, was glad of his optical reach, so none the less often the rear of the house affected him as the very jungle of his prey. The place was there more subdivided; a large "extension" in particular, where small rooms for servants had been multiplied, abounded in nooks and corners, in closets and passages, in the ramifications especially of an ample back staircase over which he leaned, many a time, to look far down —not deterred from his gravity even while aware that he might, for a spectator, have figured some solemn simpleton playing at hide-and-seek. Outside in fact he might himself make that ironic *rapprochement;* but within the walls, and in spite of the clear windows, his consistency was proof against the cynical light of New York.

It had belonged to that idea of the exasperated consciousness of his victim to become a real test for him; since he had quite put it to himself from the first that, oh distinctly! he could "cultivate" his whole perception. He had felt it as above all open to cultivation—which indeed was but another name for his manner of spending his time. He was bringing it on, bringing it to perfection, by practice; in consequence of which it had grown so fine that he was now aware of impressions, attestations of his general postulate, that couldn't have broken upon him at once. This was the case more specifically with a phenomenon at last quite frequent for him in the upper rooms, the recognition—absolutely unmistakeable, and by a turn dating from a particular hour, his resumption of his campaign after a diplomatic drop, a calculated absence of three nights—of his being definitely followed, tracked at a distance carefully taken and to the express end that he should the less confidently, less arrogantly, appear to himself merely to pursue. It worried, it finally quite broke him up, for it proved, of all the conceivable impressions, the one least suited to his book. He was kept in sight while remaining himself—as regards the essence of his position—sightless, and his only recourse then was in abrupt turns, rapid recoveries of ground.

He wheeled about, retracing his steps, as if he might so catch
in his face at least the stirred air of some other quick revolu-
tion. It was indeed true that his fully dislocalised thought of
these manœuvres recalled to him Pantaloon, at the Christmas
farce, buffeted and tricked from behind by ubiquitous Har-
lequin; but it left intact the influence of the conditions themselves each time he was re-exposed to them, so that in fact this
association, had he suffered it to become constant, would on
a certain side have but ministered to his intenser gravity. He
had made, as I have said, to create on the premises the baseless
sense of a reprieve, his three absences; and the result of the
third was to confirm the after-effect of the second.

On his return, that night—the night succeeding his last
intermission—he stood in the hall and looked up the staircase
with a certainty more intimate than any he had yet known.
"He's *there*, at the top, and waiting—not, as in general, falling
back for disappearance. He's holding his ground, and it's the
first time—which is a proof, isn't it? that something has
happened for him." So Brydon argued with his hand on the
banister and his foot on the lowest stair; in which position he
felt as never before the air chilled by his logic. He himself
turned cold in it, for he seemed of a sudden to know what
now was involved. "Harder pressed?—yes, he takes it in,
with its thus making clear to him that I've come, as they say,
'to stay.' He finally doesn't like and can't bear it, in the sense,
I mean, that his wrath, his menaced interest, now balances
with his dread. I've hunted him till he has 'turned': that, up
there, is what has happened—he's the fanged or the antlered
animal brought at last to bay." There came to him, as I say
—but determined by an influence beyond my notation!—the
acuteness of this certainty; under which however the next
moment he had broken into a sweat that he would as little
have consented to attribute to fear as he would have dared
immediately to act upon it for enterprise. It marked none the
less a prodigious thrill, a thrill that represented sudden dismay,

no doubt, but also represented, and with the selfsame throb, the strangest, the most joyous, possibly the next minute almost the proudest, duplication of consciousness.

"He has been dodging, retreating, hiding, but now, worked up to anger, he'll fight!"—this intense impression made a single mouthful, as it were, of terror and applause. But what was wondrous was that the applause, for the felt fact, was so eager, since, if it was his other self he was running to earth, this ineffable identity was thus in the last resort not unworthy of him. It bristled there—somewhere near at hand, however unseen still—as the hunted thing, even as the trodden worm of the adage *must* at last bristle; and Brydon at this instant tasted probably of a sensation more complex than had ever before found itself consistent with sanity. It was as if it would have shamed him that a character so associated with his own should triumphantly succeed in just skulking, should to the end not risk the open; so that the drop of this danger was, on the spot, a great lift of the whole situation. Yet with another rare shift of the same subtlety he was already trying to measure by how much more he himself might now be in peril of fear; so rejoicing that he could, in another form, actively inspire that fear, and simultaneously quaking for the form in which he might passively know it.

The apprehension of knowing it must after a little have grown in him, and the strangest moment of his adventure perhaps, the most memorable or really most interesting, after-wards, of his crisis, was the lapse of certain instants of con-centrated conscious *combat*, the sense of a need to hold on to something, even after the manner of a man slipping and slipping on some awful incline; the vivid impulse, above all, to move, to act, to charge, somehow and upon something— to show himself, in a word, that he wasn't afraid. The state of "holding-on" was thus the state to which he was momentarily reduced; if there had been anything, in the great vacancy, to seize, he would presently have been aware of having clutched it as he might under a shock at home have clutched the nearest chair-back. He had been surprised at any rate—of this he *was* aware—into something unprecedented since his original appropriation of the place; he had closed his eyes, held them tight, for a long minute, as with that instinct of dismay and that terror of vision. When he opened them the room, the other contiguous rooms, extraordinarily, seemed lighter—so light, almost, that at first he took the change for day. He stood firm, however that might be, just where he had paused; his resistance had helped him—it was as if there were something he had tided over. He knew after a little what this was—it had been in the imminent danger of flight. He had stiffened his will against going; without this he would have made for the stairs, and it seemed to him that, still with his eyes closed, he would have descended them, would have known how, straight and swiftly, to the bottom.

Well, as he had held out, here he was—still at the top, among the more intricate upper rooms and with the gauntlet of the others, of all the rest of the house, still to run when it should be his time to go. He would go at his time—only at his time: didn't he go every night very much at the same hour? He took out his watch—there was light for that: it was scarcely a quarter past one, and he had never withdrawn so soon. He reached his lodgings for the most part at two—with his walk of a quarter of an hour. He would wait for the last quarter—he wouldn't stir till then; and he kept his watch there with his eyes on it, reflecting while he held it that this deliberate wait, a wait with an effort, which he recognised, would serve perfectly for the attestation he desired to make. It would prove his courage—unless indeed the latter might most be proved by his budging at last from his place. What he mainly felt now was that, since he hadn't originally scuttled, he had his dignities—which had never in his life seemed so many—all to preserve and to carry aloft. This was before him in truth as a physical image, an image almost worthy of an age of greater romance. That remark indeed glimmered for him only to glow the next instant with a finer light; since what age of romance, after all, could have matched either the state of his mind or, "objectively," as they said, the wonder of his situation? The only difference would have been that, brandishing his dignities over his head as in a parchment scroll, he might then—that is in the heroic time—have proceeded downstairs with a drawn sword in his other grasp.

At present, really, the light he had set down on the mantel of the next room would have to figure his sword; which utensil, in the course of a minute, he had taken the requisite number of steps to possess himself of. The door between the rooms was open, and from the second another door opened to a third. These rooms, as he remembered, gave all three upon a common corridor as well, but there was a fourth, beyond them, without issue save through the preceding. To have moved, to have heard his step again, was appreciably a help; though even in recognising this he lingered once more a little by the chimney-piece on which his light had rested. When he next moved, just hesitating where to turn, he found himself considering a circumstance that, after his first and comparatively vague apprehension of it, produced in him the start that often attends some pang of recollection, the violent shock of having ceased happily to forget. He had come into sight of the door in which the brief chain of communication ended and which he now surveyed from the nearer threshold, the one not directly facing it. Placed at some distance to the left of this point, it would have admitted him to the last room of the four, the room without other approach or egress, had it not, to his intimate conviction, been closed *since* his former visitation, the matter probably of a quarter of an hour before. He stared with all his eyes at the wonder of the fact, arrested again where he stood and again holding his breath while he sounded its sense. Surely it had been *subsequently* closed—that is it had been on his previous passage indubitably open!

He took it full in the face that something had happened between—that he couldn't not have noticed before (by which he meant on his original tour of all the rooms that evening) that such a barrier had exceptionally presented itself. He had indeed since that moment undergone an agitation so extraordinary that it might have muddled for him any earlier view; and he tried to convince himself that he might perhaps then have gone into the room and, inadvertently, automatically, on coming out, have drawn the door after him. The difficulty was that this exactly was what he never did; it was against his whole policy, as he might have said, the essence of which was to keep vistas clear. He had them from the first, as he was well aware, quite on the brain: the strange apparition, at the far end of one of them, of his baffled "prey" (which had become by so sharp an irony so little the term now to apply!) was the form of success his imagination had most cherished, projecting into it always a refinement of beauty. He had known fifty times the start of perception that had afterwards dropped; had fifty times gasped to himself "There!" under some fond brief hallucination. The house, as the case stood, admirably lent itself; he might wonder at the taste, the native architecture of the particular time, which could rejoice so in the multiplication of doors—the opposite extreme to the modern, the actual almost complete proscription of them; but it had fairly contributed to provoke this obsession of the presence encountered telescopically, as he might say, focussed and studied in diminishing perspective and as by a rest for the elbow.

It was with these considerations that his present attention was charged—they perfectly availed to make what he saw portentous. He *couldn't*, by any lapse, have blocked that aperture; and if he hadn't, if it was unthinkable, why what else was clear but that there had been another agent? Another agent?—he had been catching, as he felt, a moment back, the very breath of him; but when had he been so close as in this simple, this logical, this completely personal act? It was so

logical, that is, that one might have *taken* it for personal; yet
for what did Brydon take it, he asked himself, while, softly
panting, he felt his eyes almost leave their sockets. Ah this
time at last they *were*, the two, the opposed projections of him,
in presence; and this time, as much as one would, the question
of danger loomed. With it rose, as not before, the question
of courage—for what he knew the blank face of the door to
say to him was "Show us how much you have!" It stared, it
glared back at him with that challenge; it put to him the two
alternatives: should he just push it open or not? Oh to have
this consciousness was to *think*—and to think, Brydon knew,
as he stood there, was, with the lapsing moments, not to have
acted! Not to have acted—that was the misery and the pang
—was even still not to act; was in fact *all* to feel the thing in
another, in a new and terrible way. How long did he pause
and how long did he debate? There was presently nothing
to measure it; for his vibration had already changed—as just
by the effect of its intensity. Shut up there, at bay, defiant,
and with the prodigy of the thing palpably proveably *done*,
thus giving notice like some stark signboard—under that
accession of accent the situation itself had turned; and
Brydon at last remarkably made up his mind on what it had
turned to.

It had turned altogether to a different admonition; to a
supreme hint, for him, of the value of Discretion! This slowly
dawned, no doubt—for it could take its time; so perfectly, on
his threshold, had he been stayed, so little as yet had he either
advanced or retreated. It was the strangest of all things that
now when, by his taking ten steps and applying his hand to a
latch, or even his shoulder and his knee, if necessary, to a
panel, all the hunger of his prime need might have been met,
his high curiosity crowned, his unrest assuaged—it was
amazing, but it was also exquisite and rare, that insistence
should have, at a touch, quite dropped from him. Discretion
—he jumped at that; and yet not, verily, at such a pitch,

because it saved his nerves or his skin, but because, much more valuably, it saved the situation. When I say he "jumped" at it I feel the consonance of this term with the fact that—at the end indeed of I know not how long—he did move again, he crossed straight to the door. He wouldn't touch it—it seemed now that he might *if* he would: he would only just wait there a little, to show, to prove, that he wouldn't. He had thus another station, close to the thin partition by which revelation was denied him; but with his eyes bent and his hands held off in a mere intensity of stillness. He listened as if there had been something to hear, but this attitude, while it lasted, was his own communication. "If you won't then—good: I spare you and I give up. You affect me as by the appeal positively for pity: you convince me that for reasons rigid and sublime—what do I know?—we both of us should have suffered. I respect them then, and, though moved and privileged as, I believe, it has never been given to man, I retire, I renounce—never, on my honour, to try again. So rest for ever—and let *me!*"

That, for Brydon was the deep sense of this last demonstration—solemn, measured, directed, as he felt it to be. He brought it to a close, he turned away; and now verily he knew how deeply he had been stirred. He retraced his steps, taking up his candle, burnt, he observed, well-nigh to the socket, and marking again, lighten it as he would, the distinctness of his footfall; after which, in a moment, he knew himself at the other side of the house. He did here what he had not yet done at these hours—he opened half a casement, one of those in the front, and let in the air of the night; a thing he would have taken at any time previous for a sharp rupture of his spell. His spell was broken now, and it didn't matter—broken by his concession and his surrender, which made it idle henceforth that he should ever come back. The empty street—its other life so marked even by the great lamplit vacancy—was within call, within touch; he stayed there as to be in it again, high above it though he was still perched; he watched as for some comforting common fact, some vulgar human note, the passage of a scavenger or a thief, some night-bird however base. He would have blessed that sign of life; he would have welcomed positively the slow approach of his friend the policeman, whom he had hitherto only sought to avoid, and was not sure that if the patrol had come into sight he mightn't have felt the impulse to get into relation with it, to hail it, on some pretext, from his fourth floor.

The pretext that wouldn't have been too silly or too compromising, the explanation that would have saved his dignity and kept his name, in such a case, out of the papers, was not definite to him: he was so occupied with the thought of recording his Discretion—as an effect of the vow he had just uttered to his intimate adversary—that the importance of this loomed large and something had overtaken all ironically his sense of proportion. If there had been a ladder applied to the front of the house, even one of the vertiginous perpendiculars employed by painters and roofers and sometimes left standing overnight, he would have managed somehow, astride of the window-sill, to compass by outstretched leg and arm that mode of descent. If there had been some such uncanny thing as he had found in his room at hotels, a workable fire-escape in the form of notched cable or a canvas shoot, he would have availed himself of it as a proof—well, of his present delicacy. He nursed that sentiment, as the question stood, a little in vain, and even—at the end of he scarce knew, once more, how long—found it, as by the action on his mind of the failure of response of the outer world, sinking back to vague anguish. It seemed to him he had waited an age for some stir of the great grim hush; the life of the town was itself under a spell—so unnaturally, up and down the whole prospect of known and rather ugly objects, the blankness and the silence lasted. Had they ever, he asked himself, the hard-faced houses, which had begun to look livid in the dim dawn, had they ever spoken so little to any need of his spirit? Great builded voids, great crowded stillnesses put on, often, in the heart of cities, for the small hours, a sort of sinister mask, and it was of this large collective negation that Brydon presently became conscious—all the more that the break of day was, almost incredibly, now at hand, proving to him what a night he had made of it.

He looked again at his watch, saw what had become of his time-values (he had taken hours for minutes—not, as in other tense situations, minutes for hours) and the strange air of the streets was but the weak, the sullen flush of a dawn in which everything was still locked up. His choked appeal from his own open window had been the sole note of life, and he could but break off at last as for a worse despair. Yet while so deeply demoralised he was capable again of an impulse denoting—at least by his present measure—extraordinary resolution; of retracing his steps to the spot where he had turned cold with the extinction of his last pulse of doubt as to there being in the place another presence than his own. This required an effort strong enough to sicken him; but he had his reason, which overmastered for the moment everything else. There was the whole of the rest of the house to traverse, and how should he screw himself to that if the door he had seen closed were at present open? He could hold to the idea that the closing had practically been for him an act of mercy, a chance offered him to descend, depart, get off the ground and never again profane it. This conception held together, it worked; but what it meant for him depended now clearly on the amount of forbearance his recent action, or rather his recent inaction, had engendered. The image of the "presence," whatever it was, waiting there for him to go—this image had not yet been so concrete for his nerves as when he stopped short of the point at which certainty would have come to him. For, with all his resolution, or more exactly with all his dread, he did stop short—he hung back from really seeing. The risk was too great and his fear too definite: it took at this moment an awful specific form.

He knew—yes, as he had never known anything—that, *should* he see the door open, it would all too abjectly be the end of him. It would mean that the agent of his shame—for his shame was the deep abjection—was once more at large and in general possession; and what glared him thus in the face was the act that this would determine for him. It would send him straight about to the window he had left open, and by that window, be long ladder and dangling rope as absent as they would, he saw himself uncontrollably insanely fatally take his way to the street. The hideous chance of this he at least could avert; but he could only avert it by recoiling in time from assurance. He had the whole house to deal with, this fact was still there; only he now knew that uncertainty alone could start him. He stole back from where he had checked himself— merely to do so was suddenly like safety—and, making blindly for the greater staircase, left gaping rooms and sounding passages behind. Here was the top of the stairs, with a fine large dim descent and three spacious landings to mark off. His instinct was all for mildness, but his feet were harsh on the floors, and, strangely, when he had in a couple of minutes become aware of this, it counted somehow for help. He couldn't have spoken, the tone of his voice would have scared him, and the common conceit or resource of "whistling in the dark" (whether literally or figuratively) have appeared basely vulgar; yet he liked none the less to hear himself go, and when he had reached his first landing—taking it all with no rush, but quite steadily—that stage of success drew from him a gasp of relief.

The house, withal, seemed immense, the scale of space again inordinate; the open rooms, to no one of which his eyes deflected, gloomed in their shuttered state like mouths of caverns; only the high skylight that formed the crown of the deep well created for him a medium in which he could advance, but which might have been, for queerness of colour, some watery under-world. He tried to think of something noble, as that his property was really grand, a splendid possession; but this nobleness took the form too of the clear delight with which he was finally to sacrifice it. They might come in now, the builders, the destroyers—they might come as soon as they would. At the end of two flights he had dropped to another zone, and from the middle of the third, with only one more left, he recognised the influence of the lower windows, of half-drawn blinds, of the occasional gleam of street-lamps, of the glazed spaces of the vestibule. This was the bottom of the sea, which showed an illumination of its own and which he even saw paved—when at a given moment he drew up to sink a long look over the banisters—with the marble squares of his childhood. By that time indubitably he felt, as he might have said in a commoner cause, better; it had allowed him to stop and draw breath, and the ease increased with the sight of the old black-and-white slabs. But what he most felt was that now surely, with the element of impunity pulling him as by hard firm hands, the case was settled for what he might have seen above had he dared that last look. The closed door, blessedly remote now, was still closed—and he had only in short to reach that of the house.

He came down further, he crossed the passage forming the access to the last flight; and if here again he stopped an instant it was almost for the sharpness of the thrill of assured escape. It made him shut his eyes—which opened again to the straight slope of the remainder of the stairs. Here was impunity still, but impunity almost excessive; inasmuch as the side-lights and the high fan-tracery of the entrance were glimmering straight into the hall; an appearance produced, he the next instant saw, by the fact that the vestibule gaped wide, that the hinged halves of the inner door had been thrown far back. Out of that again the *question* sprang at him, making his eyes, as he felt, half-start from his head, as they had done, at the top of the house, before the sign of the other door. If he had left that one open, hadn't he left this one closed, and wasn't he now in *most* immediate presence of some inconceivable occult activity? It was as sharp, the question, as a knife in his side, but the answer hung fire still and seemed to lose itself in the vague darkness to which the thin admitted dawn, glimmering archwise over the whole outer door, made a semicircular margin, a cold silvery nimbus that seemed to play a little as he looked—to shift and expand and contract.

It was as if there had been something within it, protected by indistinctness and corresponding in extent with the opaque surface behind, the painted panels of the last barrier to his escape, of which the key was in his pocket. The indistinctness mocked him even while he stared, affected him as somehow shrouding or challenging certitude, so that after faltering an instant on his step he let himself go with the sense that here *was* at last something to meet, to touch, to take, to know—something all unnatural and dreadful, but to advance upon which was the condition for him either of liberation or of supreme defeat. The penumbra, dense and dark, was the virtual screen of a figure which stood in it as still as some image erect in a niche or as some black-vizored sentinel guarding a treasure. Brydon was to know afterwards, was to recall and make out, the particular thing he had believed during the rest of his descent. He saw, in its great grey glimmering margin, the central vagueness diminish, and he felt it to be taking the very form toward which, for so many days, the passion of his curiosity had yearned. It gloomed, it loomed, it was something, it was somebody, the prodigy of a personal presence.

Rigid and conscious, spectral yet human, a man of his own substance and stature waited there to measure himself with his power to dismay. This only could it be—this only till he recognised, with his advance, that what made the face dim was the pair of raised hands that covered it and in which, so far from being offered in defiance, it was buried as for dark deprecation. So Brydon, before him, took him in; with every fact of him now, in the higher light, hard and acute—his planted stillness, his vivid truth, his grizzled bent head and white masking hands, his queer actuality of evening-dress, of dangling double eye-glass, of gleaming silk lappet and white linen, of pearl button and gold watch-guard and polished shoe. No portrait by a great modern master could have presented him with more intensity, thrust him out of his frame with more art, as if there had been "treatment," of the consummate sort, in his every shade and salience. The revulsion, for our friend, had become, before he knew it, immense—this drop, in the act of apprehension, to the sense of his adversary's inscrutable manœuvre. That meaning at least, while he gaped, it offered him; for he could but gape at his other self in this other anguish, gape as a proof that *he*, standing there for the achieved, the enjoyed, the triumphant life, couldn't be faced in his triumph. Wasn't the proof in the splendid covering hands, strong and completely spread?—so spread and so intentional that, in spite of a special verity that surpassed every other, the fact that one of these hands had lost two fingers, which were reduced to stumps, as if accidentally shot away, the face was effectually guarded and saved.

"Saved," though, *would* it be?—Brydon breathed his wonder till the very impunity of his attitude and the very insistence of his eyes produced, as he felt, a sudden stir which showed the next instant as a deeper portent, while the head raised itself, the betrayal of a braver purpose. The hands, as he looked, began to move, to open; then, as if deciding in a flash, dropped from the face and left it uncovered and presented. Horror, with the sight, had leaped into Brydon's throat, gasping there in a sound he couldn't utter; for the bared identity was too hideous as *his*, and his glare was the passion of his protest. The face, *that* face, Spencer Brydon's? —he searched it still, but looking away from it in dismay and denial, falling straight from his height of sublimity. It was unknown, inconceivable, awful, disconnected from any possibility—! He had been "sold," he inwardly moaned, stalking such game as this: the presence before him was a presence, the horror within him a horror, but the waste of his nights had been only grotesque and the success of his adventure an irony. Such an identity fitted his at *no* point, made its alternative monstrous. A thousand times yes, as it came upon him nearer now—the face was the face of a stranger. It came upon him nearer now, quite as one of those expanding fantastic images projected by the magic lantern of childhood; for the stranger, whoever he might be, evil, odious, blatant, vulgar, had advanced as for aggression, and he knew himself give ground. Then harder pressed still, sick with the force of his shock, and falling back as under the hot breath and the roused passion of a life larger than his own, a rage of personality before which his own collapsed, he felt the whole vision turn to darkness and his very feet give way. His head went round; he was going; he had gone.

III

WHAT had next brought him back, clearly—though after how long?—was Mrs Muldoon's voice, coming to him from quite near, from so near that he seemed presently to see her as kneeling on the ground before him while he lay looking up at her; himself not wholly on the ground, but half-raised and upheld—conscious, yes, of tenderness of support and, more particularly, of a head pillowed in extraordinary softness and fainly refreshing fragrance. He considered, he wondered, his wit but half at his service; then another face intervened, bending more directly over him, and he finally knew that Alice Staverton had made her lap an ample and perfect cushion to him, and that she had to this end seated herself on the lowest degree of the staircase, the rest of his long person remaining stretched on his old black-and-white slabs. They were cold, these marble squares of his youth; but *he* somehow was not, in this rich return of consciousness—the most wonderful hour, little by little, that he had ever known, leaving him, as it did, so gratefully, so abysmally passive, and yet as with a treasure of intelligence waiting all round him for quiet appropriation; dissolved, he might call it, in the air of the place and producing the golden glow of a late autumn afternoon. He had come back, yes—come back from further away than any man but himself had ever travelled; but it was strange how with this sense what he had come back *to* seemed really the great thing, and as if his prodigious journey had been all for the sake of it. Slowly but surely his consciousness grew, his vision of his state thus completing itself: he had been miraculously *carried* back—lifted and carefully borne as from where he had been picked up, the uttermost end of an interminable grey passage. Even with this he was suffered to rest, and what had now brought him to knowledge was the break in the long mild motion.

It had brought him to knowledge, to knowledge—yes, this was the beauty of his state; which came to resemble more and more that of a man who has gone to sleep on some news of a great inheritance, and then, after dreaming it away, after profaning it with matters strange to it, has waked up again to serenity of certitude and has only to lie and watch it grow. This was the drift of his patience—that he had only to let it shine on him. He must moreover, with intermissions, still have been lifted and borne; since why and how else should he have known himself, later on, with the afternoon glow intenser, no longer at the foot of his stairs—situated as these now seemed at that dark other end of his tunnel—but on a deep window-bench of his high saloon, over which had been spread, couch-fashion, a mantle of soft stuff lined with grey fur that was familiar to his eyes and that one of his hands kept fondly feeling as for its pledge of truth. Mrs Muldoon's face had gone, but the other, the second he had recognised, hung over him in a way that showed how he was still propped and pillowed. He took it all in, and the more he took it the more it seemed to suffice: he was as much at peace as if he had had food and drink. It was the two women who had found him, on Mrs Muldoon's having plied, at her usual hour, her latch-key—and on her having above all arrived while Miss Staverton still lingered near the house. She had been turning away, all anxiety, from worrying the vain bell-handle —her calculation having been of the hour of the good woman's visit; but the latter, blessedly, had come up while she was still there, and they had entered together. He had then lain, beyond the vestibule, very much as he was lying now— quite, that is, as he appeared to have fallen, but all so wondrously without bruise or gash; only in a depth of stupor. What he most took in, however, at present, with the steadier clearance, was that Alice Staverton had for a long unspeakable moment not doubted he was dead.

"It must have been that I *was*." He made it out as she held him. "Yes—I can only have died. You brought me literally to life. Only," he wondered, his eyes rising to her, "only, in the name of all the benedictions, how?"

It took her but an instant to bend her face and kiss him, and something in the manner of it, and in the way her hands clasped and locked his head while he felt the cool charity and virtue of her lips, something in all this beatitude somehow answered everything. "And now I keep you," she said.

"Oh keep me, keep me!" he pleaded while her face still hung over him: in response to which it dropped again and stayed close, clingingly close. It was the seal of their situation —of which he tasted the impress for a long blissful moment in silence. But he came back. "Yet how did you know—?"

"I was uneasy. You were to have come, you remember— and you had sent no word."

"Yes, I remember—I was to have gone to you at one to-day." It caught on to their "old" life and relation—which were so near and so far. "I was still out there in my strange darkness—where was it, what was it? I must have stayed there so long." He could but wonder at the depth and the duration of his swoon.

"Since last night?" she asked with a shade of fear for her possible indiscretion.

"Since this morning—it must have been: the cold dim dawn of to-day. Where have I been," he vaguely wailed, "where have I been?" He felt her hold him close, and it was as if this helped him now to make in all security his mild moan. "What a long dark day!"

All in her tenderness she had waited a moment. "In the cold dim dawn?" she quavered.

But he had already gone on piecing together the parts of the whole prodigy. "As I didn't turn up you came straight—?"

She barely cast about. "I went first to your hotel—where they told me of your absence. You had dined out last evening and hadn't been back since. But they appeared to know you had been at your club."

"So you had the idea of *this*—?"

"Of what?" she asked in a moment.

"Well—of what has happened."

"I believed at least you'd have been here. I've known, all along," she said, "that you've been coming."

" 'Known' it—?"

"Well, I've believed it. I said nothing to you after that talk we had a month ago—but I felt sure. I knew you *would*," she declared.

"That I'd persist, you mean?"

"That you'd see him."

"Ah but I didn't!" cried Brydon with his long wail. "There's somebody—an awful beast; whom I brought, too horribly, to bay. But it's not me."

At this she bent over him again, and her eyes were in his eyes. "No—it's not you." And it was as if, while her face hovered, he might have made out in it, hadn't it been so near, some particular meaning blurred by a smile. "No, thank heaven," she repeated—"it's not you! Of course it wasn't to have been."

"Ah but it *was*," he gently insisted. And he stared before him now as he had been staring for so many weeks. "I was to have known myself."

"You couldn't!" she returned consolingly. And then reverting, and as if to account further for what she had herself done, "But it wasn't only *that*, that you hadn't been at home," she went on. "I waited till the hour at which we had found Mrs Muldoon that day of my going with you; and she arrived, as I've told you, while, failing to bring any one to the door, I lingered in my despair on the steps. After a little, if she hadn't come, by such a mercy, I should have found means to hunt her up. But it wasn't," said Alice Staverton, as if once more with her fine intention—"it wasn't only that."

His eyes, as he lay, turned back to her. "What more then?"

She met it, the wonder she had stirred. "In the cold dim dawn, you say? Well, in the cold dim dawn of this morning I too saw you."

"Saw *me*—?"

"Saw *him*," said Alice Staverton. "It must have been at the same moment."

He lay an instant taking it in—as if he wished to be quite reasonable. "At the same moment?"

"Yes—in my dream again, the same one I've named to you. He came back to me. Then I knew it for a sign. He had come to you."

At this Brydon raised himself; he had to see her better. She helped him when she understood his movement, and he sat up, steadying himself beside her there on the window-bench and with his right hand grasping her left. "*He* didn't come to me."

"You came to yourself," she beautifully smiled.

"Ah I've come to myself now—thanks to you, dearest. But this brute, with his awful face—this brute's a black stranger. He's none of *me*, even as I *might* have been," Brydon sturdily declared.

But she kept the clearness that was like the breath of infallibility. "Isn't the whole point that you'd have been different?"

He almost scowled for it. "As different as *that*—?"

Her look again was more beautiful to him than the things of this world. "Haven't you exactly wanted to know *how* different? So this morning," she said, "you appeared to me."

"Like *him?*"

"A black stranger!"

"Then how did you know it was I?"

"Because, as I told you weeks ago, my mind, my imagination, had worked so over what you might, what you mightn't have been—to show you, you see, how I've thought of you. In the midst of that you came to me—that my wonder might be answered. So I knew," she went on; "and believed that, since the question held you too so fast, as you told me that day, you too would see for yourself. And when this morning I again saw I knew it would be because you had—and also then, from the first moment, because you somehow wanted me. *He* seemed to tell me of that. So why," she strangely smiled, "shouldn't I like him?"

It brought Spencer Brydon to his feet. "You 'like' that horror—?"

"I *could* have liked him. And to me," she said, "he was no horror. I had accepted him."

" 'Accepted'—?" Brydon oddly sounded.

"Before, for the interest of his difference—yes. And as *I*

didn't disown him, as *I* knew him—which you at last, confronted with him in his difference, so cruelly didn't, my dear —well, he must have been, you see, less dreadful to me. And it may have pleased him that I pitied him."

She was beside him on her feet, but still holding his hand— still with her arm supporting him. But though it all brought for him thus a dim light, "You 'pitied' him?" he grudgingly, resentfully asked.

"He has been unhappy, he has been ravaged," she said.

"And haven't I been unhappy? Am not I—you've only to look at me!—ravaged?"

"Ah I don't say I like him *better*," she granted after a thought. "But he's grim, he's worn—and things have happened to him. He doesn't make shift, for sight, with your charming monocle."

"No"—it struck Brydon: "I couldn't have sported mine 'downtown.' They'd have guyed me there."

"His great convex pince-nez—I saw it, I recognised the kind—is for his poor ruined sight. And his poor right hand—!"

"Ah!" Brydon winced—whether for his proved identity or for his lost fingers. Then, "He has a million a year," he lucidly added. "But he hasn't you."

"And he isn't—no, he isn't—*you!*" she murmured as he drew her to his breast.

THE VELVET GLOVE

I

HE thought he had already, poor John Berridge, tasted in their fullness the sweets of success; but nothing yet had been more charming to him than when the young Lord, as he irresistibly and, for greater certitude, quite correctly figured him, fairly sought out, in Paris, the new literary star that had begun to hang, with a fresh red light, over the vast, even though rather confused, Anglo-Saxon horizon; positively approaching that celebrity with a shy and artless appeal. The young Lord invoked on this occasion the celebrity's prized judgment of a special literary case; and Berridge could take the whole manner of it for one of the "quaintest" little acts displayed to his amused eyes, up to now, on the stage of European society—albeit these eyes were quite aware, in general, of missing everywhere no more of the human scene than possible, and of having of late been particularly awake to the large extensions of it spread before him (since so he could but fondly read his fate) under the omen of his prodigious "hit." It was because of his hit that he was having rare opportunities —of which he was so honestly and humbly proposing, as he would have said, to make the most: it was because every one in the world (so far had the thing gone) was reading *The Heart of Gold* as just a slightly too fat volume, or sitting out the same as just a fifth-act too long play, that he found himself floated on a tide he would scarce have dared to show his favourite hero sustained by, found a hundred agreeable and interesting things happen to him which were all, one way or another, affluents of the golden stream.

The great renewed resonance—renewed by the incredible luck of the play—was always in his ears without so much as a conscious turn of his head to listen; so that the queer world of his fame was not the mere usual field of the Anglo-Saxon boom, but positively the bottom of the *whole* theatric sea, unplumbed source of the wave that had borne him in the course of a year or two over German, French, Italian, Russian, Scandinavian foot-lights. Paris itself really appeared for the hour the centre of his cyclone, with reports and "returns," to say nothing of agents and emissaries, converging from the minor capitals; though his impatience was scarce the less keen to get back to London, where his work had had no such critical excoriation to survive, no such lesson of anguish to learn, as it had received at the hand of supreme authority, of that French authority which was in such a matter the only one to be artistically reckoned with. If his spirit indeed had had to reckon with it his fourth act practically hadn't: it continued to make him blush every night for the public more even than the inimitable *feuilleton* had made him blush for himself.

This had figured, however, after all, the one bad drop in his cup; so that, for the rest, his high-water mark might well have been, that evening at Gloriani's studio, the approach of his odd and charming applicant, vaguely introduced at the latter's very own request by their hostess, who, with an honest, helpless, genial gesture, washed her fat begemmed hands of the name and identity of either, but left the fresh, fair, ever so habitually assured, yet ever so easily awkward Englishman with his plea to put forth. There was that in this pleasant personage which could still make Berridge wonder what conception of profit from him might have, all incalculably, taken form in such a head—these being truly the last intrenchments of our hero's modesty. He wondered, the splendid young man, he wondered awfully, he wondered (it was unmistakable) quite nervously, he wondered, to John's ardent and acute imagination, quite beautifully, if the author of *The Heart of Gold* would mind just looking at a book by a friend of his, a great friend, which he himself believed rather clever, and had in fact found very charming, but as to which —if it really wouldn't bore Mr Berridge—he should so like the verdict of some one who knew. His friend was awfully ambitious, and he thought there was something in it—with all of which might he send the book to any address?

Berridge thought of many things while the young Lord thus charged upon him, and it was odd that no one of them was any question of the possible worth of the offered achievement—which, for that matter, was certain to be of the quality of *all* the books, to say nothing of the plays, and the projects for plays, with which, for some time past, he had seen his daily postbag distended. He had made out, on looking at these things, no difference at all from one to the other. Here, however, was something more—something that made his fellow-guest's overture *independently* interesting and, as he might imagine, important. He smiled, he was friendly and vague; said "A work of fiction, I suppose?" and that he didn't pretend ever to pronounce, that he in fact quite hated, always, to have to, not "knowing," as he felt, any better than anyone else; but would gladly look at anything, under that demur, if it would give any pleasure. Perhaps the very brightest and most diamond-like twinkle he had yet seen the star of his renown emit was just the light brought into his young Lord's eyes by this so easy consent to oblige. It was easy because the presence before him was from moment to moment referring itself back to some recent observation or memory; something caught somewhere, within a few weeks or months, as he had moved about, and that seemed to flutter forth at this stir of the folded leaves of his recent experience very much as a gathered faded flower, placed there for "pressing," might drop from between the pages of a volume opened at hazard.

He had seen him before, this splendid and sympathetic

person—whose flattering appeal was by no means *all* that made him sympathetic; he had met him, had noted, had wondered about him, had in fact imaginatively, intellectually, so to speak, quite yearned over him, in some conjunction lately, though ever so fleetingly, apprehended: which circumstance constituted precisely an association as tormenting, for the few minutes, as it was vague, and set him to sounding, intensely and vainly, the face that itself figured everything agreeable except recognition. He couldn't remember, and the young man didn't; distinctly, yes, they had been in presence, during the previous winter, by some chance of travel, through Sicily, through Italy, through the south of France, but his *Seigneurie*—so Berridge liked exotically to phrase it—had then (in ignorance of the present reasons) not noticed *him*. It was positive for the man of established identity, all the while too, and through the perfect lucidity of his sense of achievement in an air "conducting" nothing but the loudest bang, that this was fundamentally much less remarkable than the fact of his being made up to in such a quarter now. That was the disservice, in a manner, of one's having so much imagination: the mysterious values of other types kept looming larger before you than the doubtless often higher but comparatively familiar ones of your own, and if you had anything of the artist's real feeling for life the attraction and amusement of possibilities so projected were worth more to you, in nineteen moods out of twenty, than the sufficiency, the serenity, the felicity, whatever it might be, of your stale personal certitudes. You were intellectually, you were "artistically" rather abject, in fine, if your curiosity (in the grand sense of the term) wasn't worth more to you than your dignity. What *was* your dignity, "anyway," but just the consistency of your curiosity, and what moments were ever so ignoble for you as, under the blighting breath of the false gods, stupid conventions, traditions, examples, your lapses from that consistency? His *Seigneurie*, at all events, delightfully, hadn't the least real idea of what any John Berridge was talking about, and the latter felt that if he had been less beautifully witless, and thereby less true to his right figure, it might scarce have been forgiven him.

His right figure was that of life in irreflective joy and at the highest thinkable level of prepared security and unconscious insolence. What was the pale page of fiction compared with the intimately personal adventure that, in almost any direction, he would have been all so stupidly, all so gallantly, all so instinctively and, by every presumption, so prevailingly ready for? Berridge would have given six months' "royalties" for even an hour of his looser dormant consciousness—since one was oneself, after all, no worm, but an heir of all the ages too —and yet without being able to supply chapter and verse for the felt, the huge difference. His *Seigneurie* was tall and straight, but so, thank goodness, was the author of *The Heart of Gold*, who had no such vulgar "mug" either; and there was no intrinsic inferiority in being a bit inordinately, and so it might have seemed a bit strikingly, black-browed instead of being fair as the morning. Again while his new friend delivered himself our own tried in vain to place him; he indulged in plenty of pleasant, if rather restlessly headlong sound, the confessed incoherence of a happy mortal who had always many things "on," and who, while waiting at any moment for connections and consummations, had fallen into the way of talking, as they said, all artlessly, and a trifle more betrayingly, against time. He would always be having appointments, and somehow of a high "romantic" order, to keep, and the imperfect punctualities of others to wait for— though who would be of a quality to make such a pampered personage wait very much our young analyst could only enjoy asking himself. There were women who might be of a quality—half a dozen of those perhaps, of those alone, about the world; our friend was as sure of this, by the end of four minutes, as if he knew all about it.

After saying he would send him the book the young Lord indeed dropped that subject; he had asked where he might send it, and had had an "Oh, I shall remember!" on John's mention of an hotel; but he had made no further dash into literature, and it was ten to one that this would be the last the distinguished author might hear of the volume. Such again was a note of these high existences—that made one content to ask of them no whit of other consistency than that of carrying off the particular occasion, whatever it might be, in a dazzle of amiability and felicity and leaving *that* as a sufficient trace of their passage. Sought and achieved consistency was but an angular, a secondary motion; compared with the air of complete freedom it might have an effect of deformity. There was no placing this figure of radiant ease, for Berridge, in any relation that didn't appear not good enough—that is among the relations that hadn't been too good for Berridge himself. He was all right where he was; the great Gloriani somehow made that law; his house, with his supreme artistic position, was good enough for anyone, and to-night in especial there were charming people, more charming than our friend could recall from any other scene, as the natural train or circle, as he might say, of such a presence. For an instant he thought he had got the face as a specimen of imperturbability watched, with wonder, across the hushed rattle of roulette at Monte Carlo; but this quickly became as improbable as any question of a vulgar *table d'hôte*, or a steamboat deck, or a herd of fellow-pilgrims cicerone-led, or even an opera-box serving, during a performance, for frame of a type observed from the stalls. One placed young gods and goddesses only when one placed them on Olympus, and it met the case, always, that they were of Olympian race, and that they glimmered for one, at the best, through their silver cloud, like the visiting apparitions in an epic.

This was brief and beautiful indeed till something happened that gave it, for Berridge, on the spot, a prodigious extension

—an extension really as prodigious, after a little, as if he had suddenly seen the silver clouds multiply and then the whole of Olympus presently open. Music, breaking upon the large air, enjoined immediate attention, and in a moment he was listening, with the rest of the company, to an eminent tenor, who stood by the piano; and was aware, with it, that his Englishman had turned away and that in the vast, rich, tapestried room where, in spite of figures and objects so numerous, clear spaces, wide vistas and, as they might be called, becoming situations abounded, there had been from elsewhere, at the signal of unmistakable song, a rapid accession of guests. At first he but took this in, and the way that several young women, for whom seats had been found, looked charming in the rapt attitude; while even the men, mostly standing and grouped, "composed," in their stillness, scarce less impressively, under the sway of the divine voice. It ruled the scene, to the last intensity, and yet our young man's fine sense found still a resource in the range of the eyes, without sound or motion, while all the rest of consciousness was held down as by a hand mailed in silver. It was better, in this way, than the opera—John alertly thought of that: the composition sung might be Wagnerian, but no Tristram, no Iseult, no Parsifal and no Kundry of them all could ever show, could ever "act" to the music, as our friend had thus the power of seeing his dear contemporaries of either sex (armoured *they* so otherwise than in cheap Teutonic tinsel!) just continuously and inscrutably sit to it.

It made, the whole thing together, an enchantment amid which he had in truth, at a given moment, ceased to distinguish parts—so that he was himself certainly at last soaring as high as the singer's voice and forgetting, in a lost gaze at the splendid ceiling, everything of the occasion but what his intelligence poured into it. This, as happened, was a flight so sublime that by the time he had dropped his eyes again a cluster of persons near the main door had just parted to give way to a belated lady who slipped in, through the gap made for her, and stood for some minutes full in his view. It was a proof of the perfect hush that no one stirred to offer her a seat, and her entrance, in her high grace, had yet been so noiseless that she could remain at once immensely exposed and completely unabashed. For Berridge, once more, if the scenic show before him so melted into the music, here precisely might have been the heroine herself advancing to the footlights at her cue. The interest deepened to a thrill, and everything, at the touch of his recognition of this personage, absolutely the most beautiful woman now present, fell exquisitely together and gave him what he had been wanting from the moment of his taking in his young Englishman.

It was there, the missing connection: her arrival had on the instant lighted it by a flash. Olympian herself, supremely, divinely Olympian, she had arrived, could *only* have arrived, for the one person present of really equal race, our young man's late converser, whose flattering demonstration might now stand for one of the odd extravagant forms taken by nervous impatience. This charming, this dazzling woman had been one member of the couple disturbed, to his intimate conviction, the autumn previous, on his being pushed by the officials, at the last moment, into a compartment of the train that was to take him from Cremona to Mantua—where, failing a stop, he had had to keep his place. The other member, by whose felt but unseized identity he had been haunted, was the unconsciously insolent form of guaranteed happiness he had just been engaged with. The sense of the admirable intimacy that, having taken its precautions, had not reckoned with his irruption—this image had remained with him; to say nothing of the interest of aspect of the associated figures, so stamped somehow with rarity, so beautifully distinct from the common occupants of padded corners, and yet on the subject of whom, for the romantic structure he was immediately to raise, he had not had a scrap of evidence.

If he had imputed to them conditions it was all his own doing: it came from his inveterate habit of abysmal imputation, the snatching of the ell wherever the inch peeped out, without which where would have been the tolerability of life? It didn't matter now what he had imputed—and he always held that his expenses of imputation were, at the worst, a compliment to those inspiring them. It only mattered that each of the pair had been then what he really saw each now— full, that is, of the pride of their youth and beauty and fortune and freedom, though at the same time particularly preoccupied: preoccupied, that is, with the affairs, and above all with the passions, of Olympus. Who had they been, and what? Whence had they come, whither were they bound, what tie united them, what adventure engaged, what felicity, tempered by what peril, magnificently, dramatically attended? These had been his questions, all so inevitable and so impertinent, at the time, and to the exclusion of any scruples over his not postulating an inane honeymoon, his not taking the "tie," as he should doubtless properly have done, for the mere blest matrimonial; and he now retracted not one of them, flushing as they did before him again with their old momentary life. To feel his two friends renewedly in presence— friends of the fleeting hour though they had but been, and with whom he had exchanged no sign save the vaguest of salutes on finally relieving them of his company—was only to be conscious that he hadn't, on the spot, done them, so to speak, half justice, and that, for his superior entertainment, there would be ever so much more of them to come.

II

IT might already have been coming indeed, with an immense stride, when, scarce more than ten minutes later, he was

12:Q

aware that the distinguished stranger had brought the Princess straight across the room to speak to him. He had failed in the interval of any glimpse of their closer meeting; for the great tenor had sung another song and then stopped, immediately on which Madame Gloriani had made his pulse quicken to a different, if not to a finer, throb by hovering before him once more with the man in the world he most admired, as it were, looking at him over her shoulder. The man in the world he most admired, the greatest then of contemporary Dramatists —and bearing, independently, the name inscribed if not in deepest incision at least in thickest gilding on the rich recreative roll—this prodigious personage was actually to suffer "presentation" to him at the good lady's generous but ineffectual hands, and had in fact the next instant, left alone with him, bowed, in formal salutation, the massive, curly, witty head, so "romantic" yet so modern, so "artistic" and ironic yet somehow so civic, so Gallic yet somehow so cosmic, his personal vision of which had not hitherto transcended that of the possessor of a signed and framed photograph in a consecrated quarter of a writing-table.

It was positive, however, that poor John was afterward to remember of this conjunction nothing whatever but the fact of the great man's looking at him very hard, straight in the eyes, and of his not having himself scrupled to do as much, and with a confessed intensity of appetite. It was improbable, he was to recognise, that they had, for the few minutes, only stared and grimaced, like pitted boxers or wrestlers; but what had abode with him later on, none the less, was just the cherished memory of his not having so lost presence of mind as to fail of feeding on his impression. It was precious and precarious, that was perhaps all there would be of it; and his subsequent consciousness was quite to cherish this queer view of the silence, neither awkward nor empty nor harsh, but on the contrary quite charged and brimming, that represented for him his use, his unforgettable enjoyment in fact, of his

opportunity. Had nothing passed in words? Well, no misery
of murmured "homage," thank goodness; though something
must have been said, certainly, to lead up, as they put it at
the theatre, to John's having asked the head of the profession,
before they separated, if he by chance knew who the so
radiantly handsome young woman might be, the one who had
so lately come in and who wore the pale yellow dress, of the
strange tone, and the magnificent pearls. They must have
separated soon, it was further to have been noted; since it was
before the advance of the pair, their wonderful dazzling charge
upon him, that he had distinctly seen the great man, at a
distance again, block out from his sight the harmony of the
faded gold and the pearls—to speak only of that—and plant
himself there (the mere high Atlas-back of renown to Berridge now) as for communion with them. He had blocked
everything out, to this tune, effectually; with nothing of the
matter left for our friend meanwhile but that, as he had said,
the beautiful lady was the Princess. What Princess, or the
Princess of what?—our young man had afterward wondered;
his companion's reply having lost itself in the prelude of an
outburst by another vocalist who had approached the
piano.

It was after these things that she so incredibly came to him,
attended by her adorer—since he took it for absolute that the
young Lord was her adorer, as who indeed mightn't be?—and
scarce waiting, in her bright simplicity, for any form of
introduction. It may thus be said in a word that this was the
manner in which she made our hero's acquaintance, a satisfaction that she on the spot described to him as really wanting of
late to her felicity. "I've read everything, you know, and *The
Heart of Gold* three times": she put it all immediately on that
ground, while the young Lord now smiled, beside her, as if
it were quite the sort of thing he had done too; and while,
further, the author of the work yielded to the consciousness
that whereas in general he had come at last scarce to be able

to bear the iteration of those words, which affected him as a mere vain vocal convulsion, so not a breath of this association now attended them, so such a person as the Princess could make of them what she would. Unless it was to be really what *he* would!—this occurred to him in the very thick of the prodigy, no single shade of possibility of which was less prodigious than any other. It was a declaration, simply, the admirable young woman was treating him to, a profession of "artistic sympathy"—for she was in a moment to use this very term that made for them a large, clear, common ether, an element all uplifted and rare, of which they could equally partake.

If she was Olympian—as in her rich and regular young beauty, that of some divine Greek mask overpainted say by Titian, she more and more appeared to him—this offered air was that of the gods themselves: she might have been, with her long rustle across the room, Artemis decorated, hung with pearls, for her worshippers, yet disconcerting them by having under an impulse just faintly fierce, snatched the cup of gold from Hebe. It was to him, John Berridge, she thus publicly offered it; and it was his over-topping *confrère* of shortly before who was the worshipper most disconcerted. John had happened to catch, even at its distance, after these friends had joined him, the momentary deep, grave estimate, in the great Dramatist's salient watching eyes, of the Princess's so singular performance: the touch perhaps this, in the whole business, that made Berridge's sense of it most sharp. The sense of it as *prodigy* didn't in the least entail his feeling abject—any more, that is, than in the due dazzled degree; for surely there would have been supreme wonder in the eagerness of her exchange of mature glory for thin notoriety, hadn't it still exceeded everything that an Olympian of such race should have found herself bothered, as they said, to "read" at all— and most of all to read three times!

With the turn the matter took as an effect of this meeting,

Berridge was more than once to find himself almost ashamed for her—since it seemed never to occur to her to be so for herself; he was jealous of the type where she might have been taken as insolently careless of it; his advantage (unless indeed it had been his ruin) being that he could inordinately reflect upon it, could wander off thereby into kinds of licence of which she was incapable. He hadn't, for himself, waited till now to be sure of what he would do were *he* an Olympian; he would leave his own stuff snugly unread, to begin with; that would be a beautiful start for an Olympian career. He should have been as unable to write those works in short as to make anything else of them; and he should have had no more arithmetic for computing fingers than any perfect-headed marble Apollo mutilated at the wrists. He should have consented to know but the grand personal adventure on the grand personal basis: nothing short of this, no poor cognizance of confusable, pettifogging things, the sphere of earth-grubbing questions and twopenny issues, would begin to be, on any side, Olympian enough.

Even the great Dramatist, with his tempered and tested steel and his immense "assured" position, even he was not Olympian: the look, full of the torment of earth, with which he had seen the Princess turn her back, and for such a purpose, on the prized privilege of his notice, testified sufficiently to that. Still, comparatively, it was to be said, the question of a personal relation with an authority so eminent on the subject of the passions—to say nothing of the rest of his charm—might have had for an ardent young woman (and the Princess was unmistakably ardent) the absolute attraction of romance: unless, again, prodigy of prodigies, she were looking for her romance very particularly elsewhere. Yet where could she have been looking for it, Berridge was to ask himself with private intensity, in a manner to leave her so at her ease for appearing to offer *him* everything?—so free to be quite divinely gentle with him, to hover there before him in all her mild, bright, smooth sublimity and to say: "I should be so very grateful if you'd come to see me."

There succeeded this a space of time of which he was afterward to lose all account, was never to recover the history; his only coherent view of it being that an interruption, some incident that kept them a while separate, had then taken place, yet that during their separation, of half an hour or whatever, they had still somehow not lost sight of each other, but had found their eyes meeting, in deep communion, all across the great peopled room; meeting and wanting to meet, wanting —it was the most extraordinary thing in the world for the suppression of stages, for confessed precipitate intensity—to use together every instant of the hour that might be left them. Yet to use it for what?—unless, like beautiful fabulous figures in some old-world legend, for the frankest and almost the crudest avowal of the impression they had made on each other. He couldn't have named, later on, any other person she had during this space been engaged with, any more than he was to remember in the least what he had himself ostensibly done, who had spoken to him, whom he had spoken to, or whether he hadn't just stood and publicly gaped or languished.

Ah, Olympians were unconventional indeed—that was a part of their high bravery and privilege; but what it also appeared to attest in this wondrous manner was that they could communicate to their chosen in three minutes, by the mere light of their eyes, the same shining cynicism. He was to wonder of course, tinglingly enough, whether he had really made an ass of himself, and there was this amount of evidence for it that there certainly *had* been a series of moments each one of which glowed with the lucid sense that, as she couldn't like him as much as *that* either for his acted clap-trap or for his printed verbiage, what it must come to was that she liked him, and to such a tune, just for himself and quite after no other fashion than that in which every goddess in the calendar had, when you came to look, sooner or later liked some prepossessing young shepherd. The question would thus have been, for him, with a still sharper eventual ache, of whether he positively *had*, as an effect of the miracle, been petrified, before fifty pair of eyes, to the posture of a prepossessing shepherd—and would perhaps have left him under the shadow of some such imputable fatuity if his consciousness hadn't, at a given moment, cleared up to still stranger things.

The agent of the change was, as quite congruously happened, none other than the shining youth whom he now seemed to himself to have been thinking of for ever so long, for a much longer time than he had ever in his life spent at an evening party, as the young Lord: which personage suddenly stood before him again, holding him up an odd object and smiling, as if in reference to it, with a gladness that at once struck our friend as almost too absurd for belief. The object was incongruous by reason of its being, to a second and less pre-occupied glance, a book; and what had befallen Berridge within twenty minutes was that they—the Princess and he, that is—had got such millions of miles, or at least such thousands of years, away from *those* platitudes. The book, he found himself assuming, could only be *his* book (it seemed also to have a tawdry red cover); and there came to him memories, dreadfully false notes sounded so straight again by his new acquaintance, of certain altogether different persons who at certain altogether different parties had flourished volumes before him very much with that insinuating gesture, that arch expression and that fell intention. The meaning of these things—of all possible breaks of the charm at such an hour!—was that he should "signature" the ugly thing, and with a characteristic quotation or sentiment: that was the way people simpered and squirmed, the way they mouthed and beckoned, when animated by such purposes; and it already, on the spot, almost broke his heart to see such a type as that of the young Lord brought, by the vulgarest of fashions, so low. This state of quick displeasure in Berridge, however, was founded on a deeper question—the question of how in the world he was to remain for himself a prepossessing shepherd if he should consent to come back to these base actualities. It was true that even while this wonderment held him, his aggressor's perfect good conscience had placed the matter in a slightly different light.

"By an extraordinary chance I've found a copy of my friend's novel on one of the tables here—I see by the inscription that she has presented it to Gloriani. So if you'd like to glance at it—!" And the young Lord, in the pride of his association with the eminent thing, held it out to Berridge as artlessly as if it had been a striking natural specimen of some sort, a rosy round apple grown in his own orchard, or an exceptional precious stone, to be admired for its weight and lustre. Berridge accepted the offer mechanically—relieved at the prompt fading of his worst fear, yet feeling in himself a tell-tale facial blankness for the still absolutely anomalous character of his friend's appeal. He was even tempted for a moment to lay the volume down without looking at it—only with some extemporised promise to borrow it of their host and take it home, to give himself to it at an easier moment. Then the very expression of his fellow-guest's own countenance determined in him a different and a still more dreadful view; in fact an immediate collapse of the dream in which he had for the splendid previous space of time been living. The young Lord himself, in his radiant costly barbarism, figured far better than John Berridge could do the prepossessing shepherd, the beautiful mythological mortal "distinguished" by a goddess; for our hero now saw that his whole manner of dealing with his ridiculous tribute was marked exactly by the grand simplicity, the prehistoric good faith, as one might call it, of far-off romantic and "plastic" creatures, figures of exquisite Arcadian stamp, glorified rustics like those of the train of peasants in *A Winter's Tale*, who thought nothing of such treasure-trove, on a Claude Lorrain sea-strand, as a royal infant wrapped in purple: something in that fabulous style of exhibition appearing exactly what his present demonstration might have been prompted by.

The Top of the Tree, by Amy Evans—scarce credible words floating before Berridge after he had with an anguish of effort dropped his eyes on the importunate title-page—represented an object as alien to the careless grace of goddess-haunted Arcady as a washed-up "kodak" from a wrecked ship might have been to the appreciation of some islander of wholly unvisited seas. Nothing could have been more in the tone of an islander deplorably diverted from his native interests and dignities than the glibness with which John's own child of nature went on. "It's her pen-name, Amy Evans"—he couldn't have said it otherwise had he been a blue-chinned penny-a-liner—yet marking it with a disconnectedness of intelligence that kept up all the poetry of his own situation and only crashed into that of other persons. The reference put the author of *The Heart of Gold* quite into *his* place, but left the speaker absolutely free of Arcady. "Thanks awfully"—Berridge somehow clutched at that, to keep everything from swimming. "Yes, I should like to look at it," he managed, horribly grimacing now, he believed, to say; and there was in fact a strange short interlude after this in which he scarce knew what had become of anyone or of anything; in which he only seemed to himself to stand alone in a desolate place where even its desolation didn't save him from having to stare at the greyest of printed pages. Nothing here helped anything else, since the stamped greyness didn't even in itself make it impossible his eyes should follow such sentences as: "The loveliness of the face, which was that of the glorious period in which Pheidias reigned supreme, and which owed its most exquisite note to that shell-like curl of the upper lip which always somehow recalls for us the smile with which wind-blown Astarte must have risen from the salt sea to which she owed her birth and her terrible moods"; or "It was too much for all the passionate woman in her, and she let herself go, over the flowering land that had been, but was no longer, their love, with an effect of blighting desolation that might have proceeded from one of the more physical, though not more awful, convulsions of nature."

He seemed to know later on that other and much more natural things had occurred; as that, for instance, with now at last a definite intermission of the rare music that for a long time past, save at the briefest intervals, had kept all participants ostensibly attentive and motionless, and that in spite of its high quality and the supposed privilege of listening to it he had allowed himself not to catch a note of, there was a great rustling and shifting and vociferous drop to a lower plane, more marked still with the quick clearance of a way to supper and a lively dispersal of most of the guests. Hadn't he made out, through the queer glare of appearances, though they yet somehow all came to him as confused and unreal, that the Princess was no longer there, wasn't even only crowded out of his range by the immediate multiplication of her court, the obsequious court that the change of pitch had at once permitted to close round her; that Gloriani had offered her his arm, in a gallant official way, as to the greatest lady present, and that he was left with half a dozen persons more knowing than the others, who had promptly taken, singly or in couples, to a closer inspection of the fine small scattered treasures of the studio?

He himself stood there, rueful and stricken, nursing a silly red-bound book under his arm very much as if he might have been holding on tight to an upright stake, or to the nearest piece of furniture, during some impression of a sharp earth-quake-shock or of an attack of dyspeptic dizziness; albeit indeed that he wasn't conscious of this absurd, this instinctive nervous clutch till the thing that was to be more wonderful than any yet suddenly flared up for him—the sight of the Princess again on the threshold of the room, poised there an instant, in her exquisite grace, for recovery of some one or of something, and then, at recognition of him, coming straight to him across the empty place as if he alone, and nobody and nothing else, were what she incredibly wanted. She was there, she was radiantly *at* him, as if she had known and loved him for ten years—ten years during which, however, she had never quite been able, in spite of undiscouraged attempts, to cure him, as goddesses *had* to cure shepherds, of his mere mortal shyness.

"Ah no, not *that* one!" she said at once, with her divine familiarity; for she had in the flash of an eye "spotted" the particular literary production he seemed so very fondly to have possessed himself of and against which all the Amy Evans in her, as she would doubtless have put it, clearly wished on the spot to discriminate. She pulled it away from him; he let it go; he scarce knew what was happening—only made out that she distinguished the right one, the one that should have been shown him, as blue or green or purple, and intimated that her other friend, her fellow-Olympian, as Berridge had thought of him from the first, really did too clumsily bungle matters, poor dear, with his officiousness over the red one! She went on really as if she had come for that, some such rectification, some such eagerness of reunion with dear Mr Berridge, some talk, after all the tiresome music, of questions really urgent; while, thanks to the supreme strangeness of it, the high tide of golden fable floated him afresh, and her pretext and her plea, the queerness of her offered motive, melted away after the fashion of the enveloping clouds that do their office in epics and idylls.

"You didn't perhaps know I'm Amy Evans," she smiled, "or even perhaps that I write in English—which I love, I assure you, as much as you can yourself do, and which gives one (doesn't it? for who should know if not you?) the biggest of publics. I 'just love'—don't they say?—your American millions; and all the more that they really *take* me for Amy

Evans, as I've just wanted to be taken, to be loved too for myself, don't you know?—that they haven't seemed to try at all to 'go behind' (don't you say?) my poor dear little *nom de guerre*. But it's the new one, my last, *The Velvet Glove*, that I should like you to judge me by—if such a *corvée* isn't too horrible for you to think of; though I admit it's a move straight in the romantic direction—since after all (for I might as well make a clean breast of it) it's dear old discredited romance that I'm most in sympathy with. I'll send you *The Velvet Glove* to-morrow, if you *can* find half an hour for it; and then—and *then*—!" She paused as for the positive bright glory of her meaning.

It could only be so extraordinary, her meaning, whatever it was, that the need in him that would—whatever it was again!—meet it most absolutely formed the syllables on his lips as: "Will you be very, *very* kind to me?"

"Ah, 'kind,' dear Mr Berridge? 'Kind,'" she splendidly laughed, "is nothing to what—!" But she pulled herself up again an instant. "Well, to what I want to be! Just *see*," she said, "how I want to be!" It was exactly, he felt, what he couldn't *but* see—in spite of books and publics and pen-names, in spite of the really "decadent" perversity, recalling that of the most irresponsibly insolent of the old Romans and Byzantines, that could lead a creature so formed for living and breathing her Romance, and so committed, up to the eyes, to the constant fact of her personal immersion in it and genius for it, the dreadful amateurish dance of ungrammatically scribbling it, with editions and advertisements and reviews and royalties and every other futile item: since what was more of the deep essence of throbbing intercourse itself than this very act of her having broken away from people, in the other room, to whom he was as nought, of her having, with her *crânerie* of audacity and indifference, just turned her back on them all as soon as she had begun to miss him? What was more of it than her having forbidden them, by a sufficient curt ring of her own supremely silver tone, to attempt to check or criticize her freedom, than her having looked him up, at his distance, under all the noses he had put out of joint, so as to let them think whatever they might—not of herself (much she troubled to care!) but of the new champion to be reckoned with, the invincible young lion of the day? What was more of it in short than her having perhaps even positively snubbed for him the great mystified Sculptor and the great bewildered Dramatist, treated to this queer experience for the first time of their lives?

It all came back again to the really great ease of really great ladies, and to the perfect facility of everything when once they were great enough. *That* might become the delicious thing to him, he more and more felt, as soon as it should be supremely attested; it was ground he had ventured on, scenically, representationally, in the artistic sphere, but without ever dreaming he should "realize" it thus in the social. Handsomely, gallantly just now, moreover, he didn't so much as let it occur to him that the social experience would perhaps on some future occasion richly profit further scenic efforts; he only lost himself in the consciousness of all she invited him to believe. It took licence, this consciousness, the next moment, for a tremendous further throb, from what she had gone on to say to him in so many words—though indeed the words were nothing and it was all a matter but of the implication that glimmered through them: "Do you *want* very much your supper here?" And then while he felt himself glare, for charmed response, almost to the point of his tears rising with it: "Because if you don't—!"

"Because if I don't—?" She had paused, not from the faintest shade of timidity, but clearly for the pleasure of making him press.

"Why shouldn't we go together, letting me drive you home?"

"You'll come home with me?" gasped John Berridge, while

the perspiration on his brow might have been the morning dew on a high lawn of Mount Ida.

"No—you had better come with *me*. That's what I mean; but I certainly will come to you with pleasure some time if you'll let me."

She made no more than that of the most fatuous of freedoms, as he felt directly he had spoken that it might have seemed to her; and before he had even time to welcome the relief of not having then himself, for beastly contrition, to make more of it, she had simply mentioned, with her affectionate ease, that she wanted to get away, that of the bores there she might easily, after a little, have too much, and that if he'd but say the word they'd nip straight out together by an independent door and be sure to find her motor in the court. What word he had found to say, he was afterward to reflect, must have little enough mattered; for he was to have kept, of what then occurred, but a single other impression, that of her great fragrant rustle beside him over the rest of the ample room and toward their nearest and friendliest resource, the door by which he had come in and which gave directly upon a staircase. This independent image was just that of the only other of his fellow-guests with whom he had been closely concerned; he had thought of him rather indeed, up to that moment, as the Princess's fellow-Olympian—but a new momentary vision of him seemed now to qualify it.

The young Lord had reappeared within a minute on the threshold, that of the passage from the supper-room, lately crossed by the Princess herself, and Berridge felt him there, saw him there, wondered about him there, all, for the first minute, without so much as a straight look at him. He would have come to learn the reason of his friend's extraordinary public demonstration—having more right to his curiosity, or his anxiety or whatever, than anyone else; he would be taking in the remarkable appearances that thus completed it, and would perhaps be showing quite a different face for them, at

the point they had reached, than any that would have hitherto
consorted with the beautiful security of his own position. So
much, on our own young man's part, for this first flush of a
presumption that he might have stirred the germs of ire in a
celestial breast; so much for the moment during which nothing
would have induced him to betray, to a possibly rueful member of an old aristocracy, a vulgar elation or a tickled, unac-
customed glee. His inevitable second thought was, however,
it has to be confessed, another matter, which took a different
turn—for, frankly, all the conscious conqueror in him, as
Amy Evans would again have said, couldn't forego a probably
supreme consecration. He treated himself to no prolonged
reach of vision, but there was something he nevertheless fully
measured for five seconds—the sharp truth of the fact, namely,
of how the interested observer in the doorway must really
have felt about him. Rather disconcertingly, hereupon, the
sharp truth proved to be that the most amused, quite the most
encouraging and the least invidious of smiles graced the
young Lord's handsome countenance—forming, in short, his
final contribution to a display of high social candour unprecedented in our hero's experience. No, he wasn't jealous,
didn't do John Berridge the honour to be, to the extent of the
least glimmer of a spark of it, but was so happy to see his
immortal mistress do what she liked that he could positively
beam at the odd circumstance of her almost lavishing public
caresses on a gentleman not, after all, of negligible importance.

III

WELL, it was all confounding enough, but this indication in
particular would have jostled our friend's grasp of the presented cup had he had, during the next ten minutes, more
independence of thought. That, however, was out of the question when one positively felt, as with a pang somewhere deep

within, as even with a smothered cry for alarm, one's whole sense of proportion shattered at a blow and ceasing to serve. "Not *straight*, and not too fast, shall we?" was the ineffable young woman's appeal to him, a few minutes later, beneath the wide glass porch-cover that sheltered their brief wait for their chariot of fire. It was there even as she spoke; the capped charioteer, with a great clean curve, drew up at the steps of the porch, and the Princess's footman, before rejoining him in front, held open the door of the car. She got in, and Berridge was the next instant beside her; he could only say: "As you like, Princess—where you will; certainly let us prolong it; let us prolong everything; don't let us have it over—strange and beautiful as it can only be!—a moment sooner than we must." So he spoke, in the security of their intimate English, while the perpendicular imperturbable *valet-de-pied*, white-faced in the electric light, closed them in and then took his place on the box where the rigid liveried backs of the two men, presented through the glass, were like a protecting wall; such a guarantee of privacy as might come —it occurred to Berridge's inexpugnable fancy—from a vision of tall guards erect round Eastern seraglios.

His companion had said something, by the time they started, about their taking a turn, their looking out for a few of the night-views of Paris that were so wonderful; and after that, in spite of his constantly-prized sense of knowing his enchanted city and his way about, he ceased to follow or measure their course, content as he was with the particular exquisite assurance it gave him. *That* was knowing Paris, of a wondrous bland April night; that was hanging over it from vague consecrated lamp-studded heights and taking in, spread below and afar, the great scroll of all its irresistible story, pricked out, across river and bridge and radiant *place*, and along quays and boulevards and avenues, and around monumental circles and squares, in syllables of fire, and sketched and summarized, further and further, in the dim fire-dust of

endless avenues; that was all of the essence of fond and thrilled
and throbbing recognition, with a thousand things understood
and a flood of response conveyed, a whole familiar possessive
feeling appealed to and attested.

"From you, you know, it *would* be such a pleasure, and I
think—in fact I'm sure—it would do so much for the thing
in America." Had she gone on as they went, or had there
been pauses of easy and of charmed and of natural silence,
breaks and drops from talk, but only into greater confidence
and sweetness?—such as her very gesture now seemed a part
of; her laying her gloved hand, for emphasis, on the back of
his own, which rested on his knee and which took in from the
act he scarce knew what melting assurance. The emphasis, it
was true—this came to him even while for a minute he held
his breath—seemed rather that of Amy Evans; and if her
talk, while they rolled, had been in the sense of these words
(he had really but felt that they were shut intimately in together, all his consciousness, all his discrimination of meanings and indications being so deeply and so exquisitely
merged in that) the case wasn't as surely and sublimely, as
extravagantly, as fabulously romantic for him as his excited
pulses had been seeming to certify. Her hand was there on
his own, in precious living proof, and splendid Paris hung
over them, as a consecrating canopy, her purple night em-
broidered with gold; yet he waited, something stranger still
having glimmered for him, waited though she left her hand,
which expressed emphasis and homage and tenderness, and
anything else he liked indeed—since it was all then a matter of
what he next heard and what he slowly grew cold as he took
from her.

"You know they do it here so charmingly—it's a compliment a clever man is always so glad to pay a literary friend,
and sometimes, in the case of a great name like yours, it
renders such a service to a poor little book like mine!" She
spoke ever so humbly and yet ever so gaily—and still more

12:R

than before with this confidence of the sincere admirer and
the comrade. That, yes, through his sudden sharpening chill,
was what first became distinct for him; she was mentioning
somehow her explanation and her conditions—her motive,
in fine, disconcerting, deplorable, dreadful, in respect to the
experience, otherwise so boundless, that he had taken her as
having opened to him; and she was doing it, above all, with
the clearest coolness of her general privilege. What in particular she was talking about he as yet, still holding his
breath, wondered; it was something she wanted him to do
for her—which was exactly what he had hoped, but something of what trivial and, heaven forgive them both, of what
dismal order? Most of all, meanwhile, he felt the dire penetration of two or three of the words she had used; so that after
a painful minute the quaver with which he repeated them
resembled his drawing, slowly, carefully, timidly, some barbed
dart out of his flesh.

"A 'literary friend'?" he echoed as he turned his face
more to her; so that, as they sat, the whites of her eyes, near
to his own, gleamed in the dusk like some silver setting of
deep sapphires.

It made her smile—which in their relation now was like
the breaking of a cool air-wave over the conscious sore flush
that maintained itself through his general chill. "Ah, of
course you don't allow that I *am* literary—and of course if
you're awfully cruel and critical and incorruptible you won't
let it say for me what I so want it should!"

"Where are we, where, in the name of all that's damnably,
of all that's grotesquely delusive, are we?" he said, without
a sign, to himself; which was the form of his really being
quite at sea as to what she was talking about. That uncertainty
indeed he could but frankly betray by taking her up, as he
cast about him, on the particular ambiguity that his voice
perhaps already showed him to find most irritating. "Let *it*
show? 'It,' dear Princess—?"

"Why, my dear man, let your Preface show, the lovely, friendly, irresistible log-rolling Preface that I've been asking you if you wouldn't be an angel and write for me."

He took it in with a deep long gulp—he had never, it seemed to him, had to swallow anything so bitter. "You've been asking me if I wouldn't write you a Preface?"

"To *The Velvet Glove*—after I've sent it to you and you've judged if you really can. Of course I don't want you to perjure yourself; but"—and she fairly brushed him again, at their close quarters, with her fresh fragrant smile—"I do want you so to like me, and to say it all out beautifully and publicly."

"You want me to like you, Princess?"

"But, heaven help us, haven't you understood?"

Nothing stranger could conceivably have been, it struck him—if he was right now—than this exquisite intimacy of her manner of setting him down on the other side of an abyss. It was as if she had lifted him first in her beautiful arms, had raised him up high, high, high, to do it, pressing him to her immortal young breast while he let himself go, and then, by some extraordinary effort of her native force and her alien quality, setting him down exactly where she wanted him to be —which was a thousand miles away from her. Once more, so preposterously face to face with her for these base issues, he took it all in; after which he felt his eyes close, for amazement, despair and shame, and his head, which he had some time before, baring his brow to the mild night, eased of its crush-hat, sink to confounded rest on the upholstered back of the seat. The act, the ceasing to see, and if possible to hear, was for the moment a retreat, an escape from a state that he felt himself fairly flattered by thinking of it as "awkward"; the state of really wishing that his humiliation might end, and of wondering in fact if the most decent course open to him mightn't be to ask her to stop the motor and let him down.

He spoke no word for a long minute, or for considerably more than that; during which time the motor went and went, now even somewhat faster, and he knew, through his closed eyes, that the outer lights had begun to multiply and that they were getting back somewhere into the spacious and decorative quarters. He knew this, and also that his retreat, for all his attitude as of accommodating thought, his air—*that* presently and quickly came to him—of having perhaps gathered himself in, for an instant, at her behest, to turn over, in his high ingenuity, some humbugging "rotten" phrase or formula that he might place at her service and make the note of such an effort; he became aware, I say, that his lapse was but a half-retreat, with her strenuous presence and her earnest pressure and the close, cool respiration of her good faith absolutely timing the moments of his stillness and the progress of the car. Yes, it was wondrous well, he had all but made the biggest of all fools of himself, almost as big a one as *she* was still, to every appearance, in her perfect serenity, trying to make of him, and the one straight answer to it *would* be that he should reach forward and touch the footman's shoulder and demand that the vehicle itself should make an end.

That would be an answer, however, he continued intensely to see, only to inanely importunate, to utterly superfluous Amy Evans—not a bit to his at last exquisitely patient companion, who was clearly now quite taking it from him that what kept him in his attitude was the spring of the quick desire to oblige her, the charming loyal impulse to consider a little what he could do for her, say "handsomely yet conscientiously" (oh, the loveliness!) before he should commit himself. She was enchanted—*that* seemed to breathe upon him; she waited, she hung there, she quite bent over him, as Diana over the sleeping Endymion, while all the conscientious man of letters in him, as she might so supremely have phrased it, struggled with the more peccable, the more muddled and "squared," though, for her own ideal, the so much more *banal* comrade. Yes, he could keep it up now—that is he could hold out for his real reply, could meet the rather marked tension of the rest of their passage as well as she; he should be able somehow or other to make his wordless detachment, the tribute of his ostensibly deep consideration of her request, a retreat in good order. She *was*, for herself, to the last point of her guileless fatuity, Amy Evans and an asker for "lifts," a conceiver of twaddle both in herself and in him; or at least, so far as she fell short of all this platitude, it was no fault of the really affecting folly of her attempt to become a mere magazine mortal after the only fashion she had made out, to the intensification of her self-complacency, that she might.

Nothing might thus have touched him more—if to be touched, beyond a certain point, hadn't been to be squared—than the way she failed to divine the bearing of his thoughts; so that she had probably at no one small crisis of her life felt so much a promise in the flutter of her own as on the occasion of the beautiful act she indulged in at the very moment, he was afterward to recognise, of their sweeping into her great smooth empty, costly street—a desert, at that hour, of lavish lamplight and sculptured stone. She raised to her lips the hand she had never yet released and kept it there a moment pressed close against them; he himself closing his eyes to the deepest detachment he was capable of while he took in with a smothered sound of pain that this was the conferred bounty by which Amy Evans sought most expressively to encourage, to sustain and to reward. The motor had slackened and in a moment would stop; and meanwhile even after lowering his hand again she hadn't let it go. This enabled it, while he after a further moment roused himself to a more confessed consciousness, to form with his friend's a more active relation, to possess him of hers, in turn, and with an intention the straighter that her glove had by this time somehow come off. Bending over it without hindrance, he returned as firmly and fully as the application of all his recovered wholeness of feeling, under his moustache, might express, the consecration the bareness of his own knuckles had received; only after which it was that, still thus drawing out his grasp of her, and having let down their front glass by his free hand, he signified to the footman his view of their stopping short.

They had arrived; the high, closed *porte-cochère*, in its crested stretch of wall, awaited their approach; but his gesture took effect, the car pulled up at the edge of the pavement, the man, in an instant, was at the door and had opened it; quickly moving across the walk, the next moment, to press the bell at the gate. Berridge, as his hand now broke away, felt he had cut his cable; with which, after he had stepped out, he raised again the glass he had lowered and closed, its own being already down, the door that had released him. During these motions he had the sense of his companion, still radiant and splendid, but somehow momentarily suppressed, suspended, silvered over and celestially blurred, even as a summer moon by the loose veil of a cloud. So it was he saw her while he leaned for farewell on the open window-ledge; he took her in as her visible intensity of bright vagueness filled the circle that the interior of the car made for her. It was such a state as she would have been reduced to—he felt this, was certain of it—for the first time in her life; and it was he, poor John Berridge, after all, who would have created the condition.

"Good-night, Princess. I shan't see you again."

Vague was indeed no word for it—shine though she might, in her screened narrow niche, as with the liquefaction of her pearls, the glimmer of her tears, the freshness of her surprise. "You won't come in—when you've had no supper?"

He smiled at her with a purpose of kindness that could never in his life have been greater; and at first but smiled without a word. He presently shook his head, however—doubtless also with as great a sadness. "I seem to have supped to my fill, Princess. Thank you, I won't come in."

It drew from her, while she looked at him, a long, low, anxious wail. "And you won't do my Preface?"

"No, Princess, I won't do your Preface. Nothing would

induce me to say a word in print about you. I'm in fact not sure I shall ever mention you in any manner at all as long as ever I live."

He had felt for an instant as if he were speaking to some miraculously humanised idol, all sacred, all jewelled, all votively hung about, but made mysterious, in the recess of its shrine, by the very thickness of the accumulated lustre. And "Then you don't like me—?" was the marvellous sound from the image.

"Princess," was in response the sound of the worshipper, "Princess, I adore you. But I'm ashamed for you."

"Ashamed—?"

"You *are* Romance—as everything, and by what I make out every one, about you is; so what more do you want? Your Preface—the only one worth speaking of—was written long ages ago by the most beautiful imagination of man."

Humanised at least for these moments, she could understand enough to declare that she didn't. "I don't, I don't!"

"You don't need to understand. Don't attempt such base things. Leave those to us. Only live. Only be. *We'll* do the rest."

She moved over—she had come close to the window. "Ah, but, Mr Berridge—!"

He raised both hands; he shook them at her gently, in deep and soft deprecation. "Don't sound my dreadful name. Fortunately, however, you can't help yourself."

"Ah, *voyons!* I so want—!"

He repeated his gesture, and when he brought down his hands they closed together on both of hers, which now quite convulsively grasped the window-ledge. "Don't speak, because when you speak you really say things—! You *are* Romance," he pronounced afresh and with the last intensity of conviction and persuasion. "That's all you have to do with it," he continued while his hands, for emphasis, pressed hard on her own.

Their faces, in this way, were nearer together than ever,

but with the effect of only adding to the vividness of that dire non-intelligence from which, all perversely and incalculably, her very beauty now appeared to gain relief. This made for him a pang and almost an anguish; the fear of her saying something yet again that would wretchedly prove how little he moved her perception. So his eyes, of remonstrant, of suppliant intention, met hers close, at the same time that these, so far from shrinking, but with their quite other swimming plea all bedimmed now, seemed almost to wash him with the tears of her failure. He soothed, he stroked, he reassured her hands, for tender conveyance of his meaning, quite as she had just before dealt with his own for brave demonstration of hers. It was during these instants as if the question had been which of them *could* most candidly and fraternally plead. Full but of that she kept it up. "Ah, if you'd only think, if you'd only try—!"

He couldn't stand it—she was capable of believing he had edged away, excusing himself and trumping up a factitious theory, because he hadn't the wit, hadn't the hand, to knock off the few pleasant pages she asked him for and that any proper Frenchman, master of the *métier*, would so easily and gallantly have promised. Should she so begin to commit herself he'd, by the immortal gods, anticipate it in the manner most admirably effective—in fact he'd even thus make her further derogation impossible. Their faces were so close that he could practise any rich freedom—even though for an instant, while the back of the chauffeur guarded them on that side and his own presented breadth, amplified by his loose mantle, filled the whole window-space, leaving him no observation from any quarter to heed, he uttered, in a deep-drawn final groan, an irrepressible echo of his pang for what might have been, the muffled cry of his insistence. "You *are* Romance!"—he drove it intimately, inordinately home, his lips, for a long moment, sealing it, with the fullest force of authority, on her own; after which, as he broke away and the car, starting again, turned powerfully across the pavement, he had no further sound from her than if, all divinely indulgent but all humanly defeated, she had given the question up, falling back to infinite wonder. He too fell back, but could still wave his hat for her as she passed to disappearance in the great floridly-framed aperture whose wings at once came together behind her.

MORA MONTRAVERS

I

THEY were such extraordinary people to have been so odiously stricken that poor Traffle himself, always, at the best —though it was indeed just now at the worst—what his wife called horribly philosophic, fairly grimaced back, in private, at so flagrant a show of the famous, the provokedly vicious, "irony," the thing he had so often read about in clever stories, with which the usually candid countenance of their fate seemed to have begun of a sudden to bristle. Ah, that irony of fate often admired by him as a phrase and recognised as a truth— so that if he himself ever wrote a story it should certainly and most strikingly *be* about that—he fairly saw it leer at them now, could quite positively fancy it guilty of a low wink at them, in their trouble, out of that vast visage of the world that was made up for them of the separate stony stares or sympathising smirks presented by the circle of their friends. When he could get away from Jane he would pause in his worried walk—about the house or the garden, always, since he could now seldom leave her to brood alone for longer than that—and, while he shook his keys or his loose coin restlessly and helplessly in the pockets into which his hands had come to be inveterately and foolishly thrust, suffer his own familiar face, or the chance reflection of it in some gloomy glass, to respond distortedly to the grim and monstrous joke. He moved from room to room—as he easily could, at present, since their catastrophe; for when he thus sounded the depths of slumbering mirrors it was more than ever as if they were all "spare" rooms, dreary and unapplied, and as if Jane and

267

he were quartered in them, even year after year, quite as on some dull interminable visit.

The joke was at all events in its having befallen *them*, him and his admirable, anxious, conscientious wife, who, living on their sufficient means in their discreet way, liked, respected, and even perhaps a bit envied, in the Wimbledon world (with so much good old mahogany and so many Bartolozzis, to say nothing of their collection of a dozen family miniatures) to have to pick up again as best they could—which was the way Jane put it—the life that Miss Montravers, their unspeakable niece, though not, absolutely not and never, as every one would have it, their adopted daughter, had smashed into smithereens by leaving their roof, from one day to the other, to place herself immediately under the protection, or at least under the inspiration, of a little painter-man commonly called Puddick, who had no pretensions to being a gentleman and had given her lessons. If she had acted, unquestionably, according to her remarkable nature, this added no grace to the turn of the wheel of their fortune—which was, so de-deplorably, that any fledgling of their general nest (and Mora was but gone twenty-one and really clever with her brush) should *have* such a nature. It wasn't that, since her coming to them at fifteen, they had been ever, between themselves, at their ease about her—glossed over as everything had some-how come to be by the treacherous fact of her beauty. She had been such a credit to them that way that if it hadn't put them, as earnest observers, quite off their guard, the dazzle and charm of it appeared mostly to have misled their acquain-tance. That was the worst cruelty for them, that with such a personal power to please she shouldn't, even on some light irregular line, have flown, as might have been conceived, higher. These things were dreadful, were even grotesque, to say; but what wasn't so now—after his difficult, his critical, his distinctly conclusive and, above all, as he secretly ap-praised it, his unexpectedly and absurdly interesting interview with Mr Puddick? This passage, deplorably belated by Mora's own extraordinary artful action, had but just taken place, and it had sent him back to Jane saddled with the queerest and most difficult errand of his life.

He hadn't, however, on his return, at once sought her in the drawing-room—though her plan of campaign had been that they should fly their flag as high as ever, and, changing none of their refined habits, sit in that bow-windowed place of propriety, even as in a great glazed public cage, as much as ever—he had sneaked away again to tip-toe, with his pensive private humour, over the whole field; observing in her society, for the most part, the forms of black despair and grim participation, if even at the same time avoiding inconsiderate grossness; but at bottom, since his moments with Puddick, almost ready to take, as a man of the world, the impartial, the detached, in fact—hang it!—even the amused view. It hadn't as yet made a shade of difference in his tone that Mora was Jane's niece, and not even her very own, but only the child of her half-sister, whose original union with Malcolm Montravers had moreover made a break between them that had waited for healing till after the ill-starred husband's death, and the eve of that of the perfectly disillusioned wife; but in these slightly rueful, though singularly remedial, dips into thoughtful solitude he had begun at last to treat himself to luxuries that he could feel he was paying for. Mora was, accurately speaking, no sharer of his blood, and he absolutely denied her the right not alone socially to dishonour, but, beyond a mere ruffle of the surface, morally to discompose him; mixed with which rather awkwardly, not to say perhaps a bit perversely, was the sense that as the girl was showing up, unmistakably, for one of the most curious of "cases"—the term Puddick himself had used about her—she wouldn't be unlikely to reward some independent, some intelligent notice.

He had never from the first, to do himself—or to do *her*—justice, felt he had really known her, small, cool, supposedly childish, yet not a bit confiding, verily not a bit appealing, presence as she was; but clearly he should know her now, and to do so might prove indeed a job. Not that he wanted to be *too* cold-blooded about her—that is in the way of enlightened appreciation, the detachment of the simply scandalised state being another matter; for this was somehow to leave poor Jane, and poor Jane's gloom of misery, in the lurch. But once safely back from the studio, Puddick's own—where he hadn't been sure, upon his honour, that some coarse danger mightn't crop up—he indulged in a surreptitious vow that if any "fun," whether just freely or else more or less acutely speaking, was to come of the matter, he'd be blamed if he'd be wholly deprived of it. The possibility of an incalculable sort of interest—in fact, quite a refined sort, could there be refinement in such doings—had somehow come out with Puddick's at once saying: "Certainly, sir, I'll marry her if you and Mrs Traffle absolutely insist—and if Mora herself (the great point!) can be brought round to look at it in that way. But I warn you that if I do, and that if she makes that concession, I shall probably lose my hold of her—which won't be best, you know, for anyone concerned. You don't suppose I don't *want* to make it all right, do you?" the surprising young man had gone on. "The question's only of what *is* right—or what will be if we keep our heads and take time—with such an extraordinary person as Mora, don't you see? to deal with. You must grant me," Mr Puddick had wound up, "that she's a rum case."

II

WHAT he had first felt, of course, was the rare coolness of it, the almost impudent absence of any tone of responsibility; which had begun by seeming to make the little painter-man's own case as "rum," surely, as one could imagine it. He had gone, poor troubled Traffle, after the talk, straight to his own studio, or to the rather chill and vague, if scrupulously neat, pavilion at the garden-end, which he had put up eight years ago in the modest hope that it would increasingly inspire him; since it wasn't making preparations and invoking facilities that constituted swagger, but, much rather, behaving as if one's powers could boldly dispense with them. He was certain Jane would come to him there on hearing of him from the parlour-maid, to whom he had said a word in the hall. He wasn't afraid—no—of having to speak a little as he felt; but, though well aware of his wife's impatience, he wasn't keen, either, for any added intensity of effort to abound only in Mrs Traffle's sense. He required space and margin, he required a few minutes' time, to say to himself frankly that this dear dismal lady *had* no sense—none at least of their present wretched question—that was at all worth developing; since he of course couldn't possibly remark it to poor Jane. He had perhaps never remarked for his own private benefit so many strange things as between the moment of his letting himself again into the perpetually swept and garnished temple of his own perfunctory æsthetic rites, where everything was ready to his hand and only that weak tool hung up, and his glimpse of Jane, from the smaller window, as she came down the garden walk. Puddick's studio had been distinctly dirty, and Puddick himself, from head to foot, despite his fine pale little face and bright, direct, much more searching than shifting look, almost as spotty as the large morsel of rag with which he had so oddly begun to rub his fingers while standing there to receive Mora's nearest male relative; but the canvas on his easel, the thing that even in the thick of his other adventure was making so straight a push for the Academy, almost embarrassed that relative's eyes, not to say that relative's conscience, by the cleanness of its appeal. Traffle hadn't come to admire his picture or to mark how he didn't muddle where not muddling was vital; he had come to denounce his conduct, and yet now, perhaps most of all, felt the strain of having pretended so to ignore what would intensely have interested him. Thanks to this barren artifice, to the after-effect of it on his nerves, his own preposterous place, all polish and poverty, pointed such a moral as he had never before dreamed of. Spotless it might be, unlike any surface or aspect presented under the high hard Puddick north-light, since it showed no recording trace, no homely smear—since it had had no hour of history. That was the way truth showed and history came out—in spots: by them, and by nothing else, you knew the real, as you knew the leopard, so that the living creature and the living life equally had to have them. Stuffed animals and weeping woman were—well, another question. He had gathered, on the scene of his late effort, that Mora didn't weep, that she was still perfectly pleased with her shocking course; her complacency indeed remained at such a pitch as to make any question of her actual approach, on whatever basis, or any rash direct challenge of her, as yet unadvisable. He was at all events, after another moment, in presence of Jane's damp severity; *she* never ceased crying, but her tears froze as they fell—though not, unfortunately, to firm ice, any surface that would bear the weight of large argument. The only thing for him, none the less, was to carry the position with a rush, and he came at once to the worst.

"He'll do it—he's willing; but he makes a most striking point—I mean given the girl as we know her and as he of course by this time must. He keeps his advantage, he thinks, by not forcing the note—don't you see?" Traffle himself—under the quick glow of his rush—actually saw more and more. "He's feeling his way—he used that expression to me; and again I haven't to tell you, any more than he really had to tell me, that with Mora one has to sit tight. He puts on us, in short, the responsibility."

He had felt how more than ever her "done" yellow hair —done only in the sense of an elaborately unbecoming con-

formity to the spasmodic prescriptions, undulations and in-
flations of the day, not in that of any departure from its pale
straw-coloured truth—was helped by her white invalidical
shawl to intensify those reminders of their thin ideals, their
bloodless immunity, their generally compromised and missed
and forfeited frankness, that every other feature of their
domestic scene had just been projecting for him. "Responsibility—we responsible?" She gaped with the wonder of it.

"I mean that we should be if anything were to happen by
our trying to impose on her *our* view of her one redemption.
I give it you for his own suggestion—and thereby worth
thinking of."

But Jane could take nothing in. "He suggests that he
needn't marry her, and you agree with him? Pray, what is
there left to 'happen,'" she went on before he could answer,
"after her having happened so completely to disgrace herself?"

He turned his back a moment—he had shortly before
noticed a framed decoration, a "refined" Japanese thing that
gave accent, as he would have said, to the neatness of his
mouse-grey wall, and that needed straightening. Those spare
apprehensions had somehow, it was true, suddenly been
elbowed out of his path by richer ones; but he obeyed his old
habit. "She can leave him, my dear; that's what she can do—
and not, you may well believe, to come back to us."

"If she *will* come I'll take her—even now," said Jane
Traffle; "and who can ask of me more than that?"

He slid about a little, sportively, on his polished floor, as
if he would have liked to skate, while he vaguely, inaudibly
hummed. "Our difficulty is that she doesn't ask the first
blessed thing of us. We've been, you see, too stupid about her.
Puddick doesn't say it, but he knows it—that I felt. She feels
what she is—and so does he."

"What she is? She's an awful little person"—and Mrs
Traffle stated it with a cold finality she had never yet used.

12:S

"Well then, that's what she feels!—even though it's probably not the name she employs in connection with it. She has tremendously the sense of life."

"That's bad," cried Jane, "when you haven't—not even feebly—the sense of decency."

"How do you know, my dear," he returned, "when you've never had it?" And then as she but stared, since he couldn't mean she hadn't the sense of decency, he went on, really quite amazed at himself: "People must have both if possible, but if they can only have one I'm not sure that that one, as we've had it—not at all 'feebly,' as you say!—is the better of the two. What do we know about the sense of life—when it breaks out with real freedom? It has never broken out here, my dear, for long enough to leave its breath on the window-pane. But they've got it strong down there in Puddick's studio."

She looked at him as if she didn't even understand his language, and she flopped thereby into the trap set for her by a single word. "Is she living *in* the studio?"

He didn't avoid her eyes. "I don't know where she's living."

"And do I understand that you didn't ask him?"

"It was none of my business—I felt that there in an unexpected way; I couldn't somehow *not* feel it—and I suggest, my dear, accordingly, that it's also none of yours. I wouldn't answer, if you really want to know," he wound up, hanging fire an instant, but candidly bringing it out—"I wouldn't answer, if you really want to know, for their relations."

Jane's eyebrows mounted and mounted. "Whoever in the world would?"

He waited a minute, looking off at his balanced picture—though not as if now really seeing it. "I'm not talking of what the vulgar would say—or *are* saying, of course, to their fill. I'm not talking of what those relations may be. I'm talking—well," he said, "of what they mayn't."

"You mean they may be innocent?"

"I think it possible. They're, as he calls it, a 'rum' pair. They're not like us."

"If we're not like them," she broke in, "I grant you I hope not."

"We've no imagination, you see," he quietly explained—"whereas they have it on tap, for the sort of life they lead down there, all the while." He seemed wistfully to figure it out. "For us only one kind of irregularity is possible—for them, no doubt, twenty kinds."

Poor Jane listened this time—and so intently that after he had spoken she still rendered his obscure sense the tribute of a wait. "You think it's possible she's not living with him?"

"I think anything possible."

"Then what in the world did she want?"

"She wanted in the first place to get away from *us*. We didn't like her—"

"Ah, we never let her see it!"—Jane could triumphantly make *that* point.

It but had for him, however, an effect of unconscious comedy. "No, that was it—and she wanted to get away from everything we did to prevent her; from our solemn precautions *against* her seeing it. We didn't understand her, or we should have understood how much she must have wanted to. We were afraid of her in short, and she wanted not to see our contortions over it. Puddick isn't beautiful—though he has a fine little head and a face with some awfully good marks; but he's a Greek god, for statuesque calm, compared with us. He isn't afraid of her."

Jane drew herself elegantly up. "I understood you just now that it's exactly what he *is!*"

Traffle reflected. "That's only for his having to deal with her in our way. Not if he handles her in his own."

"And what, pray, is his own?"

Traffle, his hands in his pockets, resumed his walk, touching with the points of his shoes certain separations between the highly-polished planks of his floor. "Well, why should we have to know?"

"Do you mean we're to wash our hands of her?"

He only circulated at first—but quite sounding a low whistle of exhilaration. He felt happier than for a long time; broken as at a blow was the formation of ice that had somehow covered all his days, the whole ground of life, what he would have called the things under. There they were, the things under. He could see them now; which was practically what he after a little replied. "It will be so interesting." He pulled up, none the less, as he turned, before her poor scared and mottled face, her still suffused eyes, her "dressed" head parading above these miseries.

She vaguely panted, as from a dance through bush and briar. "But *what*, Sidney, will be?"

"To see what becomes of her. Without our muddling." Which was a term, however, that she so protested against his use of that he had on the spot, with more kindness than logic, to attenuate, admitting her right to ask him who could do less—less than take the stand she proposed; though indeed coming back to the matter that evening after dinner (they never really got away from it; but they had the consciousness now of false starts in other directions, followed by the captive returns that were almost as ominous of what might still be before them as the famous tragic *rentrée* of Louis XVI and Marie Antoinette from Varennes); when he brought up, for their common relief, the essential fact of the young woman's history as they had suffered it to shape itself: her coming to them bereft and homeless, addressed, packed and registered after the fashion of a postal packet; their natural flutter of dismay and apprehension, but their patient acceptance of the charge; the five flurried governesses she had had in three years, who had so bored her and whom she had so deeply disconcerted; the remarkable disposition for drawing and

daubing that she had shown from the first and that had led
them to consent to her haunting of a class, in town, that had
made her acquainted with the as yet wholly undistinguished
young artist, Walter Puddick, who, with a couple of other
keen and juvenile adventurers of the brush, "criticised," all
at their ease, according to the queer new licence of the day,
and with nobody to criticise *them*, eighty supposed daughters
of gentlemen; the uncontrolled spread of her social connection
in London, on the oddest lines, as a proof of this prosecution
of her studies; her consequent prolonged absences, her strange
explanations and deeper duplicities, and presently her bolder
defiances; with her staying altogether, at last, one fine day,
under pretext of a visit at Highgate, and writing them at the
end of the week, during which they had been without news
of her, that her visit was to Mr Puddick and his "set," and
was likely to be of long duration, as he was "looking after
her," and there were plenty of people in the set to help, and
as she, above all, wanted nothing more: nothing more, of
course, than her two hundred and seventy a year, the scant
remainder of her mother's fortune that she had come into the
use of, under that battered lady's will, on her eighteenth
birthday, and through which her admirers, every member of
the set, no doubt, wouldn't have found her least admirable.
Puddick wouldn't be paying for her, by the blessing of heaven
—*that*, Traffle recognised, would have been ground for anything; the case rather must be the other way round. She was
"treating" the set, probably, root and branch—magnificently;
so no wonder she was having success and liking it. Didn't
Jane recognise, therefore, how in the light of this fact almost
any droll *different* situation—different from the common and
less edifying turn of such affairs—might here prevail? He
could imagine even a fantastic delicacy; not on the part of the
set at large perhaps, but on that of a member or two.

What Jane most promptly recognised, she showed him in
answer to this, was that, with the tone he had so extraordinarily

begun to take on the subject, his choice of terms left her staring. Their ordeal would have to be different indeed from anything she had yet felt it for it to affect her as droll, and Mora's behaviour to repudiate at every point and in some scarce conceivable way its present appearance for it to strike her either as delicate or as a possible cause of delicacy. In fact she could have but her own word—Mora was a monster.

"Well," he laughed—quite brazen about it now—"if she is it's because she has paid for it! Why the deuce did her stars, unless to make her worship gods entirely other than Jane Traffle's, rig her out with a name that puts such a premium on adventures? 'Mora Montravers'—it paints the whole career for you. She *is*, one does feel, her name; but how couldn't she be? She'd dishonour it and its grand· air if she weren't."

"Then by that reasoning you admit," Mrs Traffle returned with more of an argumentative pounce than she had perhaps ever achieved in her life, "that she *is* misconducting herself."

It pulled him up but ten seconds. "It isn't, love, that she's misconducting herself—it's that she's conducting, positively, and by her own lights doubtless quite responsibly, Miss Montravers through the preappointed circle of that young lady's experience." Jane turned on this a desolate back; but he only went on. "It would have been better for us perhaps if she could have been a Traffle—but, failing that, I think I should, on the ground that sinning at all one should sin boldly, have elected for Montravers outright. That *does* the thing—it gives the unmistakable note. And if 'Montravers' made it probable 'Mora'—don't you see, dearest?—made it sure. Would you *wish* her to change to Puddick?" This brought her round again, but as the affirmative hadn't quite leaped to her lips he found time to continue. "Unless indeed they can make some arrangement by which he takes *her* name. Perhaps we can work it that way!"

His suggestion was thrown out as for its positive charm;

but Jane stood now, to do her justice, as a rock. "She's doing something that, surely, no girl in the world ever did before— in preferring, as I so strangely understand you, that her lover *shouldn't* make her the obvious reparation. But is her reason her dislike of his vulgar name?"

"That has no weight for *you*, Jane?" Traffle asked in reply.

Jane dismally shook her head. "Who, indeed, as you say, are *we*? Her reason—if it is her reason—is vulgarer still."

He didn't believe it could be Mora's reason, and though he had made, under the impression of the morning, a brave fight, he had after reflection to allow still for much obscurity in their question. But he had none the less retained his belief in the visibly uncommon young man, and took occasion to make of his wife an inquiry that hadn't hitherto come up in so straight a form and that sounded of a sudden rather odd. "Are you at all *attached* to her? Can you give me your word for *that*?"

She faced him again like a waning wintry moon. "Attached to Mora? Why, she's my sister's child."

"Ah, that, my dear, is no answer! Can you assure me on your honour that you're conscious of anything you can call real affection for her?"

Jane blankly brooded. "What has that to do with it?"

"I think it has everything. If we don't feel a tenderness."

"*You* certainly strike me as feeling one!" Mrs Traffle sarcastically cried.

He weighed it, but to the effect of his protesting. "No, not enough for me to demand of her to marry to spare my sensibility."

His wife continued to gloom. "What is there in what she has done to *make* us tender?"

"Let us admit then, if there's nothing, that it has made us tough! Only then we must *be* tough. If we're having the strain and the pain of it let us also have the relief and the fun."

"Oh, the 'fun'!" Jane wailed; but adding soon after: "If she'll marry him I'll forgive her."

"Ah, that's not enough!" he pronounced as they went to bed.

III

YET he was to feel too the length that even forgiving her would have to go—for Jane at least—when, a couple of days later, they both, from the drawing-room window, saw, to their liveliest astonishment, the girl alight at the gate. She had taken a fly from the station, and their attention caught her as she paused apparently to treat with the cabman of the question of his waiting for her or coming back. It seemed settled in a moment that he should wait; he didn't remount his box, and she came in and up the garden-path. Jane had already flushed, and with violence, at the apparition, and in reply to her companion's instant question had said: "Yes, I'll see her if she has come back."

"Well, she *has* come back."

"She's keeping her cab—she hasn't come to stay." Mrs Traffle had gained a far door of retreat.

"You won't speak to her?"

"Only if she has come to stay. *Then*—volumes!"

He had remained near the window, held fast there by the weight of indefinite obligation that his wife's flight from the field shifted to his shoulders. "But if she comes back to stay what can Puddick do?"

This kept her an instant. "To stay till he marries her is what I mean."

"Then if she asks for you—as she only must—am I to tell her that?"

Flushed and exalted, her hand on the door, Jane had for this question a really grand moment. "Tell her that if he will she shall come in—with your assent—for my four hundred."

"Oh, oh!" he ambiguously sounded while she whisked away, and the door from the hall was at the same time thrown open by the parlour-maid. "Miss Montravers!" announced, with a shake of anguish, that domestic, whose heightened colour and scared eyes conformed to her mistress's example. Traffle felt his own cheek, for that matter, unnaturally glow, and the very first of his observations as Mora was restored to his sight might have been that she alone of them all wore her complexion with no difference. There was little doubt moreover that this charming balance of white and pink couldn't have altered but to its loss; and indeed when they were left alone the whole immediate effect for him of the girl's standing there in immediate bright silence was that of her having come simply to reaffirm her extraordinary prettiness. It might have been just to say: "You've thought, and you think, all sorts of horrible things about me, but observe how little my appearance matches them, and in fact keep up coarse views if you can in the light of my loveliness." Yet it wasn't as if she had changed, either, even to the extent of that sharper emphasis: he afterward reflected, as he lived over this passage, that he must have taken for granted in her, with the life she was leading, so to call it, some visibility of boldness, some significant surface—of which absurd supposition her presence, at the end of three minutes, had disabused him to the point of making all the awkwardness his and leaving none at all for her. That was a side of things, the awkward, that she clearly meant never again to recognise in conversation—though certainly from the first, ever, she had brushed it by lightly enough. She was in truth exactly the same—except for her hint that they might have forgotten how pretty she *could* be; and he further made sure she would incur neither pains nor costs for any new attempt on them. The Mora they had always taken her for would serve her perfectly still; that young woman was bad enough, in all conscience, to hang together through anything that might yet happen.

So much he was to feel she had conveyed, and that it was the little person presenting herself, at her convenience, on these terms who had been all the while, in their past, their portentous inmate—since what had the portent been, by the same token, but exactly of this? By the end of three minutes more our friend's sole thought was to conceal from her that he had looked for some vulgar sign—such as, reported to Wimbledon tea-tables, could be confidentially mumbled about: he was almost as ashamed of that elderly innocence as if she had caught him in the fact of disappointment at it. Meanwhile she had expressed her errand very simply and serenely. "I've come to see you because I don't want to lose sight of you—my being no longer with you is no reason for that." She was going to ignore, he saw—and she would put it through: she was going to ignore everything that suited her, and the quantity might become prodigious. Thus it would rest upon *them*, poor things, to disallow, if they must, the grace of these negatives—in which process she would watch them flounder without help. It opened out before him—a vertiginous view of a gulf; the abyss of what the ignoring would include for the convenient general commerce; of what might lie behind, in fine, should the policy foreshadow the lurking quantity. He knew the vague void for one he should never bridge, and that to put on emphasis where Mora chose to neglect it would be work only for those who "gathered samphire" like the unfortunates in *King Lear*, or those who, by profession, planted lightning-rods at the tips of tremendous towers. He was committed to pusillanimity, which would yet have to figure for him, before he had done with it, he knew, as a gallant independence, by letting ten minutes go without mention of Jane. Mora had put him somehow into the position of having to explain that her aunt wouldn't see her—precisely that was the mark of the girl's attitude; but he'd be hanged if he'd do anything of the sort.

It was therefore like giving poor Jane basely away, his not, to any tune, speaking for her—and all the more that their visitor sat just long enough to let his helplessness grow and reach perfection. By this facility it was he who showed—and for her amusement and profit—all the change she kept him from imputing to herself. He presented her—she held him up to himself as presenting her—with a new uncle, made over, to some loss of dignity, on purpose for her; and nothing could less have suited their theory of his right relation than to have a private understanding with her at his wife's expense. However, gracefully grave and imperturbable, inimitably armed by her charming correctness, as she sat there, it would be her line in life, he was certain, to reduce many theories, solemn Wimbledon theories about the scandalous person, to the futility of so much broken looking-glass. Not naming her aunt—since *he* didn't—she had of course to start, for the air of a morning call, some other hare or two; she asked for news of their few local friends quite as if these good people mightn't ruefully have "cut" her, by what they had heard, should they have met her out on the road. She spoke of Mr Puddick with perfect complacency, and in particular held poor Traffle very much as some master's fiddle-bow might have made him hang on the semi-tone of a silver string when she referred to the visit he had paid the artist and to the latter's having wondered whether he liked what he saw. *She* liked, more and more, Mora intimated, what was offered to her own view; Puddick was going to do, she was sure, such brilliant work—so that she hoped immensely he would come again. Traffle found himself, yes—it was positive—staying his breath for this; there was, in fact, a moment, that of her first throwing off her free "Puddick," when it wouldn't have taken much more to make him almost wish that, for rounded perfection, she'd say "Walter" at once. He would scarce have guaranteed even that there hadn't been just then some seconds of his betraying that imagination in the demoralised eyes that her straight, clear, quiet beams sounded and sounded, against every presumption of what might have been. What essentially happened, at any rate, was that by the time she went she had not only settled him in the sinister attitude of having lost all interest in her aunt, but had made him give her for the profane reason of it that he was gaining so much in herself.

He rushed in again, for that matter, to a frank clearance the moment he had seen the girl off the premises, attended her, that is, back to her fly. He hadn't at this climax remarked to her that she must come again—which might have meant either of two or three incoherencies and have signified thereby comparatively little; he had only fixed on her a rolling eye— for it rolled, he strangely felt, without leaving her; which had the air of signifying heaven knew what. She took it, clearly, during the moment she sat there before her start, for the most rather than for the least it might mean; which again made him gape with the certitude that ever thereafter she would make him seem to have meant what she liked. She had arrived in a few minutes at as wondrous a recipe or as quick an aspiration for this as if she had been a confectioner using some un-precedented turn of the ladle for some supersubtle cream. He was a proved conspirator from that instant on, which was practically what he had qualified Jane, within ten minutes—if Jane had only been refreshingly sharper—to pronounce him. For what else in the world did it come to, his failure of ability to attribute any other fine sense to Mora's odd "step" than the weird design of just giving them a lead? They were to leave her alone, by her sharp prescription, and she would show them once for all how to do it. Cutting her dead wasn't leaving her alone—any idiot could do that; conversing with her affably was the privilege she offered, and the one he had so effectually embraced—he made a clean breast of this—that he had breathed to her no syllable of the message left with him by her aunt.

"Then you mean," this lady now inquired, "that I'm to

go and call upon her, at that impossible place, just as if she
were the pink of propriety and we had no exception whatever
to take to her conduct? Then you mean," Mrs Traffle had
pursued with a gleam in her eye of more dangerous portent
than any he had ever known himself to kindle there—"then
you mean that I'm to grovel before a chit of a creature on
whom I've lavished every benefit, and to whom I've actually
offered every indulgence, and who shows herself, in return
for it all, by what I make out from your rigmarole, a fiend of
insolence as well as of vice?"

The danger described by Sidney Traffle was not that of any
further act of violence from Jane than this freedom of address
to him, unprecedented in their long intercourse—this sustained and, as he had in a degree to allow, not unfounded note
of sarcasm; such a resort to which, on his wife's part, would,
at the best, mark the prospect for him, in a form flushed with
novelty, of much conscious self-discipline. What looked out
of her dear foolish face, very much with the effect of a new
and strange head boldly shown at an old and familiar pacific
window, was just the assurance that he might hope for no
abashed sense in her of differing from him on all this ground
as she had never differed on any. It was as if now, unmistakably, she *liked* to differ, the ground being her own and he
scarce more than an unwarranted poacher there. Of course it
was her own, by the fact, first, of Mora's being her, not his,
sister's child; and, second, by all the force with which her
announced munificence made it so. He took a moment to
think how he could best meet her challenge, and then reflected
that there was, happily, nothing like the truth—*his* truth, of
which it was the insidious nature to prevail. "What she
wanted, I make out, was but to give us the best pleasure she
could think of. The pleasure, I mean, of our not only recognizing how little we need worry about her, but of our seeing as
well how pleasant it may become for us to keep in touch with
her."

These words, he was well aware, left his wife—given her painful narrowness—a bristling quiver of retorts to draw from; yet it was not without a silent surprise that he saw her, with her irritated eyes on him, extract the bolt of finest point. He had rarely known her to achieve that discrimination before. "The pleasure then, in her view, you 'make out'—since you make out such wonders!—is to be all for us only?"

He found it fortunately given him still to smile. "That will depend, dear, on our appreciating it enough to make things agreeable to *her* in order to get it. But as she didn't inquire for you," he hastened to add, "I don't—no, I don't—advise your going to see her *even* for the interest I speak of!" He bethought himself. "We must wait a little."

"Wait till she gets worse?"

He felt after a little that he should be able now always to command a kindly indulgent tone. "I'll go and see her if you like."

"Why in the world should I like it? Is it your idea—for the pleasure you so highly appreciate, and heaven knows what you mean by it!—to cultivate with her a free relation of your own?"

"No"—he promptly turned—"I suggest it only as acting *for* you. Unless," he went on, "you decidedly wish to act altogether for yourself."

For some moments she made no answer; though when she at last spoke it was as if it *were* an answer. "I shall send for Mr Puddick."

"And whom will you send?"

"I suppose I'm capable of a note," Jane replied.

"Yes, or you might even telegraph. But are you sure he'll come?"

"Am I sure, you mean," she asked, "that his companion will let him? I can but try, at all events, and shall at any rate have done what I can."

"I think he's afraid of her—"

Traffle had so begun, but she had already taken him up. "And you're not, you mean—and that's why you're so eager?"

"Ah, my dear, my dear?" He met it with his strained grimace. "Let us by all means," he also, however, said, "have him if we can."

On which it was, for a little, that they strangely faced each other. She let his accommodation lie while she kept her eyes on him, and in a moment she had come up, as it were, elsewhere. "If I thought you'd see her—!"

"That I'd see her?"—for she had paused again.

"See her and go on with her—well, without my knowledge," quavered poor Jane, "I assure you you'd seem to me even worse than her. So will you promise me?" she ardently added.

"Promise you what, dear?" He spoke quite mildly.

"Not to see her in secret—which I believe would kill me."

"Oh, oh, oh, love!" Traffle smiled while she positively glared.

IV

THREE days having elapsed, however, he had to feel that things had considerably moved on his being privileged to hear his wife, in the drawing-room, where they entertained Mr Puddick at tea, put the great question straighter to that visitor than he himself, Sidney Traffle, could either have planned or presumed to do. Flushed to a fever after they had beat about the bush a little, Jane didn't flinch from her duty. "What I want to know in plain terms, if you please, is whether or no you're Mora's lover?" "Plain terms"—she did have inspirations! so that under the shock he turned away, humming, as ever, in his impatience, and, the others being seated over the vain pretence of the afternoon repast, left the young man to say what he might. It was a fool's question, and there was always a gape for the wisest (the greater the wisdom and the greater the folly) in any apprehension of such. As if he were going to say, remarkable Puddick, not less remarkable in his way than Mora—to say, that is, anything that would suit Jane; and as if it didn't give her away for a goose that she should assume he was! Traffle had never more tiptoed off to the far end of the room, whether for pretence of a sudden interest in his precious little old Copley Fielding or on any other extemporized ground, than while their guest momentarily hung fire; but though he winced it was as if he now liked to wince—the occasions she gave him for doing so were such a sign of his abdication. He had wholly stepped aside, and she could flounder as she would: he had found exactly the formula that saved his dignity, that expressed his sincerity, and that yet didn't touch his curiosity. "I see it would be indelicate for me to go further—yes, love, I do see *that*"; such was the concession he had resorted to for a snap of the particular tension of which we a moment ago took the measure. This had entailed Jane's gravely pronouncing him, for the first time in her life, ridiculous; as if, in common sense—! She used that term also with much freedom now; at the same time that it hadn't prevented her almost immediately asking him if *he* would mind writing her letter. Nothing could suit him more, from the moment she was ostensibly to run the show—as for her benefit he promptly phrased the matter—than that she should involve herself in as many inconsistencies as possible; since if he did such things in spite of his scruple this was as nothing to her needing him at every step in spite of her predominance.

His delicacy was absurd for her because Mora's indecency had made this, by her logic, the only air they could now breathe; yet he knew how it nevertheless took his presence to wind her up to her actual challenge of their guest. Face to face with that personage alone she would have failed of the assurance required for such crudity; deeply unprepared as she really was, poor dear, for the crudity to which she might, as a consequence, have opened the gates. She lived altogether thus —and nothing, to her husband's ironic view, he flattered himself, could be droller—in perpetual yearning, deprecating, in bewildered and muddled communion with the dreadful law of crudity; as if in very truth, to *his* amused sense, the situation hadn't of necessity to be dressed up to the eyes for them in every sort of precaution and paraphrase. Traffle had privately reached the point of seeing it, at its high pitch of mystery and bravery, absolutely defy any common catchword. The one his wife had just employed struck him, while he hunched his shoulders at the ominous pause she had made inevitable for sturdy Puddick, as the vulgarest, and he had time largely to blush before an answer came. He had written, explicitly on Jane's behalf, to request the favour of an interview, but had been careful not to intimate that it was to put that artless question. To have dragged a busy person, a serious person, out from town on the implication of his being treated for reward to so *bête* an appeal—no, one surely couldn't appear to have been concerned in that. Puddick had been under no obligation to come—one might honestly have doubted whether he would even reply. However, his power of reply proved not inconsiderable, as consorted with his having presented himself not a bit ruefully or sulkily, but all easily and coolly, and even to a visible degree in a spirit of unprejudiced curiosity. It was as if he had practically forgotten Traffle's own invasion of him at his studio—in addition to which who indeed knew what mightn't have happened between the Chelsea pair in a distracting or freshly epoch-making way since then?—and was ready to show himself for perfectly good-natured, but for also naturally vague about what they could want of him again. "It depends, ma'am, on the sense I understand you to attach to that word," was in any case the answer to which he at his convenience treated Jane.

12:T

"I attach to it the only sense," she returned, "that could force me—by *my* understanding of it—to anything so painful as this inquiry. I mean are you so much lovers as to make it indispensable you should immediately marry?"

"Indispensable to who, ma'am?" was what Traffle heard their companion now promptly enough produce. To which, as it appeared to take her a little aback, he added: "Indispensable to *you*, do you mean, Mrs Traffle? Of course, you see, I haven't any measure of *that*."

"Should you have any such measure"—and with it she had for her husband the effect now of quite "speaking up"— "if I were to give you my assurance that my niece will come into money when the proper means are taken of making her connection with you a little less—or perhaps I should say altogether less—distressing and irregular?"

The auditor of this exchange rocked noiselessly away from his particular point of dissociation, throwing himself at random upon another, before Mr Puddick appeared again to have made up his mind, or at least to have adjusted his intelligence; but the movement had been on Traffle's part but the instinct to stand off more and more—a vague effort of retreat that didn't prevent the young man's next response to pressure from ringing out in time to overtake him. "Is what you want me to understand then that you'll handsomely pay her if she marries me? Is it to tell me that that you asked me to come?" It was queer, Sidney felt as he held his breath, how he kept liking this inferior person the better—the better for his carrying himself so little like any sort of sneak—for every minute spent in his company. They had brought him there at the very best to patronise him, and now would simply have to reckon with his showing clearly for so much more a person "of the world" than they. Traffle, it was true, was becoming, under the precious initiation opened to him by Mora, whether directly or indirectly, much more a man of the world than over yet: as much as that at least he could turn over in his secret soul while their visitor pursued. "Perhaps you also mean, ma'am, that you suppose me to require that knowledge to determine my own behaviour—in the sense that if she comes in for money I may clutch at the way to come into it too?" He put this as the straightest of questions; yet he also, it was marked, followed up that side-issue further, as if to fight shy of what Jane wanted most to know. "Is it your idea of me that I haven't married her because she isn't rich enough, and that on what you now tell me I may think better of it? Is that how you see me, Mrs Traffle?" he asked, at his quiet pitch, without heat.

It might have floored his hostess a little, to her husband's vision, but she seemed at once to sit up, on the contrary, so much straighter, that he, after hearing her, immediately turned round. "Don't you *want*, Mr Puddick, to be able to marry a creature so beautiful and so clever?"

This was somehow, suddenly, on Jane's part, so prodigious, for art and subtlety, Traffle recognised, that he had come forward again and a remarkable thing had followed. Their guest had noticed his return and now looked up at him from over the tea-table, looked in a manner so direct, so intelligent, so quite amusedly critical, that, afresh, before he knew it, he had treated the little fact as the flicker of a private understanding between them, and had just cynically—for it was scarce covertly—smiled back at him in the independence of it. So there he was again, Sidney Traffle; after having tacitly admitted to Mora that her aunt was a goose of geese—compared to himself and *her*—he was at present putting that young woman's accomplice up to the same view of his conjugal loyalty, which might be straightway reported to the girl. Well, what was he, all the same, to do? Jane *was*, on all the ground that now spread immeasurably about them, a goose of geese: all that had occurred was that she more showily displayed it; and that she might indeed have had a momentary sense of triumph when the best that their friend first found to meet her withal proved still another evasion of the real point. "I don't think, if you'll allow me to say so, Mrs Traffle, that you've any right to ask me, in respect to Miss Montravers, what I 'want'—or that I'm under any obligation to tell you. I've come to you, quite in the dark, because of Mr Traffle's letter, and so that you shouldn't have the shadow of anything to complain of. But please remember that I've neither appealed to you in any way, nor put myself in a position of responsibility toward you."

So far, but only so far, however, had he successfully proceeded before Jane was down upon him in her new trenchant form. "It's not of your responsibility to us I'm talking, but all of your responsibility to *her*. We efface ourselves," she all effectively bridled, "and we're prepared for every reasonable sacrifice. But we do still a little care what becomes of the child to whom we gave up years of our life. If you care enough for her to live with her, don't you care enough to work out some way of making her your very own by the aid of such help as we're eager to render? Or are we to take from you, as against that, that even thus with the way made easy, she's so amazingly constituted as to prefer, in the face of the world, your actual terms of intercourse?"

The young man had kept his eyes on her without flinching, and so he continued after she had spoken. He then drank down what remained of his tea and, pushing back his chair, got up. He hadn't the least arrogance, not the least fatuity of type— save so far as it might be offensive in such a place to show a young head modelled as with such an intention of some one of the finer economic uses, and a young face already a little worn as under stress of that economy—but he couldn't help his looking, while he pulled down his not very fresh waistcoat, just a trifle like a person who had expected to be rather better regaled. This came indeed, for his host, to seeing that he looked bored; which was again, for that gentleman, a source of humiliation. What style of conversation, comparatively, on showing of it, wouldn't he and Mora all the while be having together? If they would only invite *him*, their uncle—or rather no, when it came to that, not a bit, worse luck, their uncle—if they would only invite him, their humble admirer, to tea! During which play of reflection and envy, at any rate, Mr Puddick had prepared to take his leave. "I don't think I can talk to you, really, about my 'terms of intercourse' with any lady." He wasn't superior, exactly—wasn't so in fact at all, but was nevertheless crushing, and all the more that his next word seemed spoken, in its persistent charity, for their help. "If it's important you should get at that sort of thing it strikes me you should do so by the lady herself."

Our friend, at this, no longer stayed his hand. "Mrs Traffle doesn't see her," he explained to their companion—"as the situation seems to present itself."

"You mean Mora doesn't see me, my dear!" Mrs Traffle replied with spirit.

He met it, however, with a smile and a gallant inclination. "Perhaps I mean that she only unsuccessfully tries to."

"She doesn't then take the right way!" Mora's aunt tossed off.

Mr Puddick looked at her blandly. "Then you lose a good deal, ma'am. For if you wish to learn from me how much I admire your niece," he continued straight, "I don't in the least mind answering to that that you may put my sentiments at the highest. I *adore* Miss Montravers," he brought out, after a slight catch of his breath, roundly and impatiently. "I'd do anything in the world for her."

"Then do you pretend," said Jane, with a rush, as if to break through this opening before she was checked, "then do you pretend that you're living with her in innocence?"

Sidney Traffle had a groan for it—a hunched groan in which he exhaled the anguish, as he would have called it, of his false position; but Walter Puddick only continued, in his fine unblinking way, to meet Jane's eyes. "I repudiate absolutely your charge of my 'living' with her or of her living with me. Miss Montravers is irreproachable and immaculate."

"All appearances to the contrary notwithstanding?" Mrs Traffle cried. "You'd do anything in the world for her, and she'd by the same token, I suppose, do anything in the world for you, and yet you ask me to believe that, all the while, you are, together, in this extraordinary way, doing nothing in the world——?" With which, to his further excruciation, her husband, with eyes averted from her, felt her face turn, as for a strained and unnatural intensity of meaning, upon himself. "He attempts, dear, to prove too much! But I only desire," she continued to their guest, "that you should definitely understand how far I'm willing to go."

"It *is* rather far you know," Sidney, at this, in spite of everything, found himself persuasively remarking to Puddick.

It threw his wife straight upon him, and he felt her there, more massively weighted than he had ever known her, while she said: "I'll make it four hundred and fifty. Yes, a year," she then exaltedly pursued to their visitor. "I pass you my word of honour for it. That's what I'll allow Mora as your wife."

Traffle watched him, under this—and the more that an odd spasm or shade had come into his face; which in turn made our friend wish the more to bridge somehow the dark oddity of their difference. What was all the while at bottom sharpest for him was that they might somehow pull more together. "That, you see," he fluted for conciliation, "is her aunt's really, you know, I think, rather magnificent message for her."

The young man took in clearly, during a short silence, the material magnificence—while Traffle again noted how almost any sort of fineness of appreciation could show in his face. "I'm sure I'm much obliged to you," he presently said.

"You don't refuse to let her have it, I suppose?" Mrs Traffle further proceeded.

Walter Puddick's clear eyes—clear at least as his host had hitherto judged them—seemed for the minute attached to the square, spacious sum. "I don't refuse anything. I'll give her your message."

"Well," said Jane, "that's the assurance we've wanted." And she gathered herself as for relief, on her own side, at his departure.

He lingered but a moment—which was long enough, however, for her husband to see him, as with an intenser twinge of the special impatience just noted in him, look, all unhappily, from Mora's aunt to Mora's uncle. "Of course I can't mention to her such a fact. But I wish, all the same," he said with a queer sick smile, "that you'd just simply let us alone."

He turned away with it, but Jane had already gone on. "Well, you certainly seem in sufficient possession of the right way to make us!"

Walter Puddick, picking up his hat and with his distinctly artistic and animated young back presented—though how it came to show so strikingly for such Sidney Traffle couldn't have said—reached one of the doors of the room which was not right for his egress; while Sidney stood divided between the motion of correcting and guiding him and the irresistible need of covering Jane with a last woeful reproach. For he had seen something, had caught it from the sharp flicker of trouble finally breaking through Puddick's face, caught it from the fact that—yes, positively—the upshot of their attack on him was a pair of hot tears in his eyes. They stood for queer, deep things, assuredly, these tears; they spoke portentously, since that was her note, of wonderful Mora; but there was an indelicacy in the pressure that had thus made the source of them public. "You *have* dished us now!" was what, for a Parthian shot, Jane's husband would have liked to leave with her; and what in fact he would have articulately phrased if he hadn't rather given himself to getting their guest with the least discomfort possible out of the room. Into the hall he ushered

him, and there—absurd, incoherent person as he had again to
know himself for—vaguely yet reassuringly, with an arm
about him, patted him on the back. The full force of this
victim's original uttered warning came back to him; the
probable perfect wisdom of his plea that, since he had infinitely
to manage, *their* line, the aunt's and the uncle's, was just to
let him feel his way; the gage of his sincerity as to this being
the fact of his attachment. Sidney Traffle seemed somehow to
feel the fullest force of both these truths during the moment
his young friend recognized the intention of his gesture;
and thus for a little, at any rate, while the closed door of the
drawing-room and the shelter of the porch kept them unseen
and unheard from within, they faced each other for the embarrassment that, as Traffle would have been quite ready to
put it, they had in common. Their eyes met their eyes, their
conscious grin their grin; hang it, yes, the screw *was* on
Mora's lover. Puddick's recognition of his sympathy—well,
proved that he needed something, though he didn't need in-
terference from the outside; which couldn't, any way they
might arrange it, seem delicate enough. Jane's obtrusion of
her four hundred and fifty affected Traffle thus as singularly
gross; though part of that association might proceed for him,
doubtless, from the remark in which his exasperated sensibility was, the next thing, to culminate.

"I'm afraid I can't explain to you," he first said, however,
"why it is that in spite of my indoctrination, my wife fails to
see that there's only one answer a gentleman may make to the
so intimate question she put to you."

"I don't know anything about that; I wasn't at all making
her a conventional reply. But I don't mind assuring you, on
my sacred honour—"

So Walter Puddick was going on, but his host, with a firm
touch of his arm, and very handsomely, as that host felt, or
at least desired to feel, wouldn't have it. "Ah, it's none of my
business; I accept what you've said, and it wouldn't matter to

you if I didn't. Your situation's evidently remarkable," Traffle all sociably added, "and I don't mind telling you that I, for one, have confidence in your tact. I recognised, that day I went to see you, that this was the only thing to do, and have done my best, ever since, to impress it on Mrs Traffle. She replies to me that I talk at my ease, and the appearances *are* such, I recognize, that it would be odd she shouldn't mind them. In short she had shown you how much she does mind them. I tell her," our friend pursued, "that we mustn't weigh appearances too much against realities—and that *of* those realities," he added, balancing again a little on his toes and clasping his waist with his hands, which at the same time just worked down the back of his waistcoat, "you must be having your full share." Traffle liked, as the effect of this, to see his visitor look at him harder; he felt how the ideal turn of their relation would be that he should show all the tact he *was* so incontestably showing, and yet at the same time not miss anything that would be interesting. "You see of course for yourself how little, after all, she knows Mora. She doesn't appreciate the light hand that you must have to have with her —and that, I take it," Sidney Traffle smiled, "is what you contend for with us."

"I don't contend for anything with you, sir," said Walter Puddick.

"Ah, but you do want to be let alone," his friend insisted.

The young man turned graver in proportion to this urbanity. "Mrs Traffle has closed my mouth."

"By laying on you, you mean, the absolute obligation to report her offer—?" That lady's representative continued to smile, but then it was that he yet began to see where fine freedom of thought—translated into act at least—would rather grotesquely lodge him. He hung fire, none the less, but for an instant; even though not quite saying what he had been on the point of. "I should like to feel at liberty to put it to you that if, in your place, I felt that a statement of Mrs

Traffle's overture would probably, or even possibly, dish me, I'm not sure I should make a scruple of holding my tongue about it. But of course I see that I can't very well go so far without looking to you as if my motive might be mixed. You might naturally say that I can't *want* my wife's money to go out of the house."

Puddick had an undissimulated pause for the renewed effort to do justice to so much elegant arrangement of the stiff truth of his case; but his intelligence apparently operated, and even to the extent of showing him that his companion really meant, more and more, as well—as well, that is, to *him*—as it was humanly conceivable that Mrs Traffle's husband *could* mean. "Your difficulty's different from mine, and from the appearance I incur in carrying Miss Montravers her aunt's message as a clear necessity and at any risk."

"You mean that your being conscientious about it may look as if the risk you care least to face is that of not with a little patience coming in yourself for the money?" After which, with a glitter fairly sublime in its profession of his detachment from any stupid course: "You can be sure, you know, that *I'd* be sure—!"

"Sure I'm not a pig?" the young man asked in a manner that made Traffle feel quite possessed at last of his confidence.

"Even if you keep quiet I shall know you're not, and shall believe also you won't have thought me one." To which, in the exaltation produced by this, he next added: "Isn't she, with it all—with all she has done for you I mean—splendidly fond of you?"

The question proved, however, but one of those that seemed condemned to cast, by their action, a chill; which was expressed, on the young man's part, with a certain respectful dryness. "How do you know, sir, what Miss Montravers has done for me?"

Sidney Traffle felt himself enjoy, on this, a choice of replies —one of which indeed would have sprung easiest from his lips. "Oh now, come!" seemed for the instant what he would have liked most to hear himself say; but he renounced the pleasure—even though making up for it a little by his actual first choice. "Don't I know at least that she left the honourable shelter of this house for you?"

Walter Puddick had a wait. "I never asked it of her."

"You didn't seduce her, no—and even her aunt doesn't accuse you of it. But that she should have given up—well, what she *has* given up, moderately as you may estimate it," Traffle again smiled—"surely has *something* to say about her case?"

"What has more to say than anything else," Puddick promptly returned to this, "is that she's the very cleverest and most original and most endowed, and in every way most wonderful, person I've known in all my life."

His entertainer fairly glowed, for response, with the light of it. "Thank you, then!" Traffle thus radiated.

" 'Thank you for nothing!' " cried the other with a short laugh and set into motion down the steps and the garden walk by this final attestation of the essential impenetrability even of an acutest young artist's *vie intime* with a character sketchable in such terms.

Traffle accompanied him to the gate, but wondering, as they went, if it was quite inevitable one should come back to feeling, as the result of every sort of brush with people who were really living, like so very small a boy. No, no, one must stretch to one's tallest again. It restored one's stature a little then that one didn't now mind that this demonstration would prove to Jane, should she be waiting in the drawing-room and watching for one's return, that one had retained their guest for so much privacy in the porch. "Well, take care what you do!" Traffle bravely brought out for good-bye.

"Oh, I shall tell her," Puddick replied under the effect of his renewed pat of the back; and even, standing there an instant, had a further indulgence.

"She loathes my unfortunate name of course; but she's such an incalculable creature that my information possibly may fetch her."

There was a final suddenness of candour in it that made Traffle gape. "Oh, our names, and hers—! But is her loathing of yours then all that's the matter?"

Walter Puddick stood some seconds; he might, in pursuance of what had just passed, have been going to say things. But he had decided again the next moment for the fewest possible. "No!" he tossed back as he walked off.

V

"We seem to have got so beautifully used to it," Traffle remarked more than a month later to Jane—"we seem to have lived into it and through it so, and to have suffered and surmounted the worst, that, upon my word, I scarce see what's the matter now, or what, that's so very dreadful, it's doing or has done for us. We haven't the interest of her, no," he had gone on, slowly pacing and revolving things according to his wont, while the sharer of his life, tea being over and the service removed, reclined on a sofa, perfectly still and with her eyes rigidly closed; "we've lost that, and I agree that it was great—I mean the interest of the number of ideas the situation presented us with. That has dropped—by our own act, evidently; we must have simply settled the case, a month ago, in such a way as that we shall have no more acquaintance with it; by which I mean no more of the fun of it. I, for one, confess I miss the fun—put it only at the fun of our having had to wriggle so with shame, or, call it if you like, to live so under arms, against prying questions and the too easy exposure of our false explanations; which only proves, however, that, as I say, the worst that has happened to us appears to be that we're going to find life tame again—as tame as it was before ever Mora came into it so immensely to enrich and agitate it. She has gone out of it, obviously, to leave it flat and forlorn—tasteless after having had for so many months the highest flavour. If, by her not thanking you even though she declined, by her not acknowledging in any way your—as I admit—altogether munificent offer, it seems indicated that we should hold her to have definitely enrolled herself in the deplorable 'flaunting' class, we must at least recognize that she doesn't flaunt at *us*, at whomever else she may; and that she has in short cut us as neatly and effectively as, in the event of her conclusive, her supreme contumacy, we could have aspired to cut *her*. Never was a scandal, therefore, less scandalous—more naturally a disappointment, that is, to our good friends, whose resentment of this holy calm, this absence of any echo of any convulsion, of any sensation of any kind to be picked up, strikes me as ushering in the only form of ostracism our dissimulated taint, our connection with lurid facts that *might* have gone on making us rather eminently worth while, will have earned for us. But aren't custom and use breaking us in to the sense even of *that* anti-climax, and preparing for us future years of wistful, rueful, regretful thought of the time when everything was nice and dreadful?"

Mrs Traffle's posture was now, more and more, certainly, this recumbent sightless stillness; which she appeared to have resorted to at first—after the launching, that is, of her ultimatum to Mr Puddick—as a sign of the intensity with which she awaited results. There had been no results, alas, there were none from week to week; never was the strain of suspense less gratefully crowned; with the drawback, moreover, that they could settle to nothing—not even to the alternative, that of the cold consciousness of slighted magnanimity, in which Jane had assumed beforehand that she should find her last support. Her husband circled about her couch, with his eternal dim whistle, at a discreet distance—as certain as if he turned to catch her in the act that when his back was presented in thoughtful retreat her tightened eyes opened to rest on it with peculiar sharpness. She waited for the proof that she had intervened to advantage—the advantage of Mora's social future—and she had to put up with Sidney's watching her wait. So he, on his side, lived under her tacit criticism of that attention; and had they asked themselves, the comfortless pair—as it's in fact scarce conceivable that they didn't—what it would practically have cost them to receive their niece without questions, they might well have judged their present ordeal much the dearer. When Sidney had felt his wife glare at him undetectedly for a fortnight he knew at least what it meant, and if she had signified how much he might have to pay for it should he presume again to see Mora alone, she was now, in their community of a quietude that had fairly soured on their hands, getting ready to quarrel with him for his poverty of imagination about that menace. Absolutely, the conviction grew for him, she would have liked him better to do something, even something inconsiderate of her to the point of rudeness, than simply parade there in the deference that left her to languish. The fault of this conspicuous pro- priety, which gave on her nerves, was that it did nothing to refresh their decidedly rather starved sense of their case; so that Traffle was frankly merciless—frankly, that is, for himself —in his application of her warning. There was nothing he would indeed have liked better than to call on Mora—quite, as who should say, in the friendly way to which her own last visit at Wimbledon had set so bright an example. At the same time, though he revelled in his acute reflection as to the partner of his home—"I've only to go, and then come back with some 'new fact,' *à la Dreyfus*, in order to make her sit up in a false flare that will break our insufferable spell"—he was yet determined that the flare, certain to take place sooner or later, should precede his act; so large a licence might he then obviously build upon it. His excursions to town were on

occasion, even, in truth, not other than perverse—determined, that is, he was well aware, by their calculated effect on
Jane, who could imagine in his absence, each time, that he
might be "following something up" (an expression that had
in fact once slipped from her), might be having the gumption,
in other words, to glean a few straws for their nakeder nest;
imagine it, yes, only to feel herself fall back again on the mere
thorns of consistency.

It wasn't, nevertheless, that he took all his exercise to this
supersubtle tune; the state of his own nerves treated him at
moments to larger and looser exactions; which is why,
though poor Jane's sofa still remained his centre of radiation,
the span of his unrest sometimes embraced half London. He
had never been on such fidgety terms with his club, which he
could neither not resort to, from his suburb, with an unnatural frequency, nor make, in the event, any coherent use
of; so that his suspicion of his not remarkably carrying it off
there was confirmed to him, disconcertingly, one morning
when his dash townward had been particularly wild, by the
free address of a fellow-member prone always to overdoing
fellowship and who had doubtless for some time amusedly
watched his vague gyrations—"I say, Traff, old man, what
in the world, this time, have you got 'on'?" It had never been
anything but easy to answer the ass, and was easier than ever
now—"'On'? You don't suppose I dress, do you, to come
to meet *you?*"—yet the effect of the nasty little mirror of his
unsatisfied state so flashed before him was to make him afresh
wander wide, if wide half the stretch of Trafalgar Square
could be called. He turned into the National Gallery, where
the great Masters were tantalising more by their indifference
than by any offer of company, and where he could take up
again his personal tradition of a lawless range. One couldn't
be a *raffiné* at Wimbledon—no, not with any comfort; but he
quite liked to think how he had never been anything less in
the great museum, distinguished as he thus was from those

who gaped impartially and did the place by schools. *His* sympathies were special and far-scattered, just as the places of pilgrimage he most fondly reverted to were corners un-noted and cold, where the idol in the numbered shrine sat apart to await him.

So he found himself at the end of five minutes in one of the smaller, one of the Dutch rooms—in a temple bare in very fact at that moment save for just one other of the faithful. This was a young person—visibly young, from the threshold of the place, in spite of the back presented for an instant while a small picture before which she had stopped continued to hold her; but who turned at sound of his entering footfall, and who then again, as by an alertness in this movement, engaged his eyes. With which it was remarkably given to Traffle to feel himself recognize even almost to immediate, to artless extravagance of display, two things; the first that his fellow-votary in the unprofaned place and at the odd morning hour was none other than their invincible Mora, surprised, by this extraordinary fluke, in her invincibility, and the second (oh, his certainty of *that!*) that she was expecting to be joined there by no such pale fellow-adventurer as her whilom uncle. It amazed him, as it also annoyed him, on the spot, that his heart, for thirty seconds, should be standing almost still; but he wasn't to be able afterward to blink it that he had at once quite gone to pieces, any slight subsequent success in recovering himself to the contrary notwithstanding. Their happening thus to meet was obviously a wonder—it made him feel unprepared; but what especially did the business for him, he subsequently reflected, was again the renewed degree, and for that matter the developed kind, of importance that the girl's beauty gave her. Dear Jane, at home, as he knew—and as Mora herself probably, for that matter, did—was sunk in the conviction that she was leading a life; but whatever she was doing it was clearly the particular thing she might best be occupied with. How could anything be better for a lovely creature than thus to grow from month to month in loveliness?—so that she was able to stand there before him with no more felt inconvenience than the sense of the mere tribute of his eyes could promptly rectify.

That ministered positively to his weakness—the justice he did on the spot to the rare shade of human felicity, human impunity, human sublimity, call it what one would, surely dwelling in such a consciousness. How could a girl have to think long, have to think more than three-quarters of a second, under any stress whatever, of anything in the world but that her presence was an absolute incomparable value? The prodigious thing, too, was that it had had in the past, and the comparatively recent past that one easily recalled, to content itself with counting twenty times less: a proof precisely that any conditions so determined could only as a matter of course have been odious and, at the last, outrageous to her. Goodness knew with what glare of graceless inaction this rush of recognitions was accompanied in poor Traffle; who was later on to ask himself whether he had showed to less advantage in the freshness of his commotion or in the promptly enough subsequent rage of his coolness. The commotion, in any case, had doubtless appeared more to paralyze than to agitate him, since Mora had had time to come nearer while he showed for helplessly planted. He hadn't even at the moment been proud of his presence of mind, but it was as they afterward haunted his ear that the echoes of what he at first found to say were most odious to him.

"I'm glad to take your being here for a sign you've not lost your interest in Art"—that might have passed if he hadn't so almost feverishly floundered on. "I hope you keep up your painting—with such a position as you must be in for serious work: I always thought, you know, that you'd do something if you'd stick to it. In fact, we quite miss your not bringing us something to admire as you sometimes did; we haven't, you see, much of an art-atmosphere now. I'm glad you're fond of the Dutch—that little Metsu over there that I think you were looking at is a pet thing of my own; and, if my living to do something myself hadn't been the most idiotic of dreams, something in *his* line—though of course a thousand miles behind him—was what I should have tried to go in for. You see at any rate where—missing as I say our art-atmosphere—I have to come to find one. Not such a bad place certainly"—so he had hysterically gabbled; "especially at this quiet hour —as I see you yourself quite feel. I just turned in—though it does discourage! I hope, however, it hasn't that effect on *you*," he knew himself to grin with the last awkwardness; making it worse the next instant by the gay insinuation: "I'm bound to say it isn't how you look—discouraged!"

It reeked for him with reference even while he said it—for the truth was but too intensely, too insidiously, somehow, that her confidence implied, that it in fact bravely betrayed, grounds. He was to appreciate this wild waver, in retrospect, as positive dizziness in a narrow pass—the abyss being naturally on either side; that abyss of the facts of the girl's existence which he must thus have seemed to rush into, a smirking, a disgusting tribute to them through his excessive wish to show how clear he kept of them. The terrible, the fatal truth was that she made everything too difficult—or that this, at any rate, was how she enjoyed the exquisite privilege of affecting him. She watched him, she saw him splash to keep from sinking, with a pitiless cold sweet irony; she gave him rope as a syren on a headland might have been amused at some bather beyond his depth and unable to swim. It was all the fault—his want of ease was—of the real extravagance of his idea of not letting her spy even the tip of the tail of any "freedom" with her; thanks to which fatality she had indeed the game in her own hands. She exhaled a distinction—it glanced out of every shade of selection, every turn of expression, in her dress, though she had always, for that matter, had the genius of felicity there—which was practically the "new fact" all Wimbledon had been awaiting; and yet so perverse was their relation that to mark at all any special consideration for it was to appear just to make the allusion he was most forbidding himself. It was hard, his troubled consciousness told him, to be able neither to overlook her new facts without brutality nor to recognize them without impertinence; and he was frankly at the end of his resources by the time he ceased beating the air. Then it was, yes, then it was perfectly, as if she had patiently let him show her each of his ways of making a fool of himself; when she still said nothing a moment—and yet still managed to keep him ridiculous—as if for certainty on that head. It was true that when she at last spoke she swept everything away.

"It's a great chance my meeting you—for what you so kindly think of me."

She brought that out as if he had been uttering mere vain sounds—to which she preferred the comparative seriousness of the human, or at least of the mature, state, and her unexpectedness it was that thus a little stiffened him up. "What I think of you? How do you know what I think?"

She dimly and charmingly smiled at him, for it wasn't really that she was harsh. She was but infinitely remote—the syren on her headland dazzlingly in view, yet communicating, precisely, over such an abyss. "Because it's so much more, you mean, than you know yourself? If you don't know yourself, if you know as little as, I confess, you strike me as doing," she, however, at once went on, "I'm more sorry for you than anything else; even though at the best, I dare say, it must seem odd to you to hear me so patronizing." It was borne in upon him thus that she would now make no difference, to his honour—to that of his so much more emancipated spirit at least—between her aunt and her uncle; so much should the poor uncle enjoy for his pains. He should stand or fall with fatal Jane—for at this point he was already sure Jane had been fatal; it was in fact with fatal Jane tied as a

millstone round his neck that he at present knew himself
sinking. "You try to make grabs at some idea, but the simplest
never occurs to you."

"What do you call the simplest, Mora?" he at this heard
himself whine.

"Why, my being simply a good girl. You gape at it"—he
was trying exactly not to—"as if it passed your belief; but
it's really all the while, to my own sense, what has been the
matter with me. I mean, you see, a good creature—wanting to
live at peace. Everything, however, occurs to you but that
—and in spite of my trying to show you. You never understood," she said with her sad, quiet lucidity, "what I came
to see you for two months ago." He was on the point of
breaking in to declare that the reach of his intelligence at the
juncture of which she spoke had been quite beyond expression; but he checked himself in time, as it would strike her
but as a vague weak effort to make exactly the distinction that
she held cheap. No, he wouldn't give Jane away now—he'd
suffer anything instead; the taste of what he should have to
suffer was already there on his lips—it came over him, to the
strangest effect of desolation, of desolation made certain, that
they should have lost Mora for ever, and that this present
scant passage must count for them as her form of rupture.
Jane had treated her the other day—treated her, that is,
through Walter Puddick, who would have been, when all
was said, a faithful agent—to *their* form, their form save on
the condition attached, much too stiff a one, no doubt; so that
he was actually having the extraordinary girl's answer. What
they thought of her was that she was Walter Puddick's mistress—the only difference between them being that whereas
her aunt fixed the character upon her as by the act of tying a
neatly-inscribed luggage-tag to a bandbox, he himself flourished about with *his* tag in his hand and a portentous grin for
what he could do with it if he would. She brushed aside alike,
however, vulgar label and bewildered formula; she but took

Jane's message as involving an insult, and if she treated him, as a participant, with any shade of humanity, it was indeed that she was the good creature for whom she had a moment ago claimed credit. Even under the sense of so supreme a pang poor Traffle could value his actual, his living, his wonderful impression, rarest treasure of sense, as what the whole history would most have left with him. It was all he should have of her in the future—the mere memory of these dreadful minutes in so noble a place, minutes that were shining easy grace on her part and helpless humiliation on his; wherefore, tragically but instinctively, he gathered in, as for preservation, every grain of the experience. That was it; they had given her, without intending it, still wider wings of freedom; the clue, the excuse, the pretext, whatever she might call it, for shaking off any bond that had still incommoded her. She was spreading her wings—that was what he saw—as if she hovered, rising and rising, like an angel in a vision; it was the picture that he might, if he chose, or mightn't, make Jane, on his return, sit up to. Truths, these, that for our interest in him, or for our grasp of them, press on us in succession, but that within his breast were quick and simultaneous; so that it was virtually without a wait he heard her go on. "Do try—that's really all I want to say—to keep hold of my husband."

"Your husband—?" He *did* gape.

She had the oddest charming surprise—her nearest approach to familiarity. "Walter Puddick. Don't you know I'm married?" And then, as for the life of him he still couldn't but stare: "Hasn't he told you?"

"Told us? Why, we haven't seen him—"

"Since the day you so put the case to him? Oh, I should have supposed—!" She would have supposed, obviously, that he might in some way have communicated the fact; but she clearly hadn't so much as assured herself of it. "Then there exactly he is—he doesn't seem, poor dear, to know what to do." And she had on his behalf, apparently, a moment of beautiful, anxious, yet at the same time detached and all momentary thought. "That's just then what I mean."

"My dear child," Traffle gasped, "what on earth *do* you mean?"

"Well"—and she dropped for an instant comparatively to within his reach—"that it's where you *can* come in. Where in fact, as I say, I quite wish you would!"

All his wondering attention for a moment hung upon her. "Do you ask me, Mora, to *do* something for you?"

"Yes"—and it was as if no "good creature" had ever been so beautiful, nor any beautiful creature ever so good—"to make him your care. To see that he does get it."

"Get it?" Traffle blankly echoed.

"Why, what you promised him. My aunt's money."

He felt his countenance an exhibition. "She promised it, Mora, to *you*."

"If I married him, yes—because I wasn't fit for her to speak to till I should. But if I'm now proudly Mrs Puddick—"

He had already, however, as with an immense revulsion, a long jump, taken her up: "You are, you *are*—?" He gaped at the difference it made, and in which then, immensely, they seemed to recover her.

"Before all men—and the Registrar."

"The Registrar?" he again echoed; so that, with another turn of her humour, it made her lift her eyebrows at him.

"You mean it doesn't hold if *that's* the way—?"

"It holds, Mora, I suppose, any way—that makes a real marriage. It is," he hopefully smiled, "real?"

"Could anything be more real," she asked, "than to have become such a thing?"

"Walter Puddick's wife?" He kept his eyes on her pleadingly. "Surely, Mora, it's a *good* thing—clever and charming as he is." Now that Jane had succeeded, his instinct, of a sudden, was to back her up.

Mrs Puddick's face—and the fact was it was strange, in the light of her actual aspect, to think of her and name her so—showed, however, as ready a disposition. "If he's as much as that then why were you so shocked by my relations with him?"

He panted—he cast about. "Why, we didn't doubt of his distinction—of what it was at any rate likely to become."

"You only doubted of mine?" she asked with her harder look.

He threw up helpless arms, he dropped them while he gazed at her. "It doesn't seem to me possible any one can ever have questioned your gift for doing things in your own way. And if you're now married," he added with his return of tentative presumption and his strained smile, "your own way opens out for you, doesn't it? as never yet."

Her eyes, on this, held him a moment, and he couldn't have said now what was in them. "I think it does. I'm seeing," she said—"I shall see. Only"—she hesitated but for an instant—"for that it's necessary you shall look after him."

They stood there face to face on it—during a pause that, lighted by her radiance, gave him time to take from her, somehow, larger and stranger things than either might at all intelligibly or happily have named. "Do you ask it of me?"

"I ask it of you," said Mrs Puddick after a wait that affected him as giving his contribution to her enjoyment of that title as part of her reason.

He held out, however—contribution or no contribution—another moment. "Do you beg me very hard?"

Once more she hung fire—but she let him have it. "I beg you very hard."

It made him turn pale. "Thank you," he said; and it was as if now he didn't care what monstrous bargain he passed with her—which was fortunate, for that matter, since, when she next spoke, the quantity struck him as looming large.

"I want to be free."

"How can you not?" said Sidney Traffle, feeling, to the most extraordinary tune, at one and the same time both sublime and base; and quite vague, as well as indifferent, as to which character prevailed.

"But I don't want him, you see, to suffer."

Besides the opportunity that this spread before him, he could have blessed her, could have embraced her, for "you see." "Well, I promise you he shan't suffer if I can help it."

"Thank you," she said in a manner that gave him, if possible, even greater pleasure yet, showing him as it did, after all, what an honest man she thought him. He even at that point had his apprehension of the queerness of the engagement that, as an honest man, he was taking—the engagement, since she so "wanted to be free," to relieve her, so far as he devotedly might, of any care hampering this ideal; but his perception took a tremendous bound as he noticed that their interview had within a moment become exposed to observation. A reflected light in Mora's face, caught from the quarter behind him, suddenly so advised him and caused him to turn, with the consequence of his seeing a gentleman in the doorway by which he had entered—a gentleman in the act of replacing the hat raised to salute Mrs Puddick and with an accompanying smile still vivid in a clear, fresh, well-featured face. Everything took for Sidney Traffle a sharper sense from this apparition, and he had, even while the fact of the nature of his young friend's business there, the keeping of an agreeable appointment in discreet conditions, stood out for him again as in its odd insolence of serenity and success, the consciousness that whatever his young friend was doing, whatever she was "up to," he was now quite as much in the act of backing her as the gentleman in the doorway, a slightly mature, but strikingly well-dressed, a pleasantly masterful-looking gentleman, a haunter of the best society, one could be sure, was waiting for him to go. Mora herself, promptly, had that apprehension, and conveyed it to him, the next thing, in words that amounted, with their sweet conclusive look, to a decent dismissal. "Here's what's of *real* importance to me," she seemed to say; "so, though I count on you, I needn't keep you longer." But she took time in fact just to revert. "I've asked him to go to you; and he will, I'm sure, he *will:* by which you'll have your chance, don't fear! Good-bye." She spoke as if this "chance" were what he would now at once be most yearning for; and thus it was that, while he stayed but long enough to let his eyes move again to the new, the impatient and distinctly "smart," yes, unmistakably, this time, not a bit Bohemian candidate for her attention, and then let them come back to herself as for some grasp of the question of a relation already so developed, there might have hung itself up there the prospect of an infinite future of responsibility about Walter Puddick—if only as a make-weight perhaps to the extinction of everything else. When he had turned his back and begun humbly to shuffle, as it seemed to him, through a succession of shining rooms where the walls bristled with eyes that watched him for mockery, his sense was of having seen the last of Mora as completely as if she had just seated herself in the car of a rising balloon that would never descend again to earth.

VI

It was before that aspect of the matter, at any rate, that Sidney Traffle made a retreat which he would have had to regard as the most abject act of his life hadn't he just savingly been able to regard it as the most lucid. The aftertaste of that quality of an intelligence in it sharp even to soreness was to remain with him, intensely, for hours—to the point in fact (which says all) of rendering necessary a thoughtful return to his club rather than a direct invocation of the society of his wife. He ceased, for the rest of the day there, to thresh about; that phase, sensibly, was over for him; he dropped into a deep chair, really exhausted, quite spent, and in this posture yielded to reflections too grave for accessory fidgets. They were so grave, or were at least so interesting, that it was long since he had been for so many hours without thinking of Jane—of whom he didn't even dream after he had at last inevitably, reacting from weeks of tension that were somehow ended for ever, welcomed a deep foodless doze which held him till it was time to order tea. He woke to partake, still meditatively, of that repast—yet, though late the hour and quite exceptional the length of his absence, with his domestic wantonness now all gone and no charm in the thought of how Jane would be worried. He probably shouldn't be wanton, it struck him, ever again in his life; that tap had run dry—had suffered an immense, a conclusive diversion from the particular application of its flow to Jane.

This truth indeed, I must add, proved of minor relevance on his standing before that lady, in the Wimbledon drawing-room, considerably after six o'clock had struck, and feeling himself in presence of revelations prepared not only to match, but absolutely to ignore and override, his own. He hadn't put it to himself that if the pleasure of stretching her on the rack appeared suddenly to have dropped for him this was because "it"—by which he would have meant everything else—was too serious; but *had* he done so he would at once have indulged in the amendment that he himself certainly was. His wife had in any case risen from the rack, the "bed of steel" that, in the form of her habitual, her eternal, her plaintive, aggressive sofa, had positively a pushed-back and relegated air—an air to the meaning of which a tea-service that fairly seemed to sprawl and that even at such an hour still almost unprecedentedly lingered, added the very accent of recent agitations. He hadn't been able not to consult himself a little as to the strength of the dose, or as to the protraction

of the series of doses, in which he should administer the
squeezed fruit, the expressed and tonic liquor, of his own
adventure; but the atmosphere surrounding Jane herself was
one in which he felt questions of that order immediately drop.
The atmosphere surrounding Jane had been, in fine, on no
occasion that he could recall, so perceptibly thick, so abruptly
rich, so charged with strange aromas; he could really almost
have fancied himself snuff up from it a certain strength of
transient tobacco, the trace of a lately permitted cigarette or
two at the best—rarest of accidents and strangest of discords
in that harmonious whole. Had she, gracious goodness, been
smoking with somebody?—a possibility not much less lurid
than this conceived extravagance of the tolerated, the independent pipe.

Yes, absolutely, she eyed him through a ranker medium
than had ever prevailed between them by any perversity of
his; eyed him quite as if prepared, in regular tit-for-tat
fashion, to stretch *him*, for a change, on his back, to let him
cool his heels in that posture while she sauntered in view
pointedly enough for him to tell her how he liked it. Something had happened to her in his absence that made her quite
indifferent, in other words, to what might have happened to
any one else at all; and so little had he to fear asperity on the
score of his selfish day off that she didn't even see the advantage to her, for exasperation of his curiosity, of holding him at
such preliminary arm's-length as would be represented by a
specious "scene." She would have liked him, he easily recognized, to burst with curiosity, or, better still, to grovel with
it, before she should so much as throw him a sop; but just
this artless pride in her it was that, by the very candour of
its extravagance, presently helped him to a keen induction.
He had only to ask himself what could have occurred that
would most of all things conduce to puffing her up with
triumph, and then to reflect that, thoroughly to fill that bill, as
who should say, she must have had a contrite call from

Mora. He knew indeed, consummately, how superior a resource to morbid contrition that young woman was actually
cultivating; in accordance with which the next broadest base
for her exclusive command of the situation—and she clearly
claimed nothing else—would be the fact that Walter Puddick
had been with her and that she had had him (and to the tune
of odd revelry withal to which their disordered and unremoved cups glaringly testified) all to herself. Such an interview with him as had so uplifted her that she distractedly had
failed to ring for the parlour-maid, with six o'clock ebbing in
strides—this did tell a story, Traffle ruefully recognized, with
which it might well verily yet be given her to work on him.
He was promptly to feel, none the less, how he carried the
war across her border, poor superficial thing, when he decided on the direct dash that showed her she had still to count
with him.

He didn't offer her, as he looked about, the mere obvious
"I see you've had visitors, or a visitor, and have smoked a
pipe with them and haven't bored yourself the least mite"—
he broke straight into: "He has come out here again then, the
wretch, and you've done him more justice? You've done him
a good deal, my dear," he laughed in the grace of his advantage, "if you've done him even half as much as he appears to
have done your tea-table!" For this the quick flash-light of his
imagination—that's what it *was* for her to have married an
imaginative man—was just the drop of a flying-machine into
her castle court while she stood on guard at the gate. She
gave him a harder look, and he feared he might kindle by
too great an ease—as he was far from prematurely wishing to
do—her challenge of his own experience. Her flush of presumption turned in fact, for the instant, to such a pathetically
pale glare that, before he knew it, conscious of his resources
and always coming characteristically round to indulgence as
soon as she at all gave way, he again magnanimously abdi-
cated. "He came to say it's no use?" he went on, and from

that moment knew himself committed to secrecy. It had tided
him over the few seconds of his danger—that of Jane's de-
manding of him what he had been up to. He didn't want to be
asked, no; and his not being asked guarded his not—yes—
positively lying; since what most of all now filled his spirit
was that he shouldn't himself positively *have* to speak. His
not doing so would be his keeping something all to himself—
as Jane would have liked, for the six-and-a-half minutes of
her strained, her poor fatuous chance, to keep her passage
with Puddick; or to do this, in any case, till he could feel her
resist what would certainly soon preponderantly make for
her wish to see him stare at her producible plum. It wasn't,
moreover, that he could on his own side so fully withstand
wonder; the wonder of this new singular ground of sociability
between persons hitherto seeing so little with the same eyes.
There were things that fitted—fitted somehow the fact of the
young man's return, and he could feel in his breast-pocket,
when it came to that, the presence of the very key to almost
any blind or even wild motion, as a sign of trouble, on poor
Puddick's part; but what and where was the key to the
mystery of Jane's sudden pride in his surely at the best very
queer communication? The eagerness of this pride it was, at
all events, that after a little so worked as to enable him to
breathe again for his own momentarily menaced treasure.
"They're married—they've been married a month; not a bit
as one would have wished, or by any form decent people
recognize, but with the effect, at least, he tells me, that she's
now legally his wife and he legally her husband, so that
neither can marry any one else, and that—and that—"

"And that she has taken his horrid name, under our pressure, in exchange for her beautiful one—the one that so fitted
her and that we ourselves when all was said, did like so to
keep repeating, in spite of everything, you won't deny, for
the pleasant showy thing, compared with our own and most
of our friends', it was to have familiarly about?" He took her

up with this, as she had faltered a little over the other sources of comfort provided for them by the union so celebrated; in addition to which his ironic speech gained him time for the less candid, and thereby more cynically indulgent, profession of entire surprise. And he immediately added: "They've gone in for the mere civil marriage?"

"She appears to have consented to the very least of one that would do: they looked in somewhere, at some dingy office, jabbered a word or two to a man without h's and with a pen behind his ear, signed their names, and then came out as good as you and me; very much as you and I the other day sent off that little postal-packet to Paris from our grocer's back-shop."

Traffle showed his interest—he took in the news. "Well, you know, you didn't make Church a condition."

"No—fortunately not. I was clever enough," Jane bridled, "for that."

She had more for him, her manner showed—she had that to which the bare fact announced was as nothing; but he saw he must somehow, yes, pay by knowing nothing more than he could catch at by brilliant guesses. That had after an instant become a comfort to him: it would legitimate dissimulation, just as this recognized necessity would make itself quickly felt as the mere unregarded underside of a luxury. "And they're at all events, I take it," he went on, "sufficiently tied to be divorced."

She kept him—but only for a moment. "Quite sufficiently, I gather; and that," she said, "may come."

She made him, with it, quite naturally start. "Are they thinking of it already?"

She looked at him another instant hard, as with the rich expression of greater stores of private knowledge than she could adapt all at once to his intelligence. "You've no conception—not the least!—of how he feels."

Her husband hadn't hereupon, he admitted to himself, all

artificially to gape. "Of course I haven't, love." Now that
he had decided not to give his own observation away—and
this however Puddick might "feel"—he should find it doubtless easy to be affectionate. "But he had been telling *you* all
about it?"

"He has been here nearly two hours—as you of course, so
far as that went, easily guessed. Nominally—at first—he had
come out to see you; but he asked for me on finding you
absent, and when I had come in to him seemed to want
nothing better—"

"Nothing better than to stay and stay, Jane?" he smiled
as he took her up. "Why in the world should he? What I
ask myself," Traffle went on, "is simply how in the world
you yourself could bear it." She turned away from him,
holding him now, she judged, in a state of dependence; she
reminded him even of himself, at similar moments of her own
asservissement, when he turned his back upon her to walk
about and keep her unsatisfied; an analogy markedly perceptible on her pausing a moment as under her first impression
of the scattered tea-things and then ringing to have them
attended to. Their domestic, retarded Rebecca, almost fiercely
appeared, and her consequent cold presence in the room and
inevitably renewed return to it, by the open door, for several
minutes, drew out an interval during which he felt nervous
again lest it should occur to his wife to wheel round on him
with a question. She did nothing of the sort, fortunately; she
was as stuffed with supersessive answers as if she were the
latest number of a penny periodical: it was only a matter still
of his continuing to pay his penny. She wasn't, moreover, his
attention noted, trying to be portentous; she was much
rather secretly and perversely serene—the basis of which
condition did a little tax his fancy. What on earth had Puddick
done to her—since he hadn't been able to bring her out Mora
—that had made her distinguishably happier beneath the
mere grimness of her finally scoring at home than she had

been for so many months? The best she could have learned from him—Sidney might even at this point have staked his life upon it—wouldn't have been that she could hope to make Mrs Puddick the centre of a grand rehabilitative tea-party. "Why then," he went on again, "if they were married a month ago and he was so ready to stay with you two hours, hadn't he come sooner?"

"He didn't come to tell me they were married—not on purpose for that," Jane said after a little and as if the fact itself were scarce more than a trifle—compared at least with others she was possessed of, but that she didn't yet mention.

"Well"—Traffle frankly waited now—"what in the world *did* he come to tell you?"

She made no great haste with it. "His fears."

"What fears—at present?" he disingenuously asked.

"'At present?' Why, it's just 'at present' that he feels he has got to look out." Yes, she was distinctly, she was strangely placid about it. "It's worse to have them now that she's his wife, don't you understand?" she pursued as if he were really almost beginning to try her patience. "His difficulties aren't over," she nevertheless condescended further to mention.

She was irritating, decidedly; but he could always make the reflection that if she had been truly appointed to wear him out she would long since have done so. "What difficulties," he accordingly continued, "are you talking about?"

"Those my splendid action—for he grants perfectly that it *is* and will remain splendid—have caused for him." But her calmness, her positive swagger of complacency over it, *was* indeed amazing.

"Do you mean by your having so forced his hand?" Traffle had now no hesitation in risking.

"By my having forced *hers*," his wife presently returned. "By my glittering bribe, as he calls it."

He saw in a moment how she liked what her visitor had

called things; yet it made him, himself, but want more. "She found your bribe so glittering that she couldn't resist it?"

"She couldn't resist it." And Jane sublimely stalked. "She consented to perform the condition attached—as I've mentioned to you—for enjoying it."

Traffle artfully considered. "If she has met you on that arrangement where do the difficulties come in?"

Jane looked at him a moment with wonderful eyes. "For me? They don't come in!" And she again turned her back on him.

It really tempted him to permit himself a certain impatience —which in fact he might have shown hadn't he by this time felt himself more intimately interested in Jane's own evolution than in Mrs Puddick's, or even, for the moment, in Mora's. That interest ministered to his art. "You must tell me at your convenience about yours, that is about your apparently feeling yourself now so beautifully able to sink yours. What I'm asking you about is his—if you've put them so at their ease."

"I haven't put them a bit at their ease!"—and she was at him with it again almost as in a glow of triumph.

He aimed at all possible blankness. "But surely four hundred and fifty more a year—!"

"Four hundred and fifty more is nothing to her."

"Then why the deuce did she marry him for it?—since she apparently couldn't bring herself to without it."

"She didn't marry him that she herself should get my allowance—she married him that *he* should."

At which Traffle had a bit genuinely to wonder. "It comes at any rate to the same if you pay it to her."

Nothing, it would seem, could possibly have had on Jane's state of mind a happier effect. "I shan't pay it to her."

Her husband could again but stare. "You *won't*, dear?" he deprecated.

12:X

"I don't," she nobly replied. And then as at last for one of her greater cards: "I pay it to *him*."

"But if he pays it to *her*—?"

"He doesn't. He explains."

Traffle cast about. "Explains—a—to Mora?"

"Explains to me. He *has*," she almost defiantly bridled, "perfectly explained."

Her companion smiled at her. "Ah, *that* then is what took him two hours!" He went on, however, before she could either attenuate or amplify: "It must have taken him that of course to arrange with you—as I understand?—for his monopolising the money?"

She seemed to notify him now that from her high command of the situation she could quite look down on the spiteful sarcastic touch. "We have plenty to arrange. We have plenty to discuss. We shall often—if you want to know—have occasion to meet." After which, "Mora," she quite gloriously brought forth, "hates me worse than ever."

He opened his eyes to their widest. "For settling on her a substantial fortune?"

"For having"—and Jane had positively a cold smile for it—"believed her not respectable."

"Then *was* she?" Traffle gaped.

It did turn on him the tables! "Mr Puddick continues to swear it." But even though so gracefully patient of him she remained cold.

"You yourself, however, haven't faith?"

"No," said Mrs Traffle.

"In his word, you mean?"

She had a fine little wait. "In her conduct. In his knowledge of it."

Again he had to rise to it. "With other persons?"

"With other persons. Even then."

Traffle thought. "But even when?"

"Even from the first," Jane grandly produced.

"Oh, oh, oh!" he found himself crying with a flush. He had had occasion to colour in the past for her flatness, but never for such an audacity of point. Wonderful, all round, in the light of reflection, seemed what Mora was doing for them. "It won't be her husband, at all events, who has put you up to *that!*"

She took this in as if it might have been roguishly insinuating in respect to her own wit—though not, as who should say, to make any great use of it. "It's what I read—"

"What you 'read'—?" he asked as she a little hung fire.

"Well, into the past that from far back so troubled me. I had plenty to tell *him!*" she surprisingly went on.

"Ah, my dear, to the detriment of his own wife?" our friend broke out.

It earned him, however, but her at once harder and richer look. Clearly she was at a height of satisfaction about something—it spread and spread more before him. "For all that really, you know, she *is* now his wife!"

He threw himself amazedly back. "You mean she practically isn't?" And then as her eyes but appeared to fill it out: "Is that what you've been having from him?—and is that what we've done?"

She looked away a little—she turned off again. "Of course I've wanted the full truth—as to what I've done."

Our friend could imagine that, at strict need; but wondrous to him with it was this air in her as of the birth of a new detachment. "What you've 'done,' it strikes me, might be a little embarrassing for us; but you speak as if you really quite enjoyed it!"

This was a remark, he had to note, by which she wasn't in the least confounded; so that if he had his impression of that odd novelty in her to which allusion has just been made, it might indeed have been quite a new Jane who now looked at him out of her conscious eyes. "He likes to talk to me, poor dear."

She treated his observation as if that quite met it—which

couldn't but slightly irritate him; but he hadn't in the least abjured self-control, he was happy to feel, on his returning at once: "And you like to talk with *him*, obviously—since he appears so beautifully and quickly to have brought you round from your view of him as merely low."

She flushed a little at this reminder, but it scarcely pulled her up. "I never thought him low"—she made no more of it than that; "but I admit," she quite boldly smiled, "that I did think him wicked."

"And it's now your opinion that people can be wicked without being low?"

Prodigious, really, he found himself make out while she just hesitated, the opinions over the responsibility of which he should yet see her—and all as a consequence of this one afternoon of his ill-inspired absence—ready thus unnaturally to smirk at him. "It depends," she complacently brought out, "on the kind."

"On the kind of wickedness?"

"Yes, perhaps. And"—it didn't at all baffle her—"on the kind of people."

"I see. It's all, my dear, I want to get at—for a proper understanding of the extraordinary somersault you appear to have turned. Puddick has just convinced you that *his* immoralities are the right ones?"

"No, love—nothing will ever convince me that any immoralities deserve that name. But some," she went on, "only seem wrong till they're explained."

"And those are the ones that, as you say, he has been explaining?" Traffle asked with a glittering, cheerful patience.

"He has explained a great deal, yes"—Jane bore up under it; "but I think that, by the opportunity for a good talk with him, I've at last understood even more. We weren't, you see, before," she obligingly added, "in his confidence."

"No, indeed," her husband opined, "we could scarcely be said to be. But now we are, and it makes the difference?"

"It makes the difference to *me*," Jane nobly contented herself with claiming. "If I've been remiss, however," she showed herself prepared to pursue, "I must make it up. And doubtless I *have* been."

" 'Remiss,' " he stared, "when you're in full enjoyment of my assent to our making such sacrifices for her?"

She gave it, in her superior way, a moment's thought. "I don't mean remiss in act; no, that, thank goodness, we haven't been. But remiss in feeling," she quite unbearably discriminated.

"Ah, that, *par exemple*," he protested, "I deny that I've been for a moment!"

"No"—and she fairly mused at him; "you seemed to have all sorts of ideas; while I," she conceded, "had only one, which, so far as it went, was good. But it didn't go far enough."

He watched her a moment. "I doubtless don't know what idea you mean," he smiled, "but how far does it go now?"

She hadn't, with her preoccupied eyes on him, so much as noticed the ironic ring of it. "Well, you'll see for yourself. I mustn't abandon him."

"Abandon Puddick? Who the deuce then ever said you must?"

"Didn't *you* a little," she blandly inquired, "all the while you were so great on our not 'interfering'?"

"I was great—if great you call it—only," he returned, "so far as I was great for our just a little understanding."

"Well, what I'm telling you is that I think I do at present just a little understand."

"And doesn't it make you feel just a little badly?"

"No"—she serenely shook her head; "for my intention was so good. He does justice now," she explained, "to my intention; or he will very soon—he quite let me *see* that, and it's why I'm what you call 'happy.' With which," she wound up, "there's so much more I can still do. There are bad days, you see, before him—and then he'll have only me. For if she *was* respectable," Jane proceeded, reverting as imperturbably to their question of a while back, "she's certainly not nice now."

He'd be hanged, Traffle said to himself, if he wouldn't look at her hard. "Do you mean by not coming to thank you?" And then as she but signified by a motion that this she had now made her terms with: "What else then is the matter with her?"

"The matter with her," said Jane on the note of high deliberation and competence, and not without a certain pity for his own want of light, "the matter with her is that she's quite making her preparations, by what he's convinced, for leaving him."

"Leaving him?"—he met it with treasures of surprise.

These were nothing, however, he could feel, to the wealth of authority with which she again gave it out. "Leaving him."

"A month after marriage?"

"A month after—their form; and she seems to think it handsome, he says, that she waited the month. *That*," she added, "is what he came above all that we should know."

He took in, our friend, many things in silence; but he presently had his comment. "We've done our job then to an even livelier tune than we could have hoped!"

Again this moral of it all didn't appear to shock her. "He doesn't reproach me," she wonderfully said.

"I'm sure it's very good of him then!" Traffle cried.

But her blandness, her mildness, was proof. "My dear Sidney, Walter *is* very good."

She brought it out as if she had made, quite unaided, the discovery; though even this, perhaps, was not what he most stared at. "Do you call him Walter?"

"Surely"—and she returned surprise for surprise—"isn't he my nephew?"

Traffle bethought himself. "You recognize the Registrar then for *that*."

She could perfectly smile back. "I don't know that I would if our friend weren't so interesting."

It was quite for Sidney Traffle, at this, as if he hadn't known up to that moment, filled for him with her manner of intimating her reason, what sort of a wife—for coolness and other things—he rejoiced in. Really he had to take time—and to throw himself, while he did so, into pretences. "The Registrar?"

"Don't be a goose, dear!"—she showed she could humour him at last; and it was perhaps the most extraordinary impression he had ever in his life received. "But you'll see," she continued in this spirit. "I mean how I shall interest you." And then as he but seemed to brood at her: "Interest you, I mean, in my interest—for I shan't content myself," she beautifully professed, "with your simply not minding it."

"Minding your interest?" he frowned.

"In my poor ravaged, lacerated, pathetic nephew. I shall expect you in some degree to share it."

"Oh, I'll share it if you like, but you must remember how little I'm responsible."

She looked at him abysmally. "No—it *was* mainly me. He brings that home to me, poor dear. Oh, he doesn't scare me!" —she kept it up; "and I don't know that I want him to, for it seems to clear the whole question, and really to ease me a little, that he should put everything before me, his grievance with us, I mean, and that I should know just how he has seen our attitude, or at any rate mine. I was stupid the other day when he came—he saw but a part of it then. It's settled," she further mentioned, "that I shall go to him."

"Go to him—?" Traffle blankly echoed.

"At his studio, dear, you know," Jane promptly supplied. "I want to see his work—for we had some talk about that too. He has made me care for it."

Her companion took these things in—even so many of them as there now seemed to be: they somehow left him, in point of fact, so stranded. "Why not call on *her* at once?"

"That will be useless when she won't receive me. Never, never!" said Jane with a sigh so confessedly superficial that her husband found it peculiarly irritating.

"He has brought *that* 'home' to you?" he consequently almost jibed.

She winced no more, however, than if he had tossed her a flower. "Ah, what he has made me realize is that if he has definitely lost her, as he feels, so we ourselves assuredly have, for ever and a day. But he doesn't mean to lose sight of her, and in that way——"

"In that way?"—Traffle waited.

"Well, I shall always hear whatever there may be. And there's no knowing," she developed as with an open and impartial appetite, "what that mayn't come to."

He turned away—with his own conception of this possible expansive quantity and a sore sense of how the combinations of things were appointed to take place without his aid or presence, how they kept failing to provide for him at all. It was his old irony of fate, which seemed to insist on meeting him at every turn. Mora had testified in the morning to no further use for him than might reside in his making her shuffled-off lover the benevolent business of his life; but even in this cold care, clearly, he was forestalled by a person to whom it would come more naturally. It was by his original and independent measure that the whole case had become interesting and been raised above the level of a mere vulgar scandal; in spite of which he could now stare but at the prospect of exclusion, and of his walking round it, through the coming years—to walk vaguely round and round announcing itself thus at the best as the occupation of his future—in wider and remoter circles. As against this, for warmth, there would nestle in his breast but a prize of memory, the poor little secret of the passage at the Gallery that the day had bequeathed him. He might propose to hug this treasure of consciousness, to make it, by some ingenuity he couldn't yet forecast, his very own; only it was a poor thing in view of their positive privation, and what Jane was getting out of the whole business —*her* ingenuity it struck him he could quite forecast—would certainly be a comparative riot of sympathy. He stood with his hands in his pockets and gazed a little, very sightlessly— that is with an other than ranging vision, even though not other than baffled one too—out of the glimmering square of the window. Then, however, he recalled himself, slightly shook himself, and the next moment had faced about with a fresh dissimulation. "If you talk of her leaving him, and he himself comes in for all your bounty, what then is she going to live upon?"

"On her wits, he thinks and fears; on her beauty, on her audacity. Oh, it's a picture—!" Jane was now quite un-shrinkingly able to report from her visitor. Traffle, morally fingering, as it were, the mystic medal under his shirt, was at least equally qualified, on his side, to gloom all yearningly at her; but she had meanwhile testified further to her consistent command of their position. "He believes her to be more than ever—*not* 'respectable.'"

"How, 'more than ever,' if respectable was what she *was?*"

"It was what she wasn't!" Jane returned.

He had a prodigious shrug—it almost eased him for the moment of half his impatience. "I understood that you told me a moment ago the contrary."

"Then you understood wrong. All I said was that he says she was—but that I don't believe him."

He wondered, following. "Then how does he come to describe her as less so?"

Jane straightened it out—Jane surpassed herself. "He doesn't describe her as less so than she 'was'—I only put her at that. *He*"—oh, she was candid and clear about it!— "simply puts her at less so than she might be. In order, don't you see," she luminously reasoned, "that we shall have it on our conscience that we took the case out of his hands."

"And you allowed to him then that that's how we do have it?"

To this her face lighted as never yet. "Why, it's just the point of what I tell you—that I feel I *must*."

He turned it over. "But why so if you're right?"

She brought up her own shoulders for his density. "I haven't been right. I've been wrong."

He could only glare about. "In holding her then already to have fallen—?"

"Oh, dear, no, not that! In having let it work me up. Of course I can but take from him now," she elucidated, "what he insists on."

Her husband measured it. "Of course, in other words, you can but believe she was as bad as possible and yet pretend to him he has persuaded you of the contrary?"

"Exactly, love—so that it shall make us worse. As bad as he wants us," she smiled.

"In order," Traffle said after a moment, "that he may comfortably take the money?"

She welcomed this gleam. "In order that he may comfortably take it."

He could but gaze at her again. "You *have* arranged it!"

"Certainly I have—and that's why I'm calm. He considers, at any rate," she continued, "that it will probably be Sir Bruce. I mean that she'll leave him for."

"And who in the world is Sir Bruce?"

She consulted her store of impressions. "Sir Bruce Bagley, Bart., I think he said."

Traffle fitted it in silence. "A soldier?" he then asked.

"I'm uncertain—but, as I seem to remember, a patron. He buys pictures."

Traffle could privately imagine it. "And that's how she knows him?"

Jane allowed for his simplicity. "Oh, how she 'knows' people—!"

It still held him, however, an instant. "What sort of a type?"

She seemed to wonder a little at his press of questions, but after just facing it didn't pretend to more than she knew. She was, on this basis of proper relations that she had settled, more and more willing, besides, to oblige. "I'll find out for you."

It came in a tone that made him turn off. "Oh, I don't mind." With which he was back at the window.

She hovered—she didn't leave him; he felt her there behind him as if she had noted a break in his voice or a moisture in his eyes—a tribute to a natural pang even for a not real niece. He wouldn't renew with her again, and would have been glad now had she quitted him; but there grew for him during the next moments the strange sense that, with what had so bravely happened for her—to the point of the triumph of displaying it to him inclusive—the instinct of compassion worked in her; though whether in respect of the comparative solitude to which her duties to "Walter" would perhaps more or less relegate him, or on the score of his having brought home to him, as she said, so much that was painful, she hadn't yet made up her mind. This, after a little, however, she discreetly did; she decided in the sense of consideration for his nerves. She lingered—he felt her more vaguely about; and in the silence that thus lasted between them he felt also, with its importance, the determination of their life for perhaps a long time to come. He was wishing she'd go—he was wanting not then again to meet her eyes; but still more than either of these things he was asking himself, as from time to time during the previous months he had all subtly and idly asked, what would have been the use, after all, of so much imagination as constantly worked in him. Didn't it let him into more deep holes than it pulled him out of? Didn't it make for him more tight places than it saw him through? Or didn't it at the same time, not less, give him all to himself a life, exquisite, occult, dangerous and sacred, to which everything ministered and which nothing could take away?

He fairly lost himself in that aspect—which it was clear only the vision and the faculty themselves could have hung there, of a sudden, so wantonly before him; and by the moment attention for nearer things had re-emerged he seemed to know how his wife had interpreted his air of musing melancholy absence. She had dealt with it after her own fashion; had given him a moment longer the benefit of a chance to inquire or appeal afresh; and then, after brushing him good-humouredly, in point of fact quite gaily, with her skirts, after patting and patronizing him gently with her finger-tips, very much as he had patted and patronized Walter Puddick that day in the porch, had put him in his place, on the whole matter of the issue of their trouble, or at least had left him in it, by a happy last word. She had judged him more upset, more unable to conclude or articulate, about Mora and Sir Bruce, than she, with her easier power of rebound, had been; and her final wisdom, indeed her final tenderness, would be to show him cheerful and helpful mercy. "No, then, I see I mustn't rub it in. You shan't be worried. I'll keep it all to myself, dear." With which she would have floated away—with which and some other things he was sensibly, relievingly alone. But he remained staring out at the approach of evening —and it was of the other things he was more and more conscious while the vague grey prospect held him. Even while he had looked askance in the greyness at the importunate fiend of fancy it was riding him again as the very genius of twilight; it played the long reach of its prompt lantern over Sir Bruce Bagley, the patron of promising young lives. He wondered about Sir Bruce, recalling his face and his type and his effect—his effect, so immediate, on Mora; wondered how he had proceeded, how he would still proceed, how far perhaps even they had got by that time. Lord, the fun some people did have! Even Jane, with her conscientious new care—even Jane, unmistakably, was in for such a lot.

CRAPY CORNELIA

I

THREE times within a quarter of an hour—shifting the while his posture on his chair of contemplation—had he looked at his watch as for its final sharp hint that he should decide, that he should get up. His seat was one of a group fairly sequestered, unoccupied save for his own presence, and from where he lingered he looked off at a stretch of lawn freshened by recent April showers and on which sundry small children were at play. The trees, the shrubs, the plants, every stem and twig just ruffled as by the first touch of the light finger of the relenting year, struck him as standing still in the blest hope of more of the same caress; the quarter about him held its breath after the fashion of the child who waits with the rigour of an open mouth and shut eyes for the promised sensible effect of his having been good. So, in the windless, sun-warmed air of the beautiful afternoon, the Park of the winter's end had struck White-Mason as waiting; even New York, under such an impression, was "good," good enough —for *him:* its very sounds were faint, were almost sweet, as they reached him from so seemingly far beyond the wooded horizon that formed the remoter limit of his large shallow glade. The tones of the frolic infants ceased to be nondescript and harsh, were in fact almost as fresh and decent as the frilled and puckered and ribboned garb of the little girls, which had always a way, in those parts, of so portentously flaunting the daughters of the strange native—that is of the overwhelmingly alien—populace at him.

Not that these things in particular were his matter of

meditation now; he had wanted, at the end of his walk, to sit apart a little and think—and had been doing that for twenty minutes, even though as yet to no break in the charm of procrastination. But he had looked without seeing and listened without hearing: all that had been positive for him was that he hadn't failed vaguely to feel. He had felt in the first place, and he continued to feel—yes, at forty-eight quite as much as at any point of the supposed reign of younger intensities—the great spirit of the air, the fine sense of the season, the supreme appeal of Nature, he might have said, to his time of life; quite as if she, easy, indulgent, indifferent, cynical Power, were offering him the last chance it would rest with his wit or his blood to embrace. Then with that he had been entertaining, to the point and with the prolonged consequence of accepted immobilization, the certitude that if he did call on Mrs Worthingham and find her at home he couldn't in justice to himself not put to her the question that had lapsed the other time, the last time, through the irritating and persistent, even if accidental, presence of others. What friends she had—the people who so stupidly, so wantonly stuck! If they *should*, he and she, come to an understanding, that would presumably have to include certain members of her singularly ill-composed circle, in whom it was incredible to him that he should ever take an interest. This defeat, to do himself justice—he had bent rather predominantly on *that*, you see; ideal justice to *her*, with her possible conception of what it should consist of being another and quite a different matter—he had had the fact of the Sunday afternoon to thank for; she didn't "keep" that day for him, since they hadn't, up to now, quite begun to cultivate the appointment or assignation founded on explicit sacrifices. He might at any rate look to find this pleasant practical Wednesday—should he indeed, at his actual rate, stay it before it ebbed—more liberally and intendingly given him.

The sound he at last most wittingly distinguished in his

nook was the single deep note of half-past five borne to him from some high-perched public clock. He finally got up with the sense that the time from then on *ought* at least to be felt as sacred to him. At this juncture it was—while he stood there shaking his garments, settling his hat, his necktie, his shirt-cuffs, fixing the high polish of his fine shoes as if for some reflection in it of his straight and spare and grizzled, his refined and trimmed and dressed, his altogether distinguished person, that of a gentleman abundantly settled, but of a bachelor markedly nervous—at this crisis it was, doubtless, that he at once most measured and least resented his predicament. If he should go he would almost to a certainty find her, and if he should find her he would almost to a certainty come to the point. He wouldn't put it off again—there was that high consideration for him of justice at least to himself. He had never yet denied himself anything so apparently fraught with possibilities as the idea of proposing to Mrs Worthingham—never yet, in other words, denied himself anything he had so distinctly wanted to do; and the results of that wisdom had remained for him precisely the precious parts of experience. Counting only the offers of his honourable hand, these had been on three remembered occasions at least the consequence of an impulse as sharp and a self-respect that hadn't in the least suffered, moreover, from the failure of each appeal. He had been met in the three cases—the only ones he at all compared with his present case—by the frank confession that he didn't somehow, charming as he was, cause himself to be superstitiously believed in; and the lapse of life, afterward, had cleared up many doubts.

It *wouldn't* have done, he eventually, he lucidly saw, each time he had been refused; and the candour of his nature was such that he could live to think of these very passages as a proof of how right he had been—right, that is, to have put himself forward always, by the happiest instinct, only in impossible conditions. He had the happy consciousness of having exposed the important question to the crucial test, and of having escaped, by that persistent logic, a grave mistake. What better proof of his escape than the fact that he was now free to renew the all-interesting inquiry, and should be exactly about to do so in different and better conditions? The conditions were better by as much more—as much more of his career and character, of his situation, his reputation he could even have called it, of his knowledge of life, of his somewhat extended means, of his possibly augmented charm, of his certainly improved mind and temper—as was involved in the actual impending settlement. Once he had got into motion, once he had crossed the Park and passed out of it, entering, with very little space to traverse, one of the short new streets that abutted on its east side, his step became that of a man young enough to find confidence, quite to find felicity, in the sense, in almost any sense, of action. He could still enjoy almost anything, absolutely an unpleasant thing, in default of a better, that might still remind him he wasn't so old. The standing newness of everything about him would, it was true, have weakened this cheer by too much presuming on it; Mrs Worthingham's house, before which he stopped, had that gloss of new money, that glare of a piece fresh from the mint and ringing for the first time on any counter, which seems to claim for it, in any transaction, something more than the "face" value.

This could but be yet more the case for the impression of the observer introduced and committed. On our friend's part I mean, after his admission and while still in the hall, the sense of the general shining immediacy, of the still unhushed clamour of the shock, was perhaps stronger than he had ever known it. That broke out from every corner as the high pitch of interest, and with a candour that—no, certainly—he had never seen equalled; every particular expensive object shrieking at him in its artless pride that it had just "come home." He met the whole vision with something of the grimace

produced on persons without goggles by the passage from a
shelter to a blinding light; and if he had—by a perfectly possible chance—been "snap-shotted" on the spot, would have
struck you as showing for his first tribute to the temple of
Mrs Worthingham's charming presence a scowl almost of
anguish. He wasn't constitutionally, it may at once be explained for him, a goggled person; and he was condemned in
New York to this frequent violence of transition—having to
reckon with it whenever he went out, as who should say, from
himself. The high pitch of interest, to his taste, was the pitch
of history, the pitch of acquired and earned suggestion, the
pitch of association, in a word; so that he lived by preference,
incontestably, if not in a rich gloom, which would have been
beyond his means and spirits, at least amid objects and images
that confessed to the tone of time.

He had ever felt that an indispensable presence—with a
need of it moreover that interfered at no point with his
gentle habit, not to say his subtle art, of drawing out what was
left him of his youth, of thinly and thriftily spreading the rest
of that choicest jam-pot of the cupboard of consciousness
over the remainder of a slice of life still possibly thick enough
to bear it; or in other words of moving the melancholy limits,
the significant signs, constantly a little further on, very
much as property-marks or staked boundaries are sometimes
stealthily shifted at night. He positively cherished in fact, as
against the too inveterate gesture of distressfully guarding his
eyeballs—so many New York aspects seemed to keep him at
it—an ideal of adjusted appreciation, of courageous curiosity,
of fairly letting the world about him, a world of constant
breathless renewals and merciless substitutions, make its
flaring assault on its own inordinate terms. Newness *was*
value in the piece—for the acquisitor, or at least sometimes
might be, even though the act of "blowing" hard, the act
marking a heated freshness of arrival, or other form of irruption, could never minister to the peace of those already and

long on the field; and this if only because maturer tone was after all most appreciable and most consoling when one staggered back to it, wounded, bleeding, blinded, from the riot of the raw—or, to put the whole experience more prettily, no doubt, from excesses of light.

II

IF he went in, however, with something of his more or less inevitable scowl, there were really, at the moment, two rather valid reasons for screened observation; the first of these being that the whole place seemed to reflect as never before the lustre of Mrs Worthingham's own polished and prosperous little person—to smile, it struck him, with her smile, to twinkle not only with the gleam of her lovely teeth, but with that of all her rings and brooches and bangles and other gewgaws, to curl and spasmodically cluster as in emulation of her charming complicated yellow tresses, to surround the most animated of pink-and-white, of ruffled and ribboned, of frilled and festooned Dresden china shepherdesses with exactly the right system of rococo curves and convolutions and other flourishes, a perfect bower of painted and gilded and moulded conceits. The second ground of this immediate impression of scenic extravagance, almost as if the curtain rose for him to the first act of some small and expensively mounted comic opera, was that she hadn't, after all, awaited him in fond singleness, but had again just a trifle inconsiderately exposed him to the drawback of having to reckon, for whatever design he might amiably entertain, with the presence of a third and quite superfluous person, a small black insignificant but none the less oppressive stranger. It was odd how, on the instant, the little lady engaged with her did affect him as comparatively black—very much as if that had absolutely, in such a medium, to be the graceless appearance of any item not positively of some fresh shade of a light colour or of some pretty pretension to a charming twist. Any witness of their meeting, his hostess should surely have felt, would have been a false note in the whole rosy glow; but what note so false as that of the dingy little presence that she might actually, by a refinement of her perhaps always too visible study of effect, have provided as a positive contrast or foil? whose name and intervention, moreover, she appeared to be no more moved to mention and account for than she might have been to "present"— whether as stretched at her feet or erect upon disciplined haunches—some shaggy old domesticated terrier or poodle.

Extraordinarily, after he had been in the room five minutes —a space of time during which his fellow-visitor had neither budged nor uttered a sound—he had made Mrs Worthingham out as all at once perfectly pleased to see him, completely aware of what he had most in mind, and singularly serene in face of his sense of their impediment. It was as if for all the world she didn't take it for one, the immobility, to say nothing of the seeming equanimity, of their tactless companion; at whom meanwhile indeed our friend himself, after his first ruffled perception, no more adventured a look than if advised by his constitutional kindness that to notice her in any degree would perforce be ungraciously to glower. He talked after a fashion with the woman as to whose power to please and amuse and serve him, as to whose really quite organized and indicated fitness for lighting up his autumn afternoon of life his conviction had lately strained itself so clear; but he was all the while carrying on an intenser exchange with his own spirit and trying to read into the charming creature's behaviour, as he could only call it, some confirmation of his theory that she also had her inward flutter and anxiously counted on him. He found support, happily for the conviction just named, in the idea, at no moment as yet really repugnant to him, the idea bound up in fact with the finer essence of her appeal, that she had her own vision too of her quality and her price, and that the last appearance she would have liked to bristle with was that of being forewarned and eager.

He had, if he came to think of it, scarce definitely warned her, and he probably wouldn't have taken to her so consciously in the first instance without an appreciative sense that, as she was a little person of twenty superficial graces, so she was also a little person with her secret pride. She might just have planted her mangy lion—not to say her muzzled house-dog—there in his path as a symbol that she wasn't cheap and easy; which would be a thing he couldn't possibly wish his future wife to have shown herself in advance, even if to him alone. That she could make him put himself such questions was precisely part of the attaching play of her iridescent surface, the shimmering interfusion of her various aspects; that of her youth with her independence—her pecuniary perhaps in particular, that of her vivacity with her beauty, that of her facility above all with her odd novelty; the high modernity, as people appeared to have come to call it, that made her so much more "knowing" in some directions than even he, man of the world as he certainly was, could pretend to be, though all on a basis of the most unconscious and instinctive and luxurious assumption. She was "up" to everything, aware of everything—if one counted from a short enough time back (from week before last, say, and as if quantities of history had burst upon the world within the fortnight); she was likewise surprised at nothing, and in that direction one might reckon as far ahead as the rest of her lifetime, or at any rate as the rest of his, which was all that would concern him: it was as if the suitability of the future to her personal and rather pampered tastes was what she most took for granted, so that he could see her, for all her Dresdenchina shoes and her flutter of wondrous befrilled contemporary skirts, skip by the side of the coming age as over the floor of a ball-room, keeping step with its monstrous stride and prepared for every figure of the dance.

Her outlook took form to him suddenly as a great square sunny window that hung in assured fashion over the immensity of life. There rose toward it as from a vast swarming *plaza* a high tide of motion and sound; yet it was at the same time as if even while he looked her light gemmed hand, flashing on him in addition to those other things the perfect polish of the prettiest pink finger-nails in the world, had touched a spring, the most ingenious of recent devices for instant ease, which dropped half across the scene a soft-coloured mechanical blind, a fluttered fringed awning of charmingly toned silk, such as would make a bath of cool shade for the favoured friend leaning with her there—that is for the happy couple itself—on the balcony. The great view would be the prospect and privilege of the very state he coveted—since didn't he covet it?—the state of being so securely at her side; while the wash of privacy, as one might count it, the broad fine brush dipped into clear umber and passed, full and wet, straight across the strong scheme of colour, would represent the security itself, all the uplifted inner elegance, the condition, so ideal, of being shut out from nothing and yet of having, so gaily and breezily aloft, none of the burden or worry of anything. Thus, as I say, for our friend, the place itself, while his vivid impression lasted, portentously opened and spread, and what was before him took, to his vision, though indeed at so other a crisis, the form of the "glimmering square" of the poet; yet, for a still more remarkable fact, with an incongruous object usurping at a given instant the privilege of the frame and seeming, even as he looked, to block the view.

The incongruous object was a woman's head, crowned with a little sparsely feathered black hat, an ornament quite unlike those the women mostly noticed by White-Mason were now "wearing," and that grew and grew, that came nearer and nearer, while it met his eyes, after the manner of images in the cinematograph. It had presently loomed so large that he saw nothing else—not only among the things at a considerable distance, the things Mrs Worthingham would eventually, yet unmistakably, introduce him to, but among those of this lady's various attributes and appurtenances as to which he had been in the very act of cultivating his consciousness. It was in the course of another minute the most extraordinary thing in the world: everything had altered, dropped, darkened, disappeared; his imagination had spread its wings only to feel them flop all grotesquely at its sides as he recognized in his hostess's quiet companion, the oppressive alien who hadn't indeed interfered with his fanciful flight, though she had prevented his immediate declaration and brought about the thud, not to say the felt violent shock, of his fall to earth, the perfectly plain identity of Cornelia Rasch. It was she who had remained there at attention; it was she their companion hadn't introduced; it was she he had forborne to face with his fear of incivility. He stared at her—everything else went.

"Why, it has been *you* all this time?"

Miss Rasch fairly turned pale. "I was waiting to see if you'd know me."

"Ah, my dear Cornelia"—he came straight out with it—"rather!"

"Well, it isn't," she returned with a quick change to red now, "from having taken much time to look at me!"

She smiled, she even laughed, but he could see how she had felt his unconsciousness, poor thing; the acquaintance, quite the friend of his youth, as she had been, the associate of his childhood, of his early manhood, of his middle age in fact, up to a few years back, not more than ten at the most; the associate too of so many of his associates and of almost all of his relations, those of the other time, those who had mainly gone for ever; the person in short whose noted disappearance, though it might have seemed final, had been only of recent seasons. She was present again now, all unexpectedly—he had heard of her having at last, left alone after successive deaths and with scant resources, sought economic salvation in Europe, the promised land of American thrift—she was present as this almost ancient and this oddly unassertive little rotund figure whom one seemed no more obliged to address than if she had been a black satin ottoman "treated" with buttons and gimp; a class of object as to which the policy of blindness was imperative. He felt the need of some explanatory plea, and before he could think had uttered one at Mrs Worthingham's expense. "Why, you see we weren't introduced!"

"No—but I didn't suppose I should have to be named to you."

"Well, my dear woman, you haven't—do me that justice!" He could at least make this point. "I felt all the while—!" However it would have taken him long to say what he had been feeling; and he was aware now of the pretty projected light of Mrs Worthingham's wonder. She looked as if, out for a walk with her, he had put her to the inconvenience of his stopping to speak to a strange woman in the street.

"I never supposed you knew her!"—it was to him his hostess excused herself.

This made Miss Rasch spring up, distinctly flushed, distinctly strange to behold, but not vulgarly nettled—Cornelia was incapable of that; only rather funnily bridling and laughing, only showing that this was all she had waited for, only saying just the right thing, the thing she could make so clearly a jest. "Of course if you *had* you'd have presented him."

Mrs Worthingham looked while answering at White-Mason. "I didn't want you to go—which you see you do as soon as he speaks to you. But I never dreamed—!"

"That there was anything between us? Ah, there are no end of things!" He, on his side, though addressing the younger and prettier woman, looked at his fellow-guest; to whom he even continued: "When did you get back? May I come and see you the very first thing?"

Cornelia gasped and wriggled—she practically giggled; she had lost every atom of her little old, her little young, though always unaccountable, prettiness, which used to peep so, on the bare chance of a shot, from behind indefensible features, that it almost made watching her a form of sport. He had heard vaguely of her, it came back to him (for there had been no letters; their later acquaintance, thank goodness, hadn't involved that), as experimenting, for economy, and then as settling, to the same rather dismal end, somewhere in England, at one of those intensely English places, St Leonards, Cheltenham, Bognor, Dawlish—which, awfully, *was* it?—and she now affected him for all the world as some small, squirming, exclaiming, genteelly conversing old maid of a type vaguely associated with the three-volume novels he used to feed on (besides his so often encountering it in "real life") during a far-away stay of his own at Brighton. Odder than any element of his ex-gossip's identity itself, however, was the fact that she somehow, with it all, rejoiced his sight. Indeed the supreme oddity was that the manner of her reply to his request for leave to call should have absolutely charmed his attention. She didn't look at him; she only, from under her frumpy, crapy, curiously exotic hat, and with her good little near-sighted insinuating glare, expressed to Mrs Worthingham, while she answered him, wonderful arch things, the overdone things of a shy woman. "Yes, you may call—but only when this dear lovely lady has done with you!" The moment after which she had gone.

III

FORTY minutes later he was taking his way back from the queer miscarriage of his adventure; taking it, with no conscious positive felicity, through the very spaces that had witnessed shortly before the considerable serenity of his assurance. He had said to himself then, or had as good as said it, that, since he might do perfectly as he liked, it couldn't fail for him that he must soon retrace those steps, humming, to all intents, the first bars of a wedding march; so beautifully had it cleared up that he was "going to like" letting Mrs Worthingham accept him. He was to have hummed no wedding-march, as it seemed to be turning out—he had none, up to now, to hum; and yet, extraordinarily, it wasn't in the least because she had refused him. Why then hadn't he liked as much as he had intended to like it putting the pleasant act, the act of not refusing him, in her power? Could it all have come from the awkward minute of his failure to decide sharply, on Cornelia's departure, whether or no he would attend her to the door? He hadn't decided at all—what the deuce had been in him?—but had danced to and fro in the room, thinking better of each impulse and then thinking worse. He had hesitated like an ass erect on absurd hind legs between two bundles of hay; the upshot of which must have been his giving the falsest impression. In what way that was to be for an instant considered had their common past committed him to crazy Cornelia? He repudiated with a whack on the gravel any ghost of an obligation.

What he could get rid of with scanter success, unfortunately, was the peculiar sharpness of his sense that, though mystified by his visible flurry—and yet not mystified enough for a sympathetic question either—his hostess had been, on the whole, even more frankly diverted: which was precisely an example of that newest, freshest, finest freedom in her, the air and the candour of assuming, not "heartlessly," not viciously, not even very consciously, but with a bright pampered confidence which would probably end by affecting one's nerves as the most impertinent stroke in the world, that every blest thing coming up for her in any connection was somehow matter for her general recreation. There she was again with the innocent egotism, the gilded and overflowing anarchism, really, of her doubtless quite unwitting but none the less rabid modern note. Her grace of ease was perfect, but it was all grace of ease, not a single shred of it grace of uncertainty or of difficulty—which meant, when you came to see, that, for its happy working, not a grain of provision was left by it to mere manners. This was clearly going to be the music of the future—that if people were but rich enough and furnished enough and fed enough, exercised and sanitated and mani-cured, and generally advised and advertised and made "know-ing" enough, *avertis* enough, as the term appeared to be nowadays in Paris, all they had to do for civility was to take the amused ironic view of those who might be less initiated. In *his* time, when he was young or even when he was only but a little less middle-aged, the best manners had been the best kindness, and the best kindness had mostly been some art of not insisting on one's luxurious differences, of conceal-ing rather, for common humanity, if not for common decency, a part at least of the intensity or the ferocity with which one might be "in the know."

Oh, the "know"—Mrs Worthingham was in it, all in-stinctively, inevitably and as a matter of course, up to her eyes; which didn't, however, the least little bit prevent her being as ignorant as a fish of everything that really and inti-mately and fundamentally concerned *him*, poor dear old White-Mason. She didn't, in the first place, so much as know who he was—by which he meant know who and what it was to *be* a White-Mason, even a poor and a dear and old one, "anyway." That indeed—he did her perfect justice—was of the very essence of the newness and freshness and beautiful, brave social irresponsibility by which she had originally dazzled him: just exactly that circumstance of her having no instinct for any old quality or quantity or identity, a single historic or social value, as he might say, of the New York of his already almost legendary past; and that additional one of his, on his side, having, so far as this went, cultivated blankness, cultivated positive prudence, as to her own personal background—the vagueness, at the best, with which all honest gentlefolk, the New Yorkers of his approved stock and conservative generation, were content, as for the most part they were indubitably wise, to surround the origins and antecedents and queer unimaginable early influences of persons swimming into their ken from those parts of the country that quite necessarily and naturally figured to their view as "God-forsaken" and generally impossible.

The few scattered surviving representatives of a society once "good"—*rari nantes in gurgite vasto*—were liable, at the pass things had come to, to meet, and even amid old shades once sacred, or what was left of such, every form of social impossibility, and, more irresistibly still, to find these apparitions often carry themselves (often at least in the case of the women) with a wondrous wild gallantry, equally imperturbable and inimitable, the sort of thing that reached its maximum in Mrs Worthingham. Beyond that who ever wanted to look up their annals, to reconstruct their steps and stages, to dot their i's in fine, or to "go behind" anything that was theirs? One wouldn't do that for the world—a rudimentary discretion forbade it; and yet this check from elementary undiscussable taste quite consorted with a due respect for them, or at any rate with a due respect for oneself in connection with them; as was just exemplified in what would be his own, what would be poor dear old White-Mason's, insurmountable aversion to having, on any pretext, the doubtless very queer spectre of the late Mr Worthingham presented to him. No question had he asked, or would he ever ask, should his life—that is should the success of his courtship—even intimately depend on it, either about that obscure agent of his mistress's actual affluence or about the happy headspring itself, and the apparently copious tributaries, of the golden stream.

From all which marked anomalies, at any rate, what was the moral to draw? He dropped into a Park chair again with that question, he lost himself in the wonder of why he had come away with his homage so very much unpaid. Yet it didn't seem at all, actually, as if he could say or conclude, as if he could do anything but keep on worrying—just in conformity with his being a person who, whether or no familiar with the need to make his conduct square with his conscience and his taste was never wholly exempt from that of making his taste and his conscience square with his conduct. To this latter occupation he further abandoned himself, and it didn't release him from his second brooding session till the sweet spring sunset had begun to gather and he had more or less cleared up, in the deepening dusk, the effective relation between the various parts of his ridiculously agitating experience. There were vital facts he seemed thus to catch, to seize, with a nervous hand, and the twilight helping, by their vaguely-whisked tails; unquiet truths that swarmed out after the fashion of creatures bold only at eventide, creatures that hovered and circled, that verily brushed his nose, in spite of their shyness. Yes, he had practically just sat on with his "mistress"—heaven save the mark!—as if *not* to come to the point; as if it had absolutely come up that there would be something rather vulgar and awful in doing so. The whole stretch of his stay after Cornelia's withdrawal had been consumed by his almost ostentatiously treating himself to the opportunity of which he was to make nothing. It was as if he had sat and watched himself—that came back to him: Shall I now or shan't I? Will I now or won't I? Say within the next three minutes, say by a quarter past six, or by twenty minutes past, at the furthest—always if nothing more comes up to prevent.

What had already come up to prevent was, in the strangest and drollest, or at least in the most preposterous, way in the world, that not Cornelia's presence, but her very absence, with its distraction of his thoughts, the thoughts that lumbered after her, had made the difference; and without his being the least able to tell why and how. He put it to himself after a fashion by the image that, this distraction once created, his working round to his hostess again, his reverting to the matter of his errand, began suddenly to represent a return from so far. That was simply all—or rather a little less than all; for something else had contributed. "I never dreamed you knew her," and "I never dreamed *you* did," was inevitably what had been exchanged between them—supplemented by Mrs Worthingham's mere scrap of an explanation: "Oh, yes —to the small extent you see. Two years ago in Switzerland when I was at a high place for an 'aftercure,' during twenty days of incessant rain, she was the only person in an hotel of roaring, gorging, smoking Germans with whom I couldn't have a word of talk. She and I were the only speakers of English, and were thrown together like castaways on a desert island and in a raging storm. She was ill besides, and she had no maid, and mine looked after her, and she was very grateful —writing to me later on and saying she should certainly come to see me if she ever returned to New York. She *has* returned, you see—and there she was, poor little creature!" Such was Mrs Worthingham's tribute—to which even his asking her if Miss Rasch had ever happened to speak of him caused her practically to add nothing. Visibly she had never thought again of anyone Miss Rasch had spoken of or anything Miss Rasch had said; right as she was, naturally, about her being a little clever queer creature. This was perfectly true, and yet it was probably—by being *all* she could dream of about her—what had paralysed his proper gallantry. Its effect had been not in what it simply stated, but in what, under his secretly disintegrating criticism, it almost luridly symbolized.

He had quitted his seat in the Louis Quinze drawing-room without having, as he would have described it, done anything but give the lady of the scene a superior chance not to betray a defeated hope—not, that is, to fail of the famous "pride" mostly supposed to prop even the most infatuated women at such junctures; by which chance, to do her justice, she had thoroughly seemed to profit. But he finally rose from his later station with a feeling of better success. He had by a happy turn of his hand got hold of the most precious, the least obscure of the flitting, circling things that brushed his ears. What he wanted—as justifying for him a little further consideration—was there before him from the moment he could put it that Mrs Worthingham had no data. He almost hugged that word—it suddenly came to mean so much to him. No data, he felt, for a conception of the sort of thing the New York of "his time" had been in his personal life—the New York so unexpectedly, so vividly, and, as he might say, so perversely called back to all his senses by its identity with that of poor Cornelia's time: since even she had had a time, small show as it was likely to make now, and his time and hers had been the same. Cornelia figured to him while he walked away as by contrast and opposition a massive little bundle of data; his impatience to go to see her sharpened as he thought of this: so certainly should he find out that wherever he might touch her, with a gentle though firm pressure, he would, as the fond visitor of old houses taps and fingers a disfeatured, over-papered wall with the conviction of a wainscot-edge beneath, recognize some small extrusion of history.

IV

THERE would have been a wonder for us meanwhile in his continued use, as it were, of his happy formula—brought out to Cornelia Rasch within ten minutes, or perhaps only within twenty, of his having settled into the quite comfortable chair that, two days later, she indicated to him by her fireside. He had arrived at her address through the fortunate chance of his having noticed her card, as he went out, deposited, in the good old New York fashion, on one of the rococo tables of Mrs Worthingham's hall. His eye had been caught by the pencilled indication that was to affect him, the next instant, as fairly placed there for his sake. This had really been his luck, for he shouldn't have liked to write to Mrs Worthingham for guidance—*that* he felt, though too impatient just now to analyze the reluctance. There was nobody else he could have approached for a clue, and with this reflection he was already aware of how it testified to their rare little position, his and Cornelia's—position as conscious, ironic, pathetic survivors together of a dead and buried society—that there would have been, in all the town, under such stress, not a member of their old circle left to turn to. Mrs Worthingham had practically, even if accidentally, helped him to knowledge; the last nail in the coffin of the poor dear extinct past had been planted for him by his having thus to reach his antique contemporary through perforation of the newest newness. The note of this particular recognition was in fact the more prescribed to him that the ground of Cornelia's return to a scene swept so bare of the associational charm was certainly inconspicuous. What had she then come back for?—he had asked himself that; with the effect of deciding that it probably would have been, a little, to "look after" her remnant of property. Perhaps she had come to save what little might still remain of that shrivelled interest; perhaps she had been, by those who took care of it for her, further swindled and despoiled, so that she wished to get at the facts. Perhaps on the other hand—it was a more cheerful chance—her investments, decently administered, were making larger returns, so that the rigorous thrift of Bognor could be finally relaxed.

He had little to learn about the attraction of Europe, and

rather expected that in the event of his union with Mrs Worthingham he should find himself pleading for it with the competence of one more in the "know" about Paris and Rome,
about Venice and Florence, than even she could be. He could
have lived on in *his* New York, that is in the sentimental, the
spiritual, the more or less romantic visitation of it; but had it
been positive for him that he could live on in hers?—unless
indeed the possibility of this had been just (like the famous
vertige de l'abîme, like the solicitation of danger, or otherwise
of the dreadful) the very hinge of his whole dream. However
that might be, his curiosity was occupied rather with the conceivable hinge of poor Cornelia's: it was perhaps thinkable
that even Mrs Worthingham's New York, once it should have
become possible again at all, might have put forth to this lone
exile a plea that wouldn't be in the chords of Bognor. For
himself, after all, too, the attraction had been much more of
the Europe over which one might move at one's ease, and
which therefore could but cost, and cost much, right and left,
than of the Europe adapted to scrimping. He saw himself on
the whole scrimping with more zest even in Mrs Worthingham's New York than under the inspiration of Bognor. Apart
from which it was yet again odd, not to say perceptibly
pleasing to him, to note where the emphasis of his interest
fell in this fumble of fancy over such felt oppositions as the
new, the latest, the luridest power of money and the ancient
reserves and moderations and mediocrities. These last struck
him as showing by contrast the old brown surface and tone
as of velvet rubbed and worn, shabby, and even a bit dingy,
but all soft and subtle and still velvety—which meant still
dignified; whereas the angular facts of current finance were as
harsh and metallic and bewildering as some stacked "exhibit"
of ugly patented inventions, things his mediæval mind forbade
his taking in. He had, for instance, the sense of knowing the
pleasant little old Rasch fortune—pleasant as far as it went;
blurred memories and impressions of what it had been and

what it hadn't, of how it had grown and how languished and how melted; they came back to him and put on such vividness that he could almost have figured himself testify for them before a bland and encouraging Board. The idea of taking the field in any manner on the subject of Mrs Worthingham's resources would have affected him on the other hand as an odious ordeal, some glare of embarrassment and exposure in a circle of hard unhelpful attention, of converging, derisive, unsuggestive eyes.

In Cornelia's small and quite cynically modern flat—the house had a grotesque name, "The Gainsborough," but at least wasn't an awful boarding-house, as he had feared, and she could receive him quite honourably, which was so much to the good—he would have been ready to use at once to her the greatest freedom of friendly allusion: "Have you still your old 'family interest' in those two houses in Seventh Avenue?—one of which was next to a corner grocery, don't you know? and was occupied as to its lower part by a candy-shop where the proportion of the stock of suspectedly stale popcorn to that of rarer and stickier joys betrayed perhaps a modest capital on the part of your father's, your grandfather's or whoever's tenant, but out of which I nevertheless remember once to have come as out of a bath of sweets, with my very garments, and even the separate hairs of my head, glued together. The other of the pair, a tobacconist's, further down, had before it a wonderful huge Indian who thrust out wooden cigars at an indifferent world—you could buy candy cigars too at the popcorn shop, and I greatly preferred them to the wooden; I remember well how I used to gape in fascination at the Indian and wonder if the last of the Mohicans was like him; besides admiring so the resources of a family whose 'property' was in such forms. I haven't been round there lately—we must go round together; but don't tell me the forms have utterly perished!" It was after *that* fashion he might easily have been moved, and with almost no transition, to break out to Cornelia—quite as if taking up some old talk, some old community of gossip, just where they had left it; even with the consciousness perhaps of overdoing a little, of putting at its maximum, for the present harmony, recovery, recapture (what should he call it?) the pitch and quantity of what the past had held for them.

He didn't in fact, no doubt, dart straight off to Seventh Avenue, there being too many other old things and much nearer and long subsequent; the point was only that for everything they spoke of after he had fairly begun to lean back and stretch his legs, and after she had let him, above all, light the first of a succession of cigarettes—for everything they spoke of he positively cultivated extravagance and excess, piling up the crackling twigs as on the very altar of memory; and that by the end of half an hour she had lent herself, all gallantly, to their game. It was the game of feeding the beautiful iridescent flame, ruddy and green and gold, blue and pink and amber and silver, with anything they could pick up, anything that would burn and flicker. Thick-strown with such gleanings the occasion seemed indeed, in spite of the truth that they perhaps wouldn't have proved, under cross-examination, to have rubbed shoulders in the other life so very hard. Casual contacts, qualified communities enough, there had doubtless been, but not particular "passages," nothing that counted, as he might think of it, for their "very own" together, for nobody's else at all. These shades of historic exactitude didn't signify; the more and the less that there had been made perfect terms—and just by his being there and by her rejoicing in it—with their present need to have *had* all their past could be made to appear to have given them. It was to this tune they proceeded, the least little bit as if they knowingly pretended—he giving her the example and setting her the pace of it, and she, poor dear, after a first inevitable shyness, an uncertainty of wonder, a breathlessness of courage, falling into step and going whatever length he would.

She showed herself ready for it, grasping gladly at the perception of what he must mean; and if she didn't immediately and completely fall in—not in the first half-hour, not even in the three or four others that his visit, even whenever he consulted his watch, still made nothing of—she yet understood enough as soon as she understood that, if their finer economy hadn't so beautifully served, he might have been conveying this, that and the other incoherent and easy thing by the comparatively clumsy method of sound and statement. "No, I never made love to you; it would in fact have been absurd, and I don't care—though I almost know, in the sense of almost remembering!—who did and who didn't; but you were always about, and so was I, and, little as you may yourself care who *I* did it to, I daresay you remember (in the sense of having known of it!) any old appearances that told. But we can't afford at this time of day not to help each other to have had —well, everything there was, since there's no more of it now, nor anyway of coming by it *except so;* and therefore let us *make* together, let us make over and recreate, our lost world; for which we have after all and at the worst such a lot of material. You were in particular my poor dear sisters' friend —they thought you the funniest little brown thing possible; so isn't that again to the good? You were mine only to the extent that you were so much in and out of the house—as how much, if we come to that, wasn't one in and out, south of Thirtieth Street and north of Washington Square, in those days, those spacious, sociable, Arcadian days, that we flattered ourselves we filled with the modern fever, but that were so different from any of *these* arrangements of pretended hourly Time that dash themselves forever to pieces as from the fiftieth floors of sky-scrapers."

This was the kind of thing that was in the air, whether he said it or not, and that could hang there even with such quite other things as more crudely came out; came in spite of its being perhaps calculated to strike us that these last would have been rather and most the unspoken and the indirect. They were Cornelia's contribution, and as soon as she had begun to talk of Mrs Worthingham—*he* didn't begin it!— they had taken their place bravely in the centre of the circle. There they made, the while, their considerable little figure, but all within the ring formed by fifty other allusions, fitful but really intenser irruptions that hovered and wavered and came and went, joining hands at moments and whirling round as in chorus, only then again to dash at the slightly huddled centre with a free twitch or peck or push or other taken liberty, after the fashion of irregular frolic motions in a country dance or a Christmas game.

"You're so in love with her and want to marry her!"— she said it all sympathetically and yearningly, poor crapy Cornelia; as if it were to be quite taken for granted that she knew all about it. And then when he had asked how she knew —why she took so informed a tone about it; all on the wonder of her seeming so much more "in" it just at that hour than he himself quite felt he could figure for: "Ah, how but from the dear lovely thing herself? Don't you suppose *she* knows it?"

"Oh, she absolutely 'knows' it, does she?"—he fairly heard himself ask that; and with the oddest sense at once of sharply wanting the certitude and yet of seeing the question, of hearing himself say the words, through several thicknesses of some wrong medium. He came back to it from a distance; as he would have had to come back (this was again vivid to him) should he have got round again to his ripe intention three days before—after his now present but then absent friend, that is, had left him planted before his now absent but then present one for the purpose. "Do you mean she—at all confidently!—expects?" he went on, not much minding if it couldn't but sound foolish; the time being given it for him meanwhile by the sigh, the wondering gasp, all charged with the unutterable, that the tone of his appeal set in motion. He saw his companion look at him, but it might have been with the eyes of thirty years ago; when—very likely!—he had put her some such question about some girl long since dead. Dimly at first, then more distinctly, didn't it surge back on him for the very strangeness that there had been some such passage as this between them—yes, about Mary Cardew!—in the autumn of '68?

"Why, don't you realize your situation?" Miss Rasch struck him as quite beautifully wailing—above all to such an effect of deep interest, that is, on her own part and in him.

"My situation?"—he echoed, he considered; but reminded afresh, by the note of the detached, the far-projected in it, of what he had last remembered of his sentient state on his once taking ether at the dentist's.

"Yours and hers—the situation of her adoring you. I suppose you at least know it," Cornelia smiled.

Yes, it was like the other time and yet it wasn't. *She* was like—poor Cornelia was—everything that used to be; that somehow was most definite to him. Still he could quite reply, "Do you call it—her adoring me—*my* situation?"

"Well, it's a part of yours, surely—if you're in love with her."

"Am I, ridiculous old person! in love with her?" White-Mason asked.

"I may be a ridiculous old person," Cornelia returned—"and, for that matter, of course I *am!* But she's young and lovely and rich and clever: so what could be more natural?"

"Oh, I was applying that opprobrious epithet—!" He didn't finish, though he meant he had applied it to himself. He had got up from his seat; he turned about and, taking in, as his eyes also roamed, several objects in the room, serene and sturdy, not a bit cheap-looking, little old New York objects of '68, he made, with an inner art, as if to recognize them—made so, that is, for himself; had quite the sense for the moment of asking them, of imploring them, to recognize *him*, to be for him things of his own past. Which they truly

were, he could have the next instant cried out; for it meant
that if three or four of them, small sallow carte-de-visite
photographs, faithfully framed but spectrally faded, hadn't in
every particular, frames and balloon skirts and false "property" balustrades of unimaginable terraces and all, the tone
of time, the secret for warding and easing off the perpetual
imminent ache of one's protective scowl, one would verily
but have to let the scowl stiffen or to take up seriously the
question of blue goggles, during what might remain of life.

V

WHAT he actually took up from a little old Twelfth-Street
table that piously preserved the plain mahogany circle, with
never a curl nor a crook nor a hint of a brazen flourish, what
he paused there a moment for commerce with, his back presented to crapy Cornelia, who sat taking that view of him,
during this opportunity, very protrusively and frankly and
fondly, was one of the wasted mementoes just mentioned,
over which he both uttered and suppressed a small comprehen-
sive cry. He stood there another minute to look at it, and
when he turned about still kept it in his hand, only holding
it now a little behind him. "You *must* have come back to stay
—with all your beautiful things. What else does it mean?"

" 'Beautiful'?" his old friend commented with her brow
all wrinkled and her lips thrust out in expressive dispraise.
They might at that rate have been scarce more beautiful than
she herself. "Oh, don't talk so—after Mrs Worthingham's!
They're wonderful, if you will: such things, such things! But
one's own poor relics and odds and ends are one's own at
least; and one *has*—yes—come back to them. They're all I
have in the world to come back to. They were stored, and
what I was paying—!" Miss Rasch woefully added.

He had possession of the small old picture; he hovered there; he put his eyes again to it intently; then again held it a little behind him as if it might have been snatched away or the very feel of it, pressed against him, was good to his palm. "Mrs Worthingham's things? You think them beautiful?"

Cornelia did now, if ever, show an odd face. "Why, certainly, prodigious, or whatever. Isn't that conceded?"

"No doubt every horror, at the pass we've come to, is conceded. That's just what I complain of."

"Do you *complain?*"—she drew it out as for surprise: she couldn't have imagined such a thing.

"To me her things are awful. They're the newest of the new."

"Ah, but the old forms!"

"Those are the most blatant. I mean the swaggering reproductions."

"Oh, but," she pleaded, "we can't all be *really* old."

"No, we can't, Cornelia. But *you* can—!" said White-Mason with the frankest appreciation.

She looked up at him from where she sat as he could imagine her looking up at the curate at Bognor. "Thank you, sir! If that's all you want—!"

"It *is*," he said, "all I want—or almost."

"Then no wonder such a creature as that," she lightly moralized, "won't suit you!"

He bent upon her, for all the weight of his question, his smoothest stare. "You hold she certainly won't suit me?"

"Why, what can I tell about it? Haven't you by this time found out?"

"No, but I think I'm finding." With which he began again to explore.

Miss Rasch immensely wondered. "You mean you don't expect to come to an understanding with her?" And then, as even to this straight challenge he made at first no answer: "Do you mean you give it up?"

He waited some instants more, but not meeting her eyes—only looking again about the room. "What do you think of my chance?"

"Oh," his companion cried, "what has what I think to do with it? How can I think anything but that she must like you?"

"Yes—of course. But how much?"

"Then don't you really know?" Cornelia asked.

He kept up his walk, oddly preoccupied and still not looking at her. "Do you, my dear?"

She waited a little. "If you haven't really put it to her I don't suppose she knows."

This at last arrested him again. "My dear Cornelia, she doesn't know—!"

He had paused as for the desperate tone, or at least the large emphasis of it, so that she took him up. "The more reason then to help her to find it out."

"I mean," he explained, "that she doesn't know anything."

"Anything?"

"Anything else, I mean—even if she does know *that*."

Cornelia considered of it. "But what else need she—in particular—know? Isn't that the principal thing?"

"Well"—and he resumed his circuit—"she doesn't know anything that *we* know. But nothing, ' he re-emphasized—"nothing whatever!"

"Well, can't she do without that?"

"Evidently she can—and evidently she does, beautifully. But the question is whether *I* can!"

He had paused once more with his point—but she glared, poor Cornelia, with her wonder. "Surely if you know for yourself—!"

"Ah, it doesn't seem enough for me to know for myself! One wants a woman," he argued—but still, in his prolonged tour, quite without his scowl—"to know *for* one, to know *with* one. That's what you do now," he candidly put to her.

It made her again gape. "Do you mean you want to marry *me?*"

He was so full of what he did mean, however, that he failed even to notice it. "She doesn't in the least know, for instance, how old I am."

"That's because you're so young!"

"Ah, there you are!"—and he turned off afresh and as if almost in disgust. It left her visibly perplexed—though even the perplexed Cornelia was still the exceedingly pointed; but he had come to her aid after another turn. "Remember, please, that I'm pretty well as old as you."

She had all her point at least, while she bridled and blinked, for this. "You're exactly a year and ten months older."

It checked him there for delight. "You remember my birthday?"

She twinkled indeed like some far-off light of home. "I remember everyone's. It's a little way I've always had—and that I've never lost."

He looked at her accomplishment, across the room, as at some striking, some charming phenomenon. "Well, *that's* the sort of thing I want!" All the ripe candour of his eyes confirmed it.

What could she do therefore, she seemed to ask him, but repeat her question of a moment before?—which indeed, presently she made up her mind to. "Do you want to marry *me?*"

It had this time better success—if the term may be felt in any degree to apply. All his candour, or more of it at least, was in his slow, mild, kind, considering head-shake. "No, Cornelia—not to *marry* you."

His discrimination was a wonder; but since she was clearly treating him now as if everything about him was, so she could as exquisitely meet it. "Not at least," she convulsively smiled, "until you've honourably tried Mrs Worthingham. Don't you really *mean* to?" she gallantly insisted.

He waited again a little; then he brought out: "I'll tell you presently." He came back, and as by still another mere glance over the room, to what seemed to him so much nearer. "That table *was* old Twelfth-Street?"

"Everything here was."

"Oh, the pure blessings! With you, ah, with you, I haven't to wear a green shade." And he had retained meanwhile his small photograph, which he again showed himself. "Didn't we talk of Mary Cardew?"

"Why, do you remember it?"—she marvelled to extravagance.

"You make me. You connect me with it. You connect it with *me*." He liked to display to her this excellent use she thus had, the service she rendered. "There are so many connections—there will *be* so many. I feel how, with you, they must all come up again for me: in fact you're bringing them out already, just while I look at you, as fast as ever you can. The fact that you knew every one—!" he went on; yet as if there were more in that too than he could quite trust himself about.

"Yes, I knew every one," said Cornelia Rasch; but this time with perfect simplicity. "I knew, I imagine, more than you do—or more than you did."

It kept him there, it made him wonder with his eyes on her. "Things about *them*—our people?"

"Our people. Ours only now."

Ah, such an interest as he felt in this—taking from her while, so far from scowling, he almost gaped, all it might mean! "Ours indeed—and it's awfully good they are; or that we're still here for them! Nobody else is—nobody but you: not a cat!"

"Well, I *am* a cat!" Cornelia grinned.

"Do you mean you can tell me things—?" It was too beautiful to believe.

"About what really *was*?" She artfully considered, holding him immensely now. "Well, unless they've come to you with time; unless you've learned—or found out."

"Oh," he reassuringly cried—reassuringly, it most seemed, for himself—"nothing has come to me with time, everything has gone from me. How I find out now! What creature has an idea—?"

She threw up her hands with the shrug of old days—the sharp little shrug his sisters used to imitate and that she hadn't had to go to Europe for. The only thing was that he blessed her for bringing it back. "Ah, the ideas of people now—!"

"Yes, their ideas are certainly not about *us*." But he ruefully faced it. "We've none the less, however, to live with them."

"With their ideas—?" Cornelia questioned.

"With *them*—these modern wonders; such as they are!" Then he went on: "It must have been to help me you've come back."

She said nothing for an instant about that, only nodding instead at his photograph. "What has become of yours? I mean of *her*."

This time it made him turn pale. "You remember I *have* one?"

She kept her eyes on him. "In a 'pork-pie' hat, with her hair in a long net. That was so 'smart' then; especially with one's skirt looped up, over one's hooped magenta petticoat, in little festoons, and a row of very big onyx beads over one's braided velveteen sack—braided quite plain and very broad, don't you know?"

He smiled for her extraordinary possession of these things —she was as prompt as if she had had them before her. "Oh, rather—'don't I know?' You wore brown velveteen, and, on those remarkably small hands, funny gauntlets—like mine."

"Oh, do *you* remember? But like yours?" she wondered.

"I mean like hers in my photograph." But he came back to the present picture. "This is better, however, for really showing her lovely head."

"Mary's head was a perfection!" Cornelia testified.

"Yes—it was better than her heart."

"Ah, don't say that!" she pleaded. "You weren't fair."

"Don't you think I was fair?" It interested him immensely —and the more that he indeed mightn't have been; which he seemed somehow almost to hope.

"She didn't think so—to the very end."

"She didn't?"—ah, the right things Cornelia said to him! But before she could answer he was studying again closely the small faded face. "No, she doesn't, she doesn't. Oh, her charming sad eyes and the way they *say* that, across the years, straight into mine! But I don't know, I don't know!" White-Mason quite comfortably sighed.

His companion appeared to appreciate this effect. "That's just the way you used to flirt with her, poor thing. Wouldn't you like to have it?" she asked.

"This—for my very own?" He looked up delighted. "I really may?"

"Well, if you'll give me yours. We'll exchange."

"That's a charming idea. We'll exchange. But you must come and get it at my rooms—where you'll see my things."

For a little she made no answer—as if for some feeling. Then she said: "You asked me just now why I've come back."

He stared as for the connection; after which with a smile: "Not to do *that*—?"

She waited briefly again, but with a queer little look. "I can do those things now; and—yes!—that's in a manner why. I came," she then said, "because I knew of a sudden one day —knew as never before—that I was old."

"I see. I see." He quite understood—she had notes that so struck him. "And how did you like it?"

She hesitated—she decided. "Well, if I liked it, it was on the principle perhaps on which some people like high game!"

"High game—that's good!" he laughed. "Ah, my dear, we're 'high'!"

She shook her head. "No—not you—yet. I at any rate didn't want any more adventures," Cornelia said.

He showed their small relic again with assurance. "You wanted *us*. Then here we are. Oh, how we can talk!—with all those things you know! You *are* an invention. And you'll see there are things *I* know. I shall turn up here—well, daily."

She took it in, but after a moment only answered. "There was something you said just now you'd tell me. Don't you mean to try—?"

"Mrs Worthingham?" He drew from within his coat his pocket-book and carefully found a place in it for Mary Cardew's carte-de-visite, folding it together with deliberation over which he put it back. Finally he spoke. "No—I've decided. I can't—I don't want to."

Cornelia marvelled—or looked as if she did. "Not for all she has?"

"Yes—I know all she has. But I also know all she hasn't. And, as I told you, she herself doesn't—hasn't a glimmer of a suspicion of it; and never will have."

Cornelia magnanimously thought. "No—but she knows other things."

He shook his head as at the portentous heap of them. "Too many—too many. And other indeed—*so* other. Do you know," he went on, "that it's as if *you*—by turning up for me —had brought that home to me?"

"For you," she candidly considered. "But what—since you can't marry me! can you do with me?"

Well, he seemed to have it all. "Everything. I can live with you—just this way." To illustrate which he dropped into the other chair by her fire; where, leaning back, he gazed at the flame. "I can't give you up. It's very curious. It has come over me as it did over you when you renounced Bognor. That's it—I know it at last, and I see one can like it. I'm 'high.' You needn't deny it. That's my taste. I'm old." And in spite of the considerable glow there of her little household altar he said it without the scowl.

THE BENCH OF DESOLATION

I

She had practically, he believed, conveyed the intimation, the horrid, brutal, vulgar menace, in the course of their last dreadful conversation, when, for whatever was left him of pluck or confidence—confidence in what he would fain have called a little more aggressively the strength of his position— he had judged best not to take it up. But this time there was no question of not understanding, or of pretending he didn't; the ugly, the awful words, ruthlessly formed by her lips, were like the fingers of a hand that she might have thrust into her pocket for extraction of the monstrous object that would serve best for—what should he call it?—a gage of battle.

"If I haven't a very different answer from you within the next three days I shall put the matter into the hands of my solicitor, whom it may interest you to know I've already seen. I shall bring an action for 'breach' against you, Herbert Dodd, as sure as my name's Kate Cookham."

There it was, straight and strong—yet he felt he could say for himself, when once it had come, or even, already just as it was coming, that it turned on, as if she had moved an electric switch, the very brightest light of his own very reasons. There *she* was, in all the grossness of her native indelicacy, in all her essential excess of will and destitution of scruple; and it was the woman capable of that ignoble threat who, his sharper sense of her quality having become so quite deterrent, was now making for him a crime of it that he shouldn't wish to tie himself to her for life. The vivid, lurid thing was the reality, all unmistakable, of her purpose; she had thought her case well out; had measured its odious, specious presentability; had taken, he might be sure, the very best advice obtainable at Properley, where there was always a first-rate promptitude of everything fourth-rate; it was disgustingly certain, in short, that she'd proceed. She was sharp and adroit, moreover—distinctly in certain ways a master-hand; how otherwise, with her so limited mere attractiveness, should she have entangled him? He couldn't shut his eyes to the very probable truth that if she should try it she'd pull it off. She *knew* she would—precisely; and her assurance was thus the very proof of her cruelty. That she had pretended she loved him was comparatively nothing; other women had pretended it, and other women too had really done it; but that she had pretended he could possibly have been right and safe and blest in loving *her*, a creature of the kind who could sniff that squalor of the law-court, of claimed damages and brazen lies and published kisses, of love-letters read amid obscene guffaws, as a positive tonic to resentment, as a high incentive to her course—this was what put him so beautifully in the right. It was what might signify in a woman all through, he said to himself, the mere imagination of such machinery. Truly what a devilish conception and what an appalling nature!

But there was no doubt, luckily, either, that he *could* plant his feet the firmer for his now intensified sense of these things. He was to live, it appeared, abominably worried, he was to live consciously rueful, he was to live perhaps even what a scoffing world would call abjectly exposed; but at least he was to live saved. In spite of his clutch of which steadying truth, however, and in spite of his declaring to her, with many other angry protests and pleas, that the line of conduct she announced was worthy of a vindictive barmaid, a lurking fear in him, too deep to counsel mere defiance, made him appear to keep open a little, till he could somehow turn round again, the door of possible composition. He had scoffed at her claim,

at her threat, at her thinking she could hustle and bully him—
"Such a way, my eye, to call back to life a dead love!"—yet
his instinct was ever, prudentially but helplessly, for gaining
time, even if time only more woefully to quake, and he gained
it now by not absolutely giving for his ultimatum that he
wouldn't think of coming round. He didn't in the smallest
degree mean to come round, but it was characteristic of him
that he could for three or four days breathe a little easier by
having left her under the impression that he perhaps might.
At the same time he couldn't not have said—what had con-
duced to bring out, in retort, her own last word, the word on
which they had parted—"Do you mean to say you yourself
would now be *willing* to marry and live with a man of whom
you could feel, the thing done, that he'd be all the while
thinking of you in the light of a hideous coercion?" "Never
you mind about *my* willingness," Kate had answered; "you've
known what that has been for the last six months. Leave that
to me, my willingness—I'll take care of it all right; and just
see what conclusion you can come to about your own."

He was to remember afterward how he had wondered
whether, turned upon her in silence while her odious lucidity
reigned unchecked, his face had shown her anything like the
quantity of hate he felt. Probably not at all; no man's face
could express that immense amount; especially the fair, refined, intellectual, gentleman-like face which had had—and
by her own more than once repeated avowal—so much to do
with the enormous fancy she had originally taken to him.
"Which—frankly now—would you personally *rather* I
should do," he had at any rate asked her with an intention of
supreme irony: "just sordidly marry you on top of this, or
leave you the pleasure of your lovely appearance in court and
of your so assured (since that's how you feel it) big haul of
damages? Shan't you be awfully disappointed, in fact, if I
don't let you get something better out of me than a poor
plain ten-shilling gold ring and the rest of the blasphemous

rubbish, as we should make it between us, pronounced at the altar? I take it, of course," he had swaggered on, "that your pretension wouldn't be for a moment that I should—after the act of profanity—take up my life with you."

"It's just as much my dream as it ever was, Herbert Dodd, to take up mine with *you!* Remember for me that I can do with it, my dear, that my idea is for even as much as that of you!" she had cried; "remember that for me, Herbert Dodd; remember, remember!"

It was on this she had left him—left him frankly under a mortal chill. There might have been the last ring of an appeal or a show of persistent and perverse tenderness in it, however preposterous any such matter; but in point of fact her large, clean, plain brown face—so much too big for her head, he now more than ever felt it to be, just as her head was so much too big for her body, and just as her hats had an irritating way of appearing to decline choice and conformity in respect to *any* of her dimensions—presented itself with about as much expression as his own shop-window when the broad, blank, sallow blind was down. He was fond of his shop-window with some good show on; he had a fancy for a good show and was master of twenty different schemes of taking arrangement for the old books and prints, "high-class rarities" his modest catalogue called them, in which he dealt and which his maternal uncle, David Geddes, had, as he liked to say, "handed down" to him. His widowed mother had screwed the whole thing, the stock and the connection and the rather bad little house in the rather bad little street, out of the ancient worthy, shortly before his death, in the name of the youngest and most interesting, the "delicate" one and the literary of her five scattered and struggling children. He could enjoy his happiest collocations and contrasts and effects, his harmonies and varieties of toned and faded leather and cloth, his sought colour-notes and the high clearnesses, here and there, of his white and beautifully figured price-labels, which pleased him enough in themselves almost to console him for not oftener having to break, on a customer's insistence, into the balanced composition. But the dropped expanse of time-soiled canvas, the thing of Sundays and holidays, with just his name, "Herbert Dodd, Successor," painted on below his uncle's antique style, the feeble penlike flourishes already quite archaic—this ugly vacant mask, which might so easily be taken for the mask of failure, somehow always gave him a chill.

That had been just the sort of chill—the analogy was complete—of Kate Cookham's last look. He supposed people doing an awfully good and sure and steady business, in whatever line, could see a whole front turned to vacancy that way, and merely think of the hours off represented by it. Only for this—nervously to bear it, in other words, and Herbert Dodd, quite with the literary temperament himself, was capable of that amount of play of fancy, or even of morbid analysis—you had to be on some footing, you had to feel some confidence, pretty different from his own up to now. He had never *not* enjoyed passing his show on the other side of the street and taking it in thence with a casual obliquity; but he had never held optical commerce with the drawn blind for a moment longer than he could help. It *always* looked horribly final and as if it never would come up again. Big and bare, with his name staring at him from the middle, it thus offered in its grimness a term of comparison for Miss Cookham's ominous visage. She never wore pretty, dotty, transparent veils, as Nan Drury did, and the words "Herbert Dodd"—save that she had sounded them at him there two or three times more like a Meg Merrilies or the bold bad woman in one of the melodramas of high life given during the fine season in the pavilion at the end of Properley Pier—were dreadfully, were permanently, seated on her lips. *She* was grim, no mistake.

That evening, alone in the back room above the shop, he

saw so little what he could do that, consciously demoralized for the hour, he gave way to tears about it. Her taking a stand so incredibly "low," that was what he couldn't get over. The particular bitterness of his cup was his having let himself in for a struggle on such terms—the use, on her side, of the vulgarest process known to the law: the vulgarest, the vulgarest, he kept repeating that, clinging to the help rendered him by this imputation to his terrorist of the vice he sincerely believed he had ever, among difficulties (for oh, he recognized the difficulties!) sought to keep most alien to him. He knew what he was, in a dismal, down-trodden sphere enough—the lean young proprietor of an old business that had itself rather shrivelled with age than ever grown fat, the purchase and sale of second-hand books and prints, with the back street of a long-fronted south-coast watering-place (Old Town by good luck) for the dusky field of his life. But he had gone in for all the education he could get—his educated customers would often hang about for more talk by the half-hour at a time, he actually feeling himself, and almost with a scruple, hold them there; which meant that he had had (he couldn't be blind to that) natural taste and had lovingly cultivated and formed it. Thus, from as far back as he could remember, there had been things all round him that he suffered from when other people didn't; and he had kept most of his suffering to himself —which had taught him, in a manner, *how* to suffer, and how almost to like to.

So, at any rate, he had never let go his sense of certain differences, he had done everything he could to keep it up— whereby everything that was vulgar was on the wrong side of his line. He had believed, for a series of strange, oppressed months, that Kate Cookham's manners and tone were on the right side; she had been governess—for young children—in two very good private families, and now had classes in literature and history for bigger girls who were sometimes brought by their mammas; in fact, coming in one day to look over his collection of students' manuals, and drawing it out, as so many did, for the evident sake of his conversation, she had appealed to him that very first time by her apparently pronounced intellectual side—goodness knew she didn't even then by the physical!—which she had artfully kept in view till she had entangled him past undoing. And it had all been but the cheapest of traps—when he came to take the pieces apart a bit—laid over a brazen avidity. What he now collapsed for, none the less—what he sank down on a chair at a table and nursed his weak, scared sobs in his resting arms for —was the fact that, whatever the trap, it held him as with the grip of sharp, murderous steel. There he was, there he was; alone in the brown summer dusk—brown through *his* windows—he cried and he cried. He shouldn't get out without losing a limb. The only question was which of his limbs it should be.

Before he went out, later on—for he at last felt the need to —he could, however, but seek to remove from his face and his betraying eyes, over his wash-stand, the traces of his want of fortitude. He brushed himself up; with which, catching his stricken image a bit spectrally in an old dim toilet-glass, he knew again, in a flash, the glow of righteous resentment. Who should be assured against coarse usage if a man of his really elegant, perhaps in fact a trifle over-refined or "effete" appearance, his absolutely gentlemanlike type, couldn't be? He never went so far as to rate himself, with exaggeration, a gentleman; but he would have maintained against all comers, with perfect candour and as claiming a high advantage, that he was, in spite of that liability to blubber, "like" one; which he *was* no doubt, for that matter, at several points. Like what lady then, who could ever possibly have been taken for one, was Kate Cookham, and therefore how could one have anything—anything of the intimate and private order—out with her fairly and on the plane, the only possible one, of common equality? He might find himself crippled for life; he believed verily, the more he thought, that that was what was before him. But he ended by seeing this doom in the almost redeeming light of the fact that it would all have been because he was, comparatively, too aristocratic. Yes, a man in his station couldn't afford to carry that so far—it must sooner or later, in one way or another, spell ruin. Never mind—it was the only thing he could be. Of course he should exquisitely suffer —but when hadn't he exquisitely suffered? How was he going to get through life by *any* arrangement without that? No wonder such a woman as Kate Cookham had been keen to annex so rare a value. The right thing would have been that the highest price should be paid for it—by such a different sort of logic from this nightmare of *his* having to pay.

II

WHICH was the way, of course, he talked to Nan Drury—as he had felt the immediate wild need to do; for he should perhaps be able to bear it all somehow or other with *her*—while they sat together, when time and freedom served, on one of the very last, the far westward benches of the interminable sea-front. It wasn't everyone who walked so far, especially at that flat season—the only ghost of a bustle now, save for the gregarious, the obstreperous haunters of the fluttering, far-shining Pier, being reserved for the sunny Parade of midwinter. It wasn't everyone who cared for the sunsets (which you got awfully well from there, and which were a particular strong point of the lower, the more "sympathetic" as Herbert Dodd liked to call it, Properley horizon) as he had always intensely cared, and as he had found Nan Drury care; to say nothing of his having also observed how little they directly spoke to Miss Cookham. He had taught this oppressive companion to notice them a bit, as he had taught her plenty of other things, but that was a different matter; for the reason that the "land's end" (stretching a point it carried off that name) had been, and had had to be by their lack of more sequestered resorts and conveniences, the scene of so much of what she styled their wooing-time—or, to put it more properly, of the time during which she had made the straightest and most unabashed love to *him:* just as it could henceforth but render possible, under an equal rigor, that he should enjoy there periods of consolation from beautiful, gentle, tender-souled Nan, to whom he was now at last, after the wonderful way they had helped each other to behave, going to make love, absolutely unreserved and abandoned, absolutely reckless and romantic love, a refuge from poisonous reality, as hard as ever he might.

The league-long, paved, lighted, garden-plotted, seated, and refuged Marina renounced its more or less celebrated attractions to break off short here; and an inward curve of the kindly westward shore almost made a wide-armed bay, with all the ugliness between town and country, and the further casual fringe of the coast, turning, as the day waned, to rich afternoon blooms of grey and brown and distant—it might fairly have been beautiful Hampshire—blue. Here it was that all that blighted summer, with Nan—from the dreadful May-day on—he gave himself up to the reaction of intimacy with the *kind* of woman, at least, that he liked; even if of everything else that might make life possible he was to be, by what he could make out, forever starved. Here it was that—as well as on whatever other scraps of occasions they could manage— Nan began to take off and fold up and put away in her pocket her pretty, dotty, becoming veil; as under the logic of his having so tremendously ceased, in the shake of his dark storm-gust, to be engaged to another woman. Her removal of that obstacle to a trusted friend's assuring himself whether the peachlike bloom of her finer facial curves bore the test of such further inquiry into their cool sweetness as might reinforce a mere baffled gaze—her momentous, complete surrender of so much of her charm, let us say, both marked the change in the situation of the pair and established the record of their perfect observance of every propriety for so long before. They afterward in fact could have dated it, their full clutch of their freedom and the bliss of their having so little henceforth to consider save their impotence, their poverty, their ruin; dated it from the hour of his recital to her of the—at the first blush—quite appalling upshot of his second and conclusive "scene of violence" with the mistress of his fortune, when the dire terms of his release had had to be formally, and oh! so abjectly, acceded to. She "compromised," the cruel brute, for Four Hundred Pounds down—for not a farthing less would she stay her strength from "proceedings." No jury in the land but would give her six, on the nail ("Oh, she knew quite where she was, thank you!"), and he might feel lucky to get off with so whole a skin. This was the sum, then, for which he had grovellingly compounded—under an agreement sealed by a supreme exchange of remarks.

"'Where in the name of lifelong ruin are you to *find* Four Hundred?'" Miss Cookham had mockingly repeated after him while he gasped as from the twist of her grip on his collar. "That's *your* look-out, and I should have thought you'd have made sure you knew before you decided on your base perfidy." And then she had mouthed and minced, with ever so false a gentility, her consistent, her sickening conclusion. "Of course—I may mention again—if you too distinctly object to the trouble of looking, you know where to find *me*."

"I had rather starve to death than ever go within a mile of you!" Herbert described himself as having sweetly answered; and that was accordingly where *they* devotedly but desperately were—he and she, penniless Nan Drury. Her father, of Drury & Dean, was like so far too many other of the anxious characters who peered through the dull window-glass of dusty offices at Properley, an Estate and House Agent, Surveyor,

Valuer and Auctioneer; she was the prettiest of six, with two brothers, neither of the least use, but, thanks to the manner in which their main natural protector appeared to languish under the accumulation of his attributes, they couldn't be said very particularly or positively to live. Their continued collective existence was a good deal of a miracle even to themselves, though they had fallen into the way of not unnecessarily, or too nervously, exchanging remarks upon it, and had even in a sort, from year to year, got used to it. Nan's brooding pinkness when he talked to her, her so very parted lips, considering her pretty teeth, her so very parted eyelids, considering her pretty eyes, all of which might have been those of some waxen image of uncritical faith, cooled the heat of his helplessness very much as if he were laying his head on a tense silk pillow. She had, it was true, forms of speech, familiar watchwords, that affected him as small scratchy perforations of the smooth surface from within; but his pleasure in her and need of her were independent of such things and really almost altogether determined by the fact of the happy, even if all so lonely, forms and instincts in her which claimed kinship with his own. With her natural elegance stamped on her as by a die, with her dim and disinherited individual refinement of grace, which would have made anyone wonder who she was anywhere—hat and veil and feather-boa and smart umbrella-knob and all—with her regular God-given distinction of type, in fine, she couldn't abide vulgarity much more than he could.

Therefore it didn't seem to him, under his stress, to matter particularly, for instance, if she *would* keep on referring so many things to the time, as she called it, when she came into his life—his own great insistence and contention being that she hadn't in the least entered there till his mind was wholly made up to eliminate his other friend. What that methodical fury was so fierce to bring home to him was the falsity to herself involved in the later acquaintance; whereas just his precious right to hold up his head to everything—before himself at least—sprang from the fact that she couldn't make dates fit anyhow. He hadn't so much as heard of his true beauty's existence (she had come back but a few weeks before from her two years with her terrible trying deceased aunt at Swindon, previous to which absence she had been an unnoticeable chit) till days and days, ever so many, upon his honour, after he had struck for freedom by his great first backing-out letter—the precious document, the treat for a British jury, in which, by itself, Miss Cookham's firm instructed her to recognize the prospect of a fortune. The way the ruffians had been "her" ruffians—it appeared as if she had posted them behind her from the first of her beginning her game!—and the way "instructions" bounced out, with it, at a touch, larger than life, as if she had arrived with her pocket full of them! The date of the letter, taken with its other connections, and the date of *her* first give-away for himself, his seeing her get out of the Brighton train with Bill Frankle that day he had gone to make the row at the Station parcels' office about the miscarriage of the box from Wales—those were the facts it sufficed him to point to, as he had pointed to them for Nan Drury's benefit, goodness knew, often and often enough. If he didn't seek occasion to do so for anyone else's—in open court as they said—that was his own affair, or at least his and Nan's.

It little mattered, meanwhile, if on their bench of desolation, all that summer—and it may be added for summers and summers, to say nothing of winters, there and elsewhere, to come —she did give way to her artless habit of not contradicting him enough, which led to her often trailing up and down before him, too complacently, the untimely shreds and patches of his own glooms and desperations. "Well, I'm glad I *am* in your life, terrible as it is, however or whenever I did come in!" and "*Of course* you'd rather have starved—and it seems pretty well as if we shall, doesn't it?—than have bought her

off by a false, abhorrent love, wouldn't you?" and "It isn't
as if she hadn't made up to you the way she did before you
had so much as looked at her, is it? or as if you hadn't shown
her what you felt her really to be before you had so much as
looked at *me*, is it either?" and "Yes, how on earth, pawning
the shoes on your feet, you're going to raise another shilling
—*that's* what you want to know, poor darling, don't you?"

III

HIS creditor, at the hour it suited her, transferred her base of
operations to town, to which impenetrable scene she had also
herself retired; and his raising of the first Two Hundred,
during five exasperated and miserable months, and then of
another Seventy piece-meal, bleedingly, after long delays and
under the epistolary whiplash cracked by the London solicitor
in his wretched ear even to an effect of the very report of
Miss Cookham's tongue—these melancholy efforts formed a
scramble up an arduous steep where steps were planted and
missed, and bared knees were excoriated, and clutches at wayside tufts succeeded and failed, on a system to which poor
Nan could have intelligently entered only if she had been
somehow less ladylike. She kept putting into his mouth the
sick quaver of where he should find the rest, the always inextinguishable rest, long after he had in silent rage fallen
away from any further payment at all—at first, he had but too
blackly felt, for himself, to the still quite possible non-
exclusion of some penetrating ray of "exposure." He didn't
care a tuppenny damn now, and in point of fact, after he had
by hook and by crook succeeded in being able to unload to
the tune of Two-Hundred-and-Seventy, and then simply
returned the newest reminder of his outstanding obligation
unopened, this latter belated but real sign of fight, the first he

had risked, remarkably caused nothing at all to happen; nothing at least but his being moved to quite tragically rueful wonder as to whether exactly some such demonstration mightn't have served his turn at an earlier stage.

He could by this time at any rate measure his ruin—with three fantastic mortgages on his house, his shop, his stock, and a burden of interest to carry under which his business simply stretched itself inanimate, without strength for a protesting kick, without breath for an appealing groan. Customers lingering for further enjoyment of the tasteful remarks he had cultivated the unobtrusive art of throwing in, would at this crisis have found plenty to repay them, might his wit have strayed a little more widely still, toward a circuitous egotistical outbreak, from the immediate question of the merits of this and that author or of the condition of this and that volume. He had come to be conscious through it all of strangely glaring at people when they tried to haggle—and not, as formerly, with the glare of derisive comment on their overdone humour, but with that of fairly idiotised surrender; as if they were much mistaken in supposing, for the sake of conversation, that he might take himself for saveable by the difference between sevenpence and ninepence. He watched everything impossible and deplorable happen, as in an endless prolongation of his nightmare; watched himself proceed, that is, with the finest, richest incoherence to the due preparation of his catastrophe. Everything came to seem *equally* part of this—in complete defiance of proportion; even his final command of detachment, on the bench of desolation (where each successive fact of his dire case regularly cut itself out black, yet of senseless silhouette, against the red west) in respect to poor Nan's flat infelicities, which for the most part kept no pace with the years or with change, but only shook like hard peas in a child's rattle, the same peas always, of course, so long as the rattle didn't split open with usage or from somebody's act of irritation. They represented, or they

had long done so, her contribution to the more superficial of
the two branches of intimacy—the intellectual alternative, the
one that didn't merely consist in her preparing herself for
his putting his arm round her waist.

There were to have been moments, nevertheless, all the
first couple of years, when she did touch in him, though to
his actively dissimulating it, a more or less sensitive nerve—
moments as they were too, to do her justice, when she treated
him not to his own wisdom, or even folly, served up cold, but
to a certain small bitter fruit of her personal, her unnatural,
plucking. "I wonder that since *she* took legal advice so freely,
to come down on you, you didn't take it yourself, a little,
before being so sure you stood no chance. Perhaps *your*
people would have been sure of something quite different—
perhaps, I only say, you know." She "only" said it, but she
said it, none the less, in the early time, about once a fortnight.
In the later, and especially after their marriage, it had a way
of coming up again to the exclusion, as it seemed to him, of
almost everything else; in fact during the most dismal years,
the three of the loss of their two children, the long stretch of
sordid embarrassment ending in her death, he was afterward
to think of her as having generally said it several times a day.
He was then also to remember that his answer, before she had
learnt to discount it, had been inveterately at hand: "What
would any solicitor have done or wanted to do but drag me
just into the hideous public arena"—he had always so put it
—"that it has been at anyrate my pride and my honour, the
one rag of self-respect covering my nakedness, to have loathed
and avoided from every point of view?"

That had disposed of it so long as he cared, and by the
time he had ceased to care for anything it had also lost itself
in the rest of the vain babble of home. After his wife's death,
during his year of mortal solitude, it awoke again as an echo
of far-off things—far-off, very far-off, because he felt then
not ten but twenty years older. That was by reason simply of

the dead weight with which his load of debt had settled—the persistence of his misery dragging itself out. With all that had come and gone the bench of desolation was still there, just as the immortal flush of the westward sky kept hanging its indestructible curtain. He had never got away—everything had left him, but he himself had been able to turn his back on nothing—and now, his day's labour before a dirty desk at the Gas Works ended, he more often than not, almost any season at temperate Properley serving his turn, took his slow, straight way to the Land's End and, collapsing there to rest, sat often for an hour at a time staring before him. He might in these sessions, with his eyes on the grey-green sea, have been counting again and still recounting the beads, almost all worn smooth, of his rosary of pain—which had for the fingers of memory and the recurrences of wonder the same felt break of the smaller ones by the larger that would have aided a pious mumble in some dusky altar-chapel.

If it has been said of him that when once full submersion, as from far back, had visibly begun to await him, he watched himself, in a cold lucidity, *do* punctually and necessarily each of the deplorable things that were inconsistent with his keeping afloat, so at present again he might have been held agaze just by the presented grotesqueness of that vigil. Such ghosts of dead seasons were all he *had* now to watch—such a recaptured sense for instance as that of the dismal unavailing awareness that had attended his act of marriage. He had let submersion final and absolute become the signal for it—a mere minor determinant having been the more or less contemporaneously unfavourable effect on the business of Drury & Dean of the sudden disappearance of Mr Dean with the single small tin box into which the certificates of the firm's credit had been found to be compressible. That had been his only form—or had at any rate seemed his only one. He couldn't not have married, no doubt, just as he couldn't not have suffered the last degree of humiliation and almost of want, or just as his

wife and children couldn't not have died of the little he was
able, under dire reiterated pinches, to do for them; but it *was*
"rum," for final solitary brooding, that he hadn't appeared to
see his way definitely to undertake the support of a family till
the last scrap of his little low-browed, high-toned business
and the last figment of "property" in the old tiled and tim-
bered shell that housed it had been sacrificed to creditors
mustering six rows deep.

Of course what had counted too in the odd order was that
even at the end of the two or three years he had "allowed"
her, Kate Cookham, gorged with his unholy tribute, had
become the subject of no successful siege on the part either
of Bill Frankle or, by what he could make out, of anyone else.
She had judged decent—he could do her that justice—to take
herself personally out of his world, as he called it, for good and
all, as soon as he had begun regularly to bleed; and, to whatever lucrative practice she might be devoting her great talents
in London or elsewhere, he felt his conscious curiosity about
her as cold, with time, as the passion of vain protest that she
had originally left him to. He could recall but two direct
echoes of her in all the bitter years—both communicated by
Bill Frankle, disappointed and exposed and at last quite
remarkably ingenuous sneak, who had also, from far back,
taken to roaming the world, but who, during a period, used
fitfully and ruefully to reappear. Herbert Dodd had quickly
seen, at their first meeting—everyone met everyone sooner or
later at Properley, if meeting it could always be called, either
in the glare or the gloom of the explodedly attractive Embankment—that no silver stream of which he himself had been
the remoter source could have played over the career of this
all but repudiated acquaintance. That hadn't fitted with his
first, his quite primitive raw vision of the probabilities, and
he had further been puzzled when, much later on, it had come
to him in a round-about way that Miss Cookham was supposed to be, or to have been, among them for a few days "on

the quiet," and that Frankle, who had seen her and who claimed to know more about it than he said, was cited as authority for the fact. But he hadn't himself at this juncture seen Frankle; he had only wondered, and a degree of mystification had even remained.

That memory referred itself to the dark days of old Drury's smash, the few weeks between his partner's dastardly flight and Herbert's own comment on it in the form of his standing up with Nan for the nuptial benediction of the Vicar of St Bernard's on a very cold, bleak December morning and amid a circle of seven or eight long-faced, red-nosed, and altogether dowdy persons. Poor Nan herself had come to affect him as scarce other than red-nosed and dowdy by that time, but this only added, in his then, and indeed in his lasting view, to his general and his particular morbid bravery. He had cultivated ignorance, there were small inward immaterial luxuries he could scrappily cherish even among other, and the harshest, destitutions; and one of them was represented by this easy refusal of his mind to render to certain passages of his experience, to various ugly images, names, associations, the homage of continued attention. That served him, that helped him; but what happened when, a dozen dismal years having worn themselves away, he sat single and scraped bare again, as if his long wave of misfortune had washed him far beyond everything and then conspicuously retreated, was that, thus stranded by tidal action, deposited in the lonely hollow of his fate, he felt even sustaining pride turn to nought and heard no challenge from it when old mystifications, stealing forth in the dusk of the day's work done, scratched at the door of speculation and hung about, through the idle hours, for irritated notice.

The evenings of his squalid clerkship were all leisure now, but there was nothing at all near home, on the other hand, for his imagination, numb and stiff from its long chill, to begin to play with. Voices from far off would quaver to him therefore in the stillness; where he knew for the most recurrent, little by little, the faint wail of his wife. He had become deaf to it in life, but at present, after so great an interval, he listened again, listened and listened, and seemed to hear it sound as by the pressure of some weak broken spring. It phrased for his ear her perpetual question, the one she had come to at the last as under the obsession of a discovered and resented wrong, a wrong withal that had its source much more in his own action than anywhere else. "That you didn't make *sure* she could have done anything, that you didn't make sure and that you were too afraid!"—this commemoration had ended by playing such a part of Nan's finally quite contracted consciousness as to exclude everything else.

At the time, somehow, he had made his terms with it; he had then more urgent questions to meet than that of the poor creature's taste in worrying pain; but actually it struck him—not the question, but the fact itself of the taste—as the one thing left over from all that had come and gone. So it was; nothing remained to him in the world, on the bench of desolation, but the option of taking up that echo—together with an abundance of free time for doing so. That he hadn't made sure of what might and what mightn't have been done to him, that he had been too afraid—had the proposition a possible bearing on his present apprehension of things? To reply indeed he would have had to be able to say what his present apprehension of things, left to itself, amounted to; an uninspiring effort indeed he judged it, sunk to so poor a pitch was his material of thought—though it might at last have been the feat he sought to perform as he stared at the grey-green sea.

IV

IT was seldom he was disturbed in any form of sequestered speculation, or that at his times of predilection, especially that of the long autumn blankness between the season of trippers and the season of Bath-chairs, there were westward stragglers enough to jar upon his settled sense of priority. For himself his seat, the term of his walk, was consecrated; it had figured to him for years as the last (though there were others, not immediately near it, and differently disposed, that might have aspired to the title); so that he could invidiously distinguish as he approached, make out from a distance any accident of occupation, and never draw nearer while that unpleasantness lasted. What he disliked was to compromise on his tradition, whether for a man, a woman, or a connoodling couple; it was to idiots of this last composition he most objected, he having sat there, in the past, alone, having sat there interminably with Nan, having sat there with—well, with other women when women, at hours of ease, could still care or count for him, but having never shared the place with any shuffling or snuffling strangers.

It was a world of fidgets and starts, however, the world of his present dreariness; he alone possessed in it, he seemed to make out, of the secret of the dignity of sitting still with one's fate; so that if he took a turn about or rested briefly elsewhere even foolish philanderers—though this would never have been his and Nan's way—ended soon by some adjournment as visibly pointless as their sprawl. Then, their backs turned, he would drop down on it, the bench of desolation—which was what he, and he only, made it, by sad adoption; where, for that matter, moreover, once he had settled at his end, it was marked that nobody else ever came to sit. He saw people, along the Marina, take this liberty with other resting presences; but his own struck them perhaps in general as either of too grim or just of too dingy a vicinage. He might have affected the fellow-lounger as a man evil, unsociable, possibly engaged in working out the idea of a crime; or otherwise, more probably—for on the whole he surely looked harmless —devoted to the worship of some absolutely unpractical remorse.

On a certain October Saturday he had got off as usual, early; but the afternoon light, his pilgrimage drawing to its aim, could still show him, at long range, the rare case of an established usurper. His impulse was then, as by custom, to deviate a little and wait, all the more that the occupant of the bench was a lady, and that ladies, when alone, were—at that austere end of the varied frontal stretch—markedly discontinuous; but he kept on at sight of this person's rising, while he was still fifty yards off, and proceeding, her back turned, to the edge of the broad terrace, the outer line of which followed the interspaced succession of seats and was guarded by an iron rail from the abruptly lower level of the beach. Here she stood before the sea, while our friend on his side, recognizing no reason to the contrary, sank into the place she had quitted. There were other benches, eastward and off by the course of the drive, for vague ladies. The lady indeed thus thrust upon Herbert's vision might have struck an observer either as not quite vague or as vague with a perverse intensity suggesting design.

Not that our own observer at once thought of these things; he only took in, and with no great interest, that the obtruded presence was a "real" lady; that she was dressed—he noticed such matters—with a certain elegance of propriety or intention of harmony; and that she remained perfectly still for a good many minutes; so many in fact that he presently ceased to heed her, and that as she wasn't straight before him, but as far to the left as was consistent with his missing her profile, he had turned himself to one of his sunsets again (though it wasn't quite one of his best) and let it hold him for a time that enabled her to alter her attitude and present a fuller view. Without other movement, but her back now to the sea and her face to the odd person who had appropriated her corner, she had taken a sustained look at him before he was aware she had stirred. On that apprehension, however, he became also promptly aware of her direct, her applied observation. As his sense of this quickly increased he wondered who she was and what she wanted—what, as it were, was the matter with her; it suggested to him, the next thing, that she had, under some strange idea, actually been waiting for him. Any idea about him to-day on the part of any one could only be strange.

Yes, she stood there with the ample width of the Marina between them, but turned to him, for all the world, as to show frankly that she was concerned with him. And she *was* —oh, yes—a real lady: a middle-aged person, of good appearance and of the best condition, in quiet but "handsome" black, save for very fresh white kid gloves, and with a pretty, dotty, becoming veil, predominantly white, adjusted to her countenance; which through it somehow, even to his imperfect sight, showed strong fine black brows and what he would have called on the spot character. But she was pale; her black brows were the blacker behind the flattering tissue; she still kept a hand, for support, on the terrace-rail, while the other, at the end of an extended arm that had an effect of rigidity, clearly pressed hard on the knob of a small and shining umbrella, the lower extremity of whose stick was equally, was sustainingly, firm on the walk. So this mature, qualified, important person stood and looked at the limp, undistinguished—oh, his values of aspect now!—shabby man on the bench.

It was extraordinary, but the fact of her interest, by immensely surprising, by immediately agitating him, blinded

him at first to her identity and, for the space of his long stare,
diverted him from it; with which even then, when recognition
did break, the sense of the shock, striking inward, simply
consumed itself in gaping stillness. He sat there motionless
and weak, fairly faint with surprise, and there was no instant,
in all the succession of so many, at which Kate Cookham
could have caught the special sign of his intelligence. Yet that
she did catch something he saw—for he saw her steady herself, by her two supported hands, to meet it; while, after she
had done so, a very wonderful thing happened, of which he
could scarce, later on, have made a clear statement, though he
was to think it over again and again. She moved toward him,
she reached him, she stood there, she sat down near him, he
merely passive and wonderstruck, unresentfully "impressed,"
gaping and taking it in—and all as with an open allowance on
the part of each, so that they positively and quite intimately
met in it, of the impertinence for their case, this case that
brought them again, after horrible years, face to face, of the
vanity, the profanity, the impossibility, of anything between
them but silence.

Nearer to him, beside him at a considerable interval (oh,
she was immensely considerate!) she presented him, in the
sharp terms of her transformed state—but thus the more
amply, formally, ceremoniously—with the reasons that would
serve him best for not having precipitately known her. She
was simply another and a totally different person, and the
exhibition of it to which she had proceeded with this solemn
anxiety was all, obviously, for his benefit—once he had, as he
appeared to be doing, provisionally accepted her approach.
He had remembered her as inclined to the massive and disowned by the graceful; but this was a spare, fine, worn, almost
wasted lady—who had repaired waste, it was true, however,
with something he could only appreciate as a rich accumulation of manner. She was strangely older, so far as that went
—marked by experience and as if many things had happened

to her; her face had suffered, to its improvement, contraction and concentration; and if he had granted, of old and from the first, that her eyes were remarkable, had they yet ever had for him this sombre glow? Withal, something said, she had flourished—he felt it, wincing at it, as that; she had had a life, a career, a history, something that her present waiting air and nervous consciousness couldn't prevent his noting there as a deeply latent assurance. She had flourished, she had flourished —though to learn it after this fashion was somehow at the same time not to feel she flaunted it. It wasn't thus execration that she revived in him; she made in fact, exhibitively, as he could only have put it, the matter of long ago irrelevant, and these extraordinary minutes of their reconstituted relation— how many? how few?—addressed themselves altogether to new possibilities.

Still it after a little awoke in him as with the throb of a touched nerve that his own very attitude was supplying a connection; he knew presently that he wouldn't have had her go, *couldn't* have made a sign to her for it—which was what she had been uncertain of—without speaking to him; and that therefore he was, as at the other, the hideous time, passive to whatever she might do. She was even yet, she was always, in possession of him; she had known how and where to find him and had appointed that he should see her, and, though he had never dreamed it was again to happen to him, he was meeting it already as if it might have been the only thing that the least humanly *could*. Yes, he had come back there to flop, by long custom, upon the bench of desolation *as* the man in the whole place, precisely, to whom nothing worth more than tuppence could happen; whereupon, in the grey desert of his consciousness, the very earth had suddenly opened and flamed. With this, further, it came over him that he hadn't been prepared and that his wretched appearance must show it. He wasn't fit to receive a visit—any visit; a flush for his felt misery, in the light of her opulence, broke out in his lean cheeks. But if he coloured he sat as he was—she should at least, as a visitor, be satisfied. His eyes only, at last, turned from her and resumed a little their gaze at the sea. That, however, didn't relieve him, and he perpetrated in the course of another moment the odd desperate gesture of raising both his hands to his face and letting them, while he pressed it to them, cover and guard it. It was as he held them there that she at last spoke.

"I'll go away if you wish me to." And then she waited a moment. "I mean now—now that you've seen I'm here. I wanted you to know it, and I thought of writing—I was afraid of our meeting accidentally. Then I was afraid that if I wrote you might refuse. So I thought of this way—as I knew you must come out here." She went on with pauses, giving him a chance to make a sign. "I've waited several days. But I'll do what you wish. Only I should like in that case to come back." Again she stopped; but strange was it to him that he wouldn't have made her break off. She held him in boundless wonder. "I came down—I mean I came from town—on purpose. I'm staying on still, and I've a great patience and will give you time. Only may I say it's important? Now that I do see you," she brought out in the same way, "I see how inevitable it was—I mean that I should have wanted to come. But you must feel about it as you can," she wound up—"till you get used to the idea."

She spoke so for accommodation, for discretion, for some ulterior view already expressed in her manner, that, after taking well in, from behind his hands, that this was her very voice—oh, ladylike!—heard, and heard in deprecation of displeasure, after long years again, he uncovered his face and freshly met her eyes. More than ever he couldn't have known her. Less and less remained of the figure all the facts of which had long ago so hardened for him. She was a handsome, grave, authoritative, but refined and, as it were, physically rearranged person—she, the outrageous vulgarity of whose prime assault had kept him shuddering so long as a shudder was in him. That atrocity in her was what everything had been built on, but somehow, all strangely, it was slipping from him; so that, after the oddest fashion conceivable, when he felt he mustn't let her go, it was as if he were putting out his hand to *save* the past, the hideous, real, unalterable past, exactly as she had been the cause of its being and the cause of his undergoing it. He should have been too awfully "sold" if he wasn't going to have been right about her.

"I don't mind," he heard himself at last say. Not to mind had seemed for the instant the length he was prepared to go; but he was afterward aware of how soon he must have added: "You've come on purpose to see me?" He was on the point of putting to her further: "What then do you want of me?" But he would keep—yes, in time—from appearing to show he cared. If he showed he cared, where then would be his revenge? So he was already, within five minutes, thinking his revenge uncomfortably over instead of just comfortably knowing it. What came to him, at any rate, as they actually fell to talk, was that, with such precautions, considerations, reduplications of consciousness, almost avowed feelings of her way on her own part, and light fingerings of his chords of sensibility, she was understanding, she *had* understood, more things than all the years, up to this strange eventide, had given him an inkling of. They talked, they went on—he hadn't let her retreat, to whatever it committed him and however abjectly it did so; yet keeping off and off, dealing with such surface facts as involved ancient acquaintance but kept abominations at bay. The recognition, the attestation that she *had* come down for him, that there would be reasons, that she had even hovered and watched, assured herself a little of his habits (which she managed to speak of as if, on their present ampler development, they were much to be deferred to), held them long enough to make vivid how, listen as stiffly or as serenely as he might, she sat there in fear, just as she had so stood there at first, and that her fear had really to do with her calculation of some sort of chance with him. What chance could it possibly be? Whatever it might have done, on this prodigious showing, with Kate Cookham, it made the present witness to the state of his fortunes simply exquisite: he ground his teeth secretly together as he saw he should have to take *that*. For what did it mean but that she would have liked to pity him if she could have done it with safety? Ah, however, he must give her no measure of safety!

By the time he had remarked, with that idea, that she probably saw few changes about them there that weren't for the worse—the place was going down, down and down, so fast that goodness knew where it would stop—and had also mentioned that in spite of this he himself remained faithful, with all its faults loving it still; by the time he had, after that fashion, superficially indulged her, adding a few further light and just sufficiently dry reflections on local matters, the disappearance of landmarks and important persons, the frequency of gales, the low policy of the Town Council in playing down to cheap excursionists: by the time he had so acquitted himself, and she had observed, of her own motion, that she was staying at the Royal, which he knew for the time-honoured, the conservative, and exclusive hotel, he had made out for himself one thing at least, the amazing fact that he had been landed by his troubles, at the end of time, in a "social relation," of all things in the world, and how of that luxury he was now having unprecedented experience. He had but once in his life had his nose in the Royal, on the occasion of his himself delivering a parcel during some hiatus in his succession of impossible small boys and meeting in the hall the lady who had bought of him, in the morning, a set of Crabbe; largely, he flattered himself, under the artful persuasion of his acute remarks on that author, gracefully associated by him, in this colloquy, he remembered, with a glance at Charles Lamb as well, and who went off, in a day or two, without settling, though he received her cheque from London three or four months later.

That hadn't been a social relation; and truly, deep within his appeal to himself to be remarkable, to be imperturbable and impenetrable, to be in fact quite incomparable now, throbbed the intense vision of his drawing out and draining dry the sensation he had begun to taste. He would do it, moreover—that would be the refinement of his art—not only without the betraying anxiety of a single question, but just even by seeing her flounder (since she must, in a vagueness deeply disconcerting to her) as to her real effect on him. She was distinctly floundering by the time he had brought her— it had taken ten minutes—down to a consciousness of absurd and twaddling topics, to the reported precarious state, for instance, of the syndicate running the Bijou Theatre at the Pierhead—all as an admonition that she might want him to want to know why she was thus waiting on him, might want it for all she was worth, before he had ceased to be so remark- able as not to ask her. He didn't—and this assuredly was wondrous enough—want to do anything worse to her than let her flounder; but he was willing to do that so long as it mightn't prevent his seeing at least where *he* was. He seemed still to see where he was even at the minute that followed her final break-off, clearly intended to be resolute, from make- believe talk.

"I wonder if I might prevail on you to come to tea with me to-morrow at five."

He didn't so much as answer it—though he could scarcely believe his ears. To-morrow was Sunday, and the proposal referred, clearly, to the custom of "five-o'clock" tea, known to him only by the contemporary novel of manners and the catchy advertisements of table linen. He had never in his life been present at any such luxurious rite, but he was offering practical indifference to it as a false mark of his sense that his social relation had already risen to his chin. "I gave up my very modest, but rather interesting little old book business, perhaps you know, ever so long ago."

She floundered so that she could say nothing—meet *that* with no possible word; all the less too that his tone, casual and colourless, wholly defied any apprehension of it as a reverse. Silence only came; but after a moment she returned to her effort. "If you *can* come I shall be at home. To see you otherwise than thus was, in fact, what, as I tell you, I came down for. But I leave it," she returned, "to your feeling."

He had at this, it struck him, an inspiration; which he required however a minute or two to decide to carry out; a minute or two during which the shake of his foot over his knee became an intensity of fidget. "Of course I know I still owe you a large sum of money. If it's about *that* you wish to see me," he went on, "I may as well tell you just here that I shall be able to meet my full obligation in the future as little as I've met it in the past. I can never," said Herbert Dodd, "pay up that balance."

He had looked at her while he spoke, but on finishing looked off at the sea again and continued to agitate his foot. He knew now what he had done, and why; and the sense of her fixed dark eyes on him during his speech and after didn't alter his small contentment. Yet even when she still said nothing he didn't turn round; he simply kept his corner as if *that* were his point made, should it even be the last word between them. It might have been, for that matter, from the way in which she presently rose, gathering herself, her fine umbrella and her very small smart reticule, in the construction of which shining gilt much figured, well together, and, after standing another instant, moved across to the rail of the terrace as she had done before and remained, as before, with her back to him, though this time, it well might be, under a different fear. A quarter of an hour ago she hadn't tried him, and had had that anxiety; now that she had tried him it wasn't easier—but she was thinking what she still could do. He left her to think—nothing in fact more interesting than the way she might decide had ever happened to him; but it was a part of this also that as she turned round and came nearer again he didn't rise, he gave her no help. If she got any, at least, from his looking up at her only, meeting her fixed eyes once more in silence, that was her own affair. "You must think," she said—"you must take all your time, but I shall be at home." She left it to him thus— she insisted, with her idea, on leaving him somewhere too. And on her side as well she showed an art—which resulted, after another instant, in his having to rise to his feet. He flushed afresh as he did it—it exposed him so shabbily the more; and now if she took him in, with each of his seedy items, from head to foot, he didn't and couldn't and wouldn't know it, attaching his eyes hard and straight to something quite away from them.

It stuck in his throat to say he'd come, but she had so curious a way with her that he still less could say he wouldn't, and in a moment had taken refuge in something that was neither. "Are you married?"—he put it to her with that plainness, though it had seemed before he said it to do more for him than while she waited before replying.

"No, I'm not married," she said: and then had another wait that might have amounted to a question of what this had to do with it.

He surely couldn't have told her; so that he had recourse, a little poorly as he felt, but to an "Oh!" that still left them opposed. He turned away for it—that is for the poorness, which, lingering in the air, had almost a vulgar platitude; and when he presently again wheeled about she had fallen off as for quitting him, only with a pause, once more, for a last look. It was all a bit awkward, but he had another happy thought, which consisted in his silently raising his hat as for a sign of dignified dismissal. He had cultivated of old, for the occasions of life, the right, the discriminated bow, and now, out of the grey limbo of the time when he could care for such things, this flicker of propriety leaped and worked. She might, for that matter, herself have liked it; since, receding further, only with her white face toward him, she paid it the homage of submission. He remained dignified, and she almost humbly went.

V

NOTHING in the world, on the Sunday afternoon, could have prevented him from going; he was not after all destitute of three or four such articles of clothing as, if they wouldn't particularly grace the occasion, wouldn't positively dishonour it. That deficiency might have kept him away, but no voice of the spirit, no consideration of pride. It sweetened his impatience, in fact—for he fairly felt it a long time to wait—that his pride would really most find its account in his acceptance of these conciliatory steps. From the moment he could put it in that way—that he couldn't refuse to hear what she might have, so very elaborately, to say for herself—he ought certainly to be at his ease; in illustration of which he whistled odd snatches to himself as he hung about on that cloud-dappled autumn Sunday, a mild private minstrelsy that his lips hadn't known since when? The interval of the twenty-four hours, made longer by a night of many more revivals than oblivions, had in fact dragged not a little; in spite of which, however, our extremely brushed-up and trimmed and polished friend knew an unprecedented flutter as he was ushered, at the Royal Hotel, into Miss Cookham's sitting-room. Yes, it was an adventure, and he had never had an adventure in his life; the term, for him, was essentially a term of high appreciation—such as disqualified for that figure, under due criticism, every single passage of his past career.

What struck him at the moment as qualifying in the highest degree this actual passage was the fact that at no great distance from his hostess in the luxurious room, as he apprehended it, in which the close of day had begun to hang a few shadows, sat a gentleman who rose as she rose, and whose name she at once mentioned to him. He had for Herbert Dodd all the air of a swell, the gentleman—rather red-faced and bald-headed, but moustachioed, waistcoated, necktied to the highest pitch, with an effect of chains and rings, of shining teeth in a glassily monocular smile; a wondrous apparition to have been asked to "meet" him, as in contemporary fiction, or for him to have been asked to meet. "Captain Roper, Mr Herbert Dodd" —their entertainer introduced them, yes; but with a sequel immediately afterward more disconcerting apparently to Captain Roper himself even than to her second and more breathless visitor; a "Well then, good-bye till the next time," with a hand thrust straight out, which allowed the personage so addressed no alternative but to lay aside his teacup, even though Herbert saw there was a good deal left in it, and glare about him for his hat. Miss Cookham had had her tea-tray on a small table before her, she had served Captain Roper while waiting for Mr Dodd; but she simply dismissed him now, with a high sweet unmistakable decision, a knowledge of what she was about, as our hero would have called it, which enlarged at a stroke the latter's view of the number of different things and sorts of things, in the sphere of the manners and ways of those living at their ease, that a social relation would put before one. Captain Roper would have liked to remain, would have liked more tea, but Kate signified in this direct fashion that she had had enough of him. Herbert had seen things, in his walk of life—rough things, plenty; but never things smoothed with that especial smoothness, carried out as it were by the fine form of Captain Roper's own retreat, which included even a bright convulsed leave-taking cognisance of the plain, vague individual, of no lustre at all and with the very low-class guard of an old silver watch buttoned away under an ill-made coat, to whom he was sacrificed.

It came to Herbert as he left the place a shade less remarkable—though there was still wonder enough and to spare—that he had been even publicly and designedly sacrificed; exactly so that, as the door closed behind him, Kate Cookham, standing there to wait for it, could seem to say, across the room, to the friend of her youth, only by the expression of her fine eyes: "There—see what I do for you!" "For" him —that was the extraordinary thing, and not less so that he was already, within three minutes, after this fashion, taking it in as by the intensity of a new light; a light that was one somehow with this rich inner air of the plush-draped and much-mirrored hotel, where the firelight and the approach of evening confirmed together the privacy and the loose curtains at the wide window were parted for a command of his old lifelong Parade—the field of life so familiar to him from below and in the wind and the wet, but which he had never in all the long years hung over at this vantage.

"He's an acquaintance, but a bore," his hostess explained in respect to Captain Roper. "He turned up yesterday, but I didn't invite him, and I had said to him before you came in that I was expecting a gentleman with whom I should wish to be alone. I go quite straight at my idea that way, as a rule; but you know," she now strikingly went on, "how straight I go. And he had had," she added, "his tea."

Dodd had been looking all round—had taken in, with the rest, the brightness, the distinguished elegance, as he supposed it, of the tea-service with which she was dealing and the variously-tinted appeal of certain savoury edibles on plates. "Oh, but he *hadn't* had his tea!" he heard himself the next moment earnestly reply; which speech had at once betrayed, he was then quickly aware, the candour of his interest, the unsophisticated state that had survived so many troubles. If he was so interested how could he be proud, and if he was proud how could he be so interested?

He had made her at any rate laugh outright, and was further conscious, for this, both that it was the first time of that since their new meeting, and that it didn't affect him as harsh. It affected him, however, as free, for she replied at once, still smiling and as a part of it: "Oh, I think we shall get on!"

This told him he had made some difference for her, shown her the way, or something like it, that she hadn't been sure of yesterday; which moreover wasn't what he had intended— he had come armed for showing her nothing; so that after she had gone on, with the same gain of gaiety, "You must at any rate comfortably have yours," there was but one answer for him to make.

His eyes played again over the tea-things—they seemed strangely to help him; but he didn't sit down. "I've come, as you see—but I've come, please, to understand; and if you require to be alone with me, and if I break bread with you, it seems to me I should first know exactly where I am and to what you suppose I so commit myself." He had thought it out and over and over, particularly the turn about breaking bread; though perhaps he didn't give it, in her presence—this was impossible, her presence altered so many things—quite the full sound or the weight he had planned.

But it had none the less come to his aid—it had made her perfectly grave. "You commit yourself to nothing. You're perfectly free. It's only I who commit myself."

On which, while she stood there as if all handsomely and deferentially waiting for him to consider and decide, he would have been naturally moved to ask her what she committed herself then *to*—so moved, that is, if he hadn't, before saying it, thought more sharply still of something better. "Oh, that's another thing."

"Yes, that's another thing," Kate Cookham returned. To which she added, "So *now* won't you sit down?" He sank

with deliberation into the seat from which Captain Roper
had risen; she went back to her own, and while she did so
spoke again. "I'm *not* free. At least," she said over her tea-
tray, "I'm free only for this."

Everything was there before them and around them, everything massive and shining, so that he had instinctively fallen
back in his chair as for the wondering, the resigned acceptance
of it; where her last words stirred in him a sense of odd de-
preciation. Only for "that"? "That" was everything, at this
moment, to his long inanition, and the effect, as if she had
suddenly and perversely mocked him, was to press the spring
of a protest. "Isn't 'this' then riches?"

"Riches?" she smiled over, handing him his cup—for she
had triumphed in having struck from him a question.

"I mean haven't you a lot of money?" He didn't care now
that it was out; his cup was in his hand, and what was that
but proved interest? He had succumbed to the social relation.

"Yes, I've money. Of course you wonder—but I've
wanted you to wonder. It was to make you take that in that
I came. So now you know," she said, leaning back where she
faced him, but in a straighter chair and with her arms closely
folded, after a fashion characteristic of her, as for some
control of her nerves.

"You came to show you've money?"

"That's one of the things. Not a lot—not even very much.
But enough," said Kate Cookham.

"Enough? I should think so!" he again couldn't help a bit
crudely exhaling.

"Enough for what I wanted. I don't always live like this
—not at all. But I came to the best hotel on purpose. I
wanted to show you I could. Now," she asked, "do you
understand?"

"Understand?" He only gaped.

She threw up her loosed arms, which dropped again beside
her. "I did it *for* you—I did it *for* you!"

" 'For' me—?"

"What I did—what I did here of old."

He stared, trying to see it. "When you made me pay you?"

"The Two Hundred and Seventy—all I could get from you, as you reminded me yesterday, so that I had to give up the rest. It was my idea," she went on—"it was my idea."

"To bleed me quite to death?" Oh, his ice was broken now!

"To make you raise money—since you could, you *could*. You did, you did—so what better proof?"

His hands fell from what he had touched; he could only stare—her own manner for it was different now too. "I did. I did indeed—!" And the woeful weak simplicity of it, which seemed somehow all that was left him, fell even on his own ear.

"Well then, here it is—it isn't lost!" she returned with a graver face.

" 'Here' it is," he gasped, "my poor agonized old money —my blood?"

"Oh, it's *my* blood too, you must know now!" She held up her head as not before—as for her right to speak of the thing to-day most precious to her. "I took it, but this—my being here this way—is what I've made of it! That was the idea I had!"

Her "ideas," as things to boast of, staggered him. "To have everything in the world, like this, at my wretched expense?"

She had folded her arms back again—grasping each elbow she sat firm; she knew he could see, and had known well from the first, what she had wanted to say, difficult, monstrous though it might be. "No more than at my own—but to do something with your money that you'd never do yourself."

"Myself, myself?" he wonderingly wailed. "Do you know —or don't you?—what my life has been?"

She waited, and for an instant, though the light in the

room had failed a little more and would soon be mainly that of the flaring lamps on the windy Parade, he caught from her dark eye a silver gleam of impatience. "You've suffered and you've worked—which, God knows, is what I've done! *Of course* you've suffered," she said—"you inevitably had to! We have to," she went on, "to do or to be or to get anything."

"And pray what have I done or been or got?" Herbert Dodd found it almost desolately natural to demand.

It made her cover him again as with all she was thinking of. "Can you imagine nothing, or can't you conceive—?" And then as her challenge struck deeper in, deeper down than it had yet reached and with the effect of a rush of the blood to his face, "It was *for* you, it was *for* you!" she again broke out—"and for what or whom else could it have been?"

He saw things to a tune now that made him answer straight: "I thought at one time it might be for Bill Frankle."

"Yes—that was the way you treated me," Miss Cookham as plainly replied.

But he let this pass; his thought had already got away from it. "What good then—its having been for me—has that ever done me?"

"Doesn't it do you any good *now?*" his friend returned. To which she added, with another dim play of her tormented brightness, before he could speak: "But if you won't even have your tea—!"

He had in fact touched nothing, and if he could have explained, would have pleaded very veraciously that his appetite, keen when he came in, had somehow suddenly failed. It was beyond eating or drinking, what she seemed to want him to take from her. So if he looked, before him, over the array, it was to say, very grave and graceless: "Am I to understand that you offer to repay me?"

"I offer to repay you with interest, Herbert Dodd"—and her emphasis of the great word was wonderful.

It held him in his place a minute, and held his eyes upon

her; after which, agitated too sharply to sit still, he pushed
back his chair and stood up. It was as if mere distress or
dismay at first worked in him, and was in fact a wave of deep
and irresistible emotion which made him, on his feet, sway
as in a great trouble and then, to correct it, throw himself
stiffly toward the window, where he stood and looked out
unseeing. The road, the wide terrace beyond, the seats, the
eternal sea beyond that, the lighted lamps now flaring in the
October night-wind, with the few dispersed people abroad
at the tea-hour; these things, meeting and melting into the
firelit hospitality at his elbow—or was it that portentous
amenity that melted into *them?*—seemed to form round him
and to put before him, all together, the strangest of circles
and the newest of experiences, in which the unforgettable and
the unimaginable were confoundingly mixed. "Oh, oh, oh!"
—he could only almost howl for it.

And then, while a thick blur for some moments mantled
everything, he knew she had got up, that she stood watching
him, allowing for everything, again all "cleverly" patient
with him, and he heard her speak again as with studied quiet-
ness and clearness. "I wanted to take care of you—it was what
I first wanted—and what you first consented to. I'd have
done it, oh, I'd have done it, I'd have loved you and helped
you and guarded you, and you'd have had no trouble, no
bad blighting ruin, in all your easy, yes, just your quite
jolly and comfortable life. I showed you and proved to you this
—I brought it home to you, as I fondly fancied, and it made
me briefly happy. You swore you cared for me, you wrote it
and made me believe it—you pledged me your honour and
your faith. Then you turned and changed suddenly, from
one day to another; everything altered, you broke your vows,
you as good as told me you only wanted it off. You faced me
with dislike, and in fact tried not to face me at all; you be-
haved as if you hated me—you had seen a girl, of great beauty,
I admit, who made me a fright and a bore."

This brought him straight round. "No, Kate Cookham."

"Yes, Herbert Dodd." She but shook her head, calmly and nobly, in the now gathered dusk, and her memories and her cause and her character—or was it only her arch-subtlety, her line and her "idea"?—gave her an extraordinary large assurance.

She had touched, however, the treasure of his own case— his terrible own case that began to live again at once by the force of her talking of hers, and which could always all cluster about his great asseveration. "No, no, never, never; I had never seen her then and didn't dream of her; so that when you yourself began to be harsh and sharp with me, and to seem to want to quarrel, I could have but one idea—which was an appearance you didn't in the least, as I saw it then, account for or disprove."

"An appearance—?" Kate desired, as with high astonishment, to know which one.

"How *shouldn't* I have supposed you really to care for Bill Frankle?—as, thoroughly believing the motive of your claim for my money to be its help to your marrying him, since you couldn't marry me. I was only surprised when, time passing, I made out that that hadn't happened; and perhaps," he added the next instant, with something of a conscious lapse from the finer style, "hadn't been in question."

She had listened to this only staring, and she was silent after he had said it, so silent for some instants that while he considered her something seemed to fail him, much as if he had thrown out his foot for a step and not found the place to rest it. He jerked round to the window again, and then she answered, but without passion, unless it was that of her weariness for something stupid and forgiven in him, "Oh, the blind, the pitiful folly!"—to which, as it might perfectly have applied to her own behaviour, he returned nothing. She had moreover at once gone on. "Put it then that there wasn't much to do—between your finding that you loathed me for another woman, or discovering only, when it came to the point, that you loathed me quite enough for myself."

Which, offered him in that immensely effective fashion, he recognized that he must just unprotestingly and not so very awkwardly—not so *very!*—take from her; since, whatever he had thus come to her for, it wasn't to perjure himself with any pretence that, "another woman" or no other woman, he hadn't, for years and years, abhorred her. Now he was taking tea with her—or rather, literally, seemed not to be; but this made no difference, and he let her express it as she would while he distinguished a man he knew, Charley Coote, outside on the Parade, under favour of the empty hour and one of the flaring lamps, making up to a young woman with whom (it stuck out grotesquely in his manner) he had never before conversed. Dodd's own position was that of acquiescing in this recall of what had so bitterly been—but he hadn't come back to her, of himself, to stir up, to recall or to recriminate, and for *her* it could but be the very lesson of her whole present act that if she touched anything she touched everything. Soon enough she was indeed, and all overwhelmingly, touching everything—with a hand of which the boldness grew.

"But I didn't let *that*, even, make a difference in what I wanted—which was all," she said, "and had only and passionately been, to take care of you. I had *no* money whatever —nothing then of my own, not a penny to come by anyhow; so it wasn't with mine I could do it. But I could do it with yours," she amazingly wound up—"if I could once get yours out of you."

He faced straight about again—his eyebrows higher than they had ever been in his life. "Mine? What penny of it was mine? What scrap beyond a bare, mean little living had I ever pretended to have?"

She held herself still a minute, visibly with force; only her eyes consciously attached to the seat of a chair the back of which her hands, making it tilt toward her a little, grasped as for support. "You pretended to have enough to marry me—and that was all I afterwards claimed of you when you wouldn't." He was on the point of retorting that he had absolutely pretended to nothing—least of all to the primary desire that such a way of putting it fastened on him; he was on the point for ten seconds of giving her full in the face: "I never *had* any such dream till you yourself—infatuated with me as, frankly, you on the whole appeared to be—got round me and muddled me up and made me behave as if in a way that went against the evidence of my senses." But he was to feel as quickly that, whatever the ugly, the spent, the irrecoverable truth, he might better have bitten his tongue off: there beat on him there this strange and other, this so prodigiously different beautiful and dreadful truth that no far remembrance and no abiding ache of his own could wholly falsify, and that was indeed all out with her next words. "That —*using* it for you and using you yourself for your own future —was my motive. I've led my life, which has been an affair, I assure you; and, as I've told you without your quite seeming to understand, I've brought everything fivefold back to you."

The perspiration broke out on his forehead. "Everything's mine?" he quavered as for the deep piercing pain of it.

"Everything!" said Kate Cookham.

So it told him how she had loved him—but with the tremendous effect at once of its only glaring out at him from the whole thing that it was verily she, a thousand times over, who, in the exposure of his youth and his vanity, had, on the bench of desolation, the scene of yesterday's own renewal, left for him no forward step to take. It hung there for him tragically vivid again, the hour she had first found him sequestered and accessible after making his acquaintance at his shop. And from this, by a succession of links that fairly clicked to his ear as with their perfect fitting, the fate and the pain and the payment of others stood together in a great grim order. Everything there then was *his*—to make him ask what had been Nan's, poor Nan's of the constant question of whether he need have collapsed. She was before him, she was between them, his little dead dissatisfied wife; across all whose final woe and whose lowly grave he was to reach out, it appeared, to take gifts. He saw them too, the gifts; saw them —she bristled with them—in his actual companion's brave and sincere and authoritative figure, her strangest of demonstrations. But the other appearance was intenser, as if their ghost had waved wild arms; so that half a minute hadn't passed before the one poor thing that remained of Nan, and that yet thus became a quite mighty and momentous poor thing, was sitting on his lips as for its sole opportunity.

"Can you give me your word of honour that I mightn't, under decent advice, have defied you?"

It made her turn very white; but now that she had said what she *had* said she could still hold up her head. "Certainly you might have defied me, Herbert Dodd."

"They would have told me you had no legal case?"

Well, if she was pale she was bold. "You talk of decent advice—!" She broke off, there was too much to say, and all needless. What she said instead was: "They would have told you I had nothing."

"I didn't so much as ask," her sad visitor remarked.

"Of course you didn't so much as ask."

"I couldn't be so outrageously vulgar," he went on.

"*I* could, by God's help!" said Kate Cookham.

"Thank you." He had found at his command a tone that made him feel more gentlemanlike than he had ever felt in his life or should doubtless ever feel again. It might have been enough—but somehow as they stood there with this immense clearance between them it wasn't. The clearance was like a sudden gap or great bleak opening through which there blew upon them a deadly chill. Too many things had fallen away, too many new rolled up and over him, and they made something within shake him to his base. It upset the full vessel, and though she kept her eyes on him he let that consequence come, bursting into tears, weakly crying there before her even as he had cried to himself in the hour of his youth when she had made him groundlessly fear. She turned away then— *that* she couldn't watch, and had presently flung herself on the sofa and, all responsively wailing, buried her own face on the cushioned arm. So for a minute their smothered sobs only filled the room. But he made out, through this disorder, where he had put down his hat; his stick and his new tan-coloured gloves—they had cost two-and-thruppence and would have represented sacrifices—were on the chair beside it. He picked these articles up and all silently and softly—gasping, that is, but quite on tiptoe—reached the door and let himself out.

VI

OFF there on the bench of desolation a week later she made him a more particular statement, which it had taken the remarkably tense interval to render possible. After leaving her at the hotel that last Sunday he had gone forth in his reaggravated trouble and walked straight before him, in the teeth of the west wind, close to the iron rails of the stretched Marina and with his tell-tale face turned from persons occasionally met and toward the surging sea. At the land's end, even in the confirmed darkness and the perhaps imminent big blow, his immemorial nook, small shelter as it yielded, had again received him; and it was in the course of this heedless session, no doubt, where the agitated air had nothing to add to the commotion within him, that he began to look his extraordinary fortune a bit straighter in the face and see it confess itself at once a fairy-tale and a nightmare. That, visibly, confoundingly, she was still attached to him (attached in fact was a mild word!) and that the unquestionable proof of it was in this offered pecuniary salve, of the thickest composition, for his wounds and sores and shames—these things were the fantastic fable, the tale of money in handfuls, that he seemed to have only to stand there and swallow and digest and feel himself full-fed by; but the whole of the rest was nightmare, and most of all nightmare his having thus to thank one through whom Nan and his little girls had known torture.

He didn't care for himself now, and this unextinguished and apparently inextinguishable charm by which he had held her was a fact incredibly romantic; but he gazed with a longer face than he had ever had for anything in the world at his potential acceptance of a great bouncing benefit from the person he intimately, if even in a manner indirectly, associated with the conditions to which his lovely wife and his little girls (who would have been so lovely too) had pitifully succumbed. He had accepted the social relation—which meant he had taken even that on trial—without knowing what it so dazzlingly masked; for a social relation it had become with a vengeance when it drove him about the place as now at his hours of freedom (and he actually and recklessly took, all demoralized and unstrung and unfit either for work or for anything else, other liberties that would get him into trouble) under this queer torment of irreconcilable things, a bewildered consciousness of tenderness and patience and cruelty, of great evident mystifying facts that were as little to be questioned as to be conceived or explained, and that were yet least, withal, to be lost sight of.

On that Sunday night he had wandered wild, incoherently ranging and throbbing, but this became the law of his next days as well, since he lacked more than ever all other resort or refuge and had nowhere to carry, to deposit, or contractedly let loose and lock up, as it were, his swollen consciousness, which fairly split in twain the raw shell of his sordid little boarding-place. The arch of the sky and the spread of sea and shore alone gave him space; he could roam with himself anywhere, in short, far or near—he could only never take himself back. That certitude—that this was impossible to him even should she wait there among her plushes and bronzes ten years—was the thing he kept closest clutch of; it did wonders for what he would have called his self-respect. Exactly as he had left her so he would stand off—even though at moments when he pulled up sharp somewhere to put himself an intensest question his heart almost stood still. The days of the week went by, and as he had left her she stayed; to the extent, that is, of his having neither sight nor sound of her, and of the failure of every sign. It took nerve, he said, not to return to her, even for curiosity—since how, after all, in the name of wonder, had she invested the fruits of her extortion to such advantage, there being no chapter of all the obscurity of the years to beat that for queerness? But he dropped, tired to death, on benches, half a dozen times an evening—exactly on purpose to recognize that the nerve required was just the nerve he had.

As the days without a token from her multiplied he came in as well for hours—and these indeed mainly on the bench of desolation—of sitting stiff and stark in presence of the probability that he had lost everything for ever. When he passed the Royal he never turned an eyelash, and when he met Captain Roper on the Front, three days after having been introduced to him, he "cut him dead"—another privileged consequence of a social relation—rather than seem to himself to make the remotest approach to the question of whether Miss Cookham had left Properley. He had cut people in the days of his life before, just as he had come to being himself cut—since there had been no time for him wholly without one or other face of that necessity—but had never affected such a severance as of this rare connection, which helped to give him thus the measure of his really precious sincerity. If he had lost what had hovered before him he had lost it, his only tribute to which proposition was to grind his teeth with one of those "scrunches," as he would have said, of which the violence fairly reached his ear. It wouldn't make him lift a finger, and in fact if Kate had simply taken herself off on the Tuesday or the Wednesday she would have been reabsorbed again into the darkness from which she had emerged—and no lifting of fingers, the unspeakable chapter closed, would evermore avail. That at any rate was the kind of man he still was—even after all that had come and gone, and even if for a few dazed hours certain things had seemed pleasant. The dazed hours had passed, the surge of the old bitterness had dished him (shouldn't he have been shamed if it hadn't?) and he might sit there as before, as always, with nothing at all on earth to look to. He had therefore wrongfully believed himself to be degraded; and the last word about him would be that he *couldn't* then, it appeared, sink to vulgarity as he had tried to let his miseries make him.

And yet on the next Sunday morning, face to face with him again at the land's end, what she very soon came to was: "As if I believed you didn't *know* by what cord you hold me!" Absolutely, too, and just that morning in fact, above all, he wouldn't, he quite couldn't have taken his solemn oath that he hadn't a sneaking remnant, as he might have put it to himself—a remnant of faith in tremendous things still to come of their interview. The day was sunny and breezy, the sea of a cold purple; he wouldn't go to church as he mostly went of Sunday mornings, that being in its way too a social relation—and not least when two-and-thruppenny tan-coloured gloves were new; which indeed he had the art of keeping them for ages. Yet he would dress himself as he scarce mustered resources for even to figure on the fringe of Society, local and transient, at St Bernard's, and in this trim he took his way westward; occupied largely, as he went, it might have seemed to any person pursuing the same course and happening to observe him, in a fascinated study of the motions of his shadow, the more or less grotesque shape projected, in front of him and mostly a bit to the right, over the blanched asphalt of the Parade and dangling and dancing at such a rate, shooting out and then contracting, that, viewed in themselves, its eccentricities might have formed the basis of an interesting challenge: "Find the state of mind, guess the nature of the agitation, possessing the person so remarkably represented!" Herbert Dodd, for that matter, might have been himself attempting to make by the sun's sharp aid some approach to his immediate horoscope.

It had at any rate been thus put before him that the dandling and dancing of his image occasionally gave way to perfect immobility, when he stopped and kept his eyes on it. "Suppose she should come, suppose she *should!*" it is revealed at least to ourselves that he had at these moments audibly breathed—breathed with the intensity of an arrest between hope and fear. It had glimmered upon him from early, with the look of the day, that, given all else that could happen, this would be rather, as he put it, in her line; and the possibility lived for him, as he proceeded, to the tune of a suspense almost sickening. It was, from one small stage of his pilgrimage to another, the "For ever, never!" of the sentimental case the playmates of his youth used to pretend to settle by plucking the petals of a daisy. But it came to his truly turning faint—so "queer" he felt—when, at the gained point of the long stretch from which he could always tell, he arrived within positive sight of his immemorial goal. His seat was taken and she was keeping it for him—it could only be *she* there in possession; whereby it shone out for Herbert Dodd that if he hadn't been quite sure of her recurrence she had at least been quite sure of his. *That* pulled him up to some purpose, where recognition began for them—or to the effect, in other words, of his pausing to judge if he could bear, for the sharpest note of their intercourse, this inveterate demonstration of her making him do what she liked. What settled the question for him then—and just while they avowedly watched each other, over the long interval, before closing, as if, on either side, for the major advantage—what settled it was this very fact that what she liked she liked so terribly. If it were simply to "use" him, as she had said the last time, and no matter to the profit of which of them she called it, one might let it go for that; since it could make her wait over, day after day, in that fashion, and with such a spending of money, on the hazard of their meeting again. How could she be the least sure he would ever again consent to it after the proved action on him, a week ago, of her last monstrous honesty? It was indeed positively as if he were now himself putting this influence—and for their common edification—to the supreme, to the finest test. He had a sublime, an ideal flight, which lasted about a minute. "Suppose, now that I see her there and what she has taken so characteristically for granted, suppose I just show her that she *hasn't* only confidently to wait or whistle for me, and that the length of my leash is greater than she measures, and that everything's impossible always?—show it by turning my back on her now and walking straight away. She won't be able not to understand *that!*"

Nothing had passed, across their distance, but the mute apprehension of each on the part of each; the whole expanse, at the church hour, was void of other life (he had scarce met a creature on his way from end to end) and the sun-seasoned gusts kept brushing the air and all the larger prospect clean. It was through this beautiful lucidity that he watched her watch him, as it were—watch him for what he would do. Neither moved at this high tension; Kate Cookham, her face fixed on him, only waited with a stiff appearance of leaving him, not for dignity but—to an effect of even deeper perversity—for kindness, free to choose. It yet somehow affected him at present, this attitude, as a gage of her *knowing too*—knowing, that is, that he wasn't really free, that this was the thinnest of vain parades, the poorest of hollow heroics, that his need, his solitude, his suffered wrong, his exhausted rancour, his foredoomed submission to any shown interest, all hung together too heavy on him to let the weak wings of his pride do more than vaguely tremble. They couldn't, they didn't carry him a single beat further away; according to which he stood rooted, neither retreating nor advancing, but presently correcting his own share of their bleak exchange by looking off at the sea. Deeply conscious of the awkwardness this posture gave him, he yet clung to it as the last shred of his honour, to the clear argument that it was one thing for him to have felt beneath all others, the previous days, that she was to be counted on, but quite a different for her to have felt that *he* was. His checked approach, arriving thus at no term, could in these odd conditions have established that he wasn't only if Kate Cookham had, as either of them might have said, taken it so—if she had given up the game at last by rising, by walking away and adding to the distance between them, and he had then definitely let her vanish into space. It became a fact that when she did finally rise—though after how long our record scarce takes on itself to say—it was not to confirm their separation but to put an end to it; and this by slowly approaching him till she had come within earshot. He had wondered, once aware of it in spite of his averted face, what she would say and on what note, as it were, she would break their week's silence; so that he had to recognize anew, her voice reaching him, that remarkable quality in her which again and again came up for him as her art.

"There are twelve hundred and sixty pounds, to be definite, but I have it all down for you—and you've only to draw."

They lost themselves, these words, rare and exquisite, in the wide bright genial medium and the Sunday stillness, but even while that occurred and he was gaping for it she was herself there, in her battered ladylike truth, to answer for them, to represent them, and, if a further grace than their simple syllabled beauty were conceivable, almost embarrassingly to cause them to materialize. Yes, she let her smart and tight little reticule hang as if it bulged, beneath its clasp, with the whole portentous sum, and he felt himself glare again at this vividest of her attested claims. She might have been ready, on the spot, to open the store to the plunge of his hand, or, with the situation otherwise conceived, to impose on his pauperized state an acceptance of alms on a scale unprecedented in the annals of street charity. Nothing so much counted for him, however, neither grave numeral nor elegant fraction, as the short, rich, rounded word that the breeze had picked up as it dropped and seemed now to blow about between them. "To draw—to draw?" Yes, he gaped it as if it had no sense; the fact being that even while he did so he was reading into her use of the term more romance than any word in the language had ever had for him. He, Herbert Dodd, was to live to "draw," like people, scarce hampered by the conditions of earth, whom he had remotely and circuitously heard about, and in fact when he walked back with her to where she had been sitting it was very much, for his strained nerves, as if the very bench of desolation itself were to be the scene of that exploit and he mightn't really live till he reached it.

When they had sat down together she did press the spring of her reticule, extracting from it, not a handful of gold nor a packet of crisp notes, but an oblong sealed letter, which she had thus waited on him, she remarked, on purpose to deliver, and which would certify, with sundry particulars, to the credit she had opened for him at a London bank. He took it from her without looking at it, and held it, in the same manner, conspicuous and unassimilated, for most of the rest of the immediate time, appearing embarrassed with it, nervously twisting and flapping it, yet thus publicly retaining it even while aware, beneath everything, of the strange, the quite dreadful, wouldn't it be? engagement that such inaction practically stood for. He could accept money to that amount, yes —but not for nothing in return. For what then in return? He kept asking himself for what, while she said other things and made above all, in her high, shrewd, successful way, the point that, no, he needn't pretend that his conviction of her continued personal interest in him wouldn't have tided him over any question besetting him since their separation. She put it to him that the deep instinct of where he should at last find her must confidently have worked for him, since she confessed to her instinct of where she should find *him;* which meant— oh, it came home to him as he fingered his sealed treasure!— neither more nor less than that she had now created between them an equality of experience. He wasn't to have done all the suffering, *she* was to have "been through" things he couldn't even guess at; and, since he was bargaining away his right ever again to allude to the unforgettable, so much there was of it, what her tacit proposition came to was that they were "square" and might start afresh.

He didn't take up her charge, as his so compromised "pride" yet in a manner prompted him, that he had enjoyed all the week all those elements of ease about her; the most he achieved for that was to declare, with an ingenuity contributing to float him no small distance further, that of course he had turned up at their old place of tryst, which had been, through the years, the haunt of his solitude and the goal of his walk any Sunday morning that seemed too beautiful for church; but that he hadn't in the least built on her presence there—since that supposition gave him, she would understand, wouldn't she? the air, disagreeable to him, of having come in search of her. Her quest of himself, once he had been seated there, would have been another matter—but in short, "Of course after all you did come to me, just now, didn't you?" He felt himself, too, lamely and gracelessly grin, as for the final kick of his honour, in confirmation of the record that he had then yielded but to her humility. Her humility became for him at this hour and to this tune, on the bench of desolation, a quantity more prodigious and even more mysterious than that other guaranteed quantity the finger-tips of his left hand could feel the tap of by the action of his right; though what was in especial extraordinary was the manner in which she could keep making him such allowances and yet meet him again, at some turn, as with her residuum for her clever self so great.

"Come to you, Herbert Dodd?" she imperturbably echoed. "I've been coming to you for the last ten years!"

There had been for him just before this sixty supreme seconds of intensest aspiration—a minute of his keeping his certificate poised for a sharp thrust back at her, the thrust of the wild freedom of his saying: "No, no, I *can't* give them up; I can't simply sink them deep down in my soul for ever, with no cross in all my future to mark *that* burial; so that if this is what our arrangement means I must decline to have anything to do with it." The words none the less hadn't come, and when she had herself, a couple of minutes later, spoken those others, the blood rose to his face as if, given his stiffness and her extravagance, he had just indeed saved himself.

Everything in fact stopped, even his fidget with his paper; she imposed a hush, she imposed at any rate the conscious decent form of one, and he couldn't afterward have told how long, at this juncture, he must have sat simply gazing before him. It was so long, at any rate, that Kate herself got up—and quite indeed, presently, as if her own forms were now at an end. He had returned her nothing—so what was she waiting for? She had been on the two other occasions momentarily at a loss, but never so much so, no doubt, as was thus testified to by her leaving the bench and moving over once more to the rail of the terrace. She could carry it off, in a manner, with her resources, that she was waiting with so little to wait for; she could face him again, after looking off at the sea, as if this slightly stiff delay, not wholly exempt from awkwardness, had been but a fine scruple of her courtesy. She had gathered herself in; after giving him time to appeal she could take it that he had decided and that nothing was left for her to do. "Well then," she clearly launched at him across the broad walk—"well then, good-bye."

She had come nearer with it, as if he might rise for some show of express separation; but he only leaned back motionless, his eyes on her now—he kept her a moment before him. "Do you mean that we don't—that we don't—?" But he broke down.

"Do I 'mean'—?" She remained as for questions he might ask, but it was well-nigh as if there played through her dotty veil an irrepressible irony for that particular one. "I've meant, for long years, I think, all I'm capable of meaning. I've meant so much that I can't mean more. So there it is."

"But if you go," he appealed—and with a sense as of final flatness, however he arranged it, for his own attitude—"but if you go shan't I see you again?"

She waited a little and it was strangely for him now as if —though at last so much more gorged with her tribute than she had ever been with his—something still depended on her. "Do you *like* to see me?" she very simply asked.

At this he did get up; that was easier than to say—at least with responsive simplicity; and again for a little he looked hard and in silence at his letter; which, at last, however, raising his eyes to her own for the act, while he masked their conscious ruefulness, to his utmost, in some air of assurance, he slipped into the inner pocket of his coat, letting it settle there securely. "You're too wonderful." But he frowned at her with it as never in his life. "Where does it all come from?"

"The wonder of poor me?" Kate Cookham said. "It comes from *you*."

He shook his head slowly—feeling, with his letter there against his heart, such a new agility, almost such a new range of interest. "I mean so *much* money—so extraordinarily much."

Well, she held him a while blank. "Does it seem to you

extraordinarily much—twelve-hundred-and-sixty? Because, you know," she added, "it's all."

"It's enough!" he returned with a slight thoughtful droop of his head to the right and his eyes attached to the far horizon as through a shade of shyness for what he was saying. He felt all her own lingering nearness somehow on his cheek.

"It's enough? Thank you then!" she rather oddly went on.

He shifted a little his posture. "It was more than a hundred a year—for you to get together."

"Yes," she assented, "that was what year by year I tried for."

"But that you could live all the while and have that—!" Yes, he was at liberty, as he hadn't been, quite pleasantly to marvel. All his wonderments in life had been hitherto un-answered—and didn't the change mean that here again was the social relation?

"Ah, I didn't live as you saw me the other day."

"Yes," he answered—and didn't he the next instant feel he must fairly have smiled with it?—"the other day you *were* going it!"

"For once in my life," said Kate Cookham. "I've left the hotel," she after a moment added.

"Ah, you're in—a—lodgings?" he found himself inquiring as for positive sociability.

She had apparently a slight shade of hesitation, but in an instant it was all right; as what he showed he wanted to know she seemed mostly to give him. "Yes—but far of course from here. Up on the hill." To which, after another instant, "At The Mount, Castle Terrace," she subjoined.

"Oh, I *know* The Mount. And Castle Terrace is awfully sunny and nice."

"Awfully sunny and nice," Kate Cookham took from him.

"So that if it isn't," he pursued, "like the Royal, why, you're at least comfortable."

"I shall be comfortable anywhere now," she replied with a certain dryness.

It was astonishing, however, what had become of his own. "Because I've accepted—?"

"Call it that!" she dimly smiled.

"I hope then at any rate," he returned, "you can now thoroughly rest." He spoke as for a cheerful conclusion and moved again also to smile, though as with a poor grimace, no doubt; since what he seemed most clearly to feel was that since he "accepted" he mustn't, for his last note, have accepted in sulkiness or gloom. With that, at the same time, he couldn't but know, in all his fibres, that with such a still-watching face as the dotty veil didn't disguise for him there was no possible concluding, at least on his part. On hers, on hers it was—as he had so often for a week had reflectively to pronounce things —another affair. Ah, somehow, both formidably and help-fully, her face concluded—yet in a sense so strangely en-shrouded in things she didn't tell him. What *must* she, what mustn't she, have done? What she had said—she had really told him nothing—was no account of her life; in the midst of which conflict of opposed recognitions, at any rate, it was as if, for all he could do, he himself now considerably floundered. "But I can't think—I can't think—!"

"You can't think I can have made so much money in the time and been honest?"

"Oh, you've been *honest!*" Herbert Dodd distinctly allowed.

It moved her stillness to a gesture—which, however, she had as promptly checked; and she went on the next instant as for further generosity to his failure of thought. "Everything was possible, under my stress, with my hatred."

"Your hatred—?" For she had paused as if it were after all too difficult.

"Of what I should for so long have been doing to you."

With this, for all his failures, a greater light than any yet shone upon him. "It made you think of ways—?"

"It made me think of everything. It made me work," said Kate Cookham. She added, however, the next moment: "But that's my story."

"And I mayn't hear it?"

"No—because I mayn't hear yours."

"Oh, mine—!" he said with the strangest, saddest yet after all most resigned sense of surrender of it; which he tried to make sound as if he couldn't have told it, for its splendour of sacrifice and of misery, even if he would.

It seemed to move in her a little, exactly, that sense of the invidious. "Ah, mine too, I assure you—!"

He rallied at once to the interest. "Oh, we *can* talk then?"

"Never," she most oddly replied. "Never," said Kate Cookham.

They remained so, face to face; the effect of which for him was that he had after a little understood why. That was fundamental. "Well, I see."

Thus confronted they stayed; and then, as he saw with a contentment that came up from deeper still, it was indeed she who, with her worn fine face, would conclude. "But I can take care of you."

"You *have!*" he said as with nothing left of him but a beautiful appreciative candour.

"Oh, but you'll want it now in a way—!" she responsibly answered.

He waited a moment, dropping again on the seat. So, while she still stood, he looked up at her; with the sense somehow that there were too many things and that they were all together, terribly, irresistibly, doubtless blessedly, in her eyes and her whole person; which thus affected him for the moment as more than he could bear. He leaned forward, dropping his elbows to his knees and pressing his head on his hands. So he stayed, saying nothing; only, with the sense of her own sustained, renewed and wonderful action, knowing that an arm had passed round him and that he was held. She was beside him on the bench of desolation.

A ROUND OF VISITS

I

HE had been out but once since his arrival, Mark Monteith; that was the next day after—he had disembarked by night on the previous; then everything had come at once, as he would have said, everything had changed. He had got in on Tuesday; he had spent Wednesday for the most part down town, looking into the dismal subject of his anxiety—the anxiety that, under a sudden decision, had brought him across the unfriendly sea at mid-winter, and it was through information reaching him on Wednesday evening that he had measured his loss, measured, above all, his pain. These were two distinct things, he felt, and, though both bad, one much worse than the other. It wasn't till the next three days had pretty well ebbed, in fact, that he knew himself for so badly wounded. He had waked up on Thursday morning, so far as he had slept at all, with the sense, together, of a blinding New York blizzard and of a deep sore inward ache. The great white savage storm would have kept him at the best within doors, but his stricken state was by itself quite reason enough.

He so felt the blow indeed, so gasped, before what had happened to him, at the ugliness, the bitterness, and, beyond these things, the sinister strangeness, that, the matter of his dismay little by little detaching and projecting itself, settling there face to face with him as something he must now live with always, he might have been in charge of some horrid alien thing, some violent, scared, unhappy creature whom there was small joy, of a truth, in remaining with, but whose behaviour wouldn't perhaps bring him under notice, nor otherwise compromise him, so long as he should stay to watch it. A young jibbering ape of one of the more formidable sorts, or an ominous infant panther smuggled into the great gaudy hotel and whom it might yet be important he shouldn't advertise, couldn't have affected him as needing more domestic attention. The great gaudy hotel—The Pocahontas, but carried out largely on "Du Barry" lines—made all about him, beside, behind, below, above, in blocks and tiers and superpositions, a sufficient defensive hugeness; so that, between the massive labyrinth and the New York weather, life in a lighthouse during a gale would scarce have kept him more apart. Even when in the course of that worse Thursday it had occurred to him for vague relief that the odious certified facts couldn't be all his misery, and that, with his throat and a probable temperature, a brush of the epidemic, which was for ever brushing him, accounted for something, even then he couldn't resign himself to bed and broth and dimness, but only circled and prowled the more within his high cage, only watched the more from his tenth story the rage of the elements.

In the afternoon he had a doctor—the caravanserai, which supplied everything in quantities, had one for each group of so many rooms—just in order to be assured that he was *grippé* enough for anything. What his visitor, making light of his attack, perversely told him was that he was, much rather, "blue" enough, and from causes doubtless known to himself —which didn't come to the same thing; but he "gave him something," prescribed him warmth and quiet and broth and courage, and came back the next day to readminister this last dose. He then pronounced him better, and on Saturday pronounced him well—all the more that the storm had abated and the snow had been dealt with as New York, at a push, knew how to deal with things. Oh, how New York knew how to deal—to deal, that is, with other accumulations lying passive to its hand—was exactly what Mark now ached with his impression of; so that, still threshing about in this consciousness, he had on the Saturday come near to breaking out as to what was the matter with him. The doctor brought in somehow the air of the hotel—which, cheerfully and conscientiously, by his simple philosophy, the good man wished to diffuse; breathing forth all the echoes of other woes and worries and pointing the honest moral that, especially with such a thermometer, there were enough of these to go round. Our sufferer, by that time, would have liked to tell someone; extracting, to the last acid strain of it, the full strength of his sorrow, taking it all in as he could only do by himself, and with the conditions favourable at least to this, had been his natural first need. But now, he supposed, he *must* be better; there was something of his heart's heaviness he wanted so to give out.

He had rummaged forth on the Thursday night half a dozen old photographs stuck into a leather frame, a small show-case that formed part of his usual equipage of travel— he mostly set it up on a table when he stayed anywhere long enough; and in one of the neat gilt-edged squares of this convenient portable array, as familiar as his shaving-glass or the hair-brushes, of backs and monograms now so beautifully toned and wasted, long ago given him by his mother, Phil Bloodgood handsomely faced him. Not contemporaneous, and a little faded, but so saying what it said only the more dreadfully, the image seemed to sit there, at an immemorial window, like some long effective and only at last exposed "decoy" of fate. It was *because* he was so beautifully good-looking, because he was so charming and clever and frank—besides being one's third cousin, or whatever it was, one's early school-fellow and one's later college classmate—that one had abjectly trusted him. To live thus with his unremoved, undestroyed, engaging, treacherous face, had been, as our traveller desired, to live with all of the felt pang; had been to consume it in such a single hot, sore mouthful as would so far as possible dispose of it and leave but cold dregs. Thus, if the doctor, casting about for pleasantness, had happened to notice him there, salient since he was, and possibly by the same stroke even to know him, as New York—and more or less to its cost now, mightn't one say?—so abundantly and agreeably had, the cup would have overflowed and Monteith, for all he could be sure of the contrary, would have relieved himself positively in tears.

"Oh, *he's* what's the matter with me—that, looking after some of my poor dividends, as he for the ten years of my absence had served me by doing, he has simply jockeyed me out of the whole little collection, such as it was, and taken the opportunity of my return, inevitably at last bewildered and uneasy, to 'sail,' ten days ago, for parts unknown and as yet unguessable. It isn't the beastly values themselves, however; that's only awkward and I can still live, though I don't quite know how I shall turn round; it's the horror of *his* having done it, and done it to *me*—without a mitigation or, so to speak, a warning or an excuse." That, at a hint or a jog, is what he would have brought out—only to feel afterward, no doubt, that he had wasted his impulse and profaned even a little his sincerity. The doctor didn't in the event so much as glance at his cluster of portraits—which fact quite put before our friend the essentially more vivid range of imagery that a pair of eyes transferred from room to room and from one queer case to another, in such a place as that, would mainly be adjusted to. It wasn't for *him* to relieve himself touchingly, strikingly or whatever, to such a man: such a man might much more pertinently—save for professional discretion— have emptied out there his own bag of wonders; prodigies of observation, flowers of oddity, flowers of misery, flowers of the monstrous, gathered in current hotel practice. Countless possibilities, making doctors perfunctory, Mark felt, swarmed and seethed at their doors; it showed for an incalculable world, and at last, on Sunday, he decided to leave his room.

II

EVERYTHING as he passed through the place went on—all
the offices of life, the whole bustle of the market, and withal
surprisingly scarce less that of the nursery and the play-
ground, the whole sprawl in especial of the great gregarious
fireside; it was a complete social scene in itself, on which
types might figure and passions rage and plots thicken and
dramas develop, without reference to any other sphere, or
perhaps even to anything at all outside. The signs of this met
him at every turn as he threaded the labyrinth, passing from
one extraordinary masquerade of expensive objects, one
portentous "period" of decoration, one violent phase of publicity, to another: the heavy heat, the luxuriance, the extravagance, the quantity, the colour, gave the impression of some
wondrous tropical forest, where vociferous, bright-eyed, and
feathered creatures, of every variety of size and hue, were
half smothered between undergrowths of velvet and tapestry
and ramifications of marble and bronze. The fauna and the
flora startled him alike, and among them his bruised spirit
drew in and folded its wings. But he roamed and rested, ex-
ploring and in a manner enjoying the vast rankness—in the
depth of which he suddenly encountered Mrs Folliott, whom
he had last seen, six months before, in London, and who had
spoken to him then, precisely, of Phil Bloodgood, for several
years previous her confidential American agent and factotum
too, as she might say, but at that time so little in her good
books, for the extraordinary things he seemed to be doing,
that she was just hurrying home, she had made no scruple of
mentioning, to take everything out of his hands.

Mark remembered how uneasy she had made him—how
that very talk with her had wound him up to fear, as so acute

and intent a little person she affected him; though he had affirmed with all emphasis and flourish his own confidence and defended, to iteration, his old friend. This passage had remained with him for a certain pleasant heat of intimacy, his partner, of the charming appearance, being what she was; he liked to think how they had fraternized over their difference and called each other idiots, or almost, without offence. It was always a link to have scuffled, failing a real scratch, with such a character; and he had at present the flutter of feeling that something of this would abide. *He* hadn't been hurrying home, at the London time, in any case; he was doing nothing then, and had continued to do it; he would want, before showing suspicion—that had been his attitude—to have more, after all, to go upon. Mrs Folliott also, and with a great actual profession of it, remembered and rejoiced; and, also staying in the house as she was, sat with him, under a spreading palm, in a wondrous rococo *salon*, surrounded by the pinkest, that is the fleshiest imitation Boucher panels, and wanted to know if he *now* stood up for his swindler. She would herself have tumbled on a cloud, very passably, in a fleshy Boucher manner, hadn't she been over-dressed for such an exercise; but she was quite realistically aware of what had so naturally happened—she was prompt about Bloodgood's "flight."

She had acted with energy, on getting back—she had saved what she could; which hadn't, however, prevented her losing all disgustedly some ten thousand dollars. She was lovely, lively, friendly, interested, she connected Monteith perfectly with their discussion that day during the water-party on the Thames; but, sitting here with him half an hour, she talked only of her peculiar, her cruel sacrifice—since she should never get a penny back. He had felt himself, on their meeting, quite yearningly reach out to her—so decidedly, by the morning's end, and that of his scattered sombre stations, had he been sated with meaningless contacts, with the sense of people all about him intensely, though harmlessly animated, yet at the same time raspingly indifferent. *They* would have, he and she at least, their common pang—through which fact, somehow, he should feel less stranded. It wasn't that he wished to be pitied—he fairly didn't pity himself; he winced, rather, and even to vicarious anguish, as it rose again, for poor shamed Bloodgood's doom-ridden figure. But he wanted, as with a desperate charity, to give some easier turn to the mere ugliness of the main facts; to work off his obsession from them by mixing with it some other blame, some other pity, it scarce mattered what—if it might be some other experience; as an effect of which larger ventilation it would have, after a fashion and for a man of free sensibility, a diluted and less poisonous taste.

By the end of five minutes of Mrs Folliott, however, he felt his dry lips seal themselves to a makeshift simper. She could *take* nothing—no better, no broader perception of anything than fitted her own small faculty; so that though she must have recalled or imagined that he had still, up to lately, had interests at stake, the rapid result of her egotistical little chatter was to make him wish he might rather have conversed with the French waiter dangling in the long vista that showed the oriental *café* as a climax, or with the policeman, outside, the top of whose helmet peeped above the ledge of a window. She bewailed her wretched money to excess—she who, he was sure, had quantities more; she pawed and tossed her bare bone, with her little extraordinarily gemmed and manicured hands, till it acted on his nerves; she rang all the changes on the story, the dire fatality, of her having wavered and muddled, thought of this and but done that, of her stupid failure to have pounced, when she had first meant to, in season. She abused the author of their wrongs—recognizing thus too Monteith's right to loathe him—for the desperado he assuredly had proved, but with a vulgarity of analysis and an incapacity for the higher criticism, as her listener felt it to be, which made him determine resentfully, almost grimly, that she shouldn't have the benefit of a grain of *his* vision or *his* version of what had befallen them, and of how, in particular, it had come; and should never dream thereby (though much would she suffer from that!) of how interesting he might have been. She had, in a finer sense, no manners, and to be concerned with her in any retrospect was—since their discourse was of losses—to feel the dignity of history incur the very gravest. It was true that such fantasies, or that any shade of inward irony, would be Greek to Mrs Folliott.

It was also true, however, and not much more strange, when she had presently the comparatively happy thought of "Lunch with *us*, you poor dear!" and mentioned three or four of her "crowd"—a new crowd, rather, for her, all great Sunday lunchers there and immense fun, who would in a moment be turning up—that this seemed to him as easy as anything else; so that after a little, deeper in the jungle and while, under the temperature as of high noon, with the crowd complete and "ordering," he wiped the perspiration from his brow, he felt he was letting himself go. He did that certainly to the extent of leaving far behind any question of Mrs Folliott's manners. They didn't matter there—nobody's did; and if she ceased to lament her ten thousand it was only because, among higher voices, she couldn't make herself heard. Poor Bloodgood didn't have a show, as they might have said, didn't get through at any point; the crowd was so new that—there either having been no hue and cry for him, or having been too many others, for other absconders, in the interval—they had never so much as heard of him and would have no more of Mrs Folliott's true inwardness, on that subject at least, than she had lately cared to have of Monteith's.

There was nothing like a crowd, this unfortunate knew, for making one feel lonely, and he felt so increasingly during the meal; but he got thus at least in a measure away from the terrible little lady; after which, and before the end of the hour, he wanted still more to get away from everyone else. He was in fact about to perform this manœuvre when he was checked by the jolly young woman he had been having on his left and who had more to say about the hotels, up and down the town, than he had ever known a young woman to have to say on any subject at all; she expressed herself in hotel terms exclusively, the names of those establishments playing through her speech as the *leit-motif* might have recurrently flashed and romped through a piece of profane modern music. She wanted to present him to the pretty girl she had brought with her, and who had apparently signified to her that she must do so.

"I think you know my brother-in-law, Mr Newton Winch," the pretty girl had immediately said; she moved her head and shoulders together, as by a common spring, the effect of a stiff neck or of something loosened in her back hair; but becoming, queerly enough, all the prettier for doing so. He had seen in the papers, her brother-in-law, Mr Monteith's arrival—Mr Mark P. Monteith, wasn't it?—and where he was, and she had been with him, three days before, at the time; whereupon he had said, "Hullo, what can have brought old Mark back?" He seemed to have believed—Newton had seemed—that that shirker, as he called him, never *would* come; and she guessed that if she had known she was going to meet such a former friend ("Which he claims you are, sir," said the pretty girl) he would have asked her to find out what the trouble could be. But the real satisfaction would just be, she went on, if his former friend would himself go and see him and tell him; he had appeared of late so down.

"Oh, I remember him"—Mark didn't repudiate the friendship, placing him easily; only then he wasn't married and the pretty girl's sister must have come in later; which showed, his not knowing such things, how they had lost touch. The pretty girl was sorry to have to say in return to this that her sister wasn't living—had died two years after marrying; so that Newton was up there in Fiftieth Street alone; where (in explanation of his being "down") he had been shut up for days with bad *grippe;* though now on the mend, or she wouldn't have gone to him, not she, who had had it nineteen times and didn't want to have it again. But the horrid poison just seemed to have entered into poor Newton's soul.

"That's the way it *can* take you, don't you know?" And then as, with her single twist, she just charmingly hunched her eyes at our friend, "Don't you want to go to see him?"

Mark bethought himself: "Well, I'm going to see a lady—"

She took the words from his mouth. "Of course you're going to see a lady—every man in New York is. But Newton isn't a lady, unfortunately for him, to-day; and Sunday afternoon in this place, in this weather, alone—!"

"Yes, isn't it awful?"—he was quite drawn to her.

"Oh, *you've* got your lady!"

"Yes, I've got my lady, thank goodness!" The fervour of which was his sincere tribute to the note he had had on Friday morning from Mrs Ash, the only thing that had a little tempered his gloom.

"Well then, feel for others. Fit him in. Tell him why!"

"Why I've come back? I'm glad I *have*—since it was to see *you!*" Monteith made brave enough answer, promising to do what he could. He liked the pretty girl, with her straight attack and her free awkwardness—also with her difference from the others through something of a sense and a distinction given her by so clearly having Newton on her mind. Yet it was odd to him, and it showed the lapse of the years, that Winch—as he had known him of old—could *be* to that degree on anyone's mind.

III

OUTSIDE in the intensity of the cold—it was a jump from the Tropics to the Pole—he felt afresh the force of what he had just been saying; that if it weren't for the fact of Mrs Ash's good letter of welcome, despatched, characteristically, as soon as she had, like the faithful sufferer in Fiftieth Street, observed his name, in a newspaper, on one of the hotel-lists, he should verily, for want of a connection and an abutment, have scarce dared to face the void and the chill together, but have sneaked back into the jungle and there tried to lose himself. He made, as it was, the opposite effort, resolute to walk, though hovering now and then at vague crossways, radiations of roads to nothing, or taking cold counsel of the long but still sketchy vista, as it struck him, of the northward Avenue, bright and bleak, fresh and harsh, rich and evident somehow, a perspective like a page of florid modern platitudes. He didn't quite know what he had expected for his return—not certainly serenades and deputations; but without Mrs Ash his wail would have quite lacked geniality, and it was as if Phil Bloodgood had gone off not only with so large a slice of his small *peculium*, but with all the broken bits of the past, the loose ends of old relationships, that he had supposed he might pick up again. Well, perhaps he should still pick up a few—by the sweat of his brow; no motion of their own at least, he by this time judged, would send them fluttering into his hand.

Which reflections but quickened his forecast of this charm of the old Paris inveteracy renewed—the so prized custom of nine years before, when he still believed in results from his fond frequentation of the Beaux Arts; that of walking over the river to the Rue de Marignan, precisely, every Sunday without exception, and sitting at her fireside, and often all offensively, no doubt, outstaying every one. How he had used to want those hours then, and how again, after a little, at present, the Rue de Marignan might have been before him! He had gone to her there at that time with his troubles, such as they were, and they had always worked for her amusement—which had been her happy, her clever way of taking them: she couldn't have done anything better for them in that phase, poor innocent things compared with what they might have been, than be amused by them. Perhaps that was what she would still be— with those of his present hour; now too they might inspire her with the touch she best applied and was most instinctive mistress of: this didn't at all events strike him as what he should most resent. It wasn't as if Mrs Folliott, to make up for boring him with her own plaint, for example, had had so much as a gleam of conscious diversion over his.

"I'm *so* delighted to see you, I've such immensities to tell you!"—it began with the highest animation twenty minutes later, the very moment he stood there, the sense of the Rue de Marignan in the charming room and in the things about all reconstituted, regrouped, wonderfully preserved, down to the very sitting-places in the same relations, and down to the faint sweet mustiness of generations of cigarettes; but every-thing else different, and even vaguely alien, and by a measure still other than that of their own stretched interval and of the dear delightful woman's just a little pathetic alteration of face. He had allowed for the nine years, and so, it was to be hoped, had she; but the last thing, otherwise, that would have been touched, he immediately felt, was the quality, the intensity, of her care to see him. She cared, oh, so visibly and touchingly and almost radiantly—save for her being, yes, distinctly, a little *more* battered than from even a good nine years' worth; nothing could in fact have perched with so crowning an im-patience on the heap of what she had to "tell" as that special shade of revived consciousness of having him in particular to tell it to. It wasn't perhaps much to matter how soon she brought out and caused to ring, as it were, on the little recognized marqueterie table between them (such an anciently envied treasure), the heaviest gold-piece of current history she was to pay him with for having just so felicitously come back: he knew already, without the telling, that intimate domestic tension must lately, within those walls, have reached a climax and that he could serve supremely—oh, how he was going to serve!—as the most sympathetic of all pairs of ears.

The whole thing was upon him, in any case, with the minimum of delay: Bob had had it from her, definitely, the first of the week, and it was absolutely final now, that they must set up avowedly separate lives—without horrible "proceedings" of any sort, but with her own situation, her independence, secured to her once for all. She had been coming to it, taking her time, and she had gone through—well, so old a friend would guess enough what; but she was at the point, oh, blessedly now, where she meant to stay, he'd see if she didn't; with which, in this wonderful way, he himself had arrived for the cream of it and she was just selfishly glad. Bob had gone to Washington—ostensibly on business, but really to recover breath; she had, speaking vulgarly, knocked the wind out of him and was allowing him time to turn round. Mrs Folliott, moreover, she was sure, would have gone—was certainly believed to have been seen there five days ago; and of course his first necessity, for public use, would be to patch up something with Mrs Folliott. Mark knew about Mrs Folliott?— who was only, for that matter, one of a regular "bevy." Not that it signified, however, if he didn't: she would tell him about *her* later.

He took occasion from the first fraction of a break not quite to know what he knew about Mrs Folliott—though perhaps he could imagine a little; and it was probably at this minute that, having definitely settled to a position, and precisely in his very own tapestry *bergère*, the one with the delicious little spectral "subjects" on the back and seat, he partly exhaled, and yet managed partly to keep to himself, the deep resigned sigh of a general comprehension. He knew what he was "in" for, he heard her go on—she said it again and again, seemed constantly to be saying it while she smiled at him with her peculiar fine charm, her positive gaiety of sensibility, scarce dimmed: "I'm just selfishly glad, just selfishly glad!" Well, she was going to have reason to be; she was going to put the whole case to him, all her troubles and plans, and each act of the tragi-comedy of her recent existence, as to the dearest and safest sympathiser in all the world. There would be no chance for *his* case, though it was so much for his case he had come; yet there took place within him but a mild, dumb convulsion, the momentary strain of his substituting, by the turn of a hand, one prospect of interest for another.

Squaring himself in his old *bergère*, and with his lips, during the effort, compressed to the same passive grimace that had an hour or two before operated for the encouragement of Mrs Folliott—just as it was to clear the stage completely for the present more prolonged performance—he shut straight down, as he even in the act called it to himself, on any personal claim for social consideration and rendered a perfect little agony of justice to the grounds of his friend's vividness. For it was all the justice that could be expected of him that, though, secretly, he wasn't going to be interested in her being interesting, she was yet going to be so, all the same, by the very force of her lovely material (Bob Ash *was* such a pure pearl of a donkey!) and he was going to keep on knowing she was—yes, to the very end. When after the lapse of an hour he rose to go, the rich fact that she *had* been was there between them, and with an effect of the frankly, fearlessly, harmlessly intimate fireside passage for it that went beyond even the best memories of the pleasant past. He hadn't "amused" her, no, in quite the same way as in the Rue de Marignan time—it had then been he who for the most part took frequent turns, emphatic, explosive, elocutionary, over that wonderful waxed parquet while she laughed as for the young perversity of him from the depths of the second, the matching *bergère*. To-day she herself held and swept the floor, putting him merely to the trouble of his perpetual "Brava!" But that was all through the change of basis—the amusement, another name only for the thrilled absorption, having been inevitably for *him:* as how could it have failed to be with such a regular "treat" to his curiosity? With the tea-hour now other callers were turning up, and he got away on the plea of his wanting so to think it all over. He hoped again he hadn't too queer a grin with his assurance to her, as if she would quite know what he meant, that he had been thrilled to the core. But she returned, quite radiantly, that he had carried *her* completely away; and her sincerity was proved by the final frankness of their temporary parting. "My pleasure of you is selfish, horribly, I admit; so that if *that* doesn't suit you—!" Her faded beauty flushed again as she said it.

IV

In the street again, as he resumed his walk, he saw how perfectly it would *have* to suit him and how he probably for a long time wouldn't be suited otherwise. Between them and that time, however, what mightn't for him, poor devil, on his new basis, have happened? She wasn't at any rate within any calculable period going to care so much for anything as for the so quaintly droll terms in which her rearrangement with her husband—thanks to that gentleman's inimitable fatuity— would have to be made. This was what it was to own, exactly, her special grace—the brightest gaiety in the finest sensibility; *such* a display of which combination, Mark felt as he went (if he could but have done it still more justice) she must have regaled him with! That exquisite last flush of her fadedness could only remain with him; yet while he presently stopped at a street-corner in a district redeemed from desolation but by a passage just then of a choked trolley-car that howled, as he paused for it, beneath the weight of its human accretions, he seemed to know the inward "sinking" that has been determined in a hungry man by some extravagant sight of the preparation of somebody else's dinner. Florence Ash was dining, so to speak, off the feast of appreciation, appreciation of what she had to "tell" him, that he had left her seated at; and she was welcome, assuredly—welcome, welcome, welcome, he musingly, he wistfully, and yet at the same time a trifle mechanically, repeated, stayed as he was a moment longer by the suffering shriek of another public vehicle and a sudden odd automatic return of his mind to the pretty girl, the flower of Mrs Folliott's crowd, who had spoken to him of Newton Winch. It was extraordinarily as if, on the instant, she reminded him, from across the town, that *she* had offered him dinner: it was really quite strangely, while he stood there, as if she had told him where he could go and get it. With which, none the less, it was apparently where he wouldn't find her—and what was there, after all, of nutritive in the image of Newton Winch? He made up his mind in a moment that it owed that property, which the pretty girl had somehow made imputable, to the fact of its simply being just then the one image of anything known to him that the terrible place had to offer. Nothing, he a minute later reflected, could have been so "rum" as that, sick and sore, of a bleak New York eventide, he should have had nowhere to turn if not to the said Fiftieth Street.

That was the direction he accordingly took, for when he found the number given him by the same remarkable agent of fate also present to his memory he recognized the direct intervention of Providence and how it absolutely required a miracle to explain his so precipitately taking up this loosest of connections. The miracle indeed soon grew clearer: Providence had, on some obscure system, chosen this very ridiculous hour to save him from cultivation of the sin of selfishness, the obsession of egotism, and was breaking him to its will by constantly directing his attention to the claims of others. Who could say what at that critical moment mightn't have become of Mrs Folliott (otherwise too then so sadly embroiled!) if she hadn't been enabled to air to him her grievance and her rage?—just as who could deny that it must have done Florence Ash a world of good to have put her thoughts about Bob in order by the aid of a person to whom the vision of Bob in the light of those thoughts (or in other words to whom *her* vision of Bob and nothing else) would mean so delightfully much? It was on the same general lines that poor Newton Winch, bereft, alone, ill, perhaps dying, and with the drawback of a not very sympathetic personality—as Mark remembered it at least—to contend against in almost any conceivable appeal to human furtherance, it was on these lines, very much, that the luckless case in Fiftieth Street was offered him as a source of salutary discipline. The moment for such a lesson might strike him as strange, in view of the quite special and independent opportunity for exercise that his spirit had during the last three days enjoyed there in his hotel bedroom; but evidently his languor of charity needed some admonition finer than any it might trust to chance for, and by the time he at last, Winch's residence recognized, was duly elevated to his level and had pressed the electric button at his door, he felt himself acting indeed as under stimulus of a sharp poke in the side.

V

WITHIN the apartment to which he had been admitted, moreover, the fine intelligence we have imputed to him was in the course of three minutes confirmed; since it took him no longer than that to say to himself, facing his old acquaintance, that he had never seen anyone so improved. The place, which had the semblance of a high studio light as well as a general air of other profusions and amplitudes, might have put him off a little by its several rather glaringly false accents, those of contemporary domestic "art" striking a little wild. The scene was smaller, but the rich confused complexion of the Pocahontas, showing through Du Barry paint and patches, might have set the example—which had been followed with the costliest candour—so that, clearly, Winch was in these days rich, as most people in New York seemed rich; as, in spite of Bob's depredations, Florence Ash was, as even Mrs Folliott was in spite of Phil Bloodgood's, as even Phil Bloodgood himself must have been for reasons too obvious; as in fine everyone had a secret for being, or for feeling, or for looking, everyone at least but Mark Monteith.

These facts were as nothing, however, in presence of his quick and strong impression that his pale, nervous, smiling, clean-shaven host had undergone since their last meeting some extraordinary process of refinement. He had been ill, unmistakably, and the effects of a plunge into plain clean living, where any fineness had remained, were often startling, sometimes almost charming. But independently of this, and for a much longer time, some principle of intelligence, some art of life, would discernibly have worked in him. Remembered from college years and from those two or three luckless and faithless ones of the Law School as constitutionally common, as consistently and thereby doubtless even rather powerfully coarse, clever only for uncouth and questionable things, he yet presented himself now as if he had suddenly and mysteriously been educated. There was a charm in his wide, "drawn," convalescent smile, in the way his fine fingers—had he anything like fine fingers of old?—played, and just fidgeted, over the prompt and perhaps a trifle incoherent offer of cigars, cordials, ash-trays, over the question of his visitor's hat, stick, fur coat, general best accommodation and ease; and how the deuce, accordingly, had charm, for coming out so on top, Mark wondered, "squared" the other old elements? For the short interval so to have dealt with him what force had it turned on, what patented process, of the portentous New York order in which there were so many, had it skilfully applied? Were these the things New York did when you just gave her *all* her head, and that he himself then had perhaps too complacently missed? Strange almost to the point of putting him positively off at first—quite as an exhibition of the uncanny—this sense of Newton's having all the while neither missed nor muffed anything, and having, as with an eye to the *coup de théâtre* to come, lowered one's expectations, at the start, to that abject pitch. It might have affected one verily as an act of bad faith—really as such a rare stroke of subtlety as could scarce have been achieved by a straight or natural aim.

So much as this at least came and went in Monteith's agitated mind; the oddest intensity of apprehension, admiration, mystification, which the high north-light of the March afternoon and the quite splendidly vulgar appeal of fifty overdone decorative effects somehow fostered and sharpened. Everything had already gone, however, the next moment, for wasn't the man he had come so quite over-intelligently himself to patronize absolutely bowling him over with the extraordinary speech: "See here, you know—you must be ill, or have had a bad shock, or some beastly upset: are you very sure you ought to have come out?" Yes, he after an instant believed his ears; coarse common Newton Winch, whom he had called on because he could, as a gentleman, after all afford to, coarse common Newton Winch, who had had troubles and been epidemically poisoned, lamentably sick, who bore in his face and in the very tension, quite exactly the "charm," of his manner, the traces of his late ordeal, and, for that matter, of scarce completed gallant emergence—this astonishing ex-comrade was simply writing himself at a stroke (into our friend's excited imagination at all events) the most distinguished of men. Oh, *he* was going to be interesting, if Florence Ash had been going to be; but Mark felt how, under the law of a lively present difference, that would be an effect of one's having one's self thoroughly rallied. He knew within the minute that the tears stood in his eyes; he stared through them at his friend with a sharp "Why, how do you know? How *can* you?" To which he added before Winch could speak: "I met your charming sister-in-law a couple of hours since— at luncheon, at the Pocahontas; and heard from her that you were badly laid up and had spoken of me. So I came to minister to you."

The object of this design hovered there again, considerably restless, shifting from foot to foot, changing his place, beginning and giving up motions, striking matches for a fresh cigarette, offering them again, redundantly, to his guest and then not lighting himself—but all the while with the smile of another creature than the creature known to Mark; all the while with the history of something that had happened to him ever so handsomely shining out. Mark was conscious within himself from this time on of two quite distinct processes of notation—that of his practically instant surrender to the consequences of the act of perception in his host of which the two women trained supposably in the art of pleasing had been altogether incapable; and that of some other condition on Newton's part that left his own poor power of divination nothing less than shamed. This last was signally the case on the former's saying, ever so responsively, almost radiantly, in answer to his account of how he happened to come: "Oh, then it's very interesting!" *That* was the astonishing note, after what he had been through: neither Mrs Folliott nor Florence Ash had so much as hinted or breathed to him that *he* might have incurred that praise. No wonder therefore he was now taken—with this fresh party's instant suspicion and imputation of it; though it was indeed for some minutes next as if each tried to see which could accuse the other of the greater miracle of penetration. Mark was so struck, in a word, with the extraordinarily straight guess Winch had had there in reserve for him that, other quick impressions helping, there was nothing for him but to bring out, himself: "There must be, my dear man, something rather wonderful the matter with you!" The quite more intensely and more irresistibly drawn grin, the quite unmistakably deeper consciousness in the dark, wide eye, that accompanied the not quite immediate answer to which remark he was afterward to remember.

"How do you know that—or why do you think it?"

"Because there *must* be—for you to see! I shouldn't have expected it."

"Then you take me for a damned fool?" laughed wonderful Newton Winch.

VI

HE could say nothing that, whether as to the sense of it or as to the way of it, didn't so enrich Mark's vision of him that our friend, after a little, as this effect proceeded, caught himself in the act of almost too curiously gaping. Everything, from moment to moment, fed his curiosity; such a question, for instance, as whether the quite ordinary peepers of the Newton Winch of their earlier youth could have looked under any provocation, either dark or wide; such a question, above all, as how *this* incalculable apparition came by the whole startling power of play of its extravagantly sensitive labial connections —exposed, so to its advantage (he now jumped at one explanation) by the removal of what had probably been one of the vulgarest of moustaches. With this, at the same time, the oddity of that particular consequence was vivid to him; the glare of his curiosity fairly lasting while he remembered how

he had once noted the very opposite turn of the experiment
for Phil Bloodgood. He would have said in advance that poor
Winch couldn't have afforded to risk showing his "real"
mouth; just as he would have said that in spite of the fine
ornament that so considerably muffled it Phil could only have
gained by showing his. But to have seen Phil shorn—as he
once had done—was earnestly to pray that he might promptly
again bristle; beneath Phil's moustache lurked nothing to
"make up" for it in case of removal. While he thought of
which things the line of grimace, as he could only have called
it, the mobile, interesting, ironic line the great double curve
of which connected, in the face before him, the strong nostril
with the lower cheek, became the very key to his first idea of
Newton's capture of refinement. He had shaved and was
happily transfigured. Phil Bloodgood had shaved and been
wellnigh lost; though why should one just now too precipitately drag the reminiscence in?

That question too, at the queer touch of association, played
up for Mark even under so much proof that the state of his
own soul was being with the lapse of every instant registered.
Phil Bloodgood had brought about the state of his soul—there
was accordingly that amount of connection; only it became
further remarkable that from the moment his companion had
sounded him, and sounded him, he knew, down to the last
truth of things, his disposition, his necessity to talk, the desire
that had in the morning broken the spell of his confinement,
the impulse that had thrown him so defeatedly into Mrs
Folliott's arms and into Florence Ash's, these forces seemed
to feel their impatience ebb and their discretion suddenly
grow. His companion was talking again, but just then, in-
congruously, made his need to communicate lose itself. It
was as if his personal case had already been touched by some
tender hand—and that, after all, was the modest limit of its
greed. "I know now why you came back—did Lottie mention
how I had wondered? But sit down, sit down—only let me,

nervous beast as I am, take it standing!—and believe me when
I tell you that I've now ceased to wonder. My dear chap, I
have it! It can't but have been for poor Phil Bloodgood.
He sticks out of you, the brute—as how, with what he has
done to you, shouldn't he? There was a man to see me yesterday—Tim Slater, whom I don't think you know, but who's
'on' everything within about two minutes of its happening
(I never saw such a fellow!) and who confirmed my supposition, all my own, however, mind you at first, that you're one
of the sufferers. So how the devil can you *not* feel knocked?
Why *should* you look as if you were having the time of your
life? What a hog to have played it on *you*, on *you*, of all his
friends!" So Newton Winch continued, and so the air between the two men might have been, for a momentary watcher
—which is indeed what I can but invite the reader to become
—that of a nervously displayed, but all considerate, as well as
most acute, curiosity on the one side, and that on the other,
after a little, of an eventually fascinated acceptance of so much
free and in especial of so much right attention. "Do you
mind my asking you? Because if you do I won't press; but as
a man whose own responsibilities, some of 'em at least, don't
differ much, I gather, from some of his, one would like to
know how he was ever allowed to get to the point—! But
I *do* plough you up?"

Mark sat back in his chair, moved but holding himself, his
elbows squared on each arm, his hands a bit convulsively
interlocked across him—very much in fact as he had appeared
an hour ago in the old tapestry *bergère;* but as his rigour was
all then that of the grinding effort to profess and to give, so
it was considerably now for the fear of too hysterically gush-
ing. Somehow too—since his wound was to that extent open
—he winced at hearing the author of it branded. He hadn't
so much minded the epithets Mrs Folliott had applied, for
they were to the appropriator of *her* securities. As the appropriator of his own he didn't so much want to brand him as—

just more "amusingly" even, if one would!—to make out, perhaps, with intelligent help, how such a man, in such a relation, *could* come to tread such a path: which was exactly the interesting light that Winch's curiosity and sympathy were there to assist him to. He pleaded at any rate immediately his advertising no grievance. "I feel sore, I admit, and it's a horrid sort of thing to have had happen; but when you call him a brute and a hog I rather squirm, for brutes and hogs never live, I guess, in the sort of hell in which he now must be."

Newton Winch, before the fireplace, his hands deep in his pockets, where his guest could see his long fingers beat a tattoo on his thighs, Newton Winch dangled and swung himself, and threw back his head and laughed. "Well, I must say you take it amazingly!—all the more that to see you again this way is to feel that if, all along, there was a man whose delicacy and confidence and general attitude might have marked him for a particular consideration, you'd have been the man." And they were more directly face to face again; with Newton smiling and smiling *so* appreciatively; making our friend in fact almost ask himself when before a man had ever grinned from ear to ear to the effect of its so becoming him. What he replied, however, was that Newton described in those flattering terms a client temptingly fatuous; after which, and the exchange of another protest or two in the interest of justice and decency, and another plea or two in that of the still finer contention that even the basest misdeeds had always somewhere or other, could one get at it, their propitiatory side, our hero found himself on his feet again, under the influence of a sudden failure of everything but horror—a horror determined by some turn of their talk and indeed by the very fact of the freedom of it. It was as if a far-borne sound of the hue and cry, a vision of his old friend hunted and at bay, had suddenly broken in—this other friend's, this irresistibly intelligent other companion's, practically vivid projection of that making the worst ugliness real. "Oh, it's just making my

wry face to somebody, and your letting me and caring and
wanting to know: that," Mark said, "is what does me good;
not any other hideous question. I mean I don't take any
interest in *my* case—what one wonders about, you see, is
what can be done for him. I mean, that is"—for he floundered
a little, not knowing at last quite what he did mean, a great
rush of mere memories, a great humming sound as of thick,
thick echoes, rising now to an assault that he met with his
face indeed contorted. If he didn't take care he should howl;
so he more or less successfully took care—yet with his host
vividly watching him while he shook the danger temporarily
off. "I don't mind—though it's rather *that;* my having felt
this morning, after three dismal dumb bad days, that one's
friends perhaps would be thinking of one. All I'm conscious
of now—I give you my word—is that I'd like to see him."

"You'd like to see him?"

"Oh, I don't say," Mark ruefully smiled, "that I should
like him to see *me*—!"

Newton Winch, from where he stood—and they were
together now, on the great hearth-rug that was a triumph of
modern orientalism—put out one of the noted fine hands and,
with an expressive headshake, laid it on his shoulder. "Don't
wish him that, Monteith—don't wish him that!"

"Well, but"—and Mark raised his eyebrows still higher—
"he'd see I bear up pretty well!"

"God forbid he should see, my dear fellow!" Newton
cried as for the pang of it.

Mark had for his idea, at any rate, the oddest sense of an
exaltation that grew by this use of frankness. "I'd go to him.
Hanged if I wouldn't—anywhere!"

His companion's hand still rested on him. "You'd go to
him?"

Mark stood up to it—though trying to sink solemnity as
pretentious. "I'd go like a shot." And then he added: "And
it's probably what—when we've turned round—I *shall* do."

"When 'we' have turned round?"

"Well"—he was a trifle disconcerted at the tone—"I say that because you'll have helped me."

"Oh, I do nothing but want to help you!" Winch replied —which made it right again; especially as our friend still felt himself reassuringly and sustainingly grasped. But Winch went on: "You *would* go to him—in kindness?"

"Well—to understand."

"To understand how he could swindle you?"

"Well," Mark kept on, "to try and make out with him how, after such things—!" But he stopped; he couldn't name them.

It was as if his companion knew. "Such things as you've done for him, of course—such services as you've rendered him."

"Ah, from far back. If I could tell you," our friend vainly wailed—"if I could tell you!"

Newton Winch patted his shoulder. "Tell me—tell me!"

"The sort of relation, I mean; ever so many things of a kind—!" Again, however, he pulled up; he felt the tremor of his voice.

"Tell me, tell me," Winch repeated with the same movement.

The tone in it now made their eyes meet again, and with this presentation of the altered face Mark measured as not before, for some reason, the extent of the recent ravage. "You must have been ill indeed."

"Pretty bad. But I'm better. And you do me good"— with which the light of convalescence came back.

"I don't awfully bore you?"

Winch shook his head. "You keep me up—and you see how no one else comes near me."

Mark's eyes made out that he *was* better—though it wasn't yet that nothing was the matter with him. If there was ever a man with whom there was still something the matter—!

Yet one couldn't insist on that, and meanwhile he clearly did want company. "Then there we are. I myself had no one to go to."

"You save my life," Newton renewedly grinned.

VII

"WELL, it's your own fault," Mark replied to that, "if you make me take advantage of you." Winch had withdrawn his hand, which was back, violently shaking keys or money, in his trousers pocket; and in this position he had abruptly a pause, a sensible absence, that might have represented either some odd drop of attention, some turn-off to another thought, or just simply the sudden act of listening. His guest had indeed himself—under suggestion—the impression of a sound. "Mayn't you perhaps—if you hear something—have a call?"

Mark had said it so lightly, however, that he was the more struck with his host's appearing to turn just paler; and, with it the latter now *was* listening. "You hear something?"

"I thought *you* did." Winch himself, on Mark's own pressure of the outside bell, had opened the door of the apartment —an indication then, it sufficiently appeared, that Sunday afternoons were servants', or attendants', or even trained nurses' holidays. It had also marked the stage of his convalescence, and to that extent—after his first flush of surprise —had but smoothed Monteith's way. At present he barely gave further attention; detaching himself as under some odd cross-impulse, he had quitted the spot and then taken, in the wide room, a restless turn—only, however, to revert in a moment to his friend's just-uttered deprecation of the danger boring him. "If I make you take advantage of me—that is blessedly talk to me—it's exactly what I want to do. Talk to me—talk to me!" He positively waved it on; pulling up again, however, in his own talk, to say with a certain urgency: "Hadn't you better sit down?"

Mark, who stayed before the fire, couldn't but excuse himself. "Thanks—I'm very well so. I think of things and I fidget."

Winch stood a moment with his eyes on the ground. "Are you very sure?"

"Quite—I'm all right if you don't mind."

"Then as you like!" With which, shaking to extravagance again his long legs, Newton had swung off—only with a movement that, now his back was turned, affected his visitor as the most whimsical of all the forms of his rather unnatural manner. He was curiously different with his back shown, as Mark now for the first time saw it—dangling and somewhat wavering, as from an excess of uncertainty of gait; and this impression was so strange, it created in our friend, uneasily and on the spot, such a need of explanation, that his speech was stayed long enough to give Winch time to turn round again. The latter had indeed by this moment reached one of the limits of the place, the wide studio bay, where he paused, his back to the light and his face afresh presented, to let his just passingly depressed and quickened eyes take in as much as possible of the large floor, range over it with such brief freedom of search as the disposition of the furniture permitted. He was looking for something, though the betrayed reach of vision was but of an instant. Mark caught it, however, and with his own sensibility all in vibration, found himself feeling at once that it meant something and that what it meant was connected with his entertainer's slightly marked appeal to him, the appeal of a moment before, not to remain standing. Winch knew by this time quite easily enough that he was hanging fire; which meant that they were suddenly facing each other across the wide space with a new consciousness.

Everything had changed—changed extraordinarily with the

mere turning of that gentleman's back, the treacherous aspect
of which its owner couldn't surely have suspected. If the
question was of the pitch of their sensibility, at all events, it
wouldn't be Mark's that should vibrate to least purpose.
Visibly it had come to his host that something had within the
few instants remarkably happened, but there glimmered on
him an induction that still made him keep his own manner.
Newton himself might now resort to any manner he liked.
His eyes had raked the floor to recover the position of something dropped or misplaced, and something, above all, awkward or compromising; and he had wanted his companion not
to command this scene from the hearth-rug, the hearth-rug
where he had been just before holding him, hypnotizing him
to blindness, *because* the object in question would there be
most exposed to sight. Mark embraced this with a further drop
—while the apprehension penetrated—of his power to go on,
and with an immense desire at the same time that his eyes
should seem only to look at his friend; who broke out now,
for that matter, with a fresh appeal. "Aren't you going to take
advantage of me, man—aren't you going to *take* it?"

Everything had changed, we have noted, and nothing
could more have proved it than the fact that, by the same
turn, sincerity of desire had dropped out of Winch's chords,
while irritation, sharp and almost imperious, had come in.
"That's because he sees I see something!" Mark said to
himself; but he had no need to add that it shouldn't prevent
his seeing more—for the simple reason that, in a miraculous
fashion, this was exactly what he did do in glaring out the
harder. It was beyond explanation, but the very act of blinking
thus in an attempt at showy steadiness became one and the
same thing with an optical excursion lasting the millionth of a
minute and making him aware that the edge of a rug, at the
point where an arm-chair, pushed a little out of position, over-
straddled it, happened just not wholly to have covered in
something small and queer, neat and bright, crooked and

compact, in spite of the strong toe-tip surreptitiously applied to giving it the right lift. Our gentleman, from where he hovered, and while looking straight at the master of the scene, yet saw, as by the tiny flash of a reflection from fine metal, *under* the chair. What he recognized, or at least guessed at, as sinister, made him for a moment turn cold, and that chill was on him while Winch again addressed him—as differently as possible from any manner yet used. "I beg of you in God's name to talk to me—to *talk* to me!"

It had the ring of pure alarm and anguish, but was by this turn at least more human than the dazzling glitter of intelligence to which the poor man had up to now been treating him. "It's you, my good friend, who are in deep trouble," Mark was accordingly quick to reply, "and I ask your pardon for being so taken up with my own sorry business."

"Of course I'm in deep trouble"—with which Winch came nearer again; "but turning you on was exactly what I wanted."

Mark Monteith, at this, couldn't, for all his rising dismay, but laugh out; his sense of the ridiculous so swallowed up, for that brief convulsion, his sense of the sinister. Of such convenience in pain, it seemed, was the fact of another's pain, and of so much worth again disinterested sympathy! "Your interest was then—?"

"My interest was in your being interesting. For you *are!* And my nerves—!" said Newton Winch with a face from which the mystifying smile had vanished, yet in which distinction, as Mark so persistently appreciated it, still sat in the midst of ravage.

Mark wondered and wondered—he made strange things out. "Your nerves have needed company." He could lay his hand on him now, even as shortly before he had felt Winch's own pressure of possession and detention. "As good for you yourself, that—or still better," he went on—"than I and my grievance were to have found you. Talk to *me*, talk to *me*,

Newton Winch!" he added with an immense inspiration of charity.

"That's a different matter—that others but too much can do! But I'll say this. If you want to go to Phil Bloodgood—!"

"Well?" said Mark as he stopped. He stopped and Mark had now a hand on each of his shoulders and held him at arm's-length, held him with a fine idea that was not disconnected from the sight of the small neat weapon he had been fingering in the low, luxurious morocco chair—it was of the finest orange colour—and then had laid beside him on the carpet; where, after he had admitted his visitor, his presence of mind coming back to it and suggesting that he couldn't pick it up without making it more conspicuous, he had thought, by some swing of the foot or other casual manœuvre, to dissimulate its visibility.

They were at close quarters now as not before and Winch perfectly passive, with eyes that somehow had no shadow of a secret left and with the betrayal to the sentient hands that grasped him of an intense, an extraordinary general tremor. To Mark's challenge he opposed afresh a brief silence, but the very quality of it, with his face speaking, was that of a gaping wound. "Well, you needn't take *that* trouble. You see I'm such another."

"Such another as Phil—?"

He didn't blink. "I don't know for sure, but I guess I'm worse."

"Do you mean you're guilty—?"

"I mean I shall be wanted. Only I've stayed to take it."

Mark threw back his head, but only tightened his hands. He inexpressibly understood, and nothing in life had ever been so strange and dreadful to him as his thus helping himself by a longer and straighter stretch, as it were, to the monstrous sense of his friend's "education." It had been, in its immeasurable action, the education of business, of which the fruits were all around them. Yet prodigious was the interest, for prodigious truly—it seemed to loom before Mark—must have been the system. "To 'take' it?" he echoed; and then, though faltering a little, "To take what?"

He had scarce spoken when a long sharp sound shrilled in from the outer door, seeming of so high and peremptory a pitch that with the start it gave him his grasp of his host's shoulders relaxed an instant, though to the effect of no movement in *them* but what came from just a sensibly intenser vibration of the whole man. "For *that!*" said Newton Winch.

"Then you've known—?"

"I've expected. You've helped me to wait." And then as Mark gave an ironic wail: "You've tided me over. My condition has *wanted* somebody or something. Therefore, to complete this service, will you be so good as to open the door?"

Deep in the eyes Mark looked him, and still to the detection of no glimmer of the earlier man in the depths. The earlier man had been what he invidiously remembered—yet would *he* had been the whole simpler story! Then he moved his own eyes straight to the chair under which the revolver lay and which was but a couple of yards away. He felt his companion take this consciousness in, and it determined in them another long, mute exchange. "What do you mean to do?"

"Nothing."

"On your honour?"

"*My* 'honour'?" his host returned with an accent that he felt even as it sounded he should never forget.

It brought to his own face a crimson flush—he dropped his guarding hands. Then as for a last look at him: "You're wonderful!"

"We *are* wonderful," said Newton Winch, while, simultaneously with the words, the pressed electric bell again and for a longer time pierced the warm cigaretted air.

Mark turned, threw up his arms, and it was only when he had passed through the vestibule and laid his hand on the door-knob that the horrible noise dropped. The next moment he was face to face with two visitors, a nondescript personage in a high hat and an astrakhan collar and cuffs, and a great belted constable, a splendid massive New York "officer" of the type he had had occasion to wonder at much again in the course of his walk, the type so by itself—his wide observation quite suggested—among those of the peacemakers of the earth. The pair stepped straight in—no word was said; but as he closed the door behind them Mark heard the infallible crack of a discharged pistol and, so nearly with it as to make all one violence, the sound of a great fall; things the effect of which was to lift him, as it were, with his company, across the threshold of the room in a shorter time than that taken by this record of the fact. But their rush availed little; Newton was stretched on his back before the fire; he had held the weapon horribly to his temple, and his upturned face was disfigured. The emissaries of the law, looking down at him, exhaled simultaneously a gruff imprecation, and then while the worthy in the high hat bent over the subject of their visit the one in the helmet raised a severe pair of eyes to Mark. "Don't you think, sir, you might have prevented it?"

Mark took a hundred things in, it seemed to him—things of the scene, of the moment, and of all the strange moments before; but one appearance more vividly even than the others stared out at him. "I really think I must practically have caused it."

A NOTE ON THE TEXT

In preparing these tales for publication, the editor had to choose between James's original magazine texts, those published in book form soon afterwards and those revised and rewritten for the New York Edition. The obvious choice, it seemed to him, was the original book form of the story where there was one. In that form it had the benefit of revision from magazine to volume; and in that form it was best known to James's generation. It seemed to the editor that in a chronological edition of James's shorter fictions, the New York Edition texts had no relevance, with the exception of three tales listed below which figure in the present volume. These happen to have had their first book publication in the New York Edition itself. They were "Fordham Castle," "Julia Bride" and "The Jolly Corner," serialized earlier in the magazines, but only collected by the novelist at the time that he was assembling his "definitive edition." In their case revision was not as extensive as with the stories reprinted after a lapse of many years.

The original magazine publications of the tales in this volume were as follows:

"Fordham Castle," *Harper's Magazine*, December 1904.

"Julia Bride," *Harper's Magazine*, March–April 1908.

"The Jolly Corner," *English Review*, December 1908.

"The Velvet Glove," *English Review*, March 1909.

"Mora Montravers," *English Review*, August–September 1909.

"Crapy Cornelia," *Harper's Magazine*, October 1909.

"The Bench of Desolation," *Putnam's Magazine*, October–December 1909, January 1910.

"A Round of Visits," *English Review*, April–May 1910.

No magazine publication of "The Papers" has been recorded before its appearance in *The Better Sort* (London, 1903). As mentioned above, the first book publication of "Fordham Castle," "Julia Bride" and "The Jolly Corner" was in *The Novels and Tales of Henry James* (the New York Edition, 1907–9, volumes XVI and XVII). The remaining tales in the present volume were first reprinted in *The Finer Grain* (New York and London, 1910). The text of these first book publications has been used here.

The editor wishes in particular to thank Mr Richard Garnett for his patience in dealing with endless textual questions which arose during completion of this edition of Henry James's Tales, and for his constant vigilance over the proofs. He is also deeply grateful to Mr Rupert Hart-Davis for assistance at various times beyond his responsibilities as the publisher of this edition.